RUSHIN' DEATH

RUSHIN' DEATH

A KENZIE KIRSCH MEDICAL THRILLER #5

P.D. WORKMAN

 PD WORKMAN

ISBN: 9781774683804 (KDP Hardcover)
ISBN: 9781774683798 (KDP Paperback)
ISBN: 9781774683811 (Large Print)
ISBN: 9781774683828 (Lulu Paperback)
ISBN: 9781774683835 (Kindle)
ISBN: 9781774683842 (ePub)

ALSO BY P.D. WORKMAN

FIND MORE BOOKS AT PDWORKMAN.COM

MYSTERY/SUSPENSE:

Zachary Goldman Mysteries
Private Investigator
She Wore Mourning
His Hands Were Quiet
She Was Dying Anyway
He Was Walking Alone
They Thought He was Safe
He Was Not There
Her Work Was Everything
She Told a Lie
He Never Forgot
She Was At Risk
He Drowned in Memory
Their Walls Were Empty
They Came for Him
They Sought Vengeance
She Was Their Target

Kenzie Kirsch Medical Thrillers
Unlawful Harvest
Doctored Death
Dosed to Death

Gentle Angel

Rushin' Death

Posed for Death (Coming Soon)

Death of a Corpse (Coming Soon)

Parks Pat Mysteries

Police Procedural Set in Canada

Out with the Sunset

Long Climb to the Top

Dark Water Under the Bridge

Immersed in the View

Skimming Over the Lake

Hazard of the Hills

Knows the Hills (Coming Soon)

Spanning the Creek (Coming Soon)

Sanctuary in the Stream (Coming Soon)

High-Tech Crime Solvers Series

Virtually Harmless

Stand Alone Suspense Novels

Looking Over Your Shoulder

Lion Within

Pursued by the Past

In the Tick of Time

Loose the Dogs

AND MORE AT PDWORKMAN.COM

For those seeking freedom
Wherever it might be

1

It had been too long since Kenzie had been to Burlington to see her mother. She couldn't remember for sure when the last time had been. Long enough to make her feel guilty about it. But she wasn't going to wallow in that guilt. She was on her way to Lisa Cole Kirsch's house for a surprise Christmas Day visit, and that would make up for her negligence over the past months. Lisa loved Christmastime. Kenzie could remember how she used to decorate the house; everything draped in fairy lights, Christmas trees in almost every room, garlands, nutcrackers, candles, and every other kind of Christmas decoration she could think of. It was beautiful, like stepping into a fairyland.

But she knew that wasn't how it would be when she got to the house. Walter had mentioned that Lisa didn't go "all out" for Christmas anymore. Without any children at home, she didn't see the point in going to all of the work. Kenzie could understand that, even though it made her feel a little sad.

They would have a nice afternoon and evening just visiting, reminiscing over old times and, of course, whatever Kenzie's mother managed to drag her into. There was always a cause or function or soup kitchen. Lisa Cole Kirsch's name was known all over the state, maybe all over the northeastern states, for her philanthropy. She was always working on some campaign. And Kenzie would help her out this time without any eye-rolling or complaints. That would be her gift to her mother.

Walter Kirsch, Kenzie's father, would probably be there too, even though he and Lisa had been divorced for many years and lived in different cities. They still saw each other often and kept up. They were great friends. They just weren't married anymore. Since the Senate was closed for Christmas break, there wouldn't be much lobbying for Walter to do, and he could sit back and relax for a few days. Though Walter probably wouldn't actually take much time off. Just because the Senate wasn't sitting, that didn't mean all of the backroom lobbying had ceased. It might be just the opportunity Walter needed to see people who were normally unavailable. They were off for Christmas and, if he was lucky, feeling more charitable than usual.

But he would probably be with Lisa for Christmas Day at least. When Kenzie had talked to her mother that morning, Lisa had said that she might see him.

Vermont was beautiful during the winter. Yes, it was cold, and the roads got bad, and Zachary hated the postcard-perfect views of snow-laden trees in the days leading up to Christmas. It was a difficult time of year for him and, consequently, for Kenzie. But that didn't ruin her enjoyment of the view. It looked like the inside of a snow globe.

She didn't enjoy driving Zachary's car as much as she would have enjoyed driving her sporty red convertible—her "baby"—but Zachary had suggested that she use it while he was in the hospital. It was better for winter driving and certainly held the heat better than her baby with its canvas top. Kenzie had finally conceded and left her car in the garage, taking Zachary's nondescript white compact instead. He had purchased it because it blended in so that he could conduct surveillance. He didn't want a vehicle that would stand out or be identifiable. There were white compacts everywhere, and his was never the only one parked on the street, no matter where he went.

Kenzie exited the highway and pulled into the familiar streets of Burlington. They had been her stomping grounds growing up, but felt foreign now, like they were from another life. Really, they *were* from another life. From before Amanda had died. Before Kenzie had overhauled her life and gone to medical school. Before her job at the Medical Examiner's Office. Before Zachary. She hardly even recognized her younger self when she looked back at her old life. A spoiled trust-fund kid, even if she hadn't thought she was. She thought that she was independent and had her own mind. But really, she had just been drifting. "Finding herself," Lisa had said generously. Kenzie had been rebelling against her mother's socialite life but still living on her trust fund, not needing to find work. So she went to a lot of parties, took home a lot of young men, and helped her mother out with one of her causes when Lisa managed to twist her arm hard enough. Kenzie hadn't been unique; she had been a cliche.

Now she had educated herself, supported herself by working, had her own little house, and had welcomed Zachary Goldman into her life. She rarely touched her trust fund except for charitable purposes. She didn't spend all of her time trying to make the world a better place as Lisa and Walter both did, each in their own way. Still, she tried to make her little corner of Vermont a better place, keeping the Medical Examiner's Office running smoothly, learning the practice at Dr. Wiltshire's side, helping to solve the mystery of death and bring some peace and solace to the loved ones left behind. She loved her work, found it challenging, and was happy to go home at the end of the day to her own little castle and to Zachary, when he was there.

The estate house rose up in front of Kenzie as she turned onto the long drive. She wished for a moment that she had been arriving at night. She liked how the house looked when it was lit up in the darkness. Like a lighthouse to guide her home. In the gray afternoon light, it looked empty and desolate. She wondered for a moment whether Lisa would even be there. One of the problems with showing up unannounced was that Lisa could well have other plans. She might already be out at one of the churches or soup kitchens, donning a cap and gloves to serve the city's indigent. Or she might have gone to a friend's house or be working with a committee, though both of those options seemed less likely on Christmas Day. Everyone would want to spend time with their families on Christmas Day, even if they were not home any other day.

Kenzie pulled into the parking area in front of the house. There was another car parked there ahead of her. She didn't recognize it, but she wasn't home often enough to know the vehicles of any of Lisa's regular guests. Of course, it wasn't Lisa's car; hers would be parked in the garage, sheltered from the weather and not visible to thieves. It could be Walter's car, though Kenzie would have also expected his to be parked in the garage. He was a frequent enough guest at the estate to have his own bedroom, office, and space in the garage.

She parked and shut off the engine, removing her key from the ignition. Kenzie pushed back her dark, spiraling locks, trying to make herself look tidier, and reapplied bright red lipstick. She let out a long breath to clear any tension or anxiety about going back home. She was just there for a friendly visit. She didn't have to step back into any old roles. She knew her parents well enough to tell them "no" to anything she didn't want to be involved in and to ask them to back off if they were being too intrusive, asking questions about her life or telling her what she should be doing with it. She didn't have to think about Amanda and past Christmases. Or all of the ones she had missed after leaving home, instead of going home each year like an only child should.

2

Kenzie walked up to the front door and rang the bell. She was surprised that Lisa wasn't standing at the door waiting for her. A motion detector at the entrance to the driveway alerted Lisa when someone was coming, and cameras were strategically placed so that Lisa would know who was there before ever opening the door. It was strange to have to ring the doorbell and even stranger to wait for Lisa to answer it.

Once she had been standing there for a minute, Kenzie thought that maybe she should have just gone straight in. Or rung the bell and then entered. It was, after all, her childhood home. She belonged there as much as anyone else. She wasn't a visitor. But having already stood there waiting for a full minute, she couldn't very well open the door and barge in. It would look odd.

Eventually, she could hear barking and the door opened.

Kenzie looked past Lisa as she opened the door. A dog? They had never had a dog, even in her childhood. Kenzie and Amanda had begged for a dog or other pet and Lisa had never allowed them to have anything. Dogs were messy and unruly and needed to be properly trained, walked every day, and cleaned up after. Cats shed and clawed the furniture. There was no question of being allowed a rodent that might escape into the house, or of birds or reptiles, perish the thought.

Kenzie looked at the friendly dog who came to the door and was eager to thrust her muzzle into Kenzie's hand and get some ear scratches. Kenzie turned her surprised eyes to Lisa.

"MacKenzie, this is a surprise," Lisa said, sounding more like it was an intrusion than a welcome. "You didn't tell me you were coming."

"I wanted it to be a surprise." Kenzie shook her head at the dog. "When did you get a dog? I never thought you would agree to have one in the house."

And this dog was no teacup poodle or other pampered pooch that Kenzie would have pictured any of Lisa's socialite friends with. It was a large German shepherd, mostly brown in color.

Lisa's eyes crinkled into a smile, something they had not done when she had found Kenzie waiting on her doorstep. She stepped forward and kissed Kenzie on both cheeks. "Come in and I'll tell you all about it."

Kenzie was relieved to be invited in. She had been starting to worry that Lisa didn't want her there after all and would send her smartly on her way with a brick of Christmas cake and well wishes. Lisa pushed the door open wider to allow Kenzie in. The dog pressed up against Kenzie's leg, looking for more affection.

"What's her name?" Kenzie asked as they walked through the great hall and found seats in Lisa's cozy sitting room.

Lisa sat on the couch and patted the cushion beside her, inviting the dog to jump up, which she did. Kenzie shook her head. Not only did Lisa get a dog, but it was allowed in the house and up on the furniture! It was time to check the weather in hell and be on the watch for the four horsemen of the apocalypse.

"You don't recognize her?" Lisa asked, a slight smile playing over her lips.

"Well…" Kenzie studied the animal. The dog did look like one she had seen just a couple of months earlier. But there was no way that it was the same dog. No way. "I mean… she looks like Lola."

The dog gave a small bark of acknowledgment and panted,

tongue hanging out, looking very pleased. Lisa played with the dog's ears.

"Yes, it's Lola."

"But… how did you end up with Lola? I don't understand. What is she doing here?"

"She lives here. We rescued her."

Kenzie shook her head in disbelief. "But this dog… had a deadly virus. I was sure she would be put down."

Lisa covered the dog's ears. "Don't say that in front of her," she said in good humor. "It took a lot of work to convince them to treat and release her. They wanted to you-know-what and examine her brain. I told them there was no way that they were going to do that, so they might as well put it out of their minds." Lisa said it as if it were a foregone conclusion, the same way she had told it to the scientists and medical officials who had wanted to euthanize the dog to examine her brain and any other effects of the virus on her body. Lisa's firm, take-no-prisoners approach had allowed her to cross most barriers in her life. She had been able to go places and accomplish things that Kenzie would never have expected people to allow this older, wealthy white woman to do.

"And that was all that it took?" Kenzie asked skeptically.

Lisa shrugged. "I needed to remind them that the dog had been in the papers and if a reporter following up on the story was to find out that they had put her down, even if it was for a good reason, there would be quite a backlash. I told them that they could do whatever imaging and lab tests they wanted, that I would cover all of those costs, and bring her back whenever they needed to do follow-up tests. They would look like heroes in the media instead of villains."

Kenzie nodded slowly. Lots of money, authoritative orders, and pointing out how it would look in the eyes of the public. Lisa knew how to use all the tools at her disposal.

"So… how is she? How did they treat her? There's no sign of the virus persisting?"

"I believe it was the same protocol you and Zachary were given in the hospital. They monitored her virus levels very carefully, and there has been no sign it has come back in her follow-up appointments.

Every week, initially, and every month for the next year." Lisa stroked Lola's head. "She doesn't seem to mind all of the poking and prodding. She thinks they're just giving her attention."

"Why did you do it?"

"I didn't see any reason the dog should have to be put down just because of what happened to her. It wasn't her fault. She has been very well-behaved and is very friendly. I could see that from the moment I laid eyes on her."

"I didn't think you liked dogs. You would never let us have one as kids."

"Kids and dogs." Lisa rolled her eyes. "I didn't need that headache. And with Amanda's health…"

They had put all of their time and attention into caring for Amanda when her kidney disease was diagnosed. There had been some close calls with her health as a child and she had spent a lot of time in the hospital. With Lisa always at the hospital at Amanda's side, it would have been challenging to take care of a dog, taking it out for regular walks and whatever else it needed. They could have hired someone, but that would have defeated the purpose of having a dog for the family.

Kenzie would have promised them that she would do everything necessary to take care of the dog, but Lisa was probably right with her sigh of "kids and dogs." Kenzie would never have done everything required for the dog's upkeep. Walks several times a day, feeding, vet appointments, making sure it didn't chew all of Walter's—or Lisa's—shoes. Kenzie had been a fairly reliable child, but she probably could not have kept up with everything.

"I suppose. I never expected you to get one, though."

"I never expected to get one," Lisa acknowledged, petting Lola, who was now settling down to go to sleep.

Kenzie looked around the sitting room. The first thing that she noticed was that there was no tree. Not just a smaller tree and a reduction in the number of decorations around the house. No tree at all. No lights. No garlands. No string of Christmas cards received from her friends and foundations. It could have been any time of year. Zachary could have been there without worrying about triggering flashbacks to the fateful Christmas day he had suffered when he was ten.

There hadn't been any trees in the great hall, either. Kenzie could remember years when there had been two or three huge trees, branches reaching upward, looking as though they had been decorated by a hired interior design consultant. Maybe they had been. But Kenzie thought she remembered Lisa doing all of the work. It must have been a massive effort. In the years that Kenzie lived on her own, she sometimes decorated a small tabletop tree. Still, she couldn't be bothered with a full-sized one, untangling and testing out lights, going through boxes of ornaments to find the most important ones, and then coordinating colors and textures. One little tree, preferably pre-lit, with a few personal touches...

But Lisa hadn't done even that much. Kenzie didn't see any sign of Christmas. Of course, she hadn't been through the whole house, and maybe Lisa had decorated another room. And there would be outside lights, surely.

Kenzie heard footsteps on the stairs and looked up to see Walter. Only, it wasn't her father at all.

3

Kenzie stared at the stranger, her mouth open, for several long seconds. She had no idea who he was or what he was doing in her mother's house. She had expected Walter, but this slightly pudgy, pale, gray-haired man was not Walter.

"Oh, hello," Kenzie greeted, unsure what to say.

"You have a visitor," the man observed, speaking to Lisa. "I am sorry, I did not realize."

He had perfect diction. A little too perfect. His delivery was just a bit off, as if he had to think of each word rather than letting them flowing naturally. It seemed clear that either English was his second language, or he had some other impediment to his speech. A stroke or maybe a stammer or lisp that he had trained to overcome.

"Come down here," Lisa invited. Her tone was cool, and Kenzie didn't know whether that was because of the stranger or Kenzie's unexpected presence. "Join us. Maksim, this is my daughter, Kenzie."

Maksim gave her a nod. "I am delighted to meet you."

"Thank you. And it's good to meet you... Maksim."

Kenzie looked at her mother, waiting for her to explain who Maksim was and what he was doing there. Lisa had not said anything to Kenzie about someone else being there on Christmas Day. Maybe Walter. That was all. If her mother had a new boyfriend, she hadn't said anything about him to Kenzie. If they were just on a committee or cause together, Kenzie expected Lisa to tell her what it was. That would be only natural. "This is Maksim, he is on the Kidney Transplant Foundation board," or "Maksim and I are heading to the soup kitchen to help serve Christmas dinner."

But there was no explanation forthcoming. Kenzie didn't want to pry, but she was hoping for at least a clue as to who the man was and what his business there was.

Maksim joined them, sitting on an upholstered chair to form a roughly equal triangle between the three of them. Not on the couch next to Lisa. Of course, Lola was already there, but Lisa did not indicate that she would shoo the dog off, and Maksim didn't seem to think she should.

"Have you… had a nice Christmas so far?" Kenzie asked Lisa, struggling to find something natural to talk about now that a third party had joined them.

"Yes… it's been a quiet day, which is what I expected. Other than my daughter calling me early this morning." Lisa gave her a genuine smile at that. "It was nice to hear from you."

"I was thinking about how things were when we were little, and we would wake you and Dad up early in the morning so we could open presents."

"I'll let you in on a secret," Lisa said. "Your father was never asleep. He was more excited than you were to see your faces when you opened your gifts. He would be lying there awake, waiting for you to wake up."

Kenzie laughed. "Really? He always complained about us waking him up and said we had to go back to bed and sleep until ten. And then you would get after him and say that he should be nice, and we didn't need to go back to bed."

Lisa nodded. "It was all an act. He couldn't wait to get out of bed."

Kenzie chuckled, shaking her head. Walter was a good actor. She had never guessed his secret. She supposed it was that same ability to lie and mislead people that made him such a good lobbyist. No one would ever know the truth, how much he cared about a bill and what he would or wouldn't do to get it. But it was a disconcerting attribute for a grown daughter to find out. She wondered what else in her life had just been a lie. How often had he made up a story and Lisa had gone along with it? She knew now that there had been other times. And it wasn't just innocent little things like pretending he was still tired when he really wanted to watch the girls open their presents.

There was a brief and awkward silence. What else to talk about? Kenzie wanted to know who Maksim was and why he was there. Why had he been invited to join them? She was pretty sure that "Maxim" was a French name, but he didn't strike her as French. Even though he had eradicated his accent, there was still something in his bearing that made her doubt he was French.

"Were you able to visit Zachary?" Lisa prompted.

"Yes. We had a nice visit." Kenzie glanced at Maksim, not wanting to say anything too personal in front of him. But what else was she supposed to talk about? She and Lisa were not going to sit around talking about Christmas traditions or kidney transplants, or where Walter was.

Where was he, anyway? Had Maksim deliberately arrived there when Walter was elsewhere?

"There's such a change in Zachary after Christmas Eve." Kenzie filled the silence. "The difference in his demeanor in the days before Christmas and once Christmas actually hit is amazing."

"He's that much better?"

"Yes. It's like… he's finally come through the darkness into the light."

"But he still has to stay at the hospital for longer? Obviously, he didn't come home today, or you would not be here."

"No, he'll stay there a while longer. He needs a med review to see if they can get him on a more effective cocktail. And that takes a few weeks to work through. You can't tell immediately whether these medications are working or whether they are tolerated. It takes a while for them to build up in the blood."

"It seems like he should have at least gotten a day pass."

Kenzie shook her head. "It's too early. He's doing better, but he needs time to recover now."

Maksim was listening to the conversation with a slight frown. "Your husband?" he asked. "What is he sick with?"

Kenzie looked at him, trying not to grimace or show any emotion. She and Zachary were firm believers in discussing mental illness rather than sweeping it under the rug. It would never be destigmatized if people continued to be afraid to admit to mental illness or talked about it as if it were something shameful.

But that didn't mean that it was easy. Especially talking to someone who was a complete stranger who knew nothing about Zachary's background.

"He was suicidal," she told Maksim briefly. "It's a difficult time of year for him because of past trauma. Sometimes... he needs to be hospitalized until he is stable again."

"He tried to commit suicide?"

"No. He was having suicidal thoughts and knew he was a danger to himself. So he checked himself in so he would be somewhere safe where they could help him get through it."

Maksim shook his head, clearly not impressed. Someone who, Kenzie assumed, had not had much experience with mental illness in his own family.

"So when *will* he be getting out?" Lisa asked.

"It will be at least a couple of weeks. Maybe three or four. Maybe six or eight. It depends on how things go."

"That's a long time."

"I know. It's a long time to be without him. But I want him to be well when he gets home."

"Especially since he has already been in there several weeks," Lisa pointed out. As if Kenzie might have forgotten how long he had been in already. Circumstances had conspired against Zachary this year and he'd ended up in the hospital earlier than they would have expected. Kenzie had been hoping that he would be able to get through the holiday at home this year, that it would go more smoothly than the previous year. But between the virus protocol that had sapped Zachary's physical strength and the birth of his ex-wife's twins, he had not been able to fight off the darkness.

"I know, Mother."

"Does he have a good support network? Maybe that is something that you could work on. These things go better if you are not trying to do everything yourself."

That was true, Kenzie had to admit. Feeling like she was the only thing keeping Zachary from suicide was a huge stressor. Too much for one person. As disappointed as she had been that he'd had to admit himself to the hospital, it had also been a relief not to be the one person keeping track of Zachary and his safety.

"He sees a therapist every week when he's out. More often, if he needs to. And he has some friends in town. And his… Lorne and Pat, his old foster father and his partner, they're not far away. We go there as often as we can for dinner, and they check in on Zachary. They were at the hospital today bright and early."

Lisa nodded. "That still doesn't sound like very many people. You need to make sure that you're not wearing yourself out taking care of him, MacKenzie."

"I know. I take care of myself. And I'm not the one taking care of him right now. The hospital is."

"Of course. I just worry about my daughter. You might think that's something we outgrow as our children get older, but it really isn't. I still think about you and want you to be well and safe."

"I am, Mother. I know you worry."

"And your job?" Lisa didn't look like that was something she wanted to talk about. And Kenzie supposed it was somewhat unsavory to talk about a job involving dead bodies. But Kenzie loved her job and frequently spoke details of the current cases with Zachary. On an anonymous basis, of course, never mentioning any identifying details or things the police might be holding back. Zachary was an exception—someone perfectly happy to discuss autopsy details over supper.

"Work is going well," Kenzie told her. She cast around for any details that would interest Lisa. "I've been able to participate in several postmortems and even run one or two. And we had a case that involved the FBI not long ago."

"The FBI?" Lisa darted at glance at Maksim. She pressed her lips together for a moment. "Whatever would the FBI be involved in? I thought they handled kidnapping, drugs, and guns, that kind of thing."

Maksim shifted in his seat, sending Lisa a look that Kenzie could not interpret. He was clearly not comfortable with the way the conversation was shaping up. Suicide, dead bodies, and the FBI? Who wanted to discuss those at Christmas?

"Yes. In this case, it was a serial killer," Kenzie admitted, studying them each in turn as she spoke. "We were lucky to be able to sort it out. People like that can be really difficult to catch."

"People like what?" Maksim demanded.

"Serial killers. In this case, an angel of mercy serial killer. They sometimes operate for years, even decades, without anybody realizing what's happening. Or that there even is anything going on."

"Angel of mercy," Lisa repeated. "Is that like doctors who help people to commit suicide? End of life planning?"

"No, not exactly." Kenzie didn't think it would be a good idea to get into too much detail. "Maybe I'll tell you about it sometime. Do you have… would it be okay if I get something to eat? I haven't had much today."

"Of course, dear. You know where everything is. Please help yourself."

Kenzie looked at Lisa and Maksim, then got up and left the room. They stayed where they were. Kenzie could hear the low murmur of voices as she walked away.

4

Kenzie opened the big two-doored fridge in the kitchen and scanned the items on the shelves. There was no sign of a turkey dinner, even a small one. Whatever Lisa had eaten or planned to eat for Christmas, it wasn't a traditional turkey dinner. The pickings were rather sparse. But that wasn't surprising. Lisa wasn't starving; she just didn't eat at home very often. She was always out at this dinner or that event and, if she'd had a fridge full of food, it would have just gone bad. So she had some juice, vegetables, a few prepared protein dishes, and some yogurt and bread to make toast for breakfast. Kenzie made herself a sandwich and tidied everything away. She had thought that Lisa would join in her in the kitchen after a few minutes, but she remained in the sitting room talking with Maksim. Still unsure whether he was a boyfriend or a co-worker, Kenzie felt a stab of jealousy that Lisa would be more interested in visiting with him than with her own daughter, who was, for the first time in recent memory, there on Christmas Day.

But she'd brought it upon herself. She had known that Lisa would have other commitments and that Kenzie might not even find her at home. If Lisa had other interests and other plans for Christmas, it was Kenzie's own fault for not finding out and making suitable arrangements ahead of time. It wasn't Maksim's or Lisa's fault for not knowing she was coming.

———

Kenzie had planned to spend most of the afternoon and maybe into the evening with her mother, but it didn't work out that way. The conversations were awkward and stilted and Kenzie didn't feel like Lisa wanted her there. Surprising her for Christmas had been a nice idea but, like many other ideas, it didn't work out the way she had hoped or expected.

On the way back to Roxboro, Kenzie activated her Bluetooth and called Heather, Zachary's older sister. It rang a few times, and Kenzie waited to see if it would go through to voicemail. Heather might be at the hospital visiting with Zachary. She and the other siblings Zachary had been reunited with had planned to see him in the afternoon, but Kenzie didn't know when they were planning to get there or what time they would leave. It probably depended a lot on how Zachary felt. He'd already had visitors in the morning and might be worn out. He didn't have a lot of stamina since the bout with the virus and the antiviral protocol.

"Hello?"

"Hi, Heather. It's Kenzie."

Heather probably already knew that. Kenzie's caller ID would have shown up on the screen. "Merry Christmas, Kenzie! How has your day been?"

"Pretty good." Kenzie remained noncommittal, not wanting to go into any details about it. "I just thought I'd check back in. See whether you caught up with Tyrrell and how your visit went."

There was a sigh in response. Kenzie waited for the details. Something had not worked out the way it was supposed to. She hoped that didn't mean that Zachary's spirits had taken a downturn.

"No luck with Tyrrell," Heather said. "I'm worried about him. But I guess... from talking to his ex-wife, this isn't new. He does disappear from time to time. His alcoholism."

"I was hoping that maybe he would just be late."

"Me too. But wherever he is… I hope he's having a nice day." Heather's tone was bitter. Not like her. She was usually pretty upbeat. It was Jocelyn who was the sarcastic, acid one.

"I hope he's safe," Kenzie contributed.

"Yeah." Another pause while Heather considered what to say. "I hope that he's safe too… but at the same time, I hope whatever kept him from coming was something significant, and not just the bottom of a bottle. I want him to be okay, but maybe in bed with a bad flu or in a minor fender bender."

Kenzie chuckled. "I can understand that. What did Zachary have to say about it?"

"We didn't tell him that Tyrrell was supposed to be there. It was a surprise visit, so he didn't know that Tyrrell had been in on it too. Thought it was just Joss and I."

"That makes sense." Keeping the news from Zachary that Tyrrell had disappeared, probably on a bender, was probably a good idea. It would just make him feel bad and, while they didn't want to baby him too much and keep all negative news from reaching his ears, it made sense to keep the visit as upbeat as possible and not make him feel bad that Tyrrell hadn't bothered to show up to see him or to worry about where his brother had gone and if he were in trouble. "So, how was he?"

"Good. Doing better than the last time I saw him."

"He sure appreciates you and all the work you are doing to keep things on track for him."

Heather had been keeping an eye on the private investigation business while Zachary had been in the hospital, making sure that clients were taken care of or referred to someone else who could help them. It was the first time that Zachary had had administrative support, and Kenzie didn't know how he had gotten through his previous hospitalizations without losing clients. Probably he *had* lost clients, but there had been nothing he could do about it. They would either wait until he could get back in touch with them or go on to the next name in the phone directory. The companies that had him do skip tracing and insurance investigations probably knew that he was not typically available in December. Those jobs would wait until his return.

"I enjoy it," Heather said cheerfully. "I'm glad he's given me something to do with my time. And I don't mind taking more on while he's in the hospital. I'm doing as much as possible with the skip tracing, background checks, and whatever else I can do on the computer, and keeping track of what Zachary can do when he gets back."

"You're a real help to him."

"Thanks. I hope so. Well…"

Kenzie sensed it was time to wrap the call up. "That's all I called about. Merry Christmas."

"You too. Hope you had a great day today."

Kenzie terminated the call, and for a few minutes, she just drove, thinking over the call and how her day had gone. She had thought that she would be at the family home for most of the day, on into the evening, but it had been too awkward, and she hadn't been able to visit with Lisa with Maksim there, watching with his quick, dark eyes and listening to everything they said. What was he to Lisa? The lack of introduction made the whole thing even more disconcerting. She could accept her mother having a boyfriend. It had been a long time since she and Walter had divorced, and Kenzie was not aware of any romances she'd had since then. She deserved to be happy and to pursue whatever friendships and other relationships she desired. But Lisa and Maksim hadn't acted like lovers. They didn't sit together or touch or use a special tone when talking to each other. They didn't have little jokes or shared stories between the two of them. So what *was* Maksim to Lisa?

Kenzie tried Walter's number. He might or might not know about Maksim. Kenzie wouldn't bring him up but hoped that his name or relationship with Lisa might come up in a casual conversation. Then she could at least be reassured on that count.

The phone rang several times, and Kenzie frowned. She had expected Walter to answer right away. It was a holiday; he wouldn't be working. Maybe he was just taking longer to answer. He was occupied with something else and would pick it up when he was finished. But the phone continued to ring until it finally went to voicemail.

"Dad... it's Kenzie. I guess you knew that. I'm just calling to say Merry Christmas and thought we could talk for a few minutes. So... give me a call back when you're free." She couldn't think of anything else to say and hung up.

She did not doubt that he would call her back as soon as he got the message. Maybe he was at a restaurant where he was required to turn it off. Once he was finished and turned his phone back on, he would see her message and call her back for a chat. He was good that way. He always took the opportunity to talk. It was Kenzie who shut him down and froze him out, still holding a grudge for what she saw as his part in Amanda's death. Maybe not even that. Perhaps she had forgiven him for that, but she still didn't trust his morals. He had his own ideas about what was right and wrong, and they were just too different from Kenzie's. She couldn't justify spending time with him. She didn't want anyone to think she approved of him or his decisions.

5

Kenzie settled herself in at home. She turned on the little fairy lights that she had put up, one of the few decorations that Zachary had been able to tolerate without triggering his traumatic Christmas memories. As things had turned out, she could have gone full-out on the decorations, since Zachary had never been home to see them.

She flipped through TV channels, stopping on each of the classic movies from her childhood. Sweet and sappy. They were usually comforting, but she couldn't abide them today. Her thoughts were too unsettled. She wanted Zachary home. She wanted to know that her mom was okay. If she was honest with herself, she wanted Walter to be home with Lisa. Maybe that was the real problem. Maybe it wasn't anything to do with Maksim, but just the idea that her father should be there instead. She'd been shocked when she discovered that her parents had divorced without telling her. Maybe she dreamed they would someday get back together again. They were still good friends and she never heard them fight or disagree. She didn't really understand why they couldn't be married.

There was a beep from her phone and Kenzie pulled it out, expecting it to be a message from Walter. Maybe saying that he was in a meeting or a dinner with friends and would call her back once he was free.

But it wasn't. It was a message from Rhys.

Rhys was a Black teenager Zachary had met during an investigation. Mostly nonspeaking, living with his grandmother. His mother in prison. He and Zachary kept in touch, and Kenzie and Zachary both thought Rhys had a bit of a crush on Kenzie.

Rhys had messaged Kenzie through one of her social networks, since he didn't have her phone number.

He had sent her a picture of a dog sporting a Santa hat with a big fluffy white pompom.

Kenzie tapped out a message to him. *Merry Christmas*

Rhys sent back a *Merry Christmas* graphic in an ornate font.

How are you? Did you have a good day? Kenzie asked.

There was no immediate response. No dots to show that Rhys was composing a response. Kenzie's eyes drifted back to the TV as a familiar scene played. The volume was turned down, but she could have recited the dialogue from memory.

After a few minutes, the phone alert rang again, and Kenzie looked down at it. A picture of Gloria, Rhys's mother. Not a recent photo. Kenzie had seen it before. Cropped out of a family photo.

Did you get to visit your mom today? Kenzie guessed.

Rhys sent a thumbs-up.

He wouldn't have been allowed to take his phone into the prison visit, even though it was one of his primary means of communication. No chance to take a picture of his mother on Christmas Day. If he even would have wanted one of her in her prison uniform. It was probably better to just look at the old picture of her, smiling at the camera as if there was no rift between her and her family.

That's good. And did Santa bring you something nice?

Rhys sent back a photo of a tablet computer.

Oh, very nice! Kenzie followed the message with a smiley and heart emoji.

Rhys sent a big question mark.

His messages could be difficult to parse sometimes. Zachary was usually better at figuring out what Rhys wanted to communicate than

Kenzie was. Rhys did not write complete sentences and was likelier to send a picture to express his thoughts than words. It could take several guesses sometimes.

I've had a pretty good day, Kenzie texted back, even though it wasn't exactly the truth. Zachary was doing better, and that was a big relief. Maybe she should have arranged to do something with friends to help distract her and get her through the day. But they were all doing things with their families, as Kenzie had thought she would be doing.

Z?

That one wasn't so hard to figure out. *Zachary is doing better today. Past the worst.*

Rhys sent back a gif of a happy pup jumping high into the air.

Yes. I'm happy about it too. It's hard to see someone you love so depressed.

She said it because she wanted Rhys to know that it was true of him too. That the people in his life who loved him were sad when he was depressed too. Rhys had been through a lot of trauma in his short life and he, too, had been hospitalized due to mental health issues.

Rhys sent back a gift of Charlie Brown's Snoopy kissing Lucy, with a great big heart bursting between them. Kenzie laughed.

Am I the dog or Lucy?

When Kenzie's conversation with Rhys ended, her eyes drifted to the TV, and she watched it without interest for a few minutes. But she kept looking down at the phone again, hoping to see something from Walter. Where was he? Why hadn't he called her back or messaged her yet? He was never away from his phone for that long. Even if he were having a big dinner at a club or restaurant that didn't allow phones at the table, it had been long enough. He should be done, even figuring in coffee, drinks, or a cigar after the meal. It had been hours since she had left her message.

For the first little while, she tried to push her focus back to the familiar sweet Christmas pap on the TV. But it wasn't bringing her a feeling of comfort or nostalgia. Just irritation. She liked Christmas as much as the next person, but didn't the TV networks and advertisers know how overwhelming the mythical perfect family Christmas could be to people? Not everyone was happy at Christmas, and no one had that fairy tale life where everything ended up in a happily-ever-after Christmas with everyone having discovered and accepted the true meaning of the blessed day. How were people like Zachary supposed to feel about it? Others who had lost friends or family members, who were homeless, helpless, or hopeless on a day so focused on the magic of families and home?

Of course it wasn't the fault of the TV networks. Kenzie was just disgruntled, feeling sorry for herself because she was at home without Zachary, having visited a mother who was apparently not interested in her this year, ignored by a father who couldn't be bothered to return her call. And she was one of the lucky ones. She had a safe home, no worries about war or where the next meal was coming from. She had friends and family members who would be there if she had actually needed them, instead of just being lonely for a few hours.

She started scrolling through her contact list. At first, she told herself that she was just looking for the names of friends she wanted to wish a Merry Christmas. If she were lonely, the best thing to do would be to reach out to others. Make personal connections. But the names she stopped at were not her best friends or the people she thought might be lonely.

They were the people who had some connection with her father.

She tapped the name of Shane Whittingham. She was lucky that people were cutting back on the number of phone numbers they used now. Instead of a landline at work, a landline at home, a cell phone for personal use, and a pager or cell phone for business, they were consolidating back to one phone and forwarding any other numbers to that device. Instead of Whittingham's phone ringing away on his desk in a closed office, it rang through to his cell, and the man picked up after just three rings.

"Whittingham."

"Mr. Whittingham, I don't know if you remember me. It's Kenzie Kirsch—"

"Walter's daughter. Of course I know you. Call me Shane, Kenzie. This 'mister' business is getting old. I don't need to feel any more elderly than I already am."

Kenzie laughed obligingly. "Of course, Mr.—Shane. I just wanted to wish you and your family a very Merry Christmas."

There was a slight pause before Whittingham responded, and Kenzie hoped that she hadn't put her foot in her mouth because Whittingham was divorced, estranged from his children, or something else tragic or sordid that she'd never heard about.

"Thank you, Kenzie. That's very kind. How are you? And Lisa and Walter?"

"I'm good, thanks. I don't know if you heard I work at the Medical Examiner's Office. Of course, Lisa is working on her causes, as always, and…" Kenzie hesitated, giving Whittingham an opportunity to fill in the blank. To say that he'd just been talking to Walter or that things seemed to be going well for him, something that would tell Kenzie that they had been in contact, and everything was fine.

"Good to hear it," Whittingham said heartily. "I know Walter is very proud of you. Always telling people how brilliant his daughter is."

"I didn't see him today," Kenzie offered, and again waited for Whittingham to provide more information on when he had last seen or talked to Walter. Kenzie patted herself on the back for this approach, feeling like a private investigator, like Zachary. He would probably think she was clumsy, but she was doing her best to approach the problem without alerting anyone that something might be wrong.

Of course, nothing was wrong. Lisa had a new friend. Maybe Walter had a new friend too, and he was closeted away with her, not thinking Kenzie might be trying to reach him. He could be on a transatlantic flight. Or going the opposite direction, visiting Hawaii or Asia. She hadn't talked to him recently, so she didn't know.

"Oh, I don't see him as often as I used to," Whittingham said. "Not since I retired. The occasional drink together at the club or calling to pick my brains on some political situation." She could imagine him shrugging. "Of course, being out of the business, what I know about world politics is less and less, the history becoming more or less irrelevant."

Kenzie made a noncommittal noise. "I'll bet you know more than ninety-nine percent of armchair analysts posting on Twitter."

He chuckled at that. "Well, I won't argue that. It used to be that people actually needed to know something before holding themselves out as experts. What a world we live in now."

"Yeah. Well, Merry Christmas again. Maybe we'll run into each other sometime…"

"As long as it isn't in the morgue," Whittingham teased. "I hope not to be making that journey for quite some time yet."

6

Kenzie placed a couple more similar calls. She didn't want to make too many in case word got back to Walter that his daughter was working her way through her contact list, trying to track him down. She didn't want to alarm anyone or for anyone to tell Walter that she was concerned about him. But no one had seen Walter recently or had partaken of Christmas dinner with him. She had hoped someone would repeat Walter's plans for Christmas or say they had just run into him at the grocery store or gas station. Anything that would reassure her that everything was normal in Walter's life, and he would be in touch with her sooner or later when he decided he had time.

She would even have been happy with reports that he was working on some big project and had frozen everybody else out. That would, at least, show her that there was a reason for his silence and that it wasn't intended as a statement against her in particular.

If anyone had given her positive reports about Walter, she would have been satisfied and gone on to watch the next Christmas movie rerun on the TV. Any movie, no matter how sappy.

Instead, she was left feeling like he had fallen off of the face of the earth. Where was he? Why hadn't he been at Lisa's house? Why hadn't he answered the phone or returned her call? Why hadn't he talked to anyone else?

She gave up on her pointless speculations and dialed a number she knew by heart. Lisa Cole Kirsch's private cell number.

"MacKenzie. It was so nice to see you today, dear."

Lisa's words were fine, exactly what Kenzie would have expected her to say, but they were less effusive than usual. There was no enthusiasm behind them. Lisa might have enjoyed seeing Kenzie earlier, or she might not. Her tone certainly didn't tell the tale.

"It was nice to see you too," Kenzie agreed. "Although… I felt like I had interrupted things. I'm sorry, I should have called ahead and arranged a time."

"Oh, no. You're welcome any time."

"Maksim seems nice."

There was a definite pause as Lisa tried to figure out how to respond to this. "Well… certainly. He's very charming."

Lisa's tone said just the opposite.

"Have you known him for long?"

"No… not long."

"Are the two of you dating? I'm sorry, I never ask about your personal life, and I don't even know if you are seeing anyone…"

"No. Just… business associates. Nothing personal."

"Oh, okay. I really wasn't sure, but I didn't want to say anything in front of him. Cause a situation."

"That was very thoughtful of you. I appreciate it."

And that was the wrong answer. Kenzie tried to unwind it in her head and identify precisely what was wrong with what Lisa had said. If there was no personal relationship between the two, then Kenzie's suggestion that she hadn't wanted to make things awkward should have resulted in a laugh and reassurances that nothing could be further from the truth. Lisa's answer said that it *would* have been uncomfortable for Kenzie to inquire about their relationship and that it would have been embarrassing for her. Why would it be a problem unless they *were* actually in a relationship but didn't want to talk about it in front of a third party?

"So… I called Dad earlier."

"Oh?" Lisa's reply was sharp. "How *was* your father?"

"He didn't answer."

"Oh. Well, I am sure he has been busy. You know how he is." A fake laugh.

"But it was hours ago, and he hasn't even returned my call. That's not like Dad. He always returns my calls, even if he is busy. He makes the time."

"Well…" Lisa made a little noise. "You know how he can get caught up in things."

"On Christmas Day? He can't be working today."

"He could be working any day. He's always got something on the go."

Something up his sleeve, more like.

"Who is he going to be talking to on Christmas Day? Everyone is going to want to be with their families. Not at the office. Not discussing politics."

"There are still opportunities for social functions. You don't know. Maybe he had a dinner or golf."

"Not golf. Not with a foot of snow on the course."

"Well, not golf then. But he could have something. And he will take the opportunity if he gets it."

"But dinner doesn't take hours and hours. I've been trying to reach him almost since I was at your house and I'm not getting any response. He hasn't called me back."

"Maybe he didn't get your message. There could be something wrong with his phone." Lisa gave a ladylike laugh, prim and repressed. "Did he ever tell you about the time he dropped it in the toilet?"

Kenzie laughed. "No! He didn't mention that." She thought about it. She had only tried to reach him on his cell phone, since that was what he usually answered, what he had on him all the time. But Lisa was right. There could be something wrong with his phone. It could be damaged. The carrier could be having problems. A hundred different things could go wrong with a cell phone, and then Walter

29

wouldn't have received her message. "I'll try his other numbers, I guess. You're right. It could just be a technology thing."

"Even if he doesn't answer..." Lisa trailed off.

Kenzie bit her lip. Lisa didn't think Walter would answer, even if he got Kenzie's message? Had he said something to Lisa that indicated he would be out of touch or had a problem with Kenzie? It was always Kenzie pulling away from the relationship, not Walter. He was always the one pursuing, trying to establish a closer father-daughter relationship with her. Had he said something to Lisa that indicated that had changed? Had Lisa told him to back off if he wanted Kenzie to stop running away? Turn the tables and make *her* work at the relationship?

"Do you know why he wouldn't return my call?" Kenzie challenged.

"No, no. I don't mean that. I just meant... if he doesn't, that doesn't necessarily mean anything is wrong. Just that he's busy or needs some time."

"You don't think there's anything wrong?"

Lisa gave a light laugh. "I'm sure there's not. But it isn't like I would know anything about it. He wouldn't call me. It's been years since we've had anything to do with each other."

Kenzie's jaw dropped and she had a hard time closing her mouth again. It *had been years since they'd had anything to do with each other?* She knew that wasn't true. They talked to each other all the time. More often than Kenzie talked to either of them. And Walter often stayed with Lisa when he was in town, regularly visiting her for a few days a month.

Why would Lisa say such a thing? Was it the beginning of dementia? Kenzie's mind jumped immediately to Lola. What if they were wrong? What if Lola hadn't completely cleared the virus and now Lisa had been infected? The engineered virus developed very quickly. Death occurred within a few days of the first signs of dementia.

"Mom, are you okay? Have you been feeling okay lately? The last day or two?"

"Yes, I'm fine. You saw me today. Do I look sick?"

"No, but… you haven't fallen down? Been running into things? Maybe fainted?"

"No."

"And your memory…?"

"My memory is as good as it ever was, MacKenzie," Lisa insisted firmly. "Now stop worrying about me. My, doctors can be so paranoid."

"It's just…" Kenzie didn't want to scare Lisa. Maybe she should stop in and see her again the following day. Just to make sure she wasn't having any symptoms that she had been able to mask that day. The dementia associated with the virus developed very quickly.

"Walter will be in touch, I'm sure," Lisa told her, reverting to the discussion about her ex-husband. "You don't need to worry about that. You know he loves you very much and will get back to you when he can."

"Okay." Kenzie wasn't sure what to say to this. The reassurance was thin and insubstantial. Like when they had told her in the beginning that Amanda would be fine. But Amanda had not been fine. They had all just been holding their breaths, afraid to say or do anything that might tip her health in the wrong direction. Until eventually, it was all over. "Mother… you would tell me if something was wrong, wouldn't you? If Dad is sick or you are… or if there is financial trouble or a problem with the law…"

"Oh, you have such an imagination, MacKenzie. You don't need to worry. Everything is fine."

"Are you sure?"

There was a pause that was a little too long as Lisa considered her response. "Do you remember Dr. Proctor?"

Of course Kenzie remembered Dr. Proctor. He had been a family friend. He'd seen to Amanda. He had given Kenzie good advice, encouraging her to go to medical school instead of just flushing her life down the toilet.

Only, it had turned out that he was not the kindly, wise advisor he had pretended to be. In the end… Kenzie had discovered that he wasn't what he had seemed at all.

"What would he have said?" Lisa prompted.

"I don't know… to stop worrying and do what I felt was best, I guess. That there's no point in worrying over things that haven't happened. Find out what's going on before I start panicking."

"You should listen to your heart," Lisa agreed. "You have good instincts."

7

The call with Lisa left Kenzie feeling very unsettled. She couldn't understand her mother's responses. She didn't think Lisa's strange responses the result of dementia. Was her uncharacteristic behavior when Kenzie visited her further evidence of a problem? Was it something to do with Maksim? In the past, Lisa had always been careful of anyone who showed her too much attention or tried to coerce her into donating money to organizations she hadn't fully vetted. She had protected herself from those men who would be more than happy to separate her from her money. She might come across as a kind, naive older woman in her dealings with the many charities and causes she involved herself with, but she was not naive and anyone trying to take her for a ride would find himself quickly put in his place.

If Lisa were failing mentally, someone like Maksim might have wormed his way into her good graces and be advising her in all of her decisions, guiding her hand in where the money went and who she spent time with. Someone with malice in his heart might easily funnel money away from the causes Lisa had always favored and make sure that it ended up in his own pocket instead.

Kenzie needed to follow up on Lisa's odd behavior.

And she needed to discuss it with Walter. She needed to talk to him even more urgently now. Her questions regarding who Maksim was and what Lisa had been up to lately were no longer prompted by idle curiosity, but real concern.

She had to look up the old landline number for his apartment but, when she dialed it, she got a "no such number" recording on her phone. She tried the office number she hadn't used to reach him in years, and it didn't produce an error message, but she was pretty sure that the voicemail recording she reached was exactly the same outgoing message as she had already listened to and responded to. He had that number forwarded to his cell. Why would he have more phones than just his cell phone, which, in this day and age, had more functions than a desk set ever had?

She left another message anyway, nervously mentioning Lisa and letting Walter know that she was concerned about her. Nothing dramatic or panicky; she didn't want to give her father a heart attack. She just needed him to call her. If Lisa was having symptoms, they needed to get her to the hospital immediately. The antiviral program would need to be started as early as possible, or it would be fatal.

It was late when her phone rang again. Kenzie picked it up, relieved. Walter would sort everything out. He would brush off her concerns about where he had been. He would see Lisa and evaluate whether she was behaving any differently. Maybe he would even know who Maksim was. He might be a mutual friend; someone Walter had introduced Lisa to.

But when she picked up the phone, she saw that it wasn't Walter at all. It was Dr. Wiltshire. Kenzie frowned at this.

He didn't usually call her outside of work hours. Not unless there was a death scene he thought she might want to attend with him. Kenzie was trying to get as much experience as possible in all aspects of the Medical Examiner's job. While Dr. Wiltshire could not get to every scene and would sometimes just have the forensic technicians take pictures and gather evidence for him, there were scenes that he wanted to attend to in person. And might want Kenzie to attend as part of her education.

"Doctor?" she greeted after accepting the call.

"Kenzie. How was your Christmas Day?"

"It was fine." Kenzie knew her tone was slightly clipped, but she really didn't want to talk about her day. "What's up?"

"I just wanted to make sure... I know that you have been concerned about Zachary and his health. I wanted to make sure that you were up to attending at the office tomorrow. If you need some extra time with him, I know you said that this time of year was the worst for him."

"Yes, yes, he's fine. I'll be at the office tomorrow."

"It will be busy, but we can take the time we need. You don't need to feel like you have to jump right back into it. Just taking one day off for the holiday might not be enough."

"No, no, I'm good. Zachary's worst day is Christmas Eve. Once he gets past that point, he starts to feel better."

"Mental illness doesn't usually follow the clock quite so rigidly."

"No. And he still suffers from depression. But what he went through as a child, when he lost his family and his home, that was Christmas Eve. The anniversary... is very difficult for him each year. But now that he's past that point, he'll improve, and they can make adjustments to his meds."

"So you will be in tomorrow."

"Yes. You bet. Do you know yet what we'll have to deal with?"

"I've been staying on top of what guests have arrived today. But there will be more. Those who are not found until tomorrow. Accidents that happen tonight when people are driving tired or after partaking of too much Christmas cheer. We always have a larger influx around Christmas."

It was one of the sad truths of the holiday season. More depression. People beaten down by their own expectations of themselves. Those who were in pain, missing family or loved ones who had passed or who they were estranged from. The longest, darkest nights of the year. People self-medicating with alcohol and illicit drugs. There were more suicides, more car accidents, more homeless people succumbing to the cold. Zachary was not alone in his dread of the Christmas season, though his distress might be more obvious than those who suffered silently and were able to mask their moods.

"I'll be there," she promised Dr. Wiltshire.

"I appreciate it. But keep in mind that you can adjust your schedule if something happens. People might be impatient for post-mortems to be completed, but they will take longer at this time of year. They will just have to wait."

"Thanks for your support. I'll let you know if anything changes." She thought about Lisa. Should she put off her return to work for an extra day and go see her again tomorrow?

She'd sleep on it. In all likelihood, Walter would stop in to see Lisa for breakfast or brunch and call to let Kenzie know that yes, everything was just fine, and she didn't have anything to worry about. It had just been a weird day. Lisa's mind had been on other things, or she had been short on sleep. Maksim was just—Kenzie tried to think of simple explanations for Maksim's presence—a friend of the family who had needed a place to sleep. Someone that Lisa had worked with on a board and who wanted to bend Lisa's ear on a new venture. There was a perfectly normal and natural explanation for everything that had happened or not happened on Christmas Day.

"Kenzie?" Dr. Wiltshire prompted.

"Sorry, what?"

"I'll see you tomorrow."

"Yes, yes, of course." Kenzie tried to get her head on straight. To engage with him as if she weren't distracted by any concerns about her mother. "How was your Christmas?"

"Oh." Dr. Wiltshire seemed momentarily disconcerted. "Yes, it was… very nice. A quiet Christmas at home."

She waited to see if he were going to say something more about what he had done or some gift he had received from or given to his wife. He often had amusing things to say about his wife, though Kenzie suspected that none of them were true. He just used her as a foil for his jokes.

"Get any golf clubs for Christmas?" she suggested, which should prompt one of his well-worn jokes.

"Well, as you know, I prefer not to have weapons in the house," Dr. Wiltshire replied. "I've seen the damage a nine iron can do."

"I'm sure Mrs. Wiltshire would never use one on you."

"One would hope," he agreed, "but one would not want to take any chances."

Kenzie smiled. "Tell her Merry Christmas for me."

"I will, Kenzie." His voice was warm, less strained than it had been at the beginning of the call. He sounded like he was smiling. "See you in the morning."

8

After the call with Dr. Wiltshire, Kenzie looked at the time on her phone and decided it was time to get ready for bed. She had just promised to be at the morgue bright and early. It had been a long, strange day and she needed to make sure that she got enough sleep to be functional at work the next day. Especially if they had several autopsies to do. Kenzie would try to get enough of her administrative work out of the way to be able to assist Dr. Wiltshire with an autopsy or two. She didn't exactly need to worry about making mistakes in his work like a surgeon—her patients were already dead—but it was still best to be wide awake and alert.

She took an over-the-counter sleep aid and started her bedtime routine, changing and brushing her teeth. She could never understand why Zachary was so reluctant to take something to help himself get the sleep he needed to. Without a pill, he might only get a couple of hours of sleep. Maybe none at all. If he took his prescribed sleep aid, he could get six to eight hours like a normal person, which helped keep his mood stable and made it easier to function as a private investigator. She understood that his meds were much stronger than what she took and the side effects more pronounced but, if she had to choose between a little grogginess on waking from a full night's sleep and only getting an hour or two, she would take the grogginess.

But Zachary had his own feelings and opinion on the matter, and she couldn't argue that she knew better than he did what was best for his body and brain. He had to make those decisions for himself and, medical doctor or not, she was not *his* doctor and shouldn't mix the roles of partner and practitioner.

She sat in bed reading for a while, waiting for her thoughts to slow enough that she would be able to relax and go to sleep. Worry over Lisa continued to nag at her, and her irritation at Walter not returning her calls was turning into something else. She was not just angry that he couldn't be bothered to call her, but she was also beginning to wonder whether something had happened to him.

Eventually, she put her book to the side, shut off the light, and lay as still as possible, waiting for sleep to overcome her.

Kenzie wasn't exactly bright-eyed and bushy-tailed in the morning, but she managed to drag herself out of bed and get going on her day. A hot shower helped clear the cobwebs, and a couple of cups of coffee didn't hurt.

She prepared her usual marmalade on toast, missing the morning routine with Zachary. She played a podcast on her phone so the house would not be so quiet. She had noticed she was going through podcasts a lot faster with him away. Most of them were educational, so she was learning a lot. It was hard to believe that she had lived on her own for so many years without any problem, but after a few months of living with Zachary, she felt like she was always at loose ends and the house was too quiet when he wasn't around.

Kenzie didn't feel like toast. She tossed the rest in the garbage, swigged the rest of the coffee in her cup, and put her dishes into the dishwasher. It wouldn't hurt her to get to the office a little early. She could get a head start sorting through the emails, voicemails, and remains that had arrived over Christmas. By the time Dr. Wiltshire got there, she would have everything under control and ready for him.

But Dr. Wiltshire had, perhaps, had the same idea, and Kenzie had only been there for a few minutes when he showed up.

"Oh! You're early!" Kenzie observed, looking at the time and feeling flustered.

"So are you."

"Yeah… I thought I would get a head start." She looked around, unsure what to give him since she hadn't had a chance to sort through everything yet. She liked to have things organized when he arrived, but was caught flatfooted with his early arrival.

"Pretend I'm not here," he told her, making a calming motion. "I have some personal stuff to attend to. We'll have a meeting and get a start on our day together later." He looked at his watch. "An hour, maybe? I'll get some real coffee and donuts, and we'll run through the cases for the day."

"Okay." Kenzie let out a breath. That should give her enough time to at least get a sense of what needed to be addressed. And though he'd said an hour, he would probably go to the coffee shop in an hour, which would give her another half hour before he returned and was ready to meet with her. "That should be perfect."

"Good." Dr. Wiltshire nodded. "Carry on, then. I'll be as quiet as a mouse."

He wasn't quiet as a mouse, and he didn't go directly to his office to work on whatever personal business he had to attend to. She could hear him going through the inventory in the morgue, checking in on their newest guests. Kenzie hadn't had a chance yet to make sure that they had all been logged in correctly and to identify what other paperwork they might be waiting for. She forced herself to ignore the noise of Dr. Wiltshire moving around the morgue, whistling softly through his teeth. It was his morgue, after all; he was perfectly entitled to approach the day as he wished. Kenzie liked things to be done in a certain way, but he was the one who was ultimately in charge and responsible for whatever happened here.

She checked the voicemail inboxes first, having missed important information at the beginning of the day before because her inclination was to deal with email and physical inboxes first and leave the voicemails to last. There weren't any messages from Dr. Wiltshire because, of course, he was already there. She added relevant details from the voicemail messages into her electronic notes, then worked her way through their email inboxes, printing and filing reports and assembling the information that Dr. Wiltshire would need during the day, or requests that he would need to answer. Then she went through the new log-in sheets and the remains in the morgue to ensure that everything was properly identified and accounted for and opened a new file for each new arrival.

Dr. Wiltshire went out and returned with the promised coffee and donuts, and they sat down at the table in the meeting room nearest Kenzie's desk to go through the long list of jobs to be done on old cases or the new ones that had arrived since leaving the night before Christmas.

Dr. Wiltshire scrutinized the list of names paired with the circumstances of their deaths, his brows drawn together.

"I think the best approach is to deal with as many routine cases as we can today, and then prioritize the ones that will need deeper investigation over the next few days. We should be able to get through a lot of these." His eyes scanned the list again. "Homeless death due to exposure, MVAs, unattended with no signs of violence or suspicious circumstances. Get those cleared out of the way, and then we can concentrate on the ones that are more obviously homicide."

"Won't the police be eager for us to deal with the homicides first?"

He shrugged. "Of course. But rushing them through because we have a backlog doesn't benefit anyone. We'll be able to do a more thorough investigation without worrying about running out of space if we can get the others out of here. And there's no reason to hold up the funerals for folks who were almost certainly natural causes. Families of homicide victims will understand that it will take longer if they want answers."

Kenzie nodded. "Okay." She knew she would be getting calls from the detectives assigned to the apparent homicides, but she could handle them if she knew how Dr. Wiltshire wanted to handle the investigations.

"How is your workload? Do you have a lot of paperwork to get done?"

"It's not too bad." Kenzie shrugged. She often had more to do after a weekend. They had only been shut down for one day due to Christmas and, while there was a larger than usual influx, it wasn't that much worse than a Monday. She'd been with Dr. Wiltshire for a couple of Christmases now, so she had a good feel for how long it would take to clear the stacks of paperwork and was not stressed out about it. She was more distracted by thoughts about her parents than how much administrative work there was to do.

It wasn't emergency medicine. Their patients were not going anywhere.

"Do you want to assist with clearing these patients through, then? We can set up several tables at a time, divide them between us to do the gross exam and preliminaries, and then discuss any findings and additional work to be done."

Kenzie nodded eagerly. She had led a few postmortems, taking primary control of the case rather than assisting Dr. Wiltshire. This was the next step, completing the preliminary work without his direct supervision and then collaborating on the rest of the examination. "Sure. I'd be comfortable with that."

"Excellent." Dr. Wiltshire leaned back in his chair and took a bite of the donut that had been sitting on a napkin beside his elbow. "I think that will help us clear them in the most efficient way possible. You are quite invaluable here, Kenzie. Being able to work more independently on autopsies is just one more thing to add to the resume. Though I don't mean you should be looking for work outside this office. I want to keep you here for as long as possible." He chuckled.

"I don't plan to go anywhere soon," Kenzie assured him. "It has been a great learning environment. I enjoy working with you. And I don't think I would have so many opportunities in a big city morgue. It's been nice to learn the ropes here."

"And you're learning everything from the ground up. One day, you'll be running an office of your own."

Kenzie smiled, her face warming. She was excited to be adding more tools to her toolbox. She fully intended to have a morgue of her own one day, though she didn't know how far down the road that would be. She was getting plenty of experience with Dr. Wiltshire, and that was what she needed the most.

9

On her lunch break, which amounted to a walk down the hall to the vending machine to get a bag of chips and a sandwich, Kenzie checked her phone for any messages, then tried calling her father again. Whatever he had been doing on Christmas Day, he should be back to work now, busy on the phone and computer, trying to talk people into backroom deals, to figure out how to get enough support for the bills that he wanted to go through and to block those that he didn't. Even with the Senate closed for several weeks, there was still plenty of work that could be done to prepare for when it reopened.

There was still no answer on Walter's phone, the line ringing and ringing until it went through to voicemail, and Kenzie again heard Walter's outgoing message, unchanged, inviting her to leave a message. Nothing to say that he was sick, on vacation, or would be unavailable until New Year's Day or some other reasonable-sounding date.

Where was he? Even if he was taking a real vacation for the first time in decades, why wasn't he answering his phone? Why wasn't he returning Kenzie's calls? He had said that he would always be there for her, that she only had to call him if she needed anything.

So, where was he?

Kenzie left a terse message and hung up.

She sat at her desk, unwrapped the sandwich, and examined it. She knew that if she didn't want to rely on the less-than-stellar sandwiches in the machine, she needed to either bring her lunch or go out to one of the nearby restaurants or cafes. Or even order in using one of the many food delivery services eager to take her money. But she kept sabotaging herself by not preparing ahead of time or saying that she didn't have time over her lunch hour. She didn't really get a break away from her desk. She was the public face of the Medical Examiner's Office, and people expected her to be there when they came by to fill out a form or make a request.

She knew that people would have to get used to it if she just decided to take her lunch away from her desk and left a sign telling them to come back later. But she also liked the feeling of being indispensable. That people needed her to be there throughout the workday and on into the evening, or the work of the Medical Examiner's Office would stall.

It wouldn't, of course. People would just call back another time. But logical thoughts and feelings and ego didn't always line up.

Dr. Wiltshire sailed back in after his lunch, taken away from the office rather than at his desk, and nodded to Kenzie. "When you're done there, we'll get started," he told her. Then, realizing she was holding the phone to her ear, he waved his hands to negate the statement. "When you're ready," he mouthed, and carried on to his office.

Kenzie listened to the recorded message. This time Lisa's, rather than Walter's. She tried to decide whether to leave a message for her mother about Walter. She didn't have any objective evidence that there was anything wrong. Just her father neglecting to call her back. Kenzie knew he could get immersed in his work and be distracted from the incidentals, like calling his daughter back. He'd never missed being there for Amanda when she was sick. He'd been very diligent about that. But calling Kenzie back about something unimportant might slip his mind.

Kenzie hung up without leaving a message. She glanced over her desktop and computer screen to make sure that she had completed everything she needed to and there were no half-typed messages to file or to Dr. Wiltshire that she needed to finish before leaving her desk. Then she walked down the hall to Dr. Wiltshire's office.

"I'm off," she announced. "Sorry about that."

"No, not at all!" Dr. Wiltshire insisted. "I just didn't notice you were on the phone to start with." His brows pulled down as he studied her and he readjusted his rectangular-framed glasses. "Is everything okay?"

"Just fine," Kenzie assured him quickly.

"You look upset. Are you sure?" Before Kenzie could answer, he continued. "Is it Zachary?"

"Zachary is fine. It's my—everything is fine. I'm ready if you want to get started."

Dr. Wiltshire looked at her for a moment, then nodded his agreement. Kenzie was glad that he didn't pursue it further. If she needed something from him, she would tell him. Until then, she preferred to keep her personal troubles to herself.

In autopsy, they both suited up to prevent contamination of the bodies or the evidence and protect their clothing from the various bodily fluids. Four bodies were laid out on tables for them, the most that they could do at a time. George had already done the work of stripping, washing, and preparing the bodies. The clothing was all tagged and inventoried and close at hand if they needed to look at it, and any evidence removed from the bodies—hairs, nail scrapings or clippings, particulates—had been carefully preserved and logged for them to review. Each body was draped, awaiting the doctors' examinations.

"Why don't you take those two," Dr. Wiltshire gestured to the right, "and I'll start on these."

Kenzie positioned herself at the first right-hand table and adjusted the height. She would be sore at the end of the day if she didn't take the time to do it, even if it seemed like that inch or two shouldn't make any difference. She checked the identification tags on the first body, tapped the button on the floor with her foot to activate the recording equipment that hung above her, and dictated the date, her identity, and that of the corpse's in a low, even tone. Dr. Wiltshire waited for a pause in her dictation before beginning his own recording. The equipment was good at capturing only the voice of the doctor at the table and canceling out any background, but they would try not to talk over each other anyway, just to be sure.

Kenzie's first postmortem was the homeless man who appeared to have died from exposure. Kenzie would try her best not to be influenced by what she had already been told about the victim. There had been times when the police had been wrong. When someone was initially identified as homeless when they were not. When a John Doe had not been indigent, but the unfortunate victim of a mugger who had stripped him of his wallet, watch, phone, and any other items that might identify him. The body might tell her things the police had missed.

There were no personal items logged for the victim besides the clothes he had been wearing. Kenzie took a look through the clothes with gloved hands, looking for anything that might identify who the man was or where he had come from. Worn, dirty clothes. Not filthy, encrusted with vomit or other secretions and food drippings. Just old and well-used. The brand names did not all match or suggest that they had come from the same store. They were a mix of older styles and obsolete brand names. Thrift store finds, Kenzie would bet. They were all in good repair, with no holes or rips.

When there was nothing else to glean from the clothes, Kenzie moved on to the body. The man's face was thin. His hair was short and not tangled or matted. He had facial hair, but it was no more than a few days' growth. Not weeks or months. Some minor rashes on his arm and throat. His arms were thin but muscular. Not someone who had only been sitting down begging or drinking for weeks on end, maybe someone who took casual labor jobs as they were available. Such jobs would not be available as much during the winter when construction in Vermont was generally on hiatus and landscaping consisted only of clearing snow. He had tattoos. Kenzie scrutinized them for a few minutes and took several pictures to capture the details. They might be useful in identifying him.

He had several surgical scars. Nothing too recent. Nothing that would have contributed to his death. The stitching was… less skillful than Kenzie would have expected. As if it had been done hurriedly or by someone without a lot of experience. Certainly not anyone who cared whether they left a scar. There was no frostbite on his fingers or toes. They were whole. He hadn't lost the tips of any digits over previous winters on the street.

Kenzie wondered if that meant that he hadn't been homeless for any previous winters. Maybe this was his first year on the streets and he hadn't known enough to keep himself alive. But he was emaciated. All of his ribs showed like a picket fence. There wasn't an ounce of fat on him. Muscle and bones without any padding. She'd participated in postmortems on homeless men and women before, and they didn't generally look like that. Even those who had been on the street for years went to soup kitchens, begged for money or food, and, except for those who were junkies or very sick with AIDS or cancer, didn't have the wasted look of Kenzie's John Doe. And he didn't have any needle marks.

She continued her work, dictating notes as she went along, looking for any other clues that might help the police identify the man. She finished the gross exam, front and back, and looked over at Dr. Wiltshire.

"I'm ready to begin the Y-incision. Did you want to look at him first or supervise?"

Wiltshire looked up from his table. "No, not unless you have questions or concerns."

"Nothing that I need to ask about right now. We can go over findings whenever you're ready."

"Go ahead, then." He looked back down at his own subject and continued his examination.

Kenzie took a deep breath in and let it out slowly. She continued with the procedure she had been taught in medical school and had followed more than once in the Medical Examiner's Office. She'd just never been fully on her own before.

There were no surprises with the incision and opening John Doe up. Kenzie examined the body cavity before beginning to excise any organs.

"Dr. Wiltshire."

"Yes, Dr. Kirsch?"

"He only has one kidney."

He looked up at Kenzie and nodded. "Congenital, or has it been removed?"

Kenzie had seen the surgical scars on his abdomen and didn't have to look too closely to find the internal scarring. "It was removed."

"Make a note of it. Maybe kidney disease. Maybe a donor."

Kenzie nodded. She made the appropriate notes and began removing the man's organs. There was barely any visible fat cushioning his organs either. Kenzie stopped.

"Doctor?"

"Did you find something of interest?"

"He's had one lung removed."

Wiltshire's eyebrow went up. "Interesting."

Kenzie prodded the organs that remained in the abdominal cavity. "And... one lobe of the liver."

"Most unusual. Possibly the living donor of three different organs? Very rare. At least... in North America."

Kenzie knew a good deal about organ transplants and the black-market organ trade. She knew that Dr. Wiltshire was right and that it was not unusual to pay poor farmers for their organs in other countries, notably those in Asia and India. Whatever they could donate and stay alive. Or, in some cases, more. Giving up their bodies and their lives for the money that would go to their families.

But in North America... Kenzie shook her head. It was unthinkable. The man must be a refugee. An immigrant from another country who had escaped the horrors of poverty in his own part of the world to start anew in the United States. The American dream.

"Have you ever seen that before?" she asked Dr. Wiltshire.

"No. Not here. I've only read about it in journals."

Kenzie dictated her findings and continued.

10

"How was work today?" Zachary asked after they had been through the preliminary hellos and observations about the weather and how much better he was looking. He ran one hand over his dark buzz cut. "Anything interesting?"

Kenzie recounted that she had been able to perform two autopsies pretty much on her own, and observe and assist what Dr. Wiltshire had discovered in his.

"That's great!" he observed, dark eyes alive with interest. "Dr. Wiltshire really trusts you."

Kenzie nodded. He had not hovered over her, watching her every move and making suggestions along the way. They had spoken to each other across the room and Dr. Wiltshire had checked Kenzie's work and discussed what other labs they needed to order when it was done. But he had treated her as if she was perfectly capable of completing the postmortem on her own. And, of course, she was.

"Did you find anything interesting?"

Zachary was one of the few people Kenzie could talk to about autopsies and who wasn't squeamish about them. Happy to discuss them over dinner without any sign that it made him sick or nauseated to do so. What medical examiner didn't want to be partnered with someone like that?

She described the John Doe, including the organs that had been removed, his extreme thinness, and the skin rashes that Dr. Wiltshire confirmed were the result of malnutrition.

"So do you think that it was hypothermia? Or something else?"

"I think it was starvation. Which is really scary; that's not something that you expect to see in the United States. In Vermont. Maybe in a ghetto… or an area there are a lot of illegal immigrants, you know how they sometimes live with so many people in one room or one house, living in such poverty. But here in Vermont? I didn't think I'd ever see it here."

"Other than eating disorders or neglect cases."

"Well… yes." Kenzie nodded at this. That didn't mean that she thought the John Doe had been anorexic, but Zachary was right. There were isolated cases. Eating disorders. Junkies. Adults who neglected their children or elders. But the John Doe had not appeared to fit into any of those circumstances. "But I don't think that was the case here… clearly, I can't tell by looking at his body whether he had an eating disorder and starved himself. But he doesn't fit the demographics we usually see for eating disorders. And the organ donation suggests that he was the victim of the black-market organ trade. Which we usually only see in third-world countries."

"You don't have any idea where he is from? No identification? No missing person report?"

"I have some ideas, but it hasn't all come together yet. I need to talk to Dr. Wiltshire about a few things."

Zachary nodded.

Across the common room from them, a woman started arguing loudly with her visitor. Zachary's head jerked around instantly, and Kenzie saw him angle his body so that he was between the woman and Kenzie, shielding her from anything that might happen. Even though he was probably half the woman's weight, with his pre-Christmas weight loss.

"It's okay," Kenzie said. "Just an argument."

A nurse and an orderly approached the woman, speaking to her quietly, encouraging her to settle down.

"She can flip pretty fast," Zachary said, his shoulders up almost to his ears, bracing himself, waiting for violence to break out. "Sometimes… she throws things. Attacks the staff."

They both watched, not turning all the way around to look at the woman, but watching her from the corners of their eyes, not making it obvious that they were observing. The nurse made several suggestions to the agitated patient but didn't seem to be succeeding in de-escalating the situation. The orderly stepped forward, clearly ready to intervene physically. Kenzie pulled in a breath and held it, waiting.

The woman tried to throw a punch. Zachary half-rose from his chair. Kenzie grabbed his arm to keep him from intervening.

"They know what they're doing. Let them handle it."

"I know."

But he was still right on the edge of his seat, ready to jump in at any moment. The orderly grabbed the patient by the arm, held her still, and spoke to her in a firm voice, making it clear that he would not back off and let her continue with her visit. She tried to jerk away several times, her voice rising to a wail. Eventually, the orderly managed to escort her from the visiting area back toward her room.

Once she was removed, there was a visible relaxation from all of the others in the visiting area, both patients and outsiders. Kenzie let her breath out in a puff.

"Just a little drama," she said lightly. "I imagine you've seen worse."

He nodded, but he didn't slide back in his seat or relax his shoulders. His breath was still coming in short, anxious puffs. Conversations started up again. Kenzie waited, giving Zachary time to recover.

"I don't like *you* being here—" he said. For a moment, his real intent didn't register, and all that Kenzie heard was that he didn't want her there with him, "—where you might be in danger," he finished, eyes still roaming around the room, looking for any other signs of trouble.

"I feel safe here," Kenzie assured him. "There is plenty of staff around to ensure things don't get out of hand. She didn't have any reason to be mad at me, a total stranger. She was just having a disagreement with her visitor."

"But she does sometimes." Zachary shook his head. "She *will* attack a stranger, someone who just looks at her the wrong way or who might be *thinking* about her."

"Well, it's taken care of."

Zachary rubbed his temple and made a visible effort to return to their conversation. "You think they'll be able to figure out the identity of your John Doe? Where he came from? What he was doing here?"

"We'll give them everything we can… If he's undocumented, it might be impossible to identify him. If he does have any family or friends, they won't report him missing. They won't want to draw attention to themselves and whatever is going on."

"On TV, they always identify the victim," Zachary pointed out, smiling slightly to let her know he was teasing. "Why can't you do it like on *Bones* or all of those forensic shows? They can identify a person just from their bones. Or even just one bone." He held up his index finger. He smiled more broadly, enjoying the joke. "If you can't do that, what good are you?"

Kenzie laughed. "On those shows, they always give them implants with serial numbers, rare diseases, or all of these forensic clues that point to the one house in the entire country they could have lived in. That's not actually the way it works in real life."

Zachary shook his head in mock disappointment. "I expected so much more from you."

"I'll keep working on it," Kenzie promised. She smiled. It was nice to see him breaking through his depression to be able to joke around with her.

11

Whaat about the other bodies?" Zachary asked. "Anything else of interest?"

"No, pretty routine. Unattended deaths. A motor vehicle accident. Nothing that we didn't expect to find."

"No rare poisons or plague?"

"Nope. No such luck."

"Must have been a pretty boring day."

"It was okay." Kenzie put her hand over Zachary's on the table. He twitched as if he would pull it away and then forced himself to keep it there. "How are the new meds?" she asked, "I guess it's too early to tell anything."

"The first day? Yeah, too early. Still have the old cocktail in my system and the new meds haven't had a chance to build up yet. But... no bad reactions. No heart problems or hallucinations."

Kenzie nodded. "That's always good. I hope some of these new drugs will help. It seems like there are new medications on the market every day. If they work a different way than what you have already tried... there's always the hope that it will be more effective. Maybe reduce your symptoms even more."

"Yeah. Doctors don't like to prescribe new drugs, though. They want you to stick to the old, proven ones. Even if they've been proven *not* to work."

"Your doctor seems willing to reach beyond the same old, same old."

"Sometimes. For someone like me, who is… intractable."

"They'll find something that works better. Just because you still have some symptoms, that doesn't mean the meds you are on don't help at all. Just that they don't completely eliminate the symptoms. You don't know how you would feel if you weren't on anything at all."

Zachary rolled his eyes and Kenzie knew she'd said the wrong thing. "I've had med holidays before," he reminded her. "I know what it's like to be taken off of everything." He shuddered. "I'm glad… that I'm an adult and I'm allowed to say no when they suggest something like that." He pressed his lips together. "If they tried to Title 18 me in order to withdraw all treatment and establish a baseline… I'd go to court over it."

"Of course. Yes. We both know that would be a very bad idea. I can't imagine what it would be like for you not to be taking anything."

It frustrated her when he would go off of one of his meds or would only take it when he thought he should, but he never went off of all of his antidepressants. They both knew that would be disastrous. If the hospital had tried to enforce the withdrawal of all of his meds, she would be right there beside Zachary in court, telling them what idiots they were.

"When is the last time you were on a 'med holiday'?" Kenzie asked. Such an innocuous name. Like it was something pleasant. A vacation from his mental health issues. A relaxing break.

"Not since I was a teenager." Zachary's eyes grew distant as he thought back. "After a suicide attempt." He let go of Kenzie's hand, running the thumb of his right hand over his left wrist, where the old, deep scars were still visible decades later.

"Idiot doctors."

"I'd end up in a new home with a new doctor, and they'd decide that the last doctor didn't know what he was talking about. That I'd been on antidepressants for too long or the ADHD meds were a crutch I didn't need. Foster parents weren't allowed to put kids on herbs and alternative therapies, but they would seek out quack doctors who would say that was what I needed." He shook his head. "Trying to function without any assistance… it would be great the first few days, pretending that I was normal and didn't need to take anything anymore. But once my levels started to fall…"

"I'm glad you're an adult and know that you can't do that anymore too. You won't let them do that to you again."

Zachary stretched his neck and rubbed his shoulders, which were probably cramped and stiff after the way he'd been holding them. "That was about the time I met Pat. That last med holiday."

Patrick Parker was Lorne's partner of over twenty years. Lorne Peterson had been Zachary's foster father for only a few weeks when he had first entered the foster care system at age ten, but had remained a part of Zachary's life ever since, the two of them sharing their passion for photography. Lorne had given Zachary his first camera and helped him to develop his pictures. Despite Zachary's moves among foster families, group homes, and institutions, he had always kept in touch with Lorne. Even after Lorne and his wife had divorced and Zachary had discovered that his foster father was gay. Social Services had actively discouraged Zachary from staying in touch with him, but Zachary had rebelled against those rules. Kenzie suspected that Zachary had been just as much of a support to Lorne during that dark time, facing all of the prejudices he did, as Lorne had been for Zachary. They had needed each other, as unlikely as their friendship had been.

"What did you think of Pat when you met him?" Kenzie asked curiously. Zachary had never described their meeting to her.

"I thought… the first time I met him, I didn't know he and Mr. Peterson were together. I met Pat in the building the first time I went to see him there after the separation. It was… kind of a dangerous area. This guy was harassing me. Maybe a pedophile or a trafficker, I don't know. Somebody who figured I was a likely target. Pat was there. Leaving after a visit. I practically ran into him, and he chased the jerk off and escorted me to Mr. Peterson's floor. Made sure I was safe."

"Did he know who you were?"

"No. Just being a nice guy. Helping out a kid in trouble. Then later… I knew Mr. Peterson—Lorne—was seeing someone, but I didn't know… I just assumed 'Pat' was a woman. Had no idea. Until I dropped in on Lorne one day when Pat was there, and everything clicked into place." Zachary's face flushed pink. "I didn't know… it was a much bigger deal back then. People weren't openly gay. Not people like Mr. Peterson. I didn't know how to take it. What to think."

"So how *did* you take it?" Kenzie asked curiously. Society as a whole had been so homophobic. For a teenage boy like Zachary, it must have been a shock to find out that his trusted mentor was *one of those.*

"I figured… if he was happier with Pat than he had been with Mrs. Peterson, that was good. And I knew Pat was a good guy because he'd helped me out when he didn't know anything about me. We showed him my latest photography and he thought it was good, so I knew he was okay…"

Kenzie smiled. Pat and Lorne were both good men, devoted to each other and to Zachary, a member of their chosen family. She was glad that Zachary hadn't initially been opposed to their relationship or jealous of another person in Lorne's life. His willing acceptance, as a teenager, of someone who would have typically been seen as a predator rather than a protector, said something about the kind of person Zachary was.

"I'm glad you were there for Pat," she told him, "And Lorne."

Zachary shook his head. "They were there for *me,*" he corrected. "I don't know how I would have survived without them."

12

D r. Wiltshire and Kenzie had already set up the planned workflow and autopsies for the next day so, unless there was a change in circumstances and another case had to be rushed, they already knew what they were working on and didn't have to go over it again.

After going through the usual administrative work, Kenzie moved onto her first autopsy, another John Doe. Not a homeless man, as far as she knew, but the victim of an assault. His remains had been dumped by the highway just outside the city limits. No wallet or other quick method of establishing his identity, but there would probably be a missing person report to match up to the body once his family or place of employment had had a chance to miss him.

Kenzie checked the tags on the body and dictated his file number, the date, the height and weight stats that had been noted, and her name. She pulled the drape back from the John Doe's face and gasped.

Dr. Wiltshire looked up from his autopsy, one eyebrow cocked. "Everything okay, Kenzie?"

"Yes. No. I don't know."

"That is the full range of possible answers." He moved back and forth, trying to get a good look at Kenzie's patient. "That is the body dump?"

Kenzie nodded.

"Not too much damage to the face. Does something about this victim bother you?"

"No." Kenzie swallowed. "No, I was just startled…" She tried to think of an explanation but couldn't come up with anything that made sense. "No, sorry. Everything is fine."

He studied her for a long moment before going back to his own postmortem, making observations about his patient.

Kenzie breathed several times. She fogged up the plastic visor in front of her face and felt like she couldn't get enough oxygen through the mask. But she didn't want to make a scene. Leaving the autopsy to take off her mask and get a few breaths of fresh air would attract attention to her. She didn't want to give Dr. Wiltshire anything else to worry about.

So she forced herself to take long, slow breaths, trying to slow her heart after the burst of adrenaline. Dr. Wiltshire would be sure to notice if she were breathless dictating to the recorder. She pulled the blue drape down farther, examining the man's shoulders and chest, trying to convince herself that this was an autopsy just like any other. She could just continue, following the procedures she had been trained in, and stay aloof.

She swallowed again and described the man in a flat, steady voice. She thought she could feel Dr. Wiltshire watching her for the first few seconds, but then he focused back on his own work, letting her continue without interruption.

Kenzie looked back at the familiar face. Though it was purple with antemortem bruising and sported a flattened nose, he was still immediately recognizable. No piercings. The only jewelry that was on the inventory sheet was his gold watch. If it had been a mugging, he wouldn't still have had it. Then again, if it had been a simple mugging, there would have been no reason to beat him up, the act that she assumed had led to his demise. There would have been no reason to kill him and then remove his body from the scene and dump it outside the city. Muggers didn't do that. Whatever had happened, his attacker or attackers had known him. They'd had a motive to kill him and to dispose of the body the way they had.

Unlike her previous John Doe, this one had no obvious surgical scars. He would, Kenzie suspected, have all of his organs when she opened him up. He was well-fed, none of the emaciation or other signs of malnutrition she had seen on the previous victim—a much softer body, with plenty of fat to pad it out. Still in good shape, though. He hadn't been sitting at a desk all day the past few years. Or, if he did have a desk job, he was also dedicated to an exercise regimen. His muscles were well developed. But he had the beginning of the pot belly so many men his age had.

"Livor mortis suggests that the subject was left lying primarily on his right side for some time after death," Kenzie dictated. "Compare to police photos to see if that was the position the body was in when discovered at the dump site."

There was plenty of purpling over his stomach that was not livor mortis, indicating internal bleeding. Kenzie pulled the x-ray over to do a set of films before opening the man up. Broken ribs could do a lot of damage, especially if one had punctured the man's lung. She donned a lead apron and gave Dr. Wiltshire a heads-up.

"I'm going to do some films, if you want to take a break."

"I think I will," Wiltshire said agreeably, and left his table to retreat to the attached observation room, which was shielded from the x-rays and contained a water cooler and an assortment of slightly-stale individually wrapped cookies and pairs of saltine crackers. A little something in the tummy could help if someone watching an autopsy started to feel nauseated.

Kenzie normally tuned out the observation room, focusing just on the job at hand. An observer could interrupt with a question if something were pressing, but they rarely did, just watching and listening to what the doctor had to say. There were a couple of cops in the observation room, one in uniform and one in plain clothes. Dr. Wiltshire greeted them heartily and shook hands after removing his gloves. They didn't have the mic in the observation room on, so Kenzie couldn't hear what they said to each other, but everyone seemed relaxed and pleasant. Dr. Wiltshire helped himself to a cookie, tearing off the plastic wrapper and turning to watch Kenzie as she proceeded with the x-rays. Once Kenzie had everything she needed, she gave him a nod and removed the protective apron.

Dr. Wiltshire finished eating his cookie and returned to autopsy.

"They're more interested in your fellow than mine," he observed. He looked the corpse over, then turned his eyes to the monitor as Kenzie displayed the x-ray images. "Broken nose, ribs, both knees. Multiple phalanges." He raised his brows and looked at Kenzie. "What does that suggest to you?"

"Torture?" Kenzie squinted at each of the fractured bones. "Mob? Organized crime?"

"Possibly. I would say that someone definitely wanted something from our Mr. Doe. This is not a back-alley beatdown or mugging gone bad."

Kenzie nodded. She opened her mouth to say something else to Wiltshire, then closed it again.

"Nothing else significant yet?" he asked. Kenzie was clearly just in the beginning stages of the examination, and he didn't expect her to have found anything yet.

"A lot of bruising and internal bleeding. That's all so far."

Wiltshire nodded his agreement and drifted back over to his table. Kenzie glanced once toward the observation window, then blocked it out again, turning her focus back to the job. Her whole world, for now, was that man's body and any clues it held to the cause and manner of death.

.

13

The victim's internal organs were unsurprising, unlike with the other John Doe, who had been missing half of his. A kidney ruptured by the beating. Obvious cirrhosis of the liver. Kenzie carefully removed, weighed, and dissected each organ on the watch for anything out of the ordinary. There was little in the stomach other than alcohol. The man had not had a meal recently. No big turkey dinner. That might be significant in setting the time of death once police had an identity and access to his schedule.

Kenzie opened up the small intestine and leaned in for a closer look, adjusting her face shield. "Whoa."

Dr. Wiltshire straightened up, rubbing the small of his back. "What's up?"

"You might want to see this."

Kenzie started to tease out a long white string of segments. She focused the camera on her find so they could get some pictures of it and the cops in the observation room could see it.

Wiltshire joined Kenzie at her table and looked at the monitor as she worked rather than getting into her space.

"Tapeworm," Kenzie observed.

"Yes. Think you can get the whole thing out without breaking it? It's always interesting to see how long they are."

"I think this is going to be a long one." As Kenzie remembered it, tapeworms were often two or three meters in length.

Dr. Wiltshire stared at the screen. "Interesting."

"What?"

"*Taenia saginata.* Tapeworm cases in North America are usually *Taenia solium* and are mostly found in the Latino community. *Taenia saginata,* on the other hand—beef tapeworm—is quite rare here. Mostly seen in Eastern Europe."

Kenzie nodded slowly. She wasn't surprised by this; she'd already known that the man wasn't born and raised in the USA. Eastern Europe was a surprise, though; that wasn't what she had been expecting.

"Did you inspect dental work?" Wiltshire asked.

"Not closely. He's had some work done. You think it is significant?"

"Might go back to it when you're done with the internal. See if you can tell where the work was done. We have some resources that will show where different types of work are done in the world. Amalgams or techniques used in certain countries but not in the US."

"Okay. I'll check that." Kenzie continued to pull the long body of the tapeworm from the intestine. It seemed to be folded in on itself many times. She already had more than two meters free.

She glanced up at Dr. Wiltshire to see him smiling at her.

"What?"

"Do you know how long *Taenia saginata* gets?"

"Three meters?"

Wiltshire shook his head.

"Four?"

He grinned. "Sometimes nine or more."

"You're kidding." Kenzie looked back down at her work. "Is there anything *but* tapeworm in this guy's intestines?"

"It's amazing how much tapeworm you can pack into one intestine. It might be a good idea to check for other parasites too. They can be very helpful in establishing the subject's country of origin. Parasites are limited in their distribution."

"Okay."

"Take slides of each organ. They aren't all as easy to see as tapeworms."

Kenzie looked down at the coils of the parasite, shaking her head. At least she would have something interesting to tell Zachary when she visited him.

14

Kenzie made sure that everything was properly labeled with the victim's file number and packed for shipment to the lab and that she had finished everything properly. She had stitched the Y incision closed carefully, though she wasn't sure how important that would be to the family, if the man had one. His face had been pretty messed up. They wouldn't likely want the body on display. A quick cremation would probably be preferable. She checked that her recording had been properly saved and automatically sent to the transcription company. The x-rays and other images were all saved to the file. She couldn't think of anything else she might have missed. Dr. Wiltshire talked to the cops in the observation room, and they left without needing to speak with Kenzie.

George returned the body to the cold room. Kenzie retreated to the kitchen and Dr. Wiltshire joined her in a few minutes to get himself a cup of coffee.

Kenzie stood at the counter to prepare her coffee and tried to keep her face averted without making it obvious that she was doing so.

"You did a good job," Wiltshire observed. "Very professionally done."

"Thank you."

"I'm sure the police will be able to match him to a missing person file soon. If not, between what we have so far and what shows up on the lab work, we'll be able to at least give them some information on his background that might help."

"You said that tapeworm normally comes from Eastern Europe. That's what the dental work looked like as well."

"Good work. Make sure it is all documented in his report."

Kenzie sipped her coffee, hoping he would return to his office without extending the conversation. He didn't move. Kenzie tried to settle her expression before looking at him.

"Kenzie… what's wrong?"

She swallowed.

"Is it Zachary? I've told you before, if you need to be with him… go. You can make up the time later, catch up when things quiet down."

She shook her head. "It's not Zachary."

"What, then? Was it the violence of this case?"

Kenzie had assisted in autopsies that had been just as violent as the John Doe's beating. So how could he think that was the answer?

"That man… I've seen him before."

Dr. Wiltshire's brows went way up. "Your John Doe? You mean you've seen *him* before?"

Kenzie nodded, temporarily unable to speak.

Dr. Wiltshire took Kenzie's arm gently and steered her to one of the chairs at the lunchroom table they never used. Kenzie lowered herself into it, legs shaking. Dr. Wiltshire sat down across from her.

"Tell me about it."

Kenzie coughed. She took a drink of coffee, cleared her throat, and attempted to speak clearly and unemotionally. There was a hard, hot lump in her throat, and she could barely squeak around it. Her eyes filled with tears, even though there was no excuse for it. No reason for her to be sad or angry or upset.

"At my mother's house."

He sat staring at her, waiting. Kenzie was glad that he wasn't interrogating her and making demands that she answer each question that occurred to him. Or telling her she had to call the police and report it to them. But on the other hand, it would have been easier to answer yes/no questions than to come up with the words herself.

"On Christmas Day."

Dr. Wiltshire's face drained of color. Kenzie wasn't talking about someone she'd just run into at the gas station. She wasn't talking about an old acquaintance from decades before. She had seen the dead man just two days earlier on Christmas Day at her mother's house.

He nodded to her to go on. Kenzie tried to figure out how to do that.

"I don't…" She stopped sniffing, trying to keep the tears from streaming down her cheeks. "I don't know anything about him. Just his name. Maksim. That's how she introduced him. But I don't know… how she knew him or anything about it. It was… very strange."

"She? Your mother?"

Kenzie nodded.

"You should have told me before you started the post. We could have switched."

Kenzie nodded her agreement. She had known that she should say something to him at the time, but she couldn't think of what to say or how to explain it to him. So she had just gone on with what was on the table in front of her.

"Did you talk to this man at your mother's house?"

"Yes. Just to say 'hello, nice to meet you.' He was quiet, just sat to the side while I visited my mother."

"Did he know who you were?"

"Just… her daughter. My name. We didn't talk about the office. My mother doesn't like me to talk about it. Work stuff."

"Most people don't," Wiltshire agreed with a slight smile. "A certain amount of distaste over discussing the business of death in polite company."

"Yeah."

Kenzie looked around and found a box of tissues on the shelf behind her. She wiped her eyes and blew her nose. She didn't even understand why she was crying, why she felt so upset over the autopsy of a complete stranger. Just because she knew his name and had said hello to him?

But of course, it ran deeper than that.

Her concerns over her father not being there for Christmas and not being able to reach him. And not getting an answer from Lisa the last time she had called. Were her parents mixed up in something? Why would Lisa have a Russian immigrant in her house? One who appeared to have gotten on the wrong side of the mob? And why hadn't Lisa been forthcoming about him when Kenzie had called her back later?

She'd worried that he was still there when Kenzie had called back. That he was monitoring her, preventing her from answering Kenzie's questions or giving her any additional information. And now… he was dead. That should make her feel better. Relieve her worries that one or both of her parents might be involved in something unsavory.

"Who did your mother say he was when she introduced him?"

"She… she didn't. She just said his name was Maksim. Not… where he was from or how she knew him. And he just sat there while we visited. He didn't say anything. I thought he was French."

"That's not what the body would suggest. You didn't hear him speak at all?"

"Just a sentence or two. I could tell he was foreign, but not where he was from."

"Russian accents are usually pretty easy to recognize."

"But he didn't have an accent. He had… very precise diction. Hesitations. Like he had to think about the right words ahead of time."

Wiltshire nodded slowly. "He went through some kind of speech training to get rid of his accent."

"I think so. So I couldn't tell what accent it was. Just that… he wasn't a native English speaker."

"You will need to add this information to your report."

Kenzie shook her head. "Really? But I don't know anything."

"For the completeness of the report. You're not prohibited from doing a postmortem on someone you know. It might not be encouraged. Most people would probably choose not to. But there's nothing stopping you from autopsying someone you exchanged a few words with. Vermont is a very small state. I have ended up with someone I know on the table more often than I would like to admit."

Kenzie was hesitant. She was afraid she would be forced to talk to the police about the circumstances under which she had met Maksim. She knew plenty of law enforcement officers. None of them had ever given her any trouble. They were both on the side of truth and justice. But she didn't want to implicate her father or mother in something unsavory. Neither of them would be happy having to talk to the cops because she'd happened to meet someone at Lisa's house that she would later end up autopsying.

But if Dr. Wiltshire said that was what she needed to do, then she would do it, of course. She couldn't very well hide the fact that she knew at least part of the John Doe's identity. And Lisa would, presumably, know the rest. His full name and how she had come to meet him. Once his identity was established, they would be able to talk to the people he knew and worked with, establish his schedule, and, hopefully figure out who had beaten him to death.

He deserved justice just like anyone else. Even if it was inconvenient for her or her parents.

15

After confessing to Dr. Wiltshire what she knew of the man she had autopsied, Kenzie felt better. The lump in her throat relaxed and went away, the tears dried up, and she didn't feel so nauseated and shaky. It was no big deal. She wasn't in trouble. It was just something that happened sometimes—a bizarre coincidence.

Sitting at her desk, she dialed Lisa's number, praying that she would answer this time. Though she felt better, she was still uneasy about not being able to reach either of her parents and how Maksim had been connected to Lisa. Not just a casual acquaintance, but someone who had stayed at the house with her for at least a few hours. She didn't like to think that they had been romantically involved but, of course, it was a possibility, and, if so, Kenzie should drive to her mother's house to inform her of the developments rather than just calling her on the phone. But first, she needed to know that Lisa was okay.

"Hello, MacKenzie."

"Oh, Mother." Kenzie couldn't keep the relief out of her voice. "Thank goodness. I'm so glad to hear your voice."

There was a slight hesitation. "And I'm glad to hear yours, MacKenzie. Is something wrong?"

"Well… I don't know. I just was wondering… have you seen or heard from Dad lately?"

"Walter? Well, we talk fairly regularly."

"Have you talked to him? On Christmas Day or since then?"

"I don't know."

"But—" Kenzie cut herself off. Arguing or pointing out how silly it was for Lisa to say that she didn't know whether she had talked to Walter in the past two days was not going to help anything. Kenzie could not put herself in an adversarial position. "I called him to wish him a Merry Christmas. But he didn't answer and didn't return my call."

"He probably just forgot. Caught up in one of his lobbies."

Just like Lisa got caught up in her causes.

"Yes, but I still can't get him. I've been trying a few times a day, and he's not answering the phone."

"What number are you dialing?"

As if Kenzie might have forgotten her father's phone number. Or he might have gotten it changed and not told her about it.

"I know his phone numbers."

"I don't know what to say, MacKenzie. Just keep trying. Sooner or later, he'll answer."

"You don't know where he is?"

"At his home, I assume."

"He didn't go on a vacation or something?"

Lisa laughed. "A vacation? Your father? You're kidding. When was the last time he went on a vacation?"

"I just hope there's a good explanation for him not being around. Maybe he's out of the country and has to use one of those cell phones that doesn't work in the US. And he just… didn't tell me because we haven't been talking to each other lately."

"Lately?" Lisa echoed. "As in, since Amanda died?"

Kenzie wasn't sure what to say. Of course Lisa was right. Kenzie didn't talk to her father at all if she could help it. Not since everything had come out. She should have forgiven him a long time ago but, as much as she wanted to say that it was okay and she could move on, every time she even considered letting him into her life, something else made her remember why she couldn't trust him. No matter how much he loved her, he always put himself first. His opinion mattered more than hers. His morals and ideals were, of course, the only ones that mattered, and anyone who didn't have the same ones was wrong. He made things happen. But sometimes, making things happen meant pushing other people around, letting other people get hurt in the process. And that was okay with Walter, as long as he got what he wanted in the end. He wasn't opposed to someone not in his close circle getting hurt in furtherance of one of his goals. And sometimes, even someone inside that tight circle of family and friends.

"Mom…"

"MacKenzie."

"Who is Maksim?"

"Oh." Lisa sounded surprised at the change in the direction of the conversation. "Well… that's personal, dear."

"Personal. You said it was a business relationship. I just want to know who he is."

"What do you mean?"

"I mean… his full name, for one. Where he's from. What he does. How you met. What he was doing at your house on Christmas Day—" Kenzie changed her mind about that one. "—I don't care what he was doing there Christmas Day. Unless you want to tell me. But… who is he?"

"I wish I had the answers to your questions," Lisa said vaguely, "but I don't."

"You don't… know who he is?"

"No."

"He was at your house!"

"Yes. But I don't know him. It's a long story and not one that I feel like sharing at this time. You're just going to have to be satisfied with that."

"With what? You haven't told me anything. You don't even know his last name?"

"No."

"Or that he's from Russia?"

Lisa's voice was slightly higher. "From Russia? I never told you that."

"But he is. Did you know that? Do you know anything about him?"

"No. I don't."

"Was he there when I called you back on Christmas Day? Is that why you wouldn't give me any straight answers?"

"He's not here now," Lisa said coolly.

"I know that. Was he there when I talked to you before?"

Seconds ticked by, feeling like hours. Kenzie waited while an eon went by, waiting for Lisa to say something. Lisa was not above telling a social lie, but she didn't like to. And hopefully, she didn't like the idea of lying directly to Kenzie when she asked such a specific question.

"Yes," she admitted finally.

"And that's why you talked to me like you did. Because he was there, listening to everything you said."

"Yes."

"But he's gone now, so tell me what's going on. You can be honest with me now."

"I… nothing has changed. These questions will have to wait for another time."

"Nothing has changed? It certainly has!" Kenzie fought to keep her voice down. She wanted to shake Lisa by the shoulders and shout at her to make her understand. "Maksim is dead."

Lisa gasped.

Kenzie felt bad for dropping it on her like that. But what was she supposed to do? Lisa wouldn't talk to her about it. She was somehow stuck, thinking she could not answer any of Kenzie's questions. She didn't know how serious things had gotten.

"He's dead," Kenzie repeated quietly. "I autopsied him today."

"He's dead."

"Yes. And I don't even know his name. I need you to tell me everything you know."

16

She could hear Lisa breathing on the other end of the phone— quick, shallow breaths.

Kenzie shouldn't have dumped the news on Lisa like that. And she shouldn't have broken it over the phone. She should have driven to Burlington and given Lisa that information face to face. What if she had a heart attack? There was nobody there in that big house to help her, to take care of her or call 9-1-1.

"Mom, are you okay?"

"Yes. I'm fine, MacKenzie. I'm just fine."

"Are you sure? You're not going to faint or have a heart attack on me?"

"My heart is perfectly healthy. I have it checked every year. The doctors say I am as healthy as a horse."

"A retired racehorse, maybe. You're no spring chicken."

"You're mixing your metaphors, dear."

"Yes, I am." Kenzie blew out her breath. "So what can you tell me? I need his last name. His identity. We'll need to inform his family and friends. His workplace. The police need to investigate what happened to him."

"How did he die?"

Kenzie hesitated.

"You said you did the autopsy," Lisa said, her voice stern. "How did he die?"

"He was beaten. His kidney ruptured. A broken rib lacerated his liver. He bled out."

"That doesn't sound very pleasant," Lisa said, her voice muffled.

"No. It wasn't pretty. It was probably very painful, and it wasn't immediate. Before they broke his ribs, they broke his fingers. I think it's fair to say that he was tortured. His killers wanted something from him."

There was another period of silence. Kenzie prayed that Lisa would break down and give her the information she was looking for. Who was she trying to protect by not saying anything?

"I don't know his last name," Lisa said finally. "It doesn't matter how much you ask me. I simply don't know. The only name he gave me was Maksim. Maybe that isn't even his real name. He didn't have any identification?"

"No."

"I can't help you. I don't know what his name is."

"How did you meet him?"

"He came to the house. To the door…"

"And…?"

"That's all. He introduced himself. Said his name was Maksim."

"And you let him in. That doesn't make any sense, Mother. You don't just spend Christmas Day with someone who shows up on your doorstep and tells you his name is Maksim."

Kenzie wasn't worried anymore about her mother having dementia. It was pretty clear that Lisa was being intentionally obstructive, trying to keep Kenzie from finding the answers she was looking for.

"In this case, as unlikely as it may sound, it's the truth. I don't know his last name. I don't know if Maksim is his real name."

"What did he tell you that made you let him in?"

Kenzie pictured the man standing at the front door, introducing himself in that flat, precise voice, free of any accent. Lisa opening the door wider and letting him in. Because…?

"Did he say he was a friend of Dad's?" Kenzie suggested. "Or… that he was someone you expected? A caterer or plumber? Did he pretend he knew you?"

"I think… I've said as much as I can at this point. I'm sorry I can't help you. I'm sure your policemen will be able to figure out more about him. Or Za—" Lisa cut herself off and pretended that she hadn't been about to say Zachary's name.

"Or Zachary?" Kenzie finished. "You think that Zachary could figure it out?"

"No. Zachary is in the hospital. I forgot about that for a second. There's nothing he can do."

Kenzie felt like Lisa was building up a blockade between them. She wouldn't share any information. Kenzie would have to just turn the file over to the Roxboro police without further information. She couldn't share it, not even with Zachary.

"Mother. I want to help. I want to get this figured out. How can I do that when you won't tell me anything?"

"There's nothing to tell. Let's forget all about this. Please forget you even saw him here."

―――

Kenzie was exhausted when she hung up the phone. She had been feeling fine before she started the autopsy on Maksim. But the emotional toll of the postmortem, of worrying about her parents, the emotional explanation to Dr. Wiltshire, and now the phone conversation with her mother had wrung out every last bit of strength. She had to finish her computer work, make a few notes, log off, go home, have something to eat, and then head over to the hospital to see Zachary. And she wasn't sure she could even complete one of those tasks. She wanted to lie down and sleep, to shut everything out. All of the questions, everything she had learned that day, she wanted to forget. Just to rewind and pretend none of it had happened. Start fresh.

Dr. Wiltshire approached Kenzie's desk. He was wearing his coat and outdoor gear. Ready to brave the snow and the wind again. He stopped and looked at Kenzie.

"You're still here."

Kenzie laughed. "I'm still here."

"You shouldn't be. It's been a long day. You need a nice long soak in a hot bath. Close up shop here. Do you want me to drop you somewhere?"

"No, no. I've got my car. Zachary's car. I don't need a ride."

"If you're as tired as you look, that might not be the best idea. I can drop you at your house if you like. Pick you up in the morning. You can leave your car in the garage overnight."

"No. I'll be fine. Really. I need the car tonight. I need to pop over to the hospital. For a few minutes, at least."

"Zachary would understand if you need a rest for one day."

"I know." Of course Zachary would tell her to take care of herself first. He would assure her she didn't need to visit him every day, just like he had told her several times before. But Kenzie needed it as much as he did. She needed to see that he was okay, or she wouldn't be able to sleep. She would worry about him all night, imagining everything that might have happened in her absence. Zachary depressed and beating himself up for wanting her to be there and not caring enough about her well-being. Self-harming. Even a suicide attempt. Kenzie knew she couldn't be responsible for Zachary's mental health, that it was magical thinking to believe that he wouldn't harm himself if she went to see him every day, but that he might if she missed. She could probably use an anxiety prescription herself to be able to calm down and not worry about all of the terrible things that could happen when she was away from him.

Dr. Wiltshire nodded. He put his hands flat on the top of her reception desk. "Sleep in tomorrow. Make sure you get the sleep you need. I don't want you getting run down."

The next day was Saturday. Kenzie typically only put in a few hours on a Saturday and technically didn't need to be there at all unless she was called in due to an emergent situation. "I'll come in late tomorrow," she agreed.

Dr. Wiltshire looked pleased. He had probably forgotten what day it was and thought he had talked her into something. He'd kick himself when he realized later that night. "Good. You take the time you need for yourself. Our patients aren't going to get up and walk out if they have to wait."

"They'd better not!" Kenzie agreed.

Dr. Wiltshire chuckled and walked away.

17

Kenzie wasn't proud of herself for chugging a pint of ice cream in place of a healthy supper, but she felt a lot better mentally once she did. She probably would have gotten just as much or more of a boost from a healthy, freshly prepared meal, one that wouldn't be followed by a sugar crash. But for the time being, it was what she needed. Chocolate healed a multitude of ills. Dr. Wiltshire and any other medical doctor would probably not agree, citing what chocolate ice cream was bound to do to her triglycerides, liver, and fat cells.

Even though Dr. Wiltshire's suggestion of a long soak in a hot tub sounded heavenly, Kenzie couldn't let herself crash and laze away the rest of the evening. There were a number of items on her list of things to do and Zachary would be expecting her at the hospital. It sounded a lot nicer to fall into a food coma and pamper herself the rest of the night, but she had to stay alert and focused and be productive.

Kenzie had gotten Lindsey's number from Heather. Lindsey was Tyrrell's ex-wife. Kenzie wasn't sure how Lindsey would feel about receiving a call from her asking after Zachary's brother and if she had heard anything from him or knew where he might be. It probably wouldn't be the most positive reception. But she felt like she needed to try at least that much. There wasn't much she could do. Tyrrell wasn't *her* brother and didn't normally keep in touch with her, so she couldn't exactly start a missing person investigation. There was no reason she should have heard from Tyrrell. No reason he was obligated to call her back if she reached out to him.

It felt strange to focus on the fact that Tyrrell was missing rather than on her own father. Maybe she was using it as an excuse not to deal with the questions she had about her father. She couldn't deal with his issues when she was in the process of dealing with Tyrrell's. And figuring out what to put in her report about Maksim's autopsy. Should she even indicate that his first name was Maksim, when Lisa admitted she had no idea if it was his real name?

Kenzie deliberately turned her mind away from all such questions and tapped on the phone number for Lindsey. It rang a few times and she figured it would go through to voicemail. Lindsey didn't know Kenzie and had no reason to answer a call from a stranger. Kenzie tried to decide whether she would leave a voicemail message asking Lindsey to call her back or just hang up and try again another time, hoping that Lindsey would be more inclined to answer then.

"Hello?"

"Oh, hi there. Is this Lindsey?"

"Yes. Who is this?"

"My name is Kenzie. I'm a friend of Zachary's."

"Zachary? I think you've got the wrong number."

"Zachary Goldman, Tyrrell's brother."

There were a few seconds of uncomfortable silence. "Oh. I see. Well, Tyrrell doesn't live here, so I think you're calling the wrong person. Try his cell phone."

"I guess you know that he didn't show up when he was supposed to on Christmas Day," Kenzie said, plowing ahead over Lindsey's objection.

"Considering he was supposed to be here to pick up the children, yes, I did notice that," Lindsey said dryly.

Kenzie thought about Alisha and Mason and how disappointed they must have been when their daddy didn't show up to pick them up as expected. She could hear background noise. A TV, maybe, and Mason's voice keeping a running monologue about something.

"Yeah. Sorry, that was awkward. Of course. Well… I'm just making a few calls to track Tyrrell down and make sure that he's okay."

"As I said, he's not here."

"Do you have any idea where he might be? I realize the two of you aren't together anymore, but you might know his friends or hang-outs, somewhere he's gone before…"

"I don't know where he goes when he disappears. I didn't even when we were together. I can't help you."

"So… this has happened before?" Kenzie asked tentatively. She shouldn't be surprised. Tyrrell had informed Zachary and Kenzie on their first visit that he was an alcoholic. It made sense that he might have disappeared before. Failed to show up at places where he was supposed to because he was on a binge.

"Yes. It is not the first time." Lindsey spoke crisply. "There's no point in looking for him—sorry, what was your name?"

"Kenzie. Kenzie Kirsch."

"Well, there is no point in looking for him, Kenzie. If he wanted you to know where he is, he would let you know. But that isn't what he wants. He wants to just hide from his responsibilities and shut out the rest of the world. He'll be back in a few weeks or months, saying how sorry he is about the whole thing, vowing to never do it again… but then he will. After a few months or a year, he'll drop out of sight again and start the whole cycle all over again."

"And you don't know where he goes…?"

"He doesn't want to be found."

"Okay…" Kenzie trailed off, trying to think if there was anything else she should ask Lindsey while she had the chance. Lindsey would probably block Kenzie's phone number once she got off the phone, so it was her one chance. But Lindsey had been pretty clear. There wasn't any question in her mind that Tyrrell was just off on a drunk and would resurface at some point in the future when it felt safe to do so. Or when he had hit rock bottom.

Kenzie just hoped that Tyrrell wouldn't ever turn up on her table.

"Is this the right number?" Kenzie asked, reciting Tyrrell's phone number.

"Yes. That's right. Of course, he probably hasn't paid his bill, and you'll just get an error message when you call it. He'll get another phone when he decides to join real life again."

"Thanks. I'm sorry again for bothering you. I was hoping he had a favorite hangout you might know about… or a friend to call…"

"Don't call here looking for him again." Lindsey's voice was flat. "It's not good for the kids."

Kenzie bit back the "Say 'hi' to Alisha and Mason," that had been on the tip of her tongue. They didn't need to be reminded that their father hadn't shown up and was missing in action.

She was going to stop there. She needed to get to the hospital before visiting hours were over to have a short visit with Zachary and make sure he was doing okay. There wasn't anything else she could do other than calling Tyrrell, and he hadn't responded to any call that she'd made to him already. He wasn't likely to start. Before too long, as Lindsey had said, she wouldn't even be able to get through to Tyrrell's cell if he had stopped paying for it.

But Heather might have more information than she had given Kenzie. Kenzie was sure that she would have been looking for him. And Zachary had been training Heather on private investigation skills, so it was entirely possible that she had been able to find something out that Kenzie had not.

It was worth a try.

"Hi, Kenzie," Heather, at least, had not blocked Kenzie's phone number and willingly answered the call, even knowing who it was from.

"Hi, Heather. I was just wondering, first of all, whether you had heard anything from Tyrrell?"

"No, nothing. I guess he doesn't want to talk to any of us."

"Yeah. That's what Lindsey said. I've left a couple of messages, but why would he want to talk to me? He barely even knows me. And I'm not related."

"I think Tyrrell's as comfortable with you as with anyone. I've only known him for a few months. As an adult, I mean. Since we first met in person. So I'm in the same boat. Other than sharing genes with the guy."

"And a past."

"That was a long time ago, and I don't think he remembers very much about it. He was still really young when… the fire… when we were split up. Not like with Zachary, where he remembers things we did together."

"I guess." It wasn't easy for Kenzie to understand the dynamics of their odd family relationships. She'd had one sister, Amanda, and they had been very close. They had never been separated by anything other than hospitals and Amanda's kidney disease. When Amanda had died, that was the end of it. There were no other siblings to meet. No one to reunite with. It was just over. "I was wondering… if you have done any research into where Tyrrell has disappeared to? Whether you could use any of the training Zachary has given you to figure out where he would go."

"Well…" Heather drew the word out long. "No. The stuff that I've been working on for Zach is different—tracking down people's current phone numbers and home addresses. But I already have that information for Tyrrell. The issue is that he isn't there, at home, or answering the phone. I don't know… I have no idea where I go after that. And Lindsey didn't help. I don't know where he's gone before, or I could use it as a starting point."

"Yeah. I just talked to her. Same problem."

"I don't imagine she was too happy that someone else was calling her to ask about him."

"She was a little chilly," Kenzie admitted.

"I probably would be too. Especially when he's disappointed the kids so many times. Moms want to protect their kids. Save them the heartache."

18

It was quite a bit later than Kenzie had planned when she arrived at the psych ward in the hospital. She was not going to have time for a very long visit. She arrived a bit flustered, looking at her phone to see what time it was, sweaty from her hurry from the underground parking to the reception desk at the front of psych.

"Hi," she said to Nurse Val, her voice thready in her own ears. "Sorry!" She blew out her breath, trying to settle her breathing and heart rate into something cooler and more sedate. "I'm a bit out of breath."

Kenzie placed her driver's license onto the desk so that the nurse could verify her identity, even though she had seen Kenzie there to visit Zachary a number of times now. She was still required to check ID every time as a security precaution.

She dutifully copied Kenzie's name and driver's license number into her computer log.

"How is he?" Kenzie asked.

The nurse looked at Kenzie, grimacing slightly. Kenzie's stomach did a nosedive. Was he worse? Was he reacting to one of the new meds? Or had something else happened? Maybe an altercation with the patient who had been arguing during their last visit? Zachary had said that she could flip in a minute and that she had been known to attack the staff and others. She could have easily targeted him and was probably twice his current weight.

"He's okay," Val assured quickly. "He's just… he was a little agitated when I saw him last. Probably just withdrawing from his previous medications. We have this period where he's ramping up the new meds and tapering off the old ones, where he is more likely to have problems."

"Poor guy. How long will the transition time be, do you think?"

"It's hard to say. I'd say he's coming down from his previous cocktail pretty quickly. So hopefully, he'll only have a day or two where it's really uncomfortable."

"I hope so."

The nurse nodded her agreement. She finished entering Kenzie's information and handed her driver's license back. "Sorry about all of this," she said, rolling her eyes. "I know it's a pain, especially when we already know who you are."

"It's okay. I really don't mind. I'd rather you are keeping the patients safe and have a log of everyone who comes in here."

The nurse looked at her for a moment before nodding. She too knew the history behind the increased security measures. It wasn't just routine.

"You're all set, then. Do you want someone to take you in?"

"I know my way around," Kenzie said, waving her hand. There was no need for an intern or security guard to leave what he was doing to walk Kenzie in to see Zachary.

"All right. See you later, then."

Kenzie waited for the nurse to buzz her past the door into the secure ward. She waited for it to shut behind her before moving on, consciously making sure that no one could follow her in and grab the door before it had a chance to latch securely. Then she walked into the common room and looked around. Zachary had a couple of areas that he usually hung out in, but Kenzie didn't see him immediately. She waited in case he'd just stepped out to the restroom or something quick. When he didn't appear, she headed toward his room.

One of the security guards moved to intercept her.

"Is Zachary in his room?" Kenzie asked, not letting him block her. He nodded, posture relaxing a little.

"Yeah, last I saw."

"I'm just going to see him."

"Best if you visit in the common room."

"I'll get him to."

He nodded and let Kenzie go on to Zachary's room.

Kenzie hadn't been sure whether Zachary would be sleeping, his depression getting the better of him, or restless because of his ADHD. She should have known the answer from Val's comment that he was agitated. Zachary was pacing up and down the length of the small room. When he turned around to continue walking toward the door, he saw her framed in the doorway.

"Kenzie!"

"Hey, Zach. How's it going? You're looking a little anxious, there."

He nodded. "Yeah. Don't know how I'm going to sleep tonight. What time will they take night meds around?" He looked around for a clock. Kenzie wasn't sure what time they would be taking around sleep aids and whatever else the patients needed to get through the night.

"Probably not too much longer," she assured him. "It's still visiting hours, so they won't be shuffling you off to bed yet."

"Yeah. Right," Zachary agreed, his tone staccato.

"You're having some fun with the new meds."

"Or with coming off of the old ones. Yeah." He rubbed his head. "This is why I hate taking so many pills."

That, and the way he was embarrassed when she saw how many different medications he was on. And the fact that he didn't like to feel like he was out of control, but wanted to be able to control his mental health without meds or by only taking the ones that he felt he needed from one day to the next. And the fact that he had to deal with so many different interactions and side effects. The nausea his previous morning meds caused had been quite a problem when they were trying to keep his weight up.

"Well, give it a few days, and it will be better."

"A few days?" Zachary shook his head in irritation. "I can't deal with this for a few days."

"It won't be this bad the whole time. And you'll have your night meds before too long to help you calm down for bed."

"Is it late?" He looked at his wrist like he might be wearing a watch. But of course, he didn't have a watch or even a cell phone. And there was no clock visible in the room that Kenzie could see. "Is this the time you usually come?"

"No, later than usual. Sorry. I had some other things going on with work and…" She couldn't tell him about Tyrrell. That would just make him more worried and upset, "some other personal stuff."

"Oh, that's okay. You have a life. I don't expect you to be here all the time or to be here every day at the same time," he told her quickly. "I just wondered. It's hard to keep track of what time it is here."

Even when he was medicated and stable, he still had problems with losing track of time or not being able to sleep. Kenzie could only imagine how difficult it must be with the symptoms he was experiencing.

"I'm glad I made it," Kenzie said lightly. She made a gesture in the direction of the common room. "Do you want to go visit out there? They prefer us to visit where we can be supervised."

Zachary pushed his hands down deep into his pockets as he paced. "Yeah. People bring in contraband. Even when they know it could be detrimental to the person's health." He shook his head. "Why would people do that?"

"I guess some people can be talked into it. If the person you're visiting is begging for something, they think they need…"

"Don't ever do that," he told her. "If I ask you for something, just say no. Or say yes and don't bring it; I don't care. Just don't do it."

"I don't think that's going to happen."

"You don't know. You don't know how messed up I could be if the meds are wrong. I could tell you that I really needed something. I don't know. Something that's contraindicated or an illegal drug."

Kenzie was amused by the thought of Zachary asking her for something like coke or fentanyl. There was no way. He was too straitlaced, and he knew that his family had already been hit hard by addiction. He would never take the chance of getting addicted to something like that. But there was no point in arguing about whether he would ever do such a thing.

"I won't bring you anything without clearing it with your doctor first," she promised.

Zachary nodded. "Good. Yeah."

Kenzie motioned again toward the common room. Zachary headed for the door, but stopped and looked longingly back toward his room. Kenzie shook her head, unable to understand why he would want to stay there. If it were her, she would rather be in the open space. The patient rooms were a little too small and cell-like for her.

The security guard was standing in the hallway waiting for them. He nodded when he saw that Kenzie was bringing Zachary out and started walking back toward the common room to continue supervising visits there.

"Lorne called," Zachary commented as they walked into the larger area filled with tables and chairs.

"Yeah? How are he and Pat doing?"

Kenzie stood near one of the tables he usually sat at and waited for him to sit down. But Zachary jiggled anxiously and paced a few steps away, then back.

"He sounded good. Said they had a nice Christmas. Asked how mine was. Well, no, he didn't ask how mine was because he already knew. But he said that theirs was good."

Kenzie nodded. "Good. Did Pat see his family this year?"

"Uh, yes." Zachary nodded. "Gretta and…" He frowned, trying to remember.

Kenzie waited, giving him time to dredge it up. Zachary shook his head, frowning, and gave a shrug. "Do you remember?"

"Suzanne. His sister is Suzanne."

"Right." Zachary nodded. "Pat saw Gretta and Suzanne for Christmas." He paused, thinking about it. "Mr. Peterson doesn't have anyone else."

"No parents or siblings?"

"No… not that he's ever talked about. He really doesn't talk about his family. About Pat and me. And Mrs. Peterson sometimes. But he doesn't talk about the home he came from."

Kenzie nodded. "I don't think I've ever heard him talk about them. What kind of background does he come from, do you know?"

Zachary shook his head. "He always just talks about his 'chosen' family."

"Maybe he lost his parents at an early age. Is it possible he was a foster child himself?"

Zachary blinked several times, looking as though the thought had never occurred to him before. "I don't think so… he would have said so, wouldn't he? All of the times he's talked about fostering and how I was one of his kids… he's never said he was a foster himself. And he would have, wouldn't he?"

"I would expect him to… but you never know. Maybe that's part of his past that he keeps walled off. Never talks about."

Zachary continued to pace. "He would have said. I'm sure he would have said."

Kenzie shrugged. "Okay. You're probably right. He might have lost his parents as an adult. When he was in his twenties or thirties or older. They might have been estranged and he didn't talk about it when it happened."

"Or maybe they didn't die, and he has nothing to do with them. Like with Pat and his family for the last twenty years. It was only last year that they got together for the first time, because his father had died. Until then, Gretta wasn't allowed to reach out to him."

"Yes. It was certainly not acceptable to be gay when Lorne was a young man. They might have kicked him out and told him never to come home."

"But he married Mrs. Peterson. I don't think he came out until late in their marriage. I don't think he ever told anyone when he was a teenager."

"Maybe not. Or maybe he did, and they reacted so violently that he decided he'd better toe the line and act straight to avoid being hurt. Repress his own feelings."

"Yeah." Zachary slapped his hands on his legs, not able to stay still. His brows drew down in a scowl. "It was so unfair to people like him. Why would they treat him that way? Their own kid? They knew what kind of a person he was. A good person. Even if they didn't understand his preferences."

"We don't know that they did do anything to him. We're only speculating."

He looked at her for a minute as if he were trying to work this out, then finally nodded. "Right. Yeah. Sorry, right now, my brain is…" he shook his head, searching for the right word, "uninhibited?"

"Maybe. Impressionable. Making loose associations."

"Maybe I'd better not discuss Lorne. I wouldn't want to remember things as being true that aren't. Aren't true."

Kenzie agreed. "So… anything interesting going on in the ward today?"

She looked at her phone to check the time. They wouldn't have very long to visit but, in the state Zachary was in, he probably wouldn't know the difference. He might think she was there for a long time, and he might think that she hadn't been there long enough, but his actual perception of how long it was would probably be off.

Brains chemicals were tricky things.

19

Kenzie did sleep in the next day, as she had told Dr. Wiltshire she would. Her body needed it. But eventually, she couldn't stop tossing and turning and decided it was time to get up. Her brain was, once more, working on the problem of what to do about her missing father. And about the familiar corpse in the morgue. She needed to write up her final report on Maksim.

But her father... she couldn't just forget him. She couldn't write a report and pass it on to someone else to take care of. She didn't think that police would do anything if she reported Walter missing. They would point out that she and Walter hadn't kept in touch before and he was under no obligation to call her back or let her know that he was okay. Chances were, he had just left for a Christmas vacation, and he'd get around to calling Kenzie or return to his home afterward.

And all of that could be true, but Kenzie had a feeling of dread in the pit of her stomach that told her he wasn't just on vacation somewhere. He should have been at Lisa's on Christmas Day. He should have called Kenzie to wish her a Merry Christmas no matter where he was. She had gotten used to those family traditions. Even if she didn't want Walter to call her on Christmas and her birthday, he always did. And so did her mother.

Kenzie searched out memories of when she had lived at home or, at least, in Burlington and had been more aware of what was happening in Lisa's and Walter's lives. Who were some of the people Walter had associated with? Who would he still be friends with today, decades later? She knew there were a few. Lobbying was all about relationships and Walter would not have let neglected relationships just fall by the way. He would have kept them central in his life so he could always call on them for favors or pressure where he needed them.

Kenzie looked up a few of Walter's old friends online and called them. Across the board, they said they didn't know where Walter was, but he was sure to show up soon. He was constantly popping up somewhere with a new plan or campaign underway. No one knew of any Christmas plans he'd had for travel. Walter always stayed pretty close to home for Christmas.

The higher up in the social and political strata a friend was, the more likely that Walter would have called them recently. Kenzie's mind kept returning to the governor's office, where she knew that her father had wielded some influence. He had tried to covertly record his own daughter at their instructions, so he had to hold some clout in demanding a return favor.

The problem was, the governor wouldn't be in his office over the weekend or, if he were, he wouldn't be taking any calls, particularly not from his old friend's nosy daughter. The only numbers that Kenzie could find for him online were for his office. And that wouldn't even go directly to his desk, but to a gatekeeper who would decide who could get through and who couldn't.

So Kenzie dialed another number, one that was familiar to her. Whether Lisa would take another call from her, she wasn't sure. Kenzie had probably worn out her welcome with the last call.

Lisa's tone was cool, but she answered, which was more than Kenzie had thought she would do. "MacKenzie. I hope you got everything sorted out with your... job."

"I still have to write my final report. But... yes. I'm not going to get any more information about Maksim, if that is his name, so I need to get what I did find down on paper and get it back to the police for their investigation. They'll want to know whatever I can give them. Though I'm afraid that it isn't much."

"Good, glad to hear it."

"I actually didn't call you about that. I'm sorry, I guess it's just my week to bug you."

"It is never a bother to talk to you."

Lisa's calm, flat words riled Kenzie, but she tried not to react to them. She was there for whatever information she could get, and then Lisa could go back to whatever cause she had been working on before Kenzie had interrupted her. But she hated how fake the tone was, how Lisa thought she could get away with talking that way to Kenzie and she would not understand Lisa's disdain.

"I was just wondering if you had a number for the governor."

"The governor."

Kenzie nodded impatiently. She didn't need Lisa's skepticism, and she didn't need to explain why she needed the number. She was a grown, professional woman, as was Lisa. They could treat each other like it for once.

"His number is in the phone book," Lisa pointed out. "Or whatever the internet equivalent is these days. It should not be difficult at all to find it."

"But what I need is his private number. I need to talk to him today. I can't wait until Monday and it isn't an official matter. So I need whatever number you have that might be his home phone or cell."

Lisa considered this request in silence. She was probably surprised at such an audacious ask. A well-behaved woman like Kenzie didn't go around asking for people's private numbers. Especially someone as important as the governor. Kenzie didn't have any reason to need his number. Either it was personal and unimportant and she could wait until Monday when she could reach out to him, or it was urgent and important… in which case Kenzie should let her know the details, so Lisa knew she was doing the right thing by handing the information over.

"Do you have a pencil?" Lisa said finally.

Kenzie snatched up a pen from the side table and grabbed a

magazine she had been planning to read but hadn't even opened yet. "Yes. I'm ready."

Lisa recited the number slowly and clearly for Kenzie. She scribbled it down on the magazine.

"Thank you, Mother. That will be very helpful. You've really helped me."

"I'm glad to have been of service. Perhaps someday, you'll fill me in on what this was all about."

Kenzie hoped that it would become obvious without her having to explain it. Because Walter would be back home safe and sound and they could all laugh about Kenzie's unfounded concerns.

She went ahead and called the governor's private line immediately, before she could think of the thousand reasons not to call him. She had a good reason to call him, whether he realized it or not, and she was just going to go ahead with it.

Kenzie's hand was shaking as she tapped the numbers Lisa had given her into the phone keypad.

There were a few rings before the call was connected and a rich, resonant voice she recognized spoke in her ear.

"Hello?"

"Governor Smith. I'm sorry to call you on your weekend. I'm sure this is your family time, and I don't have any right to be intruding on it."

"Who is this?"

"My name is Kenzie Kirsch. I'm Walter—"

"Oh, of course. Yes, I know who you are, Dr. Kirsch. I'm sorry, I didn't recognize your number."

"I wouldn't expect you to. I hope you don't mind that I got yours from my mother. She's not involved in this, I just asked her for the information, and she didn't know what it was about."

"And what *is* it about?" he interrupted her flow. "How can I help you, Dr. Kirsch?"

Kenzie found herself flushing. "Just Kenzie, please. I didn't call you in my capacity as a doctor or pathologist."

"Kenzie?"

Kenzie swallowed and made an effort to slow down her speech. She didn't want to sound like a babbling fool. The last thing she needed was for the governor to think she was drunk or high. "I was just wondering… whether you have heard anything from my father lately."

"From Walter." The governor thought about it. Or at least, he paused as if he were thinking about it. He might well have been trying to figure out how to get rid of Kenzie as quickly as possible. "No. It's been a couple of weeks since I spoke to Walter last. But surely you have seen or talked to him. And Lisa, of course."

"I was supposed to see him on Christmas Day." That might be stretching truth just a little. She had expected to see Walter at Lisa's house, but she hadn't made any arrangements with him. "He didn't show up—no sign of him. Mother hasn't seen him either. I wish I could say it was all just a misunderstanding and he forgot that he was supposed to be at the house… but… he's not that forgetful. There are only one or two days a year that he actually sees me. We don't get together as a family very often. There's no way he would have forgotten about it."

"Have you called him?"

"Of course. Repeatedly. And I've left him messages and sent him texts. But there hasn't been any sign of him. I was really expecting to hear from him before now. It's been four days."

The background noise Kenzie had been able to hear on the call disappeared. The governor had, she suspected, left whatever party or event he was at, escaping to a study or powder room and shutting the door.

"Kenzie, I can see why this would concern you. Can I ask… have you involved anyone else? Made a missing person report?"

"No. I've just been making phone calls, asking people he knows if they might have seen him lately. If they knew if he had any plans for the holidays. But you know Dad… he doesn't take vacations."

"No," the governor agreed, humor in his voice. "The man was a machine, never a day off. I'm surprised he even agreed to meet with you on Christmas Day. He probably still had business plans that day as well. He just expected to be able to fit you in between his other appointments."

"Yes," Kenzie agreed. "In between the main course and the dessert."

The governor chuckled. "Yes. This may seem like a strange request, Miss Kirsch—Doctor—Kenzie. But I wonder if you would leave this to me for the next step. Let me make some discreet inquiries."

"Oh, I don't expect you to do anything about this personally. I will go through channels."

"I'm asking you not to. Walter is a personal friend. I wouldn't want to see him get in any kind of trouble."

"Trouble?" Kenzie repeated.

"I don't know what he might be involved in. Politics can sometimes lead to… unusual alliances. Let me look into it and see what I can find."

"Governor… this isn't about a woman, is it?"

"What do you mean?" he asked mildly.

"Just that… if he's off somewhere with a girlfriend, that's fine. I don't care. I certainly didn't expect him to stay celibate for years after divorcing my mother. You don't need to think that you would hurt my feelings finding out that he was with a woman. Or if you know that he has a girlfriend and want to follow up with her now."

He laughed at this. "Yes, I'm sure Walter has had plenty of female company over the past years, but he is discreet. I don't know of any long-term relationships. I don't think that would get back to me. But I'll ask around and find out what's going on, if I can."

"Okay. I appreciate it. I really didn't call you because I expected you to investigate yourself. I just wanted to know if you had heard from him."

"I haven't. But I don't mind doing a little digging to see if I can find out what is going on."

20

The nice thing about going in to work on a weekend was that there weren't a lot of outside interruptions. Kenzie didn't have to deal with phone calls and people filling out forms and making requests for files. Everything was as silent as a tomb, and she could just buckle down and get caught up on any paperwork that she needed to.

Of course, when Dr. Wiltshire was there, it wasn't completely silent, but he was good about letting her work on what she needed to and not making extra requests. Unless he wanted to know if she wanted to be involved in a postmortem that he was doing. Sometimes he had catch-up work too, and fitting in a few routine unattended deaths on a Saturday or Sunday was a good way to clear the decks for the upcoming week.

Kenzie had her postmortem reports to finish. She had her dictated notes back and some of the routine labs. Dr. Wiltshire had told her that she needed to write in that she had met Maksim before and what she knew about him, which was next to nothing. She wasn't even sure of his first name. She would include their suspicion that Maksim was Eastern European. Maybe that would help match him up with a missing person report if one were filed. Kenzie was beginning to suspect that no one was going to file one. Whoever knew that

Maksim was missing either knew why or was afraid of getting into trouble. Immigrants were often reluctant to involve the police, especially when they came from parts of the world with so much corruption.

Kenzie detailed the dental work that would also help them identify Maksim, noting the amalgams that were used that were not common in the US and other work that did not seem to be up to US standards. But Dr. Wiltshire had not been surprised, saying that it was common to see a lower standard of care in eastern or undeveloped countries. Who knew if the work had even been done by a trained professional? Sometimes people just did their best to figure it out themselves or were shown by a parent or grandparent how to do work that Kenzie would have expected them to need several years of dental school for.

Would there even be any dental records if a missing person report were filed? If the work hadn't been done by a trained professional and there were no x-rays, they wouldn't have anything to match the dental work to.

Kenzie shook her head and wrote it all up in as much detail as she could anyway. No one could say that she had not been diligent in recording everything if the file were ever reviewed in light of her having a possible bias due to her previous knowledge of Maksim.

She reviewed the pictures of the tattoos on the homeless man she had autopsied and described his tattoos in as much detail as possible. The mix of Latin and Greek characters suggested it was Cyrillic. She pulled up a chart of Cyrillic letters on the computer so that she could identify them properly. A *P* in Cyrillic was not "pee", but "er," from the Greek letter *rho*, and was pronounced like a rolled "R." Instead, the Latin *P* sound was assigned to the Cyrillic letter *pe*, which was the Greek letter *pi*.

She scrutinized the tattoos for anything else that might be helpful, from the fuzzy edges that suggested their age to the colors that had been used that might be able to be localized to a particular region. They were mostly blue-black, with only occasional highlights done with reds or other colors. Maybe an expert would be able to explain the significance of the symbols or imagery.

When Kenzie had exhausted all of the information she had so far from the postmortem, she went on to the other files they had worked on during the week. The Christmas rush had brought in twice the number of suicides, accidents, and other deaths as usual. While she wanted to make sure that her first solo postmortems were as perfect as they could be, she couldn't allow herself to get behind on the other files and tasks she had either.

She started on the file for one of Dr. Wiltshire's posts and started through her checklist to ensure that it was complete. Dr. Wiltshire was very methodical in his posts and rarely missed anything, but anyone could make a mistake. Some of the tests he had ordered would take days or weeks to come in, and Kenzie needed to track those and make sure they didn't get lost in the system, but still came back in a timely manner and were logged to the file and reviewed as they should be.

She stopped at the pictures of the tattoos on Dr. Wiltshire's subject, having just logged all of the tattoos in her own case. There were a number of similarities. Like the ones on her body, the tattoos were almost entirely black or blue-black in color. Some were very intricate, and they included Cyrillic letters, as did the ones Kenzie had just logged. She examined them one at a time, surprised by the similarities.

Kenzie heard footsteps in the hall, approaching from the elevator. A familiar step. Dr. Wiltshire came into view a few seconds later. He nodded at Kenzie.

"Kenzie. How are you today?"

"I'm fine. Just going through our postmortems this week to make sure everything is on track."

"It's been a busy period. And will be again next week, by the number of bodies stacked in the cold room at the moment."

Kenzie nodded. "December and January are tough months."

He grunted his agreement and looked at the pictures Kenzie was reviewing. "Yours or mine?"

"Yours," Kenzie said, indicating the stack on her left. "And mine." She indicated the other stack.

"Ah." He leaned in slightly. "Did you have questions? Concerns?"

"There are a lot of similarities between the two subjects' tattoos."

"I would expect so," Wiltshire agreed, squinting at them. "Russian gang tattoos. Probably inked in prison."

"Both of them?"

He nodded. "Apparently so. Maybe they were rivals, and this was tit for tat, one killing in retribution for another."

"We have Russian gangs in Vermont?"

"Not many. But I've studied the typical symbology and lettering in the tattoos. Enough to recognize these."

Kenzie flipped through them, comparing the tattoos thoughtfully. "Two Russian gangsters within a day of each other."

"As I say, they are probably related."

"Mine was starvation. Yours was…" Kenzie paused, skimming through Dr. Wiltshire's preliminary report, "auto versus pedestrian."

"Ran out into traffic," Wiltshire said, nodding. "Not a particularly smart thing to do. Being a gangster doesn't lend you superhuman powers against a ton of fast-moving metal."

"Apparently not," Kenzie agreed. "Mine then yours?"

"Yes. Christmas Eve for yours. Christmas day for mine."

And then Maksim that night or the next morning. Was it related? Kenzie couldn't help shuddering. She had seen Maksim just hours before he was killed. And he hadn't been the one who had died in a car accident. He had been brutally tortured and beaten. Did that mean that Maksim had killed the first man? That he'd been the one to run into him with his vehicle and was then killed in retaliation? Or had someone else killed the first man, and Maksim had just been randomly selected for the retribution?

Had a killer been sitting in the same room as Kenzie's mother? Acting as if he were an invited guest? What exactly had happened? Why had Lisa invited the stranger into her home? Was he a stranger? Had he forced his way in? Kenzie thought that if it had been by force, then Lisa would have told her so when she asked. But Lisa had been very close-mouthed, and Kenzie didn't know why.

Wiltshire saw Kenzie's eyes on the file for Maksim. "You don't need to spend all of your time on this case," Dr. Wiltshire said, watching her face. "If it is bothering you, I can finish everything off."

"No, no, it's fine. It's just that… I can't understand why this happened. What it has to do with my mother. Why would this Russian be at her house? And be there with her for hours? Why would she let him in? Why was he even there?"

He must have thought that he would get some kind of information from Lisa. Or he had been hiding out, choosing a place no one would look for him because he had no connection to it. It sounded like an Alfred Hitchcock movie.

Who would even have thought that there were Russian gangsters in Vermont? They must have come from New York or across the border from Canada. They didn't have that kind of organized crime in Vermont.

"I can take it for you," Dr. Wiltshire offered again.

"No. I'm okay. I want to see it through to the end."

"If you're sure."

"Yes. I guess it's just one of those random things. A coincidence. Synchronicity."

"We're still waiting for labs back?"

"A few, yes." Kenzie flipped pages, refreshing her memory, even though she had just looked at them. "Just some general lab work. No DNA or anything complicated."

"So we should be able to close those next week if everything comes in on time. Do we have funeral homes for any of them?"

"No." Kenzie already knew that. "No one has claimed them. I guess if they're immigrants… maybe there isn't anyone who wants to deal with it?"

"Probably. Well, we can store them for another day or two, but then they will need to be cremated."

"Okay. What about finding relatives in Russia?"

Wiltshire shook his head. "It's not going to happen. Sometimes when we are dealing with other countries, they are very eager to identify the bodies of their countrymen and get them back. But with Russia… there's a lack of any centralized database to be able to search for fingerprints or identifying features. They don't make much effort to identify folks like this…" he indicated the two files. "Indigent. It's a different story if they are part of the oligarchy. But I don't see any sign that is the case here."

"How would we know?"

"First of all, the survivors would probably be pounding at our doors. I doubt the deceased would have prison tats. They would be well dressed and fed."

"Right."

Maksim had looked good and was apparently in good health other than his tapeworm, but Dr. Wiltshire's Russian patient had looked more like the other man Kenzie had autopsied. Thin and worn. Not in very good shape. If he were in a Russian gang like Wiltshire suggested, he would be on the lowest rungs. Soldiers.

Kenzie flipped through the file and stopped to read through the description of the soldier's injuries. He'd still had all of his organs, unlike the homeless man Kenzie had autopsied. But he had a number of fractures that had healed before the man's death.

"Yours had a lot of broken bones too. Before he was killed, I mean."

"Yes, I saw that."

"You don't think they tell us anything about his death?"

"Do you have something in mind? I wouldn't want to tell you no if you've already thought of something."

"He had broken fingers too. Like Maksim."

"Healed fingers. Whereas your Maksim had perimortem fractures. Bones that were broken immediately before his death."

"They couldn't be related?"

"I doubt it. Remind me..." Wiltshire reached for the file and Kenzie handed it to him. He glanced down the list. "Fingers, wrists, ankles..."

Kenzie nodded. Wiltshire handed the file back to her.

"Those breaks are typical of prisoners. Particularly in prisons that don't follow the same standards of care as we do in this country. Torture. Bone breaks due to being mistreated while in handcuffs and shackles. When you pit strong bone against steel or iron restraints... I'll give you a clue. It's not the restraints that break."

"Oh, okay. So another hint that your victim was in prison before he immigrated here."

"Sometime before then," Wiltshire clarified. "We don't know how long before he immigrated that was."

"I thought we didn't allow people with prison records to immigrate here. Don't they do all kinds of background checks to ensure they are… good, law-abiding members of society?"

"There are always ways around these things. Especially if you are an oligarch with more money than Go—than the governor."

"But this guy…" Kenzie gestured to the file. "He didn't have money. He was a nobody." She grimaced. "I mean—no one is a nobody. Everyone is important. But he wasn't an oligarch. He was a street soldier. Disposable to these guys."

"Disposable, maybe," Wiltshire agreed, "but not worthless. Without soldiers, there is no army. There is no power."

"Yeah. I guess you're right. So… someone with money probably paid his way? Smoothed things over so that he would be able to immigrate?"

"Probably nothing that complicated. This man probably came over in a shipping container, not through proper channels."

Kenzie smacked her forehead. "Of course. Sorry for being so dense. Yeah. He probably came over with a lot of other people just like him. Shipped like cattle."

Wiltshire shrugged. "If you lived in a port city, it probably would have occurred to you. We don't see as much of the human trafficking business in Vermont. It's still here, just like everywhere across America, but we're lucky not to have the numbers that some other states do. Or as many coming through our office."

Wiltshire's mention of the governor made Kenzie reflect on her conversation with him the night before. She had resisted calling Walter again, trying to do as the governor had asked and just to back off and let him do his thing and see if he could find out what Walter was up to. She hated the helpless feeling of having to let someone else take the lead on it. As long as she was the one making phone calls, she felt like she had some control over the outcome, even though she didn't.

She pushed these thoughts away. She needed to stay focused on the job. There was nothing she could do about her father right now. The governor would find him on a plane back from Hawaii or having stayed with a big backer in a hunting lodge without a cell signal. There was a perfectly good explanation for her inability to reach him lately.

"Do you want me to make a note of the linkages between these files? All having something to do with Russia or prison or human trafficking?"

"It's important not to establish links where there are not any. You don't know yet that any of these deaths had any connections with each other. It's best not to give the conspiracy theorists any extra fodder. We don't know that these cases have anything to do with each other."

Kenzie wanted to argue the point, but knew that she shouldn't. Dr. Wiltshire was the one with experience. He was well-respected as a medical examiner, and if he said there wasn't enough to link them together, then she had to assume he was right.

Human brains were wired to look for patterns. That was all that was going on.

21

Not being able to do anything to figure out what had happened to her father, Kenzie found herself wandering restlessly around the house looking for something to occupy her fingers or her brain. It had been easier while she was at work, with a big stack of files in front of her demanding her attention. Now that she was alone in an empty house, feeling Zachary's absence in every room, she couldn't stop thinking about it.

She didn't want to call her mother again; they had already been over the same ground enough times and Kenzie didn't actually want her to worry about what Walter was up to. Her parents had maintained a good relationship since their divorce, and she didn't want to take the chance of throwing a wrench in the works.

But there were two people she could think of who might understand what she was going through—Lorne Peterson and Patrick Parker. They had recently had a friend go missing and the police hadn't paid much attention to the missing person report they had filed. It had taken Zachary's intervention to figure out what had happened to him. Unfortunately, it had not ended well.

Kenzie hesitated to call them at first. She didn't want to bring up the tragedy that they were just starting to heal from, reopening new wounds. But there weren't many other people who would understand the limbo she found herself in. Eventually, she sat down with her phone and initiated a video call to Lorne.

They might not even be in. They could be out to dinner or the theater or another event. They did go out and do things with others in their community, so there was no guarantee Kenzie would find them home on a Saturday evening.

"Kenzie," Lorne's voice was warm, and his face on the phone screen was cheerful. He was aging well, still energetic despite the white fringe of hair and the wrinkles on his face, all of which pointed up when he smiled. "It's good to hear from you. How are you doing?"

"I'm fine. Everything is good. I'm not calling because of Zachary or because anything is wrong."

He nodded. "You can call any time you like! I talked to Zachary just the other day."

"He said something about that. That you guys had a good Christmas. Pat got to see his family."

"Yes. It was very nice. I'm sorry you and Zachary could not be there, but we know what a difficult time Christmas is for him. You come see us when he is out of the hospital and feeling up to it."

"We will, of course." Kenzie looked away from the phone screen, staring at her bookcase and trying to figure out how to introduce the topic that she wanted to. It was easier if she were not looking into his sympathetic face. "The thing is, I've had kind of a tough Christmas. Aside from what Zachary has been going through."

"You had that serial killer case too. Thank goodness you were able to sort that out before anyone else got hurt. If something had happened to you or Zachary…"

"Yeah." Kenzie had almost forgotten about that with everything else that she'd been worrying about. "I had a funny visit with my mother on Christmas Day. And it seems like… my dad might be missing."

It took a few seconds for Lorne to process this. He looked surprised, and his brows came down quickly in a frown of concern. "Your dad?" He turned his head and called over his shoulder. "Pat? You should come here."

It only took a few seconds for Pat to come into view behind

Lorne, and he leaned over to smile at Kenzie on the small screen. "Hi, Kenzie. How are you doing?"

"Her dad is missing," Lorne told Pat.

The smile disappeared from Pat's face. "Oh, no. I'm sorry." He pulled a chair over and sat down close to Lorne so that they could both lean toward each other and see the screen at the same time. "Tell me about it. What happened?"

"I don't know very much. I don't know when the last time was that someone saw him. I don't have any confirmation that he's missing. I just know that he isn't answering my calls. He usually drops in on my mom for Christmas, and I expected to see him there for an hour or two. We don't really keep in touch, but I do still care about him. Things were so weird at my mom's that day, and I called Walter to see what he thought about it and if he knew what was going on. But I can't reach him, and he doesn't return my calls. I've been leaving him messages for days, with no response."

"I can see why you'd be concerned," Pat agreed. "Did you talk to anyone else in his social circles? I assume your mother wasn't able to tell you anything?"

"She doesn't know where he is but doesn't act concerned about it. Just says, 'you know how your father is.' But I guess I don't know. He's always returned my calls before. And this time... crickets. Nothing. Total silence."

"Does he have a... girlfriend or partner?" Lorne asked.

"No, not that I know of. I asked the governor that, and he said he didn't know of anyone serious. But that doesn't mean anything. Of course he might have been seeing someone no one knew about. He didn't have to keep a relationship secret from me. I would have been happy to know he had someone to keep him company."

Lorne and Pat nodded.

"Have you talked to the police?" Lorne asked. "You must know people. You could talk to them off the books and see what action they recommend. I don't know whether a missing person report is recommended when you have so little to go on. He could just be on vacation and have his phone shut off. But maybe they could make some suggestions and initial inquiries."

"No… I haven't talked to them yet. And the governor said not to involve them yet. He was going to make some inquiries of his own."

"The governor?" Lorne's brows went up in surprise.

"He's a friend of my father's. That's why I called him. I just wanted to know if they had talked, but he said he would look into it."

"Then he'll tell you whether he thinks you should file a police report," Pat said with a nod.

"Yes. I guess. I don't think he was just putting me off… it's hard to tell sometimes. Especially with political contacts. They're so used to 'handling' people."

"Well, if he doesn't come up with anything pretty quickly, you should call him back," Lorne advised.

"Yeah. I will. It's only been a day, and I figure he might need a couple to get to all the people who might know something. And he's the governor; he must be busy even if it is Christmas vacation."

"I'm sure he is," Pat said slowly. "But this is important. You can't let it slide for too long. Those early days are critical."

There was a weighty silence as they all thought about Jose and what had happened to him. It had not been a good outcome. Would it have made a difference if the police had mobilized immediately and been able to track him? Or had it been too late the first day and by the time they started looking for him, all hope was already gone?

"I know," Kenzie agreed. She sighed. "I don't even know that there's anything wrong."

"You're not someone who usually panics at things," Pat said. "If you think that something might be wrong, that something has happened to him, then you're probably right. Don't tell yourself that you're just imagining things." He swallowed and stared off into space. "Trust your instincts."

And Kenzie's instincts said that something was wrong. It had been too long now. Too long without hearing anything from her father, who always reached out to her at Christmas and always returned her calls when she left him messages. Even when she didn't leave a message and all he had was her number on his call logs, he would still call her back.

22

T hank you," Kenzie told them. "It makes me feel like I'm not all alone and that I'm not just imagining things. I've been making myself crazy trying to talk myself out of the idea that there is something wrong."

"Have faith in yourself," Lorne advised. "You're smart and have good instincts. Don't let your doubts keep you from acting."

Kenzie nodded her thanks. Maybe she wasn't just being crazy and paranoid. She thought she knew her dad pretty well, even if she didn't see eye to eye with him on... most things.

"It's hard to know what to do," Pat said, "even when you report someone missing... it's just 'hurry up and wait.' There's nothing you can do except sit around and wait for the police to do something. And in a lot of cases... it seems like they don't do anything. That wouldn't be the case for your father, I'm sure. He's well-known and liked and has a lot of social influence, so they would be pretty diligent in looking for him. But even if they're trying, that doesn't mean they'll find anything."

"Zachary was such a help," Lorne agreed. "I didn't even plan to involve him. I figured since the police were involved, there was no point in involving a private investigator. What could he find that they didn't? But he was the one who broke the case, who really got things to move forward."

Kenzie swallowed and nodded. She also knew how that case had impacted him, and Lorne and Pat did too. Zachary would have been better off not taking that case. As it turned out, Jose had already been dead anyway. But Zachary had gotten a killer off the streets so he couldn't keep killing as he had been for years.

"I wish I could talk to Zachary about this, but I really can't. I don't want to derail his progress at the hospital. He needs to focus on getting better, not on my dad, who is probably just... taking an unscheduled vacation somewhere."

"Zach will probably be out of the hospital soon," Lorne pointed out. "He doesn't usually stay for too long once he's past Christmas Day."

"He's going to be a while. They're changing his meds around and want to ensure he's stable before going anywhere. He was having kind of a rough time with the change yesterday. And if I told him about Walter... he'd probably check himself out against medical advice, and who knows what would happen. I don't want him to crash. He needs the time to adjust and build up his reserves. They'll keep him on sleep aids for as long as he is at the hospital but, once he's home, he'll probably stop taking them unless he's having a really bad week."

"You're good to him. But you need to let him make his own decisions too. Including whether to help you with your dad."

Kenzie shook her head. "I already know how it would play out." And what was she going to do when he found out about Tyrrell being missing in action? She wouldn't be able to stop him from taking that on too. But if she were lucky. Tyrrell would bottom out and turn up again before Zachary was released. That would be the best-case scenario. "If he finds out about Tyrrell..."

Lorne and Pat both looked confused.

Kenzie hadn't meant to say it out loud. She shook her head. "Nothing. Sorry. I was just thinking about something else."

"What about Tyrrell?" Lorne asked. He had taken Tyrrell under his wing too, part of his extended family. Any sibling of Zachary's was part of his family too. "Did something happen?"

"He's… apparently gone on a drunken binge."

"Oh…" Lorne shook his head, disappointment clear in his voice. "I'm really sorry to hear that. I know he's been having a tough time lately. But I was hoping…"

"You knew he was having a hard time?"

Lorne shrugged. "I… could see the signs."

Kenzie and Zachary had seen some of the warning signs that he had gone back to drinking. But Tyrrell had denied that there was a problem and they had taken him at his word.

"Well… yeah. I guess we all did. But I was hoping that we were wrong."

"There's not really anything you can do about it until Tyrrell is ready. As much as we would all like to step in and make the decisions for him and fix everything… it won't work. It has to be his decision."

"Yes." Kenzie sat back in the easy chair, resting her head against the back. She massaged her neck with one hand, trying to release some of the tension. It had been hard keeping all of this to herself. She knew she couldn't lay it all on Zachary, so she hadn't, but it was good to let it all out to someone. "I didn't realize how much this was building up."

"It's hard to take everything on yourself. You were already seeing Zachary's therapist for couple's counseling. You know you could go back there for a session or two for yourself, too. You don't have to do it all yourself. Living with someone with mental illness is taxing enough without all the extra stuff you're dealing with."

"Yeah. I guess I could go back to Dr. Boyle. I didn't think about that. Would it be a conflict of interest for her to counsel me separately and do couple's with me and Zachary?"

"I don't think so. She's counseling him separately as well."

"That might be too much. Maybe if I'm going to go to someone, it should be someone separate, so she's not trying to keep all our issues in separate boxes…"

"She could suggest some names for you."

Kenzie nodded. "Maybe I'll do that. Thanks for the idea. In the meantime…" She yawned. "I think maybe I'm ready for bed. It's been a long day, even though it's supposed to be the weekend."

"Will you take some time off tomorrow? Or do you have to go in again?"

"I'll take tomorrow off." Kenzie thought about it. She had so much to do. If she went in for just an hour or two, it would make a big difference in how much work there was to do Monday morning.

"Take the time," Lorne said firmly. He must have seen the doubt and indecision in Kenzie's face. "You need it. If you're looking for something to do, you can come have Sunday dinner with us."

Kenzie wasn't sure how Zachary would feel about her going to have dinner with his family without him. Even calling them up for a conversation without him was iffy. She'd done it once before with disastrous results. But that had been different. She hadn't called Lorne and Pat to talk to them about Zachary. This time she'd called them to discuss her own problem, the problem of her missing father. Zachary would never tell her that she couldn't talk to them about her own problems. Just about his.

Which meant that maybe she shouldn't have mentioned Tyrrell being missing or the fact that she wasn't going to talk to Zachary about either problem because she didn't want to derail his treatment.

"I have a lot of things I want to do around here tomorrow," she told Lorne, putting him off. "I appreciate you talking me through this… but don't say anything to Zachary about it, okay? I'll tell him what he needs to know in my own time."

Pat and Lorne exchanged worried glances. Eventually, they both nodded, agreeing.

23

Talking to Lorne and Pat had helped Kenzie to calm down enough to be able to sleep. Along with an over-the-counter aid to ensure she got the full eight hours she needed.

Then she could work on the household chores she hadn't gotten to during the week and grocery shopping to stock her fridge and cupboards with real food instead of just falling back on takeout half the time. She resolved again to make lunches to take with her for the upcoming week, but had a pretty good idea that she wouldn't actually follow through on it. Maybe she was just too lazy, but it seemed like she just didn't have the energy after everything else to think about her body and what she would need to eat by noon.

She had taken a break to check her email and put her feet up for a few minutes when her phone rang and, taking it out, she saw the governor's name on the caller ID. She swiped quickly to answer it.

"Hello, sir!"

"No need to 'sir' me, Kenzie. I'm not your boss."

"Thanks for calling me back… did you find anything out?"

"It's a difficult situation. I can't really say anything to you, other than… that it would be best if you pulled back and didn't pursue it at this time."

Kenzie sat in stunned silence for a moment. She tried to wrap her mind around what this meant and how to handle it.

"Does that mean… that you talked to Walter about it?"

"I really couldn't say."

"You couldn't say."

"Sorry, no."

"But I should just stay out of it."

"Right. I'm sorry that I can't be more clear. I wish that I could."

"Did you talk to Lisa?" Kenzie tried. Lisa might have told the governor what was going on and that Kenzie needed to just stay as far away from it as possible. She couldn't understand what was going on and what Lisa knew. She had, as far as Kenzie could tell, let a stranger into her house without question and had just stayed quiet about that and about her ex-husband dropping out of sight. But she refused to give her reasons for doing so.

Kenzie kneaded her forehead with her fist.

"You really need to just let it alone," the governor repeated. "There is more at stake here than you understand. So I have to ask that you… forget about it for now. Things will work out. But you need to not interfere."

"Does this have something to do with Maksim being dead?" Kenzie asked.

There was a long pause from the governor.

"Who?" he asked eventually.

"If you've talked to Lisa, then you must know who Maksim is. And I know that he's dead because he showed up on my autopsy table. So what exactly is going on?"

"Something that is above your pay grade, Dr. Kirsch."

She knew by the use of "Dr. Kirsch" instead of Kenzie that he was dismissing her. He had done his duty as Walter's friend, but he wasn't going to give Kenzie the information she wanted. Whatever was going on, he didn't want her to be involved. So he was going to freeze her out just like Lisa.

Kenzie directed Zachary to a table by the window. It wasn't one of their usual places to sit and visit, but she wanted to be able to look out at the outside world, to feel the sun on her face and not feel like the two of them were trapped in the hospital with no way out.

Of course, she could leave any time. Whenever she wanted to, she could just get up and walk out and no one would stop her, least of all Zachary. And he too could leave when he wanted to. It would be a little more complicated to sign himself out against medical advice, but that didn't mean he couldn't do it. It might not even be against medical advice. He was no longer suicidal and was on a new cocktail, and they would probably agree that he could leave when he liked as long as they continued to monitor his symptoms and return to see a doctor if there was a problem.

But Zachary wasn't ready to leave yet, and Kenzie wasn't going to walk out before they'd had a chance for a visit.

And she couldn't really feel the sun on her face through the window because it was past sunset and all of the lights in Roxboro were coming on, twinkling like tiny fairy lights.

Zachary was not comfortable with his back to the room, so he sat with the window behind him, and Kenzie gazed at him or through the window as they talked, trying to relax all of her muscles and let the cares of the day fall away.

"How are you feeling today?" she asked Zachary, though she knew he wouldn't like too much of her focus on him and his symptoms. "I'm just wondering how the new meds are—if there are any side effects." Keeping it on his physical state rather than his emotional state. He could share more if he wanted to, but she would make it easy for him to keep his feelings to himself if he didn't feel like sharing.

"Not bad so far," Zachary said. "Dry mouth. I'm drinking lots of water. The morning nausea is better." He let out a sigh. "I really hated that."

Kenzie nodded. "Pretty difficult to enjoy food if you are so nauseated you can hardly keep anything down. I'll be really happy if we can move forward without that one."

It would be much easier to get his weight up to where it should be if he could eat in the morning. Choking down one granola bar or snack-sized yogurt in the morning was not enough to keep his calorie consumption up. She sometimes wondered if he even managed to keep that down after she left for work in the morning. He never complained about throwing up, but he wouldn't. He knew she was concerned enough about his health without adding that complication.

"They're hoping the rebound won't be as bad with the new ADHD script. And that I'll be able to sleep better. Get to sleep earlier."

"You're sleeping pretty good on this cocktail so far, aren't you?"

Zachary nodded, but tilted his head to the side slightly in a gesture that seemed to be a partial shrug. An unconscious "maybe" or "sort of." Kenzie raised her brows, inviting more information.

"I'm sleeping when I'm supposed to," he explained. "Mostly. But that's with a sleep aid each night, and I really don't like to…"

He didn't like to have to rely on a sleep aid every night. And he didn't like how they made him feel when he got up in the morning. He complained of feeling groggy for hours and unable to focus on anything unless he took the ADHD meds. Once he got home, he would probably ditch the daily regimen of the sleep aids and ADHD prescription, saving them for days when he felt like he really needed them. Something that Kenzie didn't agree with, but she couldn't fight him on it. It was his body and his choice whether to follow the recommended protocol or not. He needed to know that she trusted him and would treat him like an adult, not a child.

"It would be great if this medication will let you sleep better without taking anything else," Kenzie said, keeping her voice as neutral as possible.

24

How are *you* doing?" Zachary bounced the conversation back to Kenzie. "How was work? Things *dead* quiet as usual?"

Kenzie grinned at the joke. "Unfortunately not. Dead, but not quiet."

"That's a scary thought."

She laughed. "We're not talking about zombies here. Just that things have been *busy*. Lots of cases coming in."

"Yeah. You said that. Anything interesting?"

She loved that she could discuss her job with him, that he didn't get squeamish about it and was genuinely interested in any weird medical stuff or puzzling cases.

"We got back a bunch of reports and slides back from the lab for a bunch of stuff that we sent last week."

"Good turnaround."

"It is. I'm sure they must be busier this time of the year too, but they're staying on top of the workload."

Not that any of the samples they had sent to the lab had been for any complicated procedures. No DNA testing or trying to identify an unknown toxin.

"We found an unusual parasite profile in a few of last week's cases."

"An unusual parasite profile. What does that mean?"

"Well, we had one guy last week with a tapeworm. Very big." Kenzie watched Zachary's eyes, weighing how he would take it all. Did he want the details, or would tapeworm stories gross him out?

"How big?" Zachary prompted.

"Twelve feet long."

His eyes widened.

"I got ten feet out before I broke it. So I had to add the two pieces together, but it was all one worm."

"Is that what killed him?"

"Nope. Not even close. I think they probably had a very happy relationship. Until he died."

"But not from the tapeworm."

"No. He was... very badly beaten."

Zachary nodded slowly.

"So that was the first one. We sent slides of all of the organs and asked the lab to specifically check for parasites to see if we could narrow down where the guy was from."

"How could the parasites tell you where he was from?"

"The kind of tapeworm that he had wasn't a kind that you usually see here in North America. Usually only Eastern Europe, South America, East Africa..."

"So you knew that he didn't pick it up here. He was either from one of those areas or had traveled there and picked up this tapeworm." He paused. "But it would have to have been a long time ago, right? Because it takes time to grow to that length. He didn't just pick it up last year."

"No. Probably took decades to grow that long." Kenzie agreed with a nod. "And I knew—we had witnesses who said that he didn't have an accent, but did talk like English was his second language. Very precise and slow, like he had to think of the right words."

"So he didn't just move here recently and was learning the language."

"No. And most people don't bother to go to speech training to get rid of their accents. They do their best to learn the language, but coaching can be expensive. Most people don't do it. They just do the best they can on their own."

"But it wasn't natural enough that he had moved here as a child and learned English very young."

"No. So, he moved here some years ago, not when he was a child, and had the money for speech training. But we still didn't have any kind of ID on him, so Dr. Wiltshire figured that if we checked for other parasites, it might narrow down where he had come from."

Zachary smiled, thinking about this. "So what did you find out? Did you get anything back that you could use?"

"Yes, definitely. The various parasites he had made it most likely that he was Russian."

"Great job!"

"Well, I can't claim all of the credit for it. But it was kind of cool to be able to do that."

He nodded his agreement. His eyes flicked around the room, and Kenzie turned partway to see if there was something in particular that he was worried about. She did not see the patient who had previously made a fuss. Or anyone else that looked like they might cause any trouble.

"Everything okay?"

Zachary nodded. His eyes moved back and forth, keeping an eye on several different people. Kenzie turned back to face him fully.

"That's not the end of the story."

"Oh? What else? Did the parasites lead right back to his hometown? To the farm he grew up on?"

Kenzie laughed. "Only on TV. They're always able to narrow down where the subject was killed or came from by rare pollens and insects and all of that."

"What, then? What's the rest of the story?"

"We did slides on a number of other subjects as well. Just being thorough. They all seemed pretty routine. The kind of stuff that we see all the time."

"But...?"

"We had a couple of other subjects with tattoos that looked Russian. And they came back with the exact same parasite profile as Maksim. As the man I had done the first set of slides on."

Zachary frowned, thinking about this. He shook his head. "They all came from the same place?"

"Yeah. They did. So now we need to see if we can figure out how else they are related. It could be as simple as them all coming from the same Russian community here in Vermont, or the same area in Russia. And I don't know yet how big an area we're talking about."

"But then…" Zachary was frowning, "Why were they all killed around the same time? Who is killing off the Russians?"

Kenzie nodded, pleased to see that his brain was still as sharp as ever, keeping up with her on the questions to be answered on the cases.

"Huh." Zachary scratched the back of his neck. "There hasn't been anything in the news? I don't have internet here, don't really know what's been going on in the real world. Have there been gang wars? An outbreak of something?"

"Dr. Wiltshire thought maybe the guys with the gang tats were rivals. But when I compared the tattoos and did what research I could, it looked like they both come from the same gang."

"Infighting? Or a third party that killed both of them?"

"It *looks* like coincidence."

"Your tapeworm guy was beaten to death."

"Yes. But the others weren't. One was starvation, and one was hit by a car. Not exactly common methods of murder."

"No," Zachary admitted. He chewed his lip, thinking about it.

"I can't think of any way to tie them together," Kenzie said, shrugging. "I'd like to, but is that just because we like everything to tie up neatly? Could it just be a coincidence that they were all killed last week?"

"I don't know a lot of Russians. Do you?"

Kenzie shook her head. "No."

"Then there can't be a very big Russian community in Vermont. If neither of us can think of anyone."

Kenzie nodded her agreement.

"And more than one guy with Russian gang ink. That's not just coincidence. They didn't both just happen to come to Roxboro and happen to die within days of each other. They have to be connected. It's just too wild a coincidence."

"But we don't know how."

Zachary tapped his fingers on the table and looked around the room. "Neither of them has been identified? Nobody has claimed the bodies?"

"No."

"I would look for Russian communities in Vermont. Search them up on the internet: Russian friendship groups, cultural foundations. Maybe look for Russian restaurants or import stores if there isn't anything else. Ask about where people who are Russian gather. Go to those places and talk to people. Show the pictures and ask around. See how cooperative people are. If anyone is worried about them. If they have families here, wives and children, then they must be worried. Even if it is against the community's rules to talk to the police or outsiders, they would still be looking. Trying to get word of what happened to them."

Kenzie gazed at him. "All of that would be great… if I was a private investigator."

He gave a rueful smile. "Sorry. That's my only frame of reference. I know you're not an investigator. You do the autopsies and document everything about the body. You don't do any other investigation."

"I wish I could. I would like to find the families of these men."

Not to mention wanting to find out who Maksim was and what he was involved in so that she would know if her family was in danger. Walter off the grid and Lisa saying nothing about whatever was going on. When clearly something *was* going on.

Lisa could deny it, but Kenzie knew just enough to be worried.

People were being killed.

25

K enzie pulled out her laptop at home and settled in front of the TV, using Zachary's mobile desk. It had been almost a week without any word from Walter. She was trying to respect the governor's request and stay out of it, but she was really getting worried. She needed to know that he was okay. That was all. She didn't care what else he was involved in, as long as she knew that he was safe and sound. It was New Year's Eve, the cusp of a new year. She couldn't see herself going into it without knowing something.

New Year's Eve had always been an important day to Kenzie. Sort of the opposite of Zachary with Christmas. He couldn't see past Christmas and dreaded it for weeks ahead of time. Kenzie looked forward to the New Year. A fresh new start. Envisioning what she could accomplish over the next year. What things would look like a year from now.

She and Zachary would still be together and stronger than ever. Maybe he would be able to get through Christmas without a major depression. She would make sure next year that October and November were quiet, that nothing could happen that would jeopardize Zachary's mental health. Not a vacation this time. No retreat to a remote cabin where they could get snowed in. Not this time. Lots of quiet family time and positive experiences so that Zachary would be strong and just skate right through the difficult season. With medications that didn't make him nauseated or have other adverse side effects, he would be able to eat well and keep up his weight, which would help make him more resilient. It would be easier to bounce back from little problems.

And next year, she would know where her father was. She would arrange ahead of time for a visit with her mother and father over Christmas break. Enough of acting like a child and avoiding them, as if it would change anything that had happened fourteen years before. How many more years was she likely to have both of her parents? Maybe they would both live to be ninety, but what were the chances of that? Walter did not take good care of his health. Lisa spent too much time at banquets and fundraisers, not leaving enough time for self-care. Kenzie would give her mother a spa day. Maybe they would both take it together. A nice relaxing day or two, just regenerating.

But if the new year was going to be better, she had to do something to start it off right. It might be magical thinking, but she knew she had to do something.

The first organization she called was one that funded and assisted in Russian immigration. Kenzie wasn't sure how she was going to get any information out of them, but she wouldn't get anywhere if she didn't try.

The woman who answered the phone sounded like she was in her sixties and had a pleasant accent. Not so thick that Kenzie couldn't understand her, but enough that it was apparent where she was from. Kenzie pictured a plump grandmother in a print dress. A stereotype, maybe, but she was sure a woman like that would want to help the families of the men who had died.

"Hello," she forced herself to speak slowly and enunciate her words more clearly than she normally would. "My name is Kenzie Kirsch. My mother, Lisa Cole Kirsch, runs our family foundation, and I am looking for worthwhile organizations that would benefit from a sizable donation."

"Lisa Cole Kirsch," the grandmother repeated. "I have heard her name before."

"Maybe she's donated to you in the past?"

Wouldn't *that* be an interesting coincidence? It would, at least, get Kenzie in the door. A foundation that had received money from the Kirsch family in the past would be much more likely to be cooperative, answering Kenzie's questions even if they didn't understand why she was asking them.

"I don't know," the woman mused. "I do not think so. But she is a great philanthropist. Maybe she has."

"I wonder if you could tell me about the Russian community in Vermont? I haven't seen a lot of Russian immigrants in my area, but I am told that the community is growing. Has there been a lot of immigration lately?"

"It is a growing and thriving community," the woman agreed, sounding as if she were reading it from a pamphlet. "We have a lot to give back to Vermont for the way that we have been welcomed into the state and been provided with such great opportunities."

"Do you sponsor a certain number of immigrants each year, or how do you work?"

"The number that we can sponsor depends on the funding we get. If we can raise more funding, we can sponsor more people—and families."

"Do you get a lot of families?"

"Usually, we sponsor one of the parents, and then they can work to save money to bring the rest of the family after. In some cases, we sponsor an entire family, particularly if they are refugees, trying to escape government persecution or other powerful people in Russia."

"Is there a lot of that?"

There was a pause before the woman answered. "There is more need than we can keep up with, unfortunately. Russia can be a very difficult place to live. Very… harsh."

Kenzie nodded to herself. "Do you keep track of the people you have sponsored and what they are doing now? Of the families that you have been able to help?"

"We try to keep up with them. And many of them volunteer with the organization, spend a few hours a week or a month helping others. There are not a lot of Russians in the state, so we tend to be a very close-knit community."

"That's good. I'm sure my mother will be very happy to hear about that. It is so important to give back, isn't it? And where would we be without community?"

The woman made agreeable noises.

"Do you find that there are a lot of Russians who are here illegally?" Kenzie asked.

There was only silence in reply at first. Kenzie felt as if a cold wind had blown into the room through the phone receiver.

"We do not deal with illegal immigrants," the woman said frostily.

"No, I wasn't saying that you do. But you must become aware of Russians who did not come in... the usual way. It is such a small community, there would be gossip about it, surely?"

"I cannot comment on that. That is not anything to do with our organization."

"Of course not. I have been hearing things lately about human trafficking. People who are brought in on ship storage containers or private landings. Do you know how much—"

"I'm sorry. We do not know anything about that. I have other calls that I must take now, Miss..."

"Kirsch." Kenzie tried to think of how to get back on the woman's good side. "I think that my mother would like to make an appointment to—"

"Yes, she is welcome to call us any time. We will try to accommodate her."

And then the woman was gone.

26

Kenzie wasn't giving up. There weren't a lot of other organizations that appeared to deal with Russians or Russian immigration other than the government departments, so she turned her attention elsewhere. There were still others who might be able to help her.

She tried a street ministry. One of those small but mighty organizations that made an unexpectedly wide-reaching impact on the community. They were Catholic rather than Eastern Orthodox, so she didn't know if they would have much to do with the indigent Russian population, but it seemed like the most likely possibility.

She introduced herself as she had before, dropping Lisa's name and suggesting that the family foundation might make a sizable donation to the little street ministry. And it wasn't a lie. Kenzie could certainly direct the foundation to donate to any charity that she wanted to. Or at least, any that were not in opposition to the foundation's stated goals. Lisa would be happy to have Kenzie participate in the family foundation rather than just telling Lisa to give money to whoever she thought was deserving. Maybe it was time that she stepped up and took part. She had grown past the immature, self-centered young woman that she had been when Amanda had died, taking responsibility for her education and following the path she wanted to pursue in life. She had a job that she felt made a difference and was interesting and fulfilling. But in the process, she had left her family responsibilities behind, which was perhaps just as selfish.

"I'm looking for organizations that help the Russian community in Vermont," Kenzie said. "Particularly the indigent population… maybe immigrants who have been the victims of human trafficking, who might not have papers, and are at risk of being taken advantage of by more organized and powerful criminals."

"Well…" the young-sounding pastor seemed taken aback by her request. "I'm not sure there are many organizations who are that focused in Vermont. That would be an… underserved population. We do what we can to help those of all nationalities and backgrounds. If you are down on your luck or on the street, we're there, doing what we can."

"Do you have any familiarity with the homeless Russians on our streets?"

He considered. "I know of a few, but not very many, I'm afraid. I suspect that most of the Russians brought into this area by traffickers are not on the street where we would see them. More than likely, they are kept in safe houses by those organizations."

"Would you recognize them if they were on the street? Would you know their names or anything about their backgrounds?"

"It's possible." His voice was hesitant. "Can I ask where this is going? It seems like you have an agenda here."

Kenzie thought about it for a minute before answering, wondering whether he would hang up on her like the woman at the Russian immigration foundation. He had been helpful so far, but if she were going to get anything else out of him, she might have to disclose more to him about what she was really up to.

"I don't want to say too much," she said slowly. "So you need to keep this under your hat. It's a very sensitive issue. I'm sure that you understand that. The clients you work with are probably pretty private people who don't want their information to be bandied about."

"That's exactly right," he agreed. "We have to be very careful about what we share."

127

"There have been… some recent deaths in the Russian community—people who appear to have been either living rough or maybe in a setting where they were neglected. No one has stepped forward to identify them. I don't know if they have families around here who are just afraid to tell anyone they are missing or if something else is going on. Because it's such a small, close community… it's hard to get any information or convince people you can be trusted. I thought a ministry like yours might be able to point us in the right direction…"

"You? Meaning your family foundation?"

Kenzie thought quickly and decided she couldn't afford to reveal her position with the Medical Examiner's Office. It wasn't an official inquiry, and both Dr. Wiltshire and the governor were pretty much guaranteed not to like her stepping outside of her role at the Medical Examiner's Office to ask questions that could not be answered officially. If there were a connection between what was going on with Walter and the deaths in the Russian community, Kenzie did not want word to get back to the governor that she had been investigating when she had been told to stop.

"Yes. The foundation hopes to bring these families some peace… to see that these men are buried properly under their own names and don't just fall through the cracks."

What would she tell Lisa if word of Kenzie's inquiries got back to her? That was a problem for another day.

"I haven't heard of your foundation doing any work in this area before. Isn't the Kirsch family foundation mostly involved in medical research and advances?"

Someone was certainly up on his Vermont foundations.

"Yes," Kenzie agreed. "But we're not limited to medical matters in our charter. We pursue all quality-of-life issues. The plight of the Russian immigrants in Vermont has recently come to our attention, and we would like to look into it further. See what we can do to help Russian Vermonters."

"I'd like to meet you face to face. I'm not comfortable taking this much further on the phone. I'm sure you can understand that."

And it was probably better that Kenzie show him the men's pictures in person, leaving no electronic trail to prove that she had been meddling where she wasn't wanted. And had, in fact, been specifically told to stay out of.

Although, that was only if Walter's disappearance had something to do with the Russians. And so far, she didn't have any proof of a connection. The only connecting piece that she knew of for sure was Maksim. He *had* been at Lisa's house, Walter's ex's house, when Walter was supposed to be there. It was a tenuous connection at best.

"Okay," she agreed with the pastor. "That sounds good. Why don't you and I set up a time to meet?"

27

Kenzie might not have moved the needle forward very far on her inquiry into matters that might be connected with Walter's disappearance, but at least she had done something. It settled her conscience enough that she could go to sleep and start the new year out with the confidence that she could have a good year, which would include her father and spending more time with her family. Another step on her journey to becoming the person she eventually hoped to be.

She stayed up long enough to watch the New Year festivities in New York on the TV and then headed to bed. If Zachary had been home, maybe they would have had a drink and stayed up later, taking time to welcome the new year properly. But as it was, she didn't want to stay up late by herself. She could meet with the pastor of the street ministry the next day, visit Zachary at the hospital, and not think about work for another day. There would likely be more bodies, casualties of New Year's Eve drunk drivers, but they would wait another day.

Using pictures she had taken from her files at the Medical Examiner's Office was probably not entirely kosher. They were not to be shared with the public, and her inquiry into what had happened to them was not official, so she should probably not have printed copies for herself.

If there had been any other pictures available for her use, she would have used them. But that was the whole point. There were no other pictures because they had no idea who the men were. If she were going to find out who they were and if there were any other connections to Walter, she needed to show him the pictures. The only pictures she had. She printed off a picture of Walter at the same time. There were plenty of photos of him around, even if she hadn't had any herself.

Pastor Clark was much as Kenzie had pictured him when she had talked to him on the phone. A young man, under thirty years of age, with dark hair and an earnest manner. He shook Kenzie's hand with a strong grip and thanked her for taking the time to meet with him, even though it had been her request, not his.

"At this time of year, not many people are thinking about the city's homeless," he told her. "Yes, there are those who will serve at a soup kitchen or community program feeding the hungry on Christmas and Easter, but the need is much greater than that. There is more to taking care of the homeless than just donating some canned goods during a Christmas drive or serving a turkey dinner on Christmas Day. The homeless are here all year, and December and January are very hard on them. The darkness, the bitter cold, seeing other people who have so much at Christmas and just waste it on food they'll never eat and toys they'll never use. It's hard to be homeless."

Kenzie nodded. She felt a little guilty that she was one of the privileged ones, looking for her father, who was also one of the privileged ones, ultra-wealthy and probably oblivious to the plight of the homeless. She had always resented her mother insisting that they should help in soup kitchens and other programs on Christmas Day. Why did she always have to spend part of *her* holiday on those people?

She tried to swallow the guilt, the self-centeredness, the privilege.

She could be a better person. Maturity took some work.

"I can't say I've been the best example of that," she admitted.

"Well, you're here now," he said simply. "It's your holiday and you're spending it looking into someone else's troubles."

She was and she wasn't. It was still just because of Walter. Would she have felt the need to do anything if none of the corpses in the morgue had any connection with him? If he hadn't dropped out of sight? If she hadn't seen Maksim at her mother's house?

"I told you that this was about some men in the Russian community who had died, right?" She knew that was what she had told the pastor, but she wanted to remind him. To prepare him for what he was going to see.

"Yes," he nodded. "Yes, I understand that."

"So these pictures, you might find them disturbing."

"Are they… that bad?" he asked uncertainly.

"No. They're not gory." Were they? Kenzie was used to looking at corpses. Would he see something different from what she did when he looked at them? "There is no blood. One of them was beaten, and he has a broken nose and black eye. Another was hit by a car and has scrapes from hitting the pavement."

He nodded slowly. "Okay. That doesn't sound too bad."

She paused, searching his face, making sure that he was ready.

"I've probably seen worse on the homeless we serve in our ministry," he assured her. "They are frequently the targets of violence, unfortunately."

She showed him the first picture. The man who had died of starvation. A thin, pinched face, but no violence. A good picture to start him on and ensure he wasn't too squeamish.

Pastor Clark studied the picture, his mouth tightening and face grim. He shook his head. "I've never seen that man, to my knowledge."

Kenzie flipped to the next one, the car accident victim.

He shook his head again. "No."

Kenzie was pretty sure that it would be three for three. As much as she had hoped that someone working on the street would at least recognize the victims, it was apparent that these men had not been part of Pastor Clark's flock.

She showed him Maksim's and he frowned, brows coming down. Kenzie waited. "You know him?" she prompted.

"I don't know. I feel like I might have seen him before, but I don't know where."

Kenzie held the picture steady, waiting for him to work through the memory and come up with the solution, but he shook his head.

"I'm sorry. I'll think about it, but right now, I can't think of where I might have run into him. He isn't someone who is usually in my circles, but… I might have seen him somewhere before. *He* wasn't homeless."

"No. Not as far as I know."

His clothing had been too expensive for him to be homeless. His skin was pampered, the pores in his face small, and plenty of elasticity remained in his skin. Not someone who spent much time in the elements or harsh conditions. Not too thin, like the other two men. Kenzie was sure he had never been homeless. If he was part of the Russian mob, he was much higher up in the organization than the foot soldiers.

"Sorry," the pastor apologized. He shrugged. "I wish I could have helped."

"Do you know of anyone who might be able to help me? Someone who might have a better chance of recognizing them?"

"We have an old Russian woman who helps out with hygiene kits. I can see if she would be willing to look at the pictures. Or knows if anyone has recently disappeared from the community. I don't know how tightly knit the Russian community is here. To be honest, I was surprised to hear you asking about Russians. We don't get a lot of them."

"Yeah. I didn't realize that there was any real community here before either. I don't remember any Russians in my school classes, growing up or in medical school. I've never really had any Russian friends."

"The world is changing. Vermont is still very white, with west

European ancestry, but it's not going to stay that way forever. We are seeing some changes to the demographics, though they are slow."

"I appreciate your help, even if you couldn't identify them. I still hope to be able to, but… not yet, I guess."

"Good luck. I'll check with Marissa and see whether she can help you."

Kenzie sat in the car after talking to the pastor, watching the people coming and going from the ministry. She shouldn't be surprised that the man hadn't been able to identify any of the victims, but she couldn't help the disappointment that washed through her. She had hoped to at least take a step toward finding out what had happened to her father. Someone would recognize one of the Russians and would be able to tell her how they connected up with Walter. But it had been nothing but another dead end.

Kenzie's phone vibrated, and she looked down at it, expecting to see a call or text from the pastor, maybe telling her that the Russian woman, Marissa, didn't want to meet with her.

The caller ID was "unknown." Kenzie didn't usually answer numbers or names she didn't recognize or had unknown or blocked numbers. But she had been contacting the various charities asking questions, and she still hadn't heard back from Walter. He could have a new number if something had happened to his regular phone and he'd had to pick up a burner while waiting for it to be repaired. If it was a telemarketer, it was easy enough just to hang up. Kenzie swiped to accept the call.

"Hello?"

"You have been causing trouble."

Kenzie's heart thudded hard. "What? Who is this?"

The voice was low and threatening. "If you don't back off, bad things are going to happen. Is that what you want? For bad things to happen to people you care about?"

"I don't know what you're talking about," Kenzie protested. Clearly, her inquiries had become known to someone. But which ones? And who would be in danger? Her parents? Zachary? Other friends or workmates?

"Go back to work and stop asking questions. Just do your job and stay in your own lane."

"It's a holiday today."

He spat out something that she did not understand. "Don't be stupid! When you go back to work tomorrow. Do your job. Leave everything else alone."

"Who is this? I don't know what questions you're talking about. It's my job to ask questions."

"It is not." His words were crisp and clear and, for the first time, she thought she detected a slight accent in the way he pronounced the words. That was not the way that someone who was raised on American English would answer. "It isn't," or even "no, it ain't," but not the three words pronounced separately like that. It was too perfect.

"Just do your job," the man told her for the third time, and he hung up.

28

Nothing had changed. Kenzie was still sitting in her car watching people coming and going from the street ministry, looking for anyone who might be a Russian immigrant or someone from another of the eastern European countries. Even though her heater was blasting warm air at the top setting and she was wearing a warm winter coat, she was cold. Sweat had collected under her armpits and was now freezing.

She could just ignore the call, of course. Most threatening phone calls were nothing more than that. Just calls. People who didn't have any intention of following up on their threats. They didn't have the motivation to do anything about their anger; they just wanted to express it.

Probably no one was in danger. The call was intended to keep her from making any further inquiries about the men who had died.

She could stop and just leave it alone. The men who had been killed did not appear to have friends or families in the community looking for them. There were no matching missing person reports, or Kenzie would have gotten a call from a police detective. The men were alone and unattached. Kenzie could simply pass the files on through the usual procedures. The bodies would be handled by the state. There was plenty of other work to be done in the Medical

Examiner's Office. There was no point in Kenzie getting stuck on an odd set of coincidences.

If there were something going on in the Russian immigrant community, then that would soon become obvious. Another death. A police investigation. Someone would turn something up. Kenzie's postmortems had been thorough. Her reports were complete. There was no need to ask more questions.

Except in connection with Walter.

There might be no connection between the Russians and Walter's disappearance, so she could continue to ask questions about him without upsetting whoever it was that didn't want her poking into the men's identities or histories. Her father was a different matter. She couldn't very well be expected not to stop calling him or making inquiries with his friends as to whether anyone knew why he had disappeared or where he was.

But if she ignored the call and something happened to Kenzie or someone close to her, it might be too late to figure out who the caller had been. The best bet was to have someone look into it immediately. Find out whether the call was traceable. Narrow down who it had been who had called her and made threats. Make sure that it wasn't someone who could go on and harm her, Lisa, or someone else in Kenzie's life.

Kenzie powered the phone off. That would, she hoped, prevent any information from being overwritten. She wouldn't call 9-1-1 or one of the cops that she knew directly, in case that would corrupt the bits of data on her phone.

It was probably nothing. Just an empty threat.

Probably.

It was a holiday, so there was less staff at the police station above Kenzie's morgue than usual. A skeleton crew to ensure everything continued going smoothly, but not the usual bustle of activity.

Kenzie approached the officer manning the desk and nodded a friendly greeting.

"Hi, I don't know if you know me. I'm Dr. Kenzie Kirsch from the Medical Examiner's Office?" Kenzie made a downward gesture to indicate the morgue.

"Oh." He nodded politely. "Well, good to meet you, doctor."

"I was wondering who is in today? I'd like to talk to Sergeant Campbell, but I suppose he'll be home with his family today."

"Actually," the officer swiveled in his chair to check a duty roster. "He is in today."

"Oh, that's great. Would you find out if he could see me?"

"Dr. Kirsch?"

"Right."

"Give me a moment. Have a seat." He gestured toward the chairs under the window.

Kenzie obeyed, sitting down so that he had the privacy to make the call to Sergeant Campbell. She pulled out her phone and then realized that she couldn't distract herself by playing with it, since she had turned it off in hopes of preserving any data. She looked for something else to occupy her attention. There were no magazines. A few public service posters around the waiting area. But she was finished reading those in a minute. All the things she thought of doing were on her phone. Her email, games, social networks… how had she become so dependent on one device for her entertainment?

She opened her purse to see if she had a notepad and pen to make a list of things she needed to follow up on. She saw, with relief, that she had her iPad with her. Her iPad was almost as good as her phone. It might not have everything loaded onto it, but she could access her mail accounts and social networks and it did have solitaire and Angry Birds installed. And there was a practically endless list of other games and apps she could install.

She had not even finished reading through her email when the desk sergeant called her.

"Ma'am? Doctor? Come this way, and I'll take you to Sergeant Campbell's office."

Kenzie stood up and went with him. She already knew the way to Campbell's office, but allowed herself to be escorted there. The young man needed something to do on such a quiet day.

He rapped on Campbell's open door, then gestured for Kenzie to enter. "Dr. Kirsch, sir."

"Thank you." Campbell stood up at his desk and reached across to shake Kenzie's hand, wrapping both of his around hers in a warm greeting. "It's good to see you, Kenzie; how are you?" They both sat down.

"I'm fine. I have a small problem I thought I'd better talk to you about."

"Of course. Anything. And how is Zachary?"

Campbell had been Zachary's friend long before he was hers. Kenzie appreciated how he dealt with Zachary, always upfront and tactful, not hiding behind euphemisms or pretending that he didn't know about Zachary's battle with mental illness.

"He's still in the hospital." Campbell had seen him there when he had investigated a death in the psych unit. "He's doing a lot better now and will be out... sometime in the next few weeks. When he's ready."

"Good. Good to hear it. He's had a difficult time."

Kenzie nodded and swallowed the lump in her throat. "But he's on the mend. Until the next thing. I didn't know what to do about this..." Kenzie put her phone on Campbell's desk. "I had a threatening phone call. I think it might be related to one or more of the autopsies that we've done recently. I don't like to make a big deal. I'm sure it was probably all just hot air. But I didn't want to take the chance of losing any evidence that can be obtained now."

Campbell nodded. He eyed the phone.

"When did you receive the call?"

"Within the last hour."

"Have you made or received any calls since?"

"No. I shut it off. I didn't want to take the chance that anything could be overwritten. I don't know if that's a thing with phones like it is with computers, but..."

"You did the right thing. I'll send it to our forensic team to figure out what they can. I assume the caller ID was blocked."

"Yes. But you can still pull the service provider's logs, right? And it will be on there?"

"Yes." Campbell shuffled through papers in the file drawer of his desk. "Let's get you to file an incident report and give permission for your logs to be released to us. Save ourselves having to get a warrant."

"Of course," Kenzie agreed, receiving the forms from him.

"What did this guy say to you? Male, I assume?"

"Yes. He said… just to do my job and not ask any questions or someone I knew could be hurt."

"Vague."

Kenzie nodded and sighed. "My first instinct was just to ignore it. But… if it was a serious threat…"

"Best to be sure. Especially since you are a civil servant. If it was just a civilian receiving a random threat, I might not be inclined to do anything. But with you being involved in law enforcement, it is possible that your work is a threat to this man's illicit business, and also possible that he could be serious about retaliating."

Kenzie began to work her way through the form. "How much detail do you want?"

"As much as you can give. Male, you said. Give me the estimated age. How he spoke. Timbre. Accent?"

"Not an accent, exactly. But I think he normally has one and was trying to keep me from detecting it. Which is… something that one of the men I recently autopsied did as well. He'd obviously had some kind of speech training to eliminate the accent."

29

O ne of the men you recently autopsied…?" Campbell shook his head. "He *spoke* to you?"

Kenzie realized how crazy that sounded and shook her head, laughing. "Oh, no, no, not like that. It was somebody that I had met before, when visiting my mother. He had no accent, but the care and the occasional pauses in his speech made me think that he wasn't a native English speaker."

"And you autopsied him?"

"Yes. It's in my report," she added quickly, to allay any concerns about its propriety. "That's what Dr. Wiltshire said to do. Vermont is too small of a place to avoid seeing anyone you know on the table. Sooner or later, you will know someone who comes through."

"I imagine so," he agreed. "I wasn't concerned about whether you were allowed, though. Just that… it would be difficult to do that with someone you knew."

"I'd only met him. Very briefly. He's not a friend."

"Oh, well, that's good, then. It would be like me having to arrest a friend. Sooner or later, it happens, but that doesn't mean you want to or it is very comfortable."

Kenzie nodded. It would have been different if it had been a friend. She'd had nightmares about pulling back the drape from a body and finding someone she knew underneath. A dream that had become more frequent with her father missing.

"Any more detail about the voice? And what did he say that he was calling about? You said it might be related to your work, so I assume he said something to make you think that, not that he was just your average kook."

"It was… Not an old voice. But not like a teenager's either. Thirties, maybe. Could be older or younger than that. Pleasant. Not gravelly. Nothing really distinctive about it. No speech impediment or accent, other than the feeling that English was his second language. The way that he spoke each word separately, rather than running them together and using contractions like native English speakers do."

Campbell jotted down a few notes on the pad of paper in front of him.

"And he didn't exactly say what he was calling about… but he kept telling me to do my job and not ask any questions, so I thought it must be something to do with a death investigation. Someone who didn't want me to discover something he had been involved in. Like you said."

"And do you have a suspicion about what case he's talking about? Is there one that you *have* been asking a lot of questions about?"

Kenzie studied Campbell for a moment. She knew he was a good cop, a straight arrow, not someone who could easily be influenced or corrupted. But she was still uneasy talking to him about the details. The governor had told her to back off, and Kenzie was still asking questions. About her father, about the Russians, trying to tie the disparate pieces together. If word got back to him that Kenzie had disregarded his instruction…

"I don't know for sure. There are… several cases involving Russians. Like the one I told you, the fellow that I had talked to. I think they might be related." She hesitated, wondering whether she should say anything about her father. She decided to leave him out of it. She had already mentioned her mother, which had probably been a mistake. "So I've been trying to find some contacts who would be knowledgeable about the Russian community here. Who could identify the men, knew what they had been involved in."

"That sounds like police work."

"Well… I haven't been holding myself out as a law enforcement officer. And I've been quite discreet. Just some preliminary attempts to get the bodies identified. That's an important part of my job, you know."

"You need to keep to your side of the fence, though. If you have questions that need to be investigated, you boot them upstairs. Let us deal with those. I don't want you to end up in the middle of some mess. You've been threatened now, so you're on notice that you've gone too far."

Kenzie felt her cheeks flushing. She shrugged and looked away from Campbell, pretending she was concentrating on the form he had placed in front of her.

"How do you know these bodies are Russian if you don't know their identities?" he asked.

Kenzie told him about the parasites and the Russian prison tattoos. He looked very serious hearing these details.

"So you know that they are probably involved in organized crime, and you thought it would be a good idea to go off and investigate it on your own?"

"We don't know for sure that those are gang tattoos. Dr. Wiltshire thought they might be, but we'll need confirmation from an expert. But these men, the two with tattoos, they don't look like mob. I don't think they are."

"You'd be surprised. You can't tell whether someone is connected just by looking at them. The most baby-faced kid could have a brother or father that brought him into the organization. Or a mother, for that matter. It's dangerous to assume just because the person doesn't look like what you might have seen on TV."

"That wasn't it, though. They were so malnourished. The first one, I am sure died of starvation. The second one was hit by a car, but I wouldn't be surprised if he was hallucinating from the lack of food and water. If they were Russian mob, they wouldn't be starving, would they? They would have everything they need."

Campbell pursed his lips and considered. He grunted an acknowledgment of her explanation and jotted some more notes on the pad in front of him.

"Yes, I agree," he said eventually. "That does not sound like they are in the mob *here*, though they might have been back home. And they might still have connections here who have concerns about how they were treated. You don't know. You can't take the chance of attracting the attention of these guys."

"No. And I won't. I'll stop asking questions to try to identify them. I'll pass everything I know on to you. But it isn't very much."

"Exactly what steps did you take to try to identify them?"

Kenzie told him about the Russian immigration foundation and the street ministry. She didn't say that she had been asking questions under the guise of the Kirsch family foundation. But she hadn't mentioned the Medical Examiner's Office or the police department either. She hadn't held herself out to be a professional. Somehow—she felt a chill at the thought—someone had managed to tie her inquiries back to her job at the Medical Examiner's Office. Someone had looked hard enough to make the connection between the Kirsch family foundation and Kenzie Kirsch of the Medical Examiner's Office.

It wasn't like she had avoided social media or kept anything about her identity under the radar. Anyone with a computer and an internet connection could probably track her to the medical examiner's office. And, apparently, to her private cell phone number as well.

"All right. And you're going to stop now, right? No more questions. No more saying that you're interested in the Russian immigrant community or flashing the pictures of dead men."

Kenzie nodded her agreement. "I won't."

"The third man that you mentioned, tell me more about him. He was not malnourished like the other two?"

"No. So I guess he would be more involved in the organization's administration. He must have had a higher position, even if he doesn't have tattoos."

"What do you know about him?"

Kenzie sat back in her seat and closed her eyes briefly, picturing him first in her mother's sitting room and then on the table in autopsy.

"He seemed... polished. Refined. My mother is very much a *proper lady* and he fit in there. I felt like something was wrong with him being there, but I couldn't identify what was wrong; other than that she hadn't introduced him to me properly. Normally... she would say where she knew someone from, what project they were working on together, where I might run into them again, or something they might be able to help me with. Or vice versa. But she didn't say anything, so I was uncomfortable. Not because he came across as being a thug or involved in crime somehow."

"You'll send me your report, so I'll have all of his vital information and a picture of him?"

"Yes, sure. Of course. There wasn't anything else remarkable about him... other than having twelve feet of tapeworm in his gut."

Campbell made a choking sound. Kenzie laughed at the green tinge to his skin.

"More people than you would think have parasites. But this was pretty amazing. It must have been growing for a very long time, and it is a species that we don't usually see here in North America."

"I'm glad to hear that. How did he get it?"

"They come from meat that hasn't been properly cooked. Once you have one, it just keeps growing, being nourished by what you eat."

"He wouldn't have had any symptoms? Had it looked at by a doctor?"

"Not necessarily. It's possible that he would have some digestive symptoms, but most people have some complaints. Not significant enough to have anything done about it, obviously."

"And I guess you know his name, if he was introduced to you. I thought that he was unidentified, like the others."

"Lisa said that his name is Maksim. I thought it was French. I asked her about him again after he ended up on my table, and she said she didn't know any more than that. Just a first name."

"And how did she meet him?"

"She wouldn't talk about it. I didn't have any luck getting any information out of her."

Campbell's brows drew down. "Really. Why would she not tell you everything she knows?"

"I don't know. Maybe one of your detectives will have an easier time getting it out of her. Good luck."

"You'd better give me her information too."

Kenzie finished filling in the basics on the incident form and signed a waiver that Campbell put in front of her for the phone log data from her service provider.

"We'll want your phone for a day or two. You might want to get a burner so that you have something in case of emergencies until you get it back."

"Okay." Kenzie swallowed, feeling a little sick. She hated to leave her phone with him. It was such a big part of her life. Everything was on there.

But it was also in the cloud, her iPad, and her computer at home. She wouldn't lose anything and, in a couple of days, she would have her phone back as good as new. It was worth the sacrifice if it would help to keep her family members safe.

30

As she left the police station, Kenzie thought about who she needed to inform about her burner number. Zachary did not have his phone in the hospital, so he did not need to know her new number or that she'd had reason to hand her phone over to the police. Dr. Wiltshire shouldn't be calling her before she got to work the next day, so she could tell him then.

Well, he shouldn't be calling her, but he might if there was a call that he wanted or needed her to attend at. Kenzie grumbled to herself and added him to the list of people who needed to be notified.

Her mother? She probably wouldn't need to contact Kenzie before she got her phone back. Except if she heard from Walter. Or if she got a call from the police. If either of those things happened, she would want to call Kenzie. So she would have to be notified.

There was no way to notify Walter, since there was no way to reach him. Kenzie would leave a message on his phone. Then if he ever decided to turn up and call her, he could.

Tyrrell? He wouldn't be calling her. She had a few friends who might want her temporary number, but she wanted to keep the numbers low. The fewer people she had to tell, the better. Lorne and Pat? It would probably be a good idea to notify them. And Heather. She could just send them all an email message. She wouldn't tell them that the police had it, just that it was in for repairs, so she had another number temporarily.

No one needed to know that the reason behind the burner was that she had been threatened.

One of the problems with calling Lisa was that she would always have assignments for Kenzie. Little things that *if Kenzie could just take a quick minute* to take care of, it would help Lisa *immensely* with her work. People that Lisa wanted her to call to encourage to donate to a cause or attend at a dinner. Thank you notes that she could write. An old friend that hadn't heard from Kenzie in ages, who would feel more disposed to help the foundation with something if they had a chance to gossip with Kenzie about old times for a few minutes, and perhaps be reminded of the expensive medical care Amanda had needed when she was sick. The Kirsch family had been able to afford her treatments, but so many people needed financial aid. Wouldn't it be nice if they didn't have to dig themselves huge pits of debt to get the care that they needed?

Lisa did not disappoint. Even though all Kenzie wanted to do was to give Lisa her burner number in case she urgently needed to reach Kenzie in the next couple of days, particularly if she saw or was in contact with Walter, Lisa was prepared with a list of demands.

Which was why Kenzie had to make her way to the offices of the Kirsch family foundation in Burlington to sign paperwork and get caught up on things she should have handled weeks before. Kenzie was motivated by her sense of guilt. If she was going to use the Kirsch family foundation name when making inquiries about home-less Russians, then the least she could do was keep up with the minor obligations she had to the foundation. Even if Lisa didn't have any idea what Kenzie had been doing in the name of the foundation.

Kenzie explained to Hillary, the administrator who ran the foun-dation office, that if she got any calls from the Russian immigration foundation or the street ministry, they would be directed to Kenzie.

Under no circumstances was anyone else to handle them or to imply that the foundation didn't have any interest in these matters.

"You'll need to fill out charity profiles for them," Hillary instructed her. "They go into the database so that we know what work has been done, research, officers, contacts, who it is handling inquiries, all of that. You cannot deal with another foundation without filling out a charity profile."

So Kenzie was forced to sit down at the computer station designated for her use and create a profile for each organization she had been in contact with, even though she doubted that she would ever hear anything from either of them. But she needed to be sure that those inquiries were directed to Kenzie and not to Lisa if they did call. She updated her own contact information with the burner phone number as an alternate number.

In an effort to make the profiles look as legitimate as possible—she would probably send each of them a little money since they had answered her questions and she didn't like to get their hopes up and then not follow through—she went to each of the websites to collect the information she needed to fill out as many of the fields as she could in the profiles. She clicked back to the database and started typing in "Russian" to find the charity profile she had just created.

More than one organization popped up on the screen. Apparently, the foundation had looked into more than one charity geared toward the Russian community in the past. Kenzie clicked on a Russian culture society, curious to see what had been done. This was not a charity she had come across when she had been trying to find charities that had something to do with the Russian community in Vermont.

The profile was pretty sparse so far. There was no website referred to, so that was probably why Kenzie had not come across them in her online search. She clicked through the information that had been entered manually. Her eyes stopped on a contact name.

Maksim.

Her heart thudded hard as she stared at the name, her cursor hovering over it.

A coincidence?

A common Russian name?

She had first met the man at Lisa's house. What were the chances that Lisa had connections to two men named Maksim?

There was no last name. Kenzie clicked on Maksim. His personal profile popped up on the screen. There were a lot of blanks, but there was a picture of his face, confirming to Kenzie that it was the same Maksim she had met. There could be no doubt at all. There was a promo picture of Lisa handing Maksim an oversize replica check, five figures long.

So Lisa had given him money already. He was a recipient. He hadn't just come to her house and introduced himself on Christmas Day. She had known who he was and maybe had invited him over. Maybe Kenzie was wrong and there was a relationship between them? Maybe they had met through the foundation and gotten along so well that Lisa had decided to pursue a personal relationship. She had invited him over for Christmas Day so she wouldn't be alone. Maybe Walter had already informed her that he wouldn't be coming over and, since Kenzie had not announced her intention to visit, Lisa assumed that she would be by herself and had wanted some company. She didn't tell Kenzie anything more than the man's name because she hadn't wanted to explain the convoluted backstory, that they had been helping Maksim's charity and then she and Maksim had decided to see more of each other.

Who Lisa chose to spend time with was her own business. She didn't have to tell Kenzie or explain anything to her. She could have told Kenzie to mind her own business, but had instead said that she didn't know the man.

Of course she did.

Kenzie shook her head, looking at the picture of the check passing from Lisa's grip to Maksim's.

31

Or was it?

Kenzie double clicked the picture to open it into a separate window and enlarged it. The name on the check was not Maksim's foundation, but the Kirsch family foundation. Lisa wasn't making a donation to Maksim's organization, but the reverse—Maksim was funding the family foundation.

A donor.

Money going from the Russian culture society to the Kirsch family foundation. And then where? What program was the family foundation putting it into?

Kenzie didn't know the database structure very well but, clicking around, she was able to find the records of money coming in and going out. She could see the Russian's money being deposited into a segregated account and then... nothing. It had not gone out again but was still sitting in the account. Whatever the money was for, it hadn't been paid out yet.

That wasn't surprising. The foundation could be putting money into anything from a scholarship to a building fund or a hundred other options. If the project had not yet started or was not ready to be funded, then the money would stay in the foundation's account, earning interest until it was time.

Kenzie clicked through various fields that were supposed to describe the purpose of the money and what it was that the Russian culture society did, but those fields were empty. The information that had been filled out was pretty sparse. Why? Lisa and Hillary were bulldogs about ensuring that the computer information was up to date and they had every bit of information they might need at their fingertips. If a donor called with questions about how their money had been used, or the IRS called with questions about who money had come from or where it had gone next, all of the information was right there, along with confirmation that they had done all of their research to ensure that the recipient was legitimate and properly registered for tax reasons.

So why was all of that information missing for the Russian culture society? Had it been promised but never delivered? Was it sitting around the office somewhere in hard copy and had not been typed into the computer yet? Or was something going on that shouldn't be?

Hillary hovered behind Kenzie. "Do you need help with anything? Are you finding everything you need?"

"Yes," Kenzie said vaguely. She clicked on Maksim's name to pop his picture up on the screen. "Do you know this man? Maksim? He made a donation to the foundation."

Hillary leaned forward, adjusting her glasses. "Oh yes, I remember him. He seemed like a nice man."

"What was the money for?"

Hillary shook her head. "Lisa was taking care of that. I don't know the details. She said she would take care of it."

"It's still sitting in the bank."

Hillary nodded. "It's in a segregated account. Lisa insisted on that. So it isn't going into general admin or overhead. It has all been set aside."

"But you don't know who it was supposed to go to after that."

"No, you'll have to ask your mother for the details."

"Has she said anything about this in the last week? About Maksim or the donation?"

"No. But it's the holidays. No one has really been working. The office has been closed." Hillary had made a special trip into the office to deal with Kenzie after her mother had twisted her arm enough to make her come. "We'll open next week and if there is something to be done, we'll take care of it."

"There isn't much information about that charity in here—nothing on the ownership or board of directors. There is no website. No business plan. No financial statements. I checked the IRS database and I don't even see them named as a registered charity. Unless it is under some other name."

"They don't have to be a charity to give us money," Hillary pointed out. "We are registered and will use it for charitable purposes."

"It's a society, though. Doesn't that mean it is a charity?"

Hillary shook her head. "No." She didn't try to explain it any further. Kenzie rubbed her head. She'd always thought that a society had to be a registered charity.

"But you don't know what the money is earmarked for."

"No. I thought it was something to do with your father, but Lisa didn't tell me anything about it. I just thought that from... bits of overheard conversation."

"Walter."

"Yes."

Kenzie thought this through. Walter's business was lobbying. He did not run the charity that bore his name. What did the Russians want Walter to do with the money? Was it to be paid to some company sponsoring a bill that affected the Russian community? Or trying to defeat a bill?

"Do you know where Walter is?"

Hillary's brows went up. "Do *I* know where he is? Don't you?"

"No. I don't. I've been trying to reach him, but he hasn't returned my calls."

"Last I heard, he was in Roxboro. I assumed that meant he was with you. Or at least visiting you."

"No," Kenzie shook her head vehemently. She didn't repeat that she had been trying to reach Walter. *What was he doing in Roxboro?*

For that matter, what had *Maksim* been doing in Roxboro?

Kenzie had seen Maksim last in Burlington, at Lisa's house. But he had died in Roxboro, or proximate enough to it that they were the closest Medical Examiner's Office. It was another connection in the Maksim-Lisa-Walter triangle.

But what did it mean?

32

When Kenzie had finished digging up everything she could at the foundation about Maksim and his organization, which was basically nothing, she headed for home. But she dialed Lisa's number on the burner phone as she traveled down the highway, letting it play over the Bluetooth speakers.

"Hello?" Lisa's voice was cautious, as if she didn't know who it was. Kenzie had *just* given her the burner number, but it apparently hadn't clicked in.

"It's Kenzie, Mother."

"Oh, MacKenzie. Right, on your new phone."

"Temporary phone. I'll be back on my old one again in a few days." She didn't want Lisa to erase her old number from all of her contact lists and then be confused when Kenzie tried to get her to go back to them.

"Yes, that's what you said," Lisa agreed.

"I finished everything you needed me to do at the foundation."

"Oh, good. Thank you for doing that. It is so easy to let things get behind, and you have been quite busy between your work and Zachary's health. And your vacation, of course…"

If Lisa was implying that Kenzie had taken a nice relaxing vacation away from her family foundation responsibilities, she needed to think again. Kenzie and Zachary had been sidelined by a virus and then a brutal antivirus protocol, which they had been happy to follow, since the other option was rapid dementia and death, and then Kenzie had booked a Thanksgiving resort vacation in the mountains to help them to rest and regenerate. Which had ended up being more work when first the owner of the resort had died and then a vacationer in another of the cabins. It had not been what Kenzie had hoped at all.

Of course, none of that was Lisa's fault, and Kenzie hadn't told her any of the details of what had happened, so she couldn't blame Lisa for thinking Kenzie and Zachary had just taken a vacation and not dealt with any responsibilities she had to the family foundation.

"Well, it's all caught up now," she assured Lisa through gritted teeth.

"Excellent. We really should get together for dinner one day, MacKenzie. Since Zachary is in the hospital right now, you must be taking most of your meals alone, and that can be lonely. You and I could have something nice. Enjoy ourselves one day."

Kenzie wanted to keep Lisa in a good mood, so she didn't argue that they weren't really compatible and probably wouldn't enjoy dinner together quite as much as Lisa imagined.

"Mmm, that would be nice. Mother… while I was there, at the foundation…"

"Yes?"

"I was doing some work on the computer, updating some information in the database."

"That's good. But Hillary can do it if you give her the information. That is her job."

"I was there, so I should be the one to do it. She already had to make a special trip to the office just to see me, which isn't really fair. Anyway… I came across the record for a Russian friendship society."

There was a pause, but only a very small one, before Lisa's "Mmm-hmm?" as if she thought it only mildly interesting that Kenzie had uncovered Maksim's charity.

"I saw Maksim in the database. You said you hadn't met him before and didn't know who he was, but you have information about him and his charity in the database. You have tens of thousands of dollars in the bank that came from him. So… explain to me what is going on?"

"I didn't tell you I had never met him before," Lisa said dismissively.

"I'm pretty sure you did. You said he introduced himself to you at your door on Christmas Day, and you let him in."

"Yes, that's right," Lisa agreed.

"But you knew who he was."

"Yes."

"Then why would he introduce himself to you again?"

"It's just a formality, MacKenzie. I don't see why it is of any concern to you."

"What is the money for?"

There was a much longer pause. Kenzie waited for the excuses. *It's none of your business. You don't need to know that. It is foundation business, not yours.* But Lisa had just been pushing her to take part in the foundation, to make herself useful there instead of only doing what she absolutely had to, letting things go for months at a time until her participation became critical. So it was her business. She was doing exactly what Lisa had told her to do—taking an interest. Asking questions about the way things worked. Informing herself about the activities of the foundation.

"The details are confidential," Lisa said eventually. "We need to take care not to say anything that could get out…"

"I'm not going public. I'm asking what's going on. Why did the foundation get this donation? What is it supposed to be going to?"

"It has to do with some lobbying on behalf of the Russian community. Honest people who have immigrated to the United States and yet are in danger of their civil rights being violated. The government has identified them as a threat. Little old ladies knitting scarves for their grandchildren. They just want to be allowed to live free of any… persecution or prejudice."

"Little old ladies?" Kenzie repeated.

It had certainly not been little old ladies who had been ending up on her table.

"Men, women, and children. They have immigrated legally, they have all of their papers, yet they are still at risk of having everything taken away from them."

"What? Who is taking what away from them?"

"There are a lot of details that I don't understand," Lisa confessed. "Your father knows what it is all about. He is the one that is supposed to be directing the funds."

"But he isn't. It's just sitting there in the bank. Because he hasn't shown up."

"He will, MacKenzie. You don't need to worry about that. Things are just a little… difficult right now. They will all get straightened out in the end."

"People are being killed, Mother. I don't think this is just a minor blip that we can ignore, and everything will come to rights."

"What do you mean, people are being killed? Maksim?"

"He's just one of them. I have *a number* of dead Russians in the morgue. Explain that to me. Explain what is going on that could possibly justify turning a blind eye to these deaths in the hopes that everything will just come right in the end?"

"I don't know anything about that. I don't know anything about deaths, other than that you told me that Maksim was dead. But… I haven't heard anything from anyone else."

"You're waiting for someone else to verify it? You think that I just made it up?"

"No, of course not. I'm just not sure… what to do next. If someone will be stepping in and taking over for him. I'm not sure what to do next."

"I think you need to tell the police what is going on with Walter. And what Maksim was up to. Things don't look good. You don't want the foundation mixed up in something questionable."

"No. It isn't. We haven't even touched that money."

That was the first confirmation that Kenzie had that her mother knew that there might be something illegal going on. She had not just put the money from Maksim's organization into operating funds. She hadn't touched it. She could show anyone who inquired that they had merely held on to the money after receiving it. And if it turned out that it came from dirty sources, the foundation could always return it or turn it over to the feds. They had not done anything questionable.

"Why? Where do you think it came from? If it is just earmarked for widows and orphans, then what is going on here? Where is Dad? Why was Maksim beaten to death? You know something, Mother, and I think you need to talk to the police and tell them what you know."

"I can't go to the police, MacKenzie."

There was a slight crack in Lisa's voice. She *couldn't* go to the police? Why not? She didn't just say she didn't want to go to the police. Lisa was always very precise. She picked her words carefully. She wouldn't say that she *couldn't* go to the police if she just didn't want to deal with them. Or was too busy to take herself to the police station.

"Why not?"

"I don't want anyone else to die."

Kenzie swallowed. She wished she had bought a bottle of water at the last gas station. She had nothing to moisten her mouth, which was suddenly as dry as a desert. "Have you been threatened?"

"No. Not me personally. But... there are things going on that I don't understand. I don't know who these people are or why anyone has died. You know that I would never get involved in anything shady, MacKenzie. You *know* that."

"Of course I do," Kenzie assured her. Lisa had known about the gray market kidney transplant Amanda had received, but Kenzie believed that the only one who knew anything about what had really happened was Walter. And he probably hadn't known anything for sure at the time. He had just chosen to close his eyes to anything that didn't sound right because his daughter desperately needed that kidney. He wouldn't take any chances in waiting, so he had pushed ahead with something that had been too good to be true, ignoring what might be happening behind the scenes. But Lisa would never have approved if she had known where the kidney came from. She campaigned for kidney research, improvements in transplants, and a hundred other causes adjacent to organ donation, but Lisa had never done anything Kenzie knew to have even a whiff of impropriety. "Did someone call you? Did someone tell you that more people would die if you talked to the police?"

"No. Nobody has threatened me outright. There has just been… innuendo… things that didn't feel quite right. And Maksim showing up on Christmas Day." She trailed off, not finishing the thought that Kenzie had.

"And Dad *not* showing up."

"Yes. Maksim said he would stay and wait. He wanted to talk to Walter and he would wait until he got there. In the house, out of the house, it didn't matter. He would stay there until he saw Walter."

"And you weren't about to let him stand around outside for hours or sit in his car waiting."

"Of course not. That would have been rude. A good host would never…" Her voice again slid off into nothing. A good host would never allow a mobster to wait around outside the house? A good host always made sure that everyone felt as comfortable as possible, even if they were on their way to the slaughter?

"You expected Daddy to be there."

"Yes. He always stops in on Christmas Day, even if it is only for a few minutes."

"Did you talk to him on the phone? Get a message or text from him? Did he ever say why he hadn't shown up?"

"No. I haven't heard anything."

"In a week. He's never called or messaged you. And you can't go to the police to report him missing?"

"No. I don't live with him. I don't have any responsibility for him. He could be off sailing in the Caribbean."

Never mind that Walter had never done anything like that.

"I talked to the governor," Kenzie told Lisa.

There was an answering gasp. As if Kenzie might have just ruined everything. Pulled the trigger on her father's execution.

"I was just asking him if he'd talked to Dad lately. If they had done anything together. I was trying to find anyone who could tell me that he was okay and that I didn't need to keep looking. Keep calling."

"What did he say?" Lisa sounded breathless.

"He said he would look into it and call me back."

"And… then he didn't?"

"He did call me back, but he told me not to do anything. Not to talk to anybody about it. Just to let it go and everything would be fine."

"But you didn't," Lisa snapped. "You were looking for answers at the foundation. You are calling me again and asking me questions. Why won't you just leave it be? What if asking questions gets Walter hurt?"

"I'm sorry." Kenzie tried to lick her lips but was still too dry. "I don't want to get anyone hurt, especially Walter or you. That's why I went to the police today."

33

She knew before she said it that it was the wrong thing to say. But Kenzie didn't want to lie to her mother. She didn't want to keep what she had done a secret. She wanted instead to show Lisa that she could trust the police. Kenzie did. Calling them had been the right thing to do.

"You did what?" Lisa demanded. "You called the police? Why would you do that? After the governor himself told you to step back and leave it alone?"

"I didn't say anything to them about Dad. That was what the governor asked me to leave alone, and I did. I haven't filed a missing person report, even though I think one of us should. I haven't called any of his other friends. I haven't called the governor every day to see if he has an update. I've just been waiting. Trying to wait."

"Then why did you go to the police? What did you tell them?"

"I told them that I was threatened. That's why the police have my phone."

There was a sob on the other end of the line. Kenzie felt terrible. She had called Lisa to try to find out more about Maksim. She hadn't called to upset Lisa and make her feel as bad as Kenzie herself felt. Kenzie had been ignoring the feeling of dread that sat in her gut every day, the knowledge that somewhere, her father was dead, or he would have called her back. Somewhere along the line, she was going to learn that Walter had been beaten to death, just like Maksim.

And Hillary had said that Walter was in Roxboro last she had heard. So maybe he would end up on Kenzie's autopsy table once they found his body. Some hiker or dog walker would come across his body in the snow, preserved by the cold, and would see that he was brought to Kenzie's morgue for processing.

"You were threatened?" Lisa asked, barely able to get the words out.

Kenzie felt irrationally like apologizing. For what? For being threatened? For telling Lisa? For wanting her father back? "Someone called me on my phone. Told me to stop investigating or people close to me would be hurt."

"Oh, MacKenzie... I'm so sorry that happened. This is terrible. It has gone much too far. When will it end?"

"I don't know. I don't understand what's going on. How all of these things are connected, if they are. Maksim's death. The others. Dad being... gone. There are connections between them all, but I can't see the big picture."

"I'm worried about you. You'll stop now, won't you? You won't ask any more questions about Walter, or Maksim, or any other Russians. You won't ask anything about the money. Just... go home, take care of Zachary, go to work, and take care of all of the routine jobs... and don't *find* anything."

"You think I should hold back on anything I find at work? In an autopsy?"

"There are... there are too many people who know what you have been up to. I don't want someone coming after you, or Zachary, or me. I don't want them to use us as leverage to get Walter to do what they want."

"Is that what's happening?"

There was too long a silence. Kenzie couldn't stand it. Couldn't stand wondering how much her mother knew and how much she had already faced. What difficult choices had she been required to make? Choosing between her daughter or her ex-husband? Being forced to use money for things that she knew were unethical? They had been putting pressure on her before Kenzie had even known that there was anything wrong. She must have felt so alone.

"Everybody speaks in half sentences. *If,* but no *then.* Telling me how much better I will feel if I cooperate and do the things they want me to. I can't sleep. I can't eat. I keep telling them that I don't know anything. That I don't know what they're talking about. It keeps them at a distance for a while… but not forever. I don't know whether…" Lisa ran out of steam again.

"You don't know whether…" Kenzie repeated softly.

There were too many ways to finish that sentence, and she was afraid of all of them. How had Lisa gotten caught in the middle of this? Kenzie felt a flash of anger toward her father. *He* was the one who had caused this. It was something to do with his lobbying, with people he'd had contact with in backroom negotiations, everything done under a cloak of secrecy. That wasn't the way that Lisa worked. She would never be like that. She was an open book. Anyone who wanted to know what kind of a person she was had only to look at all of the good works she had done. She was tireless in her charitable work, trying to keep anyone from having to go through what Amanda had gone through and what the family had gone through because of Amanda's disease. She was always doing something, helping someone, making something better. *That* was the kind of person Lisa Cole Kirsch was.

"I don't know whether your father is… alive. Whether they have him or whether he is hiding. They don't tell me. They just tell me to cooperate, and then everything will go back to the way that it was."

Kenzie's eyes filled with tears at the heartbreaking throb in her mother's voice.

"But things will never go back to how they were," Lisa said. "You know they won't."

Kenzie knew that she would never be the same again. She would never take her parents for granted again. She would never complain about going home to visit her mother or having to fill out paperwork and endorse documents at the foundation office. She would never complain about how she had grown away from her father since finding out about Amanda's transplanted kidney. How he didn't have the same ethics as she did. She swore she would never complain again. She didn't have anything to complain about concerning how she was raised. She had learned from Zachary how traumatic childhood experiences could be and how abusive his parents had been. She had grown up in a world he couldn't even imagine.

"We'll find Daddy," Kenzie told Lisa. "I'll find out what happened to him, and we'll bring him home again. He'll be back to aggravating you before you know it!"

Lisa gave a little laugh of appreciation. "But you know you can't do anything, MacKenzie. Neither of us can do anything that might put him into further danger."

34

Kenzie felt guilty ending the call with her mother, knowing that Lisa was by herself, lonely and scared for her ex-husband and daughter, and that she wasn't in a position where she could do anything but wait and worry. But Kenzie couldn't stay on the phone with Lisa for the rest of the day. It wouldn't do either of them any good.

She hadn't thought to write down all of the phone numbers she might need when she had been on the computer at the foundation. She could have logged in to her contacts list and written down all the ones she might need in the next couple of days. She didn't realize how much she relied on just having those numbers on her phone. She didn't have to memorize them, didn't even have to look them up and punch in the numbers. All she had to do was search for the person she wanted to call, pick their name from her favorites, or tell her phone who she wanted to call. She had no idea what anyone's number was anymore.

And that included Campbell. She had his cell number in her contact list, but since she was in the car with a new phone that had no information on it and no internet browser, that was useless to her until she got home. She knew the police department general switch-board, so she called that number and asked for Campbell, hoping he would still be at his desk. The odds were not good. As far as she could tell, he had just gone into work for a couple of hours on a holiday, like Kenzie sometimes did on the weekend, to tie up loose ends that she couldn't get to while doing the rest of her job. And she had added to Campbell's work by telling him about the threat she had received.

"Campbell," he answered gruffly.

"Oh, you're still there. It's Kenzie. Sorry to bother you again."

His voice was more relaxed once he knew who it was. "No problem, Kenzie. And I'm not at the office anymore. I just have my office phone forwarded in case something pops on this investigation. I'm afraid I don't have anything for you yet. How are things on your end? Feeling better now that you've got us looking into those threats?"

"Yes," Kenzie lied. "Thank you so much for helping out with that."

"I'm happy to do it. Besides, I've mostly passed it on to the detectives to see what they can uncover. Easy enough for me to do."

She knew there was a lot more to coordinating an investigation than just assigning it to someone else, but she would let it go. He was trying to let her off the hook.

She was bursting to tell Campbell what she had learned. It might not be much, but knowing something about who Maksim was and the connection between him and the family foundation—that was something, at least. Finding out that Lisa had known since Christmas Day that something was wrong. Maybe even before then. When had she first gotten an inkling that the Russian might be up to something sinister? Had she known that it would send shock waves through her life? That he and his organization would hold Walter hostage, in word if not actually physically holding him? That her family, the thing that was most precious to her, would be threatened?

But she couldn't tell Campbell anything she had learned from Lisa. Lisa would not stand for it. She wanted her communications with Kenzie to be completely clean. There couldn't be any sign that she was giving Kenzie information that Kenzie was then acting upon.

"So, what else can I do for you?" Campbell asked. "Did you think of something else to add to your report?"

"No. I was just wondering… if you could give me some background on the Russian community here. In Roxboro or all of Vermont. Are they... do the police have much to do with them? Are there crimes that you are aware of but maybe not able to make arrests on yet...?"

Campbell cleared his throat noisily. "That's not really something that I can confide in you about. Of course there are criminals in any community. And there are always crimes that the police are aware of, where we are watching a situation but don't yet have the proof we need to make arrests. It can take months or years to build some cases. Civilians think we are ignoring their complaints and not doing anything because they don't see the behind-the-scenes work. They think that if they make a report, we should act on it immediately. And we do. But there are so many things that need to be taken into account. We can't just run out and arrest someone like you see them do on TV. Or if we do, without the evidence that we need, they will be right back on the streets the next time we turn around. And more cautious and cagey this time."

"Dr. Wiltshire said that a couple of the dead men had Russian gang tattoos. Is that something you see a lot of here?"

"They are known. I can't tell you how many people around here have tattoos or are involved in gangs or organized crime. Or how many people are hiding their Russian connections. They don't have any tattoos and manage to fly under the radar. They're more like... moles. Getting things done quietly behind the scenes and never showing their faces. There is a lot of money flowing into these organizations, and despite all of the money laundering laws and know-your-client rules, we can't stem the flow. We need stricter laws. We need ways to cut off the flow of money from billionaire oligarchs in Russia, to stop it from being used for illegal purposes here."

Kenzie nodded along with Campbell's words. She didn't know much about organized crime, but money had to be at its heart. A complex organization could not survive without it.

"So, how do you do that? How can you stop the money?"

"First, we have to know how it is getting in. Do they have someone on the inside who is funneling money to them even though it is illegal? Are they working within a fraudulent bank system? Are they using other currencies that don't have the same controls? Offshore accounts? Multiple layers of shell corporations?"

"Charities?" Kenzie suggested.

"Charities. Could be. They're pretty well regulated, but it's possible for an organization to use a charity to launder their money. They look like legitimate organizations, like they are doing good in the community, helping families and schools when, really, they are just cleaning money from illegal trafficking."

"Do you know of any scams like that?"

Campbell didn't answer for a minute. "Well, there are always scams like that going on. I can't say that I specifically know of this one or that one, but we've always got our eyes on something. And so do the feds. They're the ones more likely to be involved with organized crime. They have ways of digging into organizations that a little police force like ours doesn't. They have the manpower and the training. Know what to look for and where."

"Are you working with them on this—on any cases involving Russians?"

"I couldn't share anything like that with you."

"What are the Russians involved in around here? Is it mostly drugs?"

"There is plenty of drug trafficking going on, by the Russians and other groups. And human trafficking, both for prostitution and unpaid labor."

Kenzie paid attention to the mention of unpaid labor, thinking of the first John Doe that she had autopsied. All muscles and bone. Worked and starved to death. And the one who had been hit by a car had been similarly malnourished. What was it that Dr. Wiltshire had said about him? That he had run out into traffic?

Had he been trying to escape something? Was he being chased? People didn't normally run out into traffic for no reason. There were plenty of vehicle versus pedestrian accidents but, usually, it was someone jaywalking, drunk, or distracted by a phone. Not running directly into a busy street, as the witnesses had described. Maybe the man had been hoping that with so many people around, he would be able to get away from the traffickers. But he hadn't been able to escape the slave labor. Not the way that he had wanted to.

"Do we have a lot of that in Vermont? Human trafficking?"

"It's everywhere, Kenzie. There is no way to escape it. When you plug one hole, something else springs up. We work hard with the community, hotels, truckers, and other organizations that might unintentionally be enabling trafficking, trying to get people to pay attention to what's going on around them and to report when they see signs of trafficking. But people are still afraid to contact the police. Especially to report something that is only suspicious. They don't have proof and, as far as they are concerned, when they do report something, the police don't take any action."

"Because they can't see what's happening behind the scenes to see that the police are investigating and gathering evidence."

"Right," Campbell agreed. "We can't tell people what we are doing, so they think we are doing nothing. Then why bother to report it?"

"Is there anything else the Russians are doing...?"

"They have their fingers in *all* of the pies. Why wouldn't they be doing everything they can to make money? Power and money are what it's all about. That's what everyone wants. More and more power and money. And they'll do whatever they can to get it."

Kenzie was silent, trying to imagine how Walter was involved in all of this. He was not Russian. He was not involved in human trafficking or any other illegal business. While he might not have the same ethics as Kenzie, she was sure that he wouldn't be involved in anything that was clearly criminal. If there were shades of gray, there was no telling what he might be up to, but she didn't believe for a minute that he would willingly get involved in the prostitution or slave trades.

"So is that all you called about?" Campbell asked. "Just learning about the Russian underground? Of course, there are plenty of Russian immigrants who don't have anything to do with organizations like these. People just living their lives like every other American. Who would be horrified at being grouped together with the Russian mob."

"Of course," Kenzie said quickly. "I never intended to imply that all Russians were criminals or gangsters. I was just surprised… that they are here, in small-town Vermont."

"All right. Well, I need to spend some quality time with the family now, so I'll have to let you go."

"Oh, sure," Kenzie agreed, feeling bad that she had been keeping him from family time. She could have waited another day.

But could Walter?

35

After the day she'd had, Kenzie found it soothing to return to the familiar clean lines of the hospital corridors. Even though she wasn't practicing medicine in the hospital, she still felt like she belonged there just as much as she did in the Medical Examiner's Office. Lots of time spent in those halls as a student, learning the ins and outs of medicine and the hospital administrative structure. It always felt a little like coming home. Maybe also because she had spent so much time in the hospital as a teen visiting Amanda. She'd spent many, many hours in hospitals over the years.

Kenzie waited for the nurse receptionist to verify her driver's license and check her in. She wasn't even impatient with the waiting. It was just part of the routine she went through in visiting Zachary, and the routine soothed her and helped her to slip into "visiting" mode, leaving the rest of her worries behind.

In the psych ward, it was all about Zachary. How he was doing. Their relationship. Sharing with each other and enjoying each other's company, knowing that one day, a few more weeks down the road, they would be going home together and taking their lives back up again. Until that happened, Kenzie felt like she was only living half a life. Waiting for her other half to join her.

The nurse finished recording Kenzie's information and smiled at her. "All set." She handed Kenzie her driver's license back again. "Have a nice visit."

"Thanks." Kenzie nodded and headed into the unit. She found Zachary on one of his favorite chairs in the visitor room, looking around at the people and the window. He smiled when he saw her and gave her a brief hug before sitting back down.

"Kenzie. I was hoping you would come…"

"Of course. I'll always come to see you."

"I know you will if you can, but there are other things going on in your life too. I thought you might be extra busy today."

She had to think for a minute about why he would expect her to be extra busy that day. The morning had been a very long time ago, but then she remembered that it was still New Year's Day. Although it was a holiday, it was also a day that there might be an influx of new bodies.

"Oh, yeah. No, luckily I didn't have to be in today. But I imagine we'll have plenty on our plates for the next couple of weeks. Still getting caught up from the Christmas season, and then New Year's accidents too. I wish I could say that drinking and driving was now so socially unacceptable that people just don't do it anymore, but I don't think I'll ever be able to say that."

Zachary nodded. He looked away and, for a moment Kenzie wondered if he was thinking about Tyrrell and if he was safe, if he'd made it through New Year's okay. But he still didn't know about Tyrrell's bender. As far as he knew, Tyrrell was still safe at home like he should be.

"Everything is okay?" Zachary asked.

Kenzie nodded. "Sure. Everything is okay. Why?"

"You just look… tired. Worried."

"I just had a lot to do today. Not at the office, but… well, I went to Burlington and finally took care of a bunch of stuff that my mother has been wanting me to do."

Zachary cocked his head slightly. She knew she didn't talk to him much about her family or obligations with them, so it was only natural he would be curious about this. "For your trust?"

"Not the trust, the family foundation."

He still looked expectant. Kenzie shrugged and let out a sigh. "So the trust is a different entity than the family foundation. The trust administers the money that comes to me from the time I turned eighteen until my parents die. For things like education, major expenses, travel—personal stuff. Sort of like an allowance for grown-ups. The family foundation is what my mother uses for charitable work. It receives grants and donations and does fundraising, and the money it receives goes into the charities and causes that Lisa directs it to. So that's family money that is going to other places, not to me. And of course, if I want to direct money to a worthy cause, I can do that too because I'm on the board of the foundation and have the power to make those decisions. Mother has to approve them as well, but I can't see her ever fighting a donation I wanted to make unless it was something illegal or immoral. She'd be happy for me to be a lot more involved in the foundation than I am."

Zachary nodded slowly. "I see. I didn't know how it was all set up."

"I don't talk about it a lot," Kenzie admitted. "I've neglected my duties as a director and officer of the foundation. Lisa lets it slide, but I really should be more diligent about it. It is supposed to be for all of us to use, not just her."

"All of you?"

"Me and my parents. It is supposed to be all dependents of my paternal grandfather, but it has come down to just my parents and me. And one day, just me…" She didn't suggest that maybe one day she would have children who could also use the foundation for good causes. That might be too much for Zachary. They were not married. They had only been intimate for a short time and were still in couple's therapy working through the effects of Zachary's traumatic upbringing and the assault he had suffered. Suggesting that the two of them might have children who would take over the foundation after her might feel like too much pressure to Zachary. She didn't want to overwhelm him and have him pull away because of it.

Not that he wouldn't like children. She knew that he longed for them. He'd wanted children with Bridget when they had been married, but she had refused him. Only to go on and have children with Gordon after her divorce from Zachary. The whole thing was a minefield Kenzie wasn't willing to step into as part of a casual conversation. Maybe someday, when it was planned, and maybe under the supervision of their therapist.

"It's cool to be able to do that," Zachary said. "To decide that someone or something is worth funding, and then just… do it."

"It can be fun," Kenzie admitted. She'd never gotten quite the charge out of it that Lisa seemed to get. But maybe that was just because she hadn't put very much time and effort into it. It was Lisa's life work, not Kenzie's. "Really rewarding to see the faces of people that you have helped. Though I prefer to do it anonymously most of the time, so people don't know exactly where the money has come from. Then you see more genuine responses, and people don't feel obligated to you. You don't get that whole… scripted response."

"What would you like to give money to?"

"I don't know. I've been looking at a few charities the last few days. But I haven't decided yet."

"And your mom does stuff that is mostly… kidney related."

"Yes. Because of Amanda's kidney disease. So she tries to ensure that other people don't have to go through what we did. Though, you can't really do that."

"You can't stop people from getting kidney disease."

"She tries! Gives lots of money to research on prevention, gene therapy, early treatment, all that kind of thing. But, no. You can't prevent people from getting kidney disease, no matter how hard you try. But you can try to make it easier on them."

Zachary's eyes flicked around the room. Alert, watching for trouble. Kenzie waited for him to turn his attention back to her.

"How has your day been today? I don't suppose they do anything special around here for New Year's?"

There hadn't been much done by the psych ward for Christmas, so she couldn't imagine them making a big deal about the new year.

"No. I knew what day it was today, but they don't announce it or make a big deal out of it. Anything you change here can agitate people. They're used to things happening the same way every day. And holidays where you are supposed to feel a certain way, like

Christmas, or to do something specific, like New Year's, add that much more pressure. People get more depressed because they aren't with their families or don't have families or friends. And the whole New Year's resolution thing… it's hard to look at your life and see all the things you want to change or thought you had overcome but didn't, or that you're never going to be able to overcome. It's not just resolutions to go on a diet or to exercise every day."

"No. That makes sense. So they just let it pass without observing it?"

"Pretty much. If they mention it, it's just in passing. Not a big deal."

"It's good that they're careful. Do you remember New Year's a couple of years ago?"

Zachary looked at her for a moment, then smiled and flushed a little bit pinker. "No… not exactly. There's sort of a blank there when I was unconscious."

"I remember it quite clearly. It started out okay; we had a nice supper… but then things went a little off the rails."

"Off the road," Zachary corrected.

Kenzie grimaced. "Yes, off the road."

"Not the best first date."

"Pretty memorable."

"Not for me."

Kenzie laughed. The accident had certainly started their relationship and the new year off with a *bang*.

Zachary stretched and straightened as if feeling to make sure that everything was in place and working the way it was supposed to. After the accident, he had been paralyzed until the swelling around his spinal cord had been reduced. Even just that brief paralysis and inflammation had meant that he needed physiotherapy to regain full use of his legs. She couldn't see any continuing problems but, every now and then, she was reminded of what Zachary had been through when he talked about being clumsy or awkward because of the accident.

"You were lucky," Kenzie asserted. "We both were. I've seen the results of accidents like that, and not everyone walks away from them."

"I didn't walk away," Zachary reminded her.

"No… but you walked away from the hospital. I've seen other results on the table."

Zachary nodded. "I was lucky," he agreed.

36

Kenzie glanced at the phone display before picking up the receiver, but did not recognize the number. There was no name.

"Medical Examiner's Office," she announced.

"Yes…" the voice was slow and careful. "Is this Dr. Kirsch?"

"Yes, it is," Kenzie responded, slowing her words in case he had had trouble understanding her.

"Dr. Kenzie Kirsch."

"That's right. How can I help you, sir?"

His English was heavily accented. Kenzie's heart picked up speed. A Russian accent. And with everything else that had happened, just hearing the thick Russian accent worried her. What more could happen?

But maybe he was just calling to claim one of the bodies. That would be really helpful. They would be able to identify the deceased and get more insight into what might have led to their deaths.

"I think we can help each other."

"Okay…"

"We must get together to meet."

Kenzie recited the address of the morgue. "We're in the basement. Hit the B elevator button when you get here—"

"No," his voice was a hiss. "I cannot come there. That would be very bad. You must come to me."

"I'm sorry, I don't conduct business outside of this office."

"I think... this is perhaps more *personal* than business."

"What is it regarding?"

He didn't answer immediately. Maybe the English construction was too difficult for him to understand.

"What is it about?" she tried.

"I need to speak with you."

"I know. But what do you want to speak about?"

"I will tell you that when I see you. Will you meet me today? At the sandwich shop. *It's a Wrap.*"

Kenzie knew the place well. She was slightly reassured that the Russian stranger wanted to meet in a busy public place. What could happen if she met him out in public? It would be different if he insisted on meeting her in some lonely place where anything could happen. She could be murdered, assaulted, or kidnapped. But in the sandwich shop? Nothing could happen to her there.

"Okay," she conceded, "I could meet you there. But I'd like to know what it is about. Is it something about the results of an autopsy?"

"Perhaps."

"Mr...?"

He didn't respond.

"I don't know your name. What am I supposed to call you?"

"Oh. Alexei. You may call me Alexei."

"Alexei. I need you to tell me more about why you want to meet. I will meet with you; *It's a Wrap* is a good place to meet, and they have great sandwiches. But I want to know what it is about."

"Today? At noon? You would like a sandwich?"

"I can meet with you at noon," Kenzie conceded. "But will you please tell me how to recognize you? And what it is that we will be meeting about?"

"I will know you. Pretty lady with curly dark hair."

Kenzie felt a little chill at the description. Not only did he have her number and know her name, but he knew the neighborhood around the morgue and he had seen her or a picture of her so that he would be able to recognize her.

"Yes, but I would like to know what you look like too. What if someone else comes up to me at the shop? How will I know it is you?"

She would, hopefully, recognize his voice and there wouldn't be more than one Russian man looking for her at the sandwich shop, but she wanted more information before then. And if one Russian knew that she had been making inquiries and had information for her, there were bound to be others who knew she had been making inquiries and didn't want her to talk to anyone else about them.

"I will wear black coat. Long. With a green scarf. You will remember? Green scarf?"

That would help, at least.

"Yes, okay. Noon today at *It's a Wrap*?"

"Yes. I will see you there?"

"Sure. I'll be there."

"It will be good to see you. Walter Kirsch's daughter."

Kenzie swallowed. "Yes. Yes, I am. Do you know Walter?"

"Does anyone of importance in Vermont *not* know Walter?"

Kenzie shook her head, irritated at his question.

"Do you know where he is now?"

"Perhaps that is something we can discuss."

"Do you?" Kenzie pressed.

"You see him every Christmas, do you not?"

"No. Not every year. Sometimes I see him at—" Kenzie cut herself off. If Alexei didn't already know that Walter visited his ex-wife regularly, she didn't want to tell him. She needed to keep her mother safe as much as she was able. "Sometimes I see him and sometimes I don't. Sometimes he just calls me."

"For this to work, you must tell me the truth," he said heavily.

"I don't know who you are. Why would I tell you anything?"

"We want to help each other, do we not? So you must tell me the truth. About everything."

"I don't know that I want to help you. I don't know what you want or who you are. You're going to have to do something to prove your goodwill to me. Maybe you have some information that I need."

"Perhaps," he agreed, sounding pleased.

"Good… I really need to understand what is going on right now."

"We will help each other."

He hung up without saying goodbye. Kenzie set her handset back in the cradle and stared at the phone for a few minutes, trying to figure out what to do. She would meet Alexei there. Nothing could happen to her in the middle of the lunch crowd at *It's a Wrap*. Maybe he had some information that would provide the police detectives with information to solve the cases of the recently dead Russians. Or maybe by meeting with him, she would find something out about Walter.

She would have arranged to take Zachary with her if he had been available. Or to have him watching while she met with the mysterious Russian. But he wasn't available and Kenzie could not put off the meeting until he was. She wrestled with an alternative solution to ensure she wasn't walking into a dangerous situation, even though she felt she would be safe in such a busy public place. *It's a Warp* over the lunch hour was like Grand Central Station. Nothing could happen there without a dozen witnesses.

George was in preparing the subjects for the afternoon post-mortems. Kenzie busied herself inventorying supplies in the morgue, even though she knew that the cupboards and drawers were properly stocked. She scratched the back of her head, trying to figure out how to approach the topic with him.

"That's heavy work," she said, watching him move and prep another body.

George glanced at her. Kenzie was a lot smaller than he was, and she moved bodies around too. They both knew what it was like and had figured out the best ways to get leverage when moving dead weight. "Yep," he agreed.

"I was wondering… maybe you'd like to get a sandwich or something at *It's a Wrap* at lunchtime?"

His brows came down while he considered this, moving the body from side to side as he washed it down. "I thought you had a boyfriend."

"I do!" Kenzie's face burned. "That's not what this is about. I just wanted… I need a favor, actually…"

He blinked at her and waited for her to fill him in.

"I am meeting someone there today."

"Uh…"

"A stranger, someone I don't know." Kenzie hurried on, wanting to get the weirdness out of the way. "It's not a date or anything romantic. I think that he has some information that I need. About my dad. And…" Kenzie ran her fingers through her curls, anxious. Remembering how Alexei had described her. Her mouth was dry and she knew she wasn't doing a very good job at explaining to George what she needed and why she needed it. "He called me with information. And he wants to meet at *It's a Wrap*. So that's good because it's a safe place, it's crowded, lots of people will be around to see and no one will suspect that there is anything illicit going on. But I'm just a little bit nervous. I'd like to have someone there as backup, just in case."

"You don't know what could happen," George pointed out unnecessarily. "This guy could come with a gun. Or try to grab you and throw you in a van."

"I know. I don't think he would do anything like that with so many witnesses, but sometimes people are crazy. They don't think. And I would just like to be sure that I've got someone on my side in case something does go sideways." She shrugged at George. "Your size would help deter anyone…"

"And I get a sandwich."

Kenzie nodded, relieved. He wouldn't be asking about the sandwich if he wasn't planning to come. She didn't need to twist his arm or explain in more detail. "Of course. You get a sandwich."

"And does it have to be a wrap? It could be a foot-long, right? And it could be something like… meatball sub?"

"Sure. Whatever kind you like."

It wasn't like it was a fancy restaurant and he might break her budget with his choice of wines. They were sandwiches. He could have two if he wanted.

George shrugged. "Okay," he agreed.

37

Kenzie tried to look busy, as if she were doing all the work she usually did, but she couldn't focus on her administrative tasks. She was just waiting for the clock to change over to 12:00. Or 11:50, so she could be at *It's a Wrap* at 12:00.

Was she being stupid agreeing to meet with someone that she didn't know when he hadn't provided her with much of an explanation? It was. There was no question of that. She was being careful and taking precautions, but it was probably still a stupid thing to do. Maybe she should have called Campbell to get a couple of cops to hang around in plain clothes and be ready to take any necessary action. Campbell would probably like to know what was going on.

But that would mean telling him about Walter being missing and the governor had told her not to discuss it. And she had also been told by Lisa not to talk to anyone about it for fear that something might happen to Walter if she were in touch with or overheard by the wrong people. Word spread fast in little communities, and the Russian community in Roxboro certainly qualified.

It was 11:42. Kenzie started to tidy up and put things away. She stacked her files neatly in a basket, grabbed her purse from her drawer, and pulled on her winter clothing. *It's a Wrap* was close, but it was January. It was not warm.

George appeared at her desk. He had a coat and big, heavy boots on. He stood there for a moment, watching her get ready.

"I don't have a gun," he told her.

"Oh. No, I don't think you need one. I don't expect there to be any violence. Maybe this guy will be there, maybe he won't. But I don't think he's going to try anything."

It hadn't occurred to Kenzie before that it might be a ploy to get her away from her desk for a while too. She cleared anything sensitive off of the desk and locked it in her drawer. She locked the screen on her computer. Everything looked fine. No one would be able to just walk in there and mess with her stuff.

George nodded. Kenzie took a deep breath and blew it out. "It is making me nervous. Sorry."

"Can't see why it would."

She looked at his face and saw that he was joking. "Yeah, why would meeting a complete stranger be stressful?"

"You need to be careful. Don't give him any personal information. Your personal cell or your address."

"No, you're right. That wouldn't be a very good idea."

They were mostly silent on their walk over to the sandwich shop. Kenzie looked around, waiting for someone to approach her. There were, of course, all sorts of strangers around her, all bundled up in their winter coats, many of which were black. She looked for the green scarf. There couldn't be that many men wearing green scarves.

There were a *lot* of people to watch. Kenzie tried to keep track of them all. She watched the door for new arrivals, but it wasn't always easy to see each person's clothing. Some scarves had a little green on them or were somewhere between teal and green and Kenzie didn't know whether to count them. Some people did their scarves up under their coats, which made them harder to see, but Kenzie assumed that the man she was supposed to be meeting would not do that. He would want his scarf to be visible.

No one approached her. Kenzie kept an eye on the time, watching the minutes tick by. Where was he? She was in the right place at the right time. Had he wanted to get her away from her desk? To be sure where she was so that he could be somewhere else and know he would not be interrupted? Was it all just a big joke?

A few times, George made an appearance, met her eyes, and then melted into the background again. She didn't know what to tell him. Clearly, something had gone wrong. Kenzie bought him his meatball sub, and he ate it at one of the crowded tables, watching her the whole time.

But nothing happened. No one tried to kidnap Kenzie or even to talk to her, other than a few people she knew from the police station, who all nodded and were friendly.

There was no sign of the Russian with a green scarf.

Eventually, it was closer to 1:00 than 12:00, and Kenzie decided there was no point in waiting any longer. The servers had asked her several times if she wanted something to eat, and she finally accepted and had one of them prepare her a barbecue chicken wrap. She ate it slowly, keeping her eyes open in case the man finally made an appearance, but he did not. It was a bust.

"Let's head back to the office," Kenzie eventually told George.

He shrugged and went with her. Kenzie stepped out of the warm sandwich shop into the cold, brisk winter air outside. Alexei certainly wouldn't have been waiting outside for her. Not for that long. Sooner or later, he would have come inside looking for her, if just to get out of the frigid air. Kenzie looked around, hoping for some sign of him hurrying toward the shop, delayed because he had blown a tire or missed the bus. But no one she could see matched the description he had given or the picture she had built in her head of him.

She saw a movement out of the corner of her eye as she walked by the alley that ran behind *It's a Wrap* and turned her head to see what it was, expecting to see a bird or blowing piece of garbage.

Kenzie froze.

A man was lying in the alley, possibly drunk or passed out. And he was wearing a green scarf. A loose end flapping in the wind was what had caught her attention.

38

A t first, Kenzie's brain couldn't accept what she saw. She was sure it was a prank or the filming of a movie scene. Something other than real life. It was all faked, with an actor and stage makeup. Someone was setting her up to see if she would freak out over this. But who would play a joke like that on her?

She grabbed George's arm to pull him to a stop and to make sure that he saw the same thing as she did. He looked, squinting and leaning forward.

"Just some drunk," he told Kenzie. "Come on. We need to get back to the office. Let someone else deal with it."

"No. No, that's who I was supposed to meet. What happened? We have to figure out what is going on here!"

"Kenzie…" He tried to take another step toward the office, to convince her that this wasn't something they needed to deal with. But Kenzie knew that it was. Even if this wasn't the man she was supposed to meet with, as a medical doctor she could not walk by. She was obligated to stop and help.

"No. Come on. I have to look. Come with me. In case… it's a trick."

He rolled his eyes and shook his head slightly, looking like he would not, but he walked down the alley with her, looking away from the man. Did he think he could avoid this by pretending not to see him?

Kenzie looked down at the man, whose face was a cyanotic blue. Her heart sank. It was not a joke and it was not someone who had just had too much to drink or who had slipped and bumped his head. She pushed his shoulder with her foot at first, as if she might be able to wake him up. "Sir? Sir, are you okay? Can you wake up?"

There was no response. Kenzie bent down and grasped his shoulder, giving it a hard shake, calling to him again. But she knew there wasn't going to be any response. The limbs were too heavy. There was no resistance in the muscles.

Kenzie knelt, conceding that this wasn't just an actor and he wasn't going to jump up and tell her that she had been pranked. He was never going to be jumping up again. But she still had to go through the motions to do everything she had been trained to do.

"Would you please call 9-1-1?" she asked George. "That would be really helpful."

She felt for a pulse. Pried open the man's eye. Pulled open his coat and rubbed his sternum hard, checking for a pain response. But as expected, she could not detect any sign of life.

"What's wrong with him?" George asked as he began the conversation with the 9-1-1 dispatcher.

"He's dead."

George stopped and looked at her. "He's *drunk*," he said, as if to correct her.

"No. He's not drunk. He's dead." In pulling open his coat, she had moved the green scarf a little and could see the bruises around the man's neck. "Probably strangulation. I'll call Dr. Wiltshire and see if he wants to come over for the scene survey... but we'll need police dispatched. They'll need to tape off the area and start on their inquiries. We'll need to gather any forensic evidence..."

George looked at her in disbelief for another minute, then finally returned to the insistent operator trying to get the details from him. "Uh... cancel the ambulance. I guess we need the police."

It wasn't long before a couple of officers showed up. It was handy to be so close to the police station. They hardly even needed to get into their car to come over, though they did since that was the easiest way to transport the crime scene tape and other miscellany they would need to mark the perimeter of the crime scene and open an investigation.

"Ma'am, you'll need to be on the other side of the tape," one young officer told Kenzie as he got started.

"I'm Dr. Kenzie Kirsch—"

"There's nothing you can do for him at the moment, ma'am. If you'll just go to the other side of the tape, the detectives will want to speak to you."

"I'm with the Medical Examiner's Office."

"Someone from the Medical Examiner's Office will be here soon."

"No, *I* am. *I'm* with the Medical Examiner's Office."

He frowned at her. "I thought you were the one who called the body in."

"I did. But I am also with the Medical Examiner's Office. So I actually need to be here as part of the investigation."

"Can you do that?"

"What?"

"Be a witness and part of the death investigation?"

Kenzie hadn't worked that one through. "Yes, of course," she bluffed. "It isn't like I had anything to do with his death. I'm just the one who found him and called it in." She remembered what Dr. Wiltshire had said about her involvement with Maksim's autopsy. "Vermont is too small to never see someone you've met before on the morgue table. Sooner or later…"

The cop frowned at this, his lips thinning. But he shrugged, giving his head a shake. "Fine, you can stay here, but I expect to see someone else backing you up. And you will need to talk to the detectives."

"Okay." Kenzie had already sent a text message to Dr. Wiltshire, who had already started with the next postmortem. Hopefully, he would see it and either call her back or send someone else over to help her out. She didn't want to be standing around in the cold for two hours before someone bothered to show up.

39

The police detectives showed up and stood well back of the corpse, suited up to avoid contaminating the scene.

"You're here from the Medical Examiner's Office?" one of them questioned. Kenzie squinted at his name bar. Sanchez.

"I am with the Medical Examiner's Office," she agreed slowly. "But I was already at the scene. I was the one who found the body and called it in. The cop who put up the tape said that someone else would have to do the site review and sign off on the body. So…"

Sanchez scowled. "That seems pretty stupid when you're already here."

Kenzie shrugged. "I didn't want to argue with him. I don't want to screw up anything in the investigation."

"Tell me how you found the body. Last I heard, your department wasn't required to go out and scout out their own corpses." Sanchez looked at his partner, expecting a laugh, and then at Kenzie and George. "What? Is the whole audience dead?"

"This isn't a comedy club," George said. "Come on. Are you going to let us go or not?"

"Who are you?"

"George, also from the Medical Examiner's Office. I was here

191

with Dr. Kirsch when she discovered the body. So you have a corroborating witness. Can we just get this over with?"

"I'll get your story," Sanchez pointed at Kenzie, "and then yours." He indicated George.

George didn't move. Kenzie nodded to the side, indicating that he should walk away and leave them alone. George stayed there, looking at Sanchez, waiting for the questions.

"I need to interview you separately," Sanchez said.

George looked at him. "Go ahead."

"You need to go over there and let us interview Dr. Kirsch." Sanchez pointed to where he wanted George to go.

"You want me to walk through here?" George indicated the center of the area that had been taped off, just a couple of feet from the body.

Sanchez rolled his eyes. "No. Fine. Go around, stick to the perimeter. Look where you're putting your big feet."

George kept to the perimeter. Kenzie watched his retreat. "There's not much to tell," she explained to the detectives. "I was at *It's a Wrap* for lunch. George was with me. We were walking back to the Medical Examiner's Office and something caught my eye. I looked over here and saw that… someone was lying on the pavement. I made George come over with me to ensure that I wasn't a trap, so I didn't get jumped by him or a second guy. I asked George to call it in. When I verified that he was dead, we canceled an ambulance and asked for the police."

"He was dead when you got here?"

"Yes."

"How long had he been dead?"

"I don't have any equipment with me to make that determination. It had been a while."

"How do you know that?"

"Judging by skin temperature. Which is not very accurate, especially in these conditions. But he was quite cool to the touch. I would need my equipment from the Medical Examiner's Office to give a more accurate estimate. And the sooner I can get that stuff, the better."

"Why don't you send George to get it?"

Kenzie glanced in George's direction. "Could I do that?"

"I'll send him over after talking with him and confirming your story. Then you can do the preliminaries and sign off. If we have to wait for a second death investigator to make it here, it could be another hour or two."

"Well… yes, it could," Kenzie agreed. With Dr. Wiltshire already elbow-deep into another autopsy, she couldn't say how long it would be before he could break away. And the staffing was pretty light with people on vacation. They would have to either wait for Dr. Wiltshire or call someone in, and either route could take a couple of hours.

Sanchez nodded to Kenzie. "Wait here." He walked around the perimeter to talk to George. Their discussion was very brief. Sanchez apparently asked George to get Kenzie's equipment. He nodded and looked over at her. In a moment, he was calling her on her cell phone rather than walking back over to her.

"What do you need me to bring?"

"The usual death kit. There isn't anything very unusual here. Just the basics. And make sure the techs are on their way to take any evidence."

"Okay. Do you want me to talk to Dr. Wiltshire?"

"Uh…" Kenzie tried to figure out what to do about him. She had already sent him a text, but he hadn't replied. He might not have seen it. If George told him what was going on when he got to the morgue, he would take the brunt of any irritation over the chain of events. Dr. Wiltshire would not want to leave his postmortem, but might feel obligated to do so, even though Kenzie was qualified to do the initial site survey. "Yeah, I suppose you'd better tell him. I already sent him a message, but he might not have seen it. Tell him he doesn't have to come, though. I'm happy to take care of it."

George chuckled. "I'll tell him, but I'm not promising anything."

"Thanks. I appreciate it."

He nodded and hung up. She watched him walk away from the site back toward the police building.

It took longer than expected for his next call to come through to her. She supposed she was expecting things to happen more quickly than was natural. It always seemed like things took longer when you were waiting. Finally, her phone rang and she picked it up. It was coming from one of the office numbers.

"Hi, George?"

"Actually, it's me, Kenzie." Dr. Wiltshire sounded like he was on speakerphone. Clear, but loud, with other sounds from the room.

"Oh… hi, Doctor."

"What is this about you going out to find more bodies? Don't you think that we have enough to deal with already?" While his words were good-humored, she thought she could sense tension in his voice. Which made sense. She'd gone off-script, stumbling across a body on her own. He was sure to be wondering what was going on.

"Sorry about that. It certainly wasn't how I expected to spend my lunch hour or afternoon."

"No, I don't imagine it was. I've sent George back with the van and your kit. As long as you are comfortable with it, you can do the site review and you and George can handle the transport. If there is anything you have concerns about, though, you should wait for me."

"I'm okay going ahead with it. There isn't much to investigate at the scene. I don't see any other evidence to be gathered, but I'll leave that to the tech boys."

"If there is anything to be found, I'm sure they'll find it. I would come straight over, especially since you are so close, but I'm sort of… busy right now."

Kenzie could well imagine. It wasn't exactly something Dr. Wiltshire could leave in the middle of. And she didn't want to wait until he finished the autopsy.

"I should be fine. It looks pretty straightforward. I'll get a temperature reading so we can set the time of death as closely as possible, but otherwise, there isn't much to do here."

"No point in wasting extra resources on it, then," Wiltshire agreed. "Get back here as quickly as you can. We'll see if we can fit him in this afternoon."

"You want to go ahead with the post that quickly?" Kenzie was surprised. They already had a full dance card for the next few days, with everyone who had arrived in the morgue carefully prioritized.

"I think the situation warrants it." Dr. Wiltshire dropped his voice. "George said something about you wanting to go over there with him at lunch because you were meeting someone who might have information on a case."

Kenzie swallowed. She had known that George might read Dr. Wiltshire in on why he had been there with her, but she'd hoped to be the one to break the news to him herself. She wasn't quite sure how she would explain herself to him.

"Uh… well, that's what I told him. Yes."

"You know that our part of the investigation is in the morgue. We leave everything else to the police. Why would you be going to the restaurant to talk to someone about it?"

"I'll explain it to you when I get back," Kenzie promised. That would give her a few more minutes to come up with something that sounded coherent but would not get her into too much trouble. She wasn't quite sure how she was going to do that but, hopefully, she would come up with something before then. "George kind of got… an abridged version."

"I see. Well, I look forward to hearing the full-length version."

"I'll see you in a few minutes, then," Kenzie agreed. Though she wasn't quite looking forward to it herself.

40

Only a couple of minutes later, the medical examiner van rolled up to the taped-off area. George climbed out, bringing Kenzie her kit so that she could properly examine the stranger in the field before transporting him back to the office. She ran through the checklist in her head as she approached the body and proceeded, trying to go slowly so that she wouldn't forget anything important. She was going to be in enough trouble with Dr. Wiltshire without forgetting to do something vital.

"Sorry, I had to tell Dr. Wiltshire what was going on," George apologized, staying on the other side of the tape.

"Of course. I wouldn't expect you to lie to him."

"It's just that I know he's kind of ticked off about it. I didn't say something because I wanted to get you in trouble."

"I know, George. It's fine. I'll go through everything with Dr. Wiltshire. You don't need to hide anything."

She looked up from the body to look him in the face and he was apparently reassured.

"Okay. I just didn't want you to think…"

"No. It's fine. I would have to go through everything anyway. Just give me a few minutes to concentrate here. There isn't a lot to do, but I need to stay focused."

George nodded and stayed quiet. She wished he would return to the van to prepare the body bags and gurney, but he didn't; he just stood there watching her. Kenzie inserted the probe to take the man's internal temperature and watched the numbers flash across the screen before settling on the final reading. Kenzie shook her head. Despite his cold skin, it had not been long since the man died. She had expected his temperature to be quite a bit lower with how cold it was outside. She would have to run the formulas when she returned to the office to establish the window. But she knew it was going to be much more recent than she had hoped.

Alexei had been killed while she had been waiting for him inside. Maybe if she hadn't waited so long for him to show up…

But would she have been able to stop him from getting killed? It wasn't like he'd been bleeding out in the alleyway and she could have saved him if she'd been there to apply pressure to his wounds and call an ambulance. He had been strangled. That would have been quick, and there was nothing she could have done to help him, even if she'd arrived there a minute later. And if she had arrived a minute earlier… she might have been a victim herself. Maybe she had been saved simply because it had been busy inside the sandwich shop and George had been standing guard.

She couldn't decide whether Alexei had intended to help her or whether he was trying to get information about Walter from her. Or maybe he was doing a balancing act, trying to achieve both ends.

She noted the temperature, pulled out an HDSLR camera and started taking photographs of the body and surrounding area. The techs would take more, but she liked to take her own. It was better to have too many photos than not enough. She zoomed in on the ligature mark around the man's throat, still red rather than purple or blue.

The forensic techs got there while she was doing her examination and stood back, waiting for her to finish and give them any specific instructions. Kenzie checked the body quickly for anything else of note, then stepped back.

"Ligature strangulation," she told them. "The site looks pretty clean. I don't see anything on or around him, but I'll let you take a look before we move the body, just to be sure."

"Choked with the scarf?" one of the techs inquired.

"No. Too wide and soft. I'm sure it would be possible, but not very easy. The mark on his neck is from something thin."

"A necklace or a tool?"

Kenzie shook her head. "We'll have to look at it carefully under the microscope, see if there is any trace left behind or a link or weave to the bruise. But I think it probably wasn't a necklace. They're much more fragile than TV cop shows would have you think. And it would have been likely to leave a cut. I don't see any blood or abrasion, just a bruise."

"Something else, then." The tech turned his head back and forth, scanning the ground for anything that might fit the bill. Kenzie had looked around too, but didn't see anything.

"I think probably a cord," Kenzie said. "I don't know what kind, but something flexible and strong."

"Something the killer brought with him and took away with him?"

"We should check the dumpsters," Kenzie realized. "In case he discarded it here."

"If he brought it with him, he probably took it away."

They probably did not want to get stuck looking through the garbage in the dumpsters. At least it was winter. Not the sweltering summer, when everything would start rotting the instant it was put out in the bin. Any perishable foodstuffs would freeze pretty quickly.

"Check the closest dumpsters just to be sure," Kenzie said, giving a grimace of sympathy. "If the weapon was dumped, it will be near the top. This has just happened in the last hour."

"Well, that's something," the tech grumbled.

They were quiet while they worked together to identify any items in the alley that might be evidence in the case, setting up evidence numbers and scales before photographing each from several different angles. Always more than they would ever need. An investigator could never tell which pictures would be key to solving the case or proving it to the jury. Something that had seemed small and insignificant at the scene could end up being a vital piece of evidence.

They went over the Russian's coat, scarf, hair, and shoes, looking for any trace evidence. Then the first tech gave Kenzie a nod. "You can go ahead and move the body. We'll have another look to ensure there isn't something underneath or on his back."

Kenzie motioned to George, and he retrieved the appropriate cadaver bags from the van. They laid out the outer shell, then the inner one on top of that. Both were used to moving bodies around at the morgue, but it was a little more difficult on the pavement than from the gurney to a morgue table and back. They shifted the body on top of the bags and rolled him onto his side so the techs could check his back for any trace. One of them painstakingly brushed gravel and debris into a collection envelope. He sealed it and shrugged at Kenzie. "I don't see anything out of place. Nothing to indicate that he has been lying anywhere other than this."

Kenzie and George proceeded to tuck the Russian into the bags, then lifted the corpse from the ground to the gurney that George had brought over.

Kenzie was relieved to leave the cold alley behind. She would be able to warm up at the office and get the rust out of her joints.

But then she was going to have to face Dr. Wiltshire and his questions.

41

D r. Wiltshire was still busy in autopsy, so Kenzie elected not to talk to him right away. She would let George prep Alexei's body while she processed a few emails and made sure that everything was in order at her desk so that she could help with the postmortem without guilt. She would get Julie from upstairs to cover the desk until the end of the day.

She immersed herself in her inbox and task list, working through them as efficiently as possible. It was hard to stay focused on her work while her brain was still trying to deal with what had just happened that afternoon. Finding a dead body while she was out on her lunch break was not routine. It might be routine for her to deal with dead bodies at work, but that wasn't the same thing. All the time she was trying to work through her administrative work, she was trying to compose a narrative in her head of what had happened from the time she got the phone call from Alexei. But even going all the way back to the time that the phone had rung didn't give a full picture of what was happening. It was connected to the autopsies she had already done on the other Russians, to her missing father, and now to another murder occurring only moments before she arrived on the scene. Every time she thought about it, she started to shake.

How was she supposed to deal with this?

In fact, she wasn't supposed to. She was supposed to let the police know everything she knew and let them take care of it. And she had. Almost. She had to hold back the information about Walter because that was what the governor had asked her to do, but now she second-guessed herself, wondering if that was the best course of action. Maybe she should ignore the governor's request and lay everything out for Campbell or whatever detective he assigned to the case.

Kenzie stopped and stared at the screen, stopping what she was doing.

It was a short email, curt and to the point.

MacKenzie, you are not safe. Stop asking questions.

She looked at the email address, but it wasn't from anyone she knew or even a recognizable address. It was a long stream of letters, numbers, and symbols that Kenzie knew meant it had been routed through some kind of anonymizer service. Whoever had sent her the warning had wanted to stay behind the scenes, where he was safe.

Kenzie clicked on the reply button but just got a "no-reply" address from the anonymizer service. There was no way for her to respond to the sender asking for more information or confirm that she would or would not stop asking questions.

She was not the one who had gone out of her way to find Alexei. She had minded her own business and had been doing routine work at the Medical Examiner's Office when he had reached out to her to ask her to meet. That wasn't her fault. That wasn't her asking questions; someone else wanted to tell her what was happening.

Or maybe to find out what she knew about what was going on.

Either way, Alexei had been taken out of the picture. He wasn't going to find out what she knew and he wasn't going to be revealing anything more to her… other than what she might find in his postmortem.

Kenzie dragged the email over to a personal folder to file it for later use. She had to think about how she wanted to handle it. Not that there was anything for her to do. Either she stopped asking questions about her father and the Russians, or she didn't. She couldn't talk to anyone about it, argue the point with him.

She had already resolved not to put anyone in her family at risk.

She needed to follow through on that resolution and not let herself be derailed as she had been by the Russian's unexpected call.

Kenzie did the best she could to stay on task and make sure she was on top of everything going on in the office. Eventually, Julie made her way downstairs and stood by Kenzie's desk, smiling cheerfully.

"Hi, Kenzie! Did you have a good Christmas?"

Kenzie had almost forgotten all about Christmas. It seemed like a long time ago. So much had happened since then. It was the last thing she was prepared to answer.

"Sure, yes. I had a good Christmas." Kenzie gave Julie a warm smile, hoping she wouldn't ask a bunch of follow-up questions on what she had done and what gifts she had gotten. "How was yours?"

"Really good. My boyfriend and I just cocooned for a few days, didn't have anything to do with anyone but each other, and it was *so* great. I really think it made us a lot closer."

"That sounds nice."

Julie nodded vigorously. "It really was. I would recommend it to anyone starting out in a new relationship or trying to reconnect with an old one. We went to this retreat center—"

Kenzie blocked out the rest. The last thing she needed was to go on another retreat. She motioned for Julie to come around the desk and made sure that all of her own piles had been moved to the side so that Julie had plenty of space.

"You already know how to manage everything here. I don't think there is anything out of the ordinary that you need to be aware of. Uh, unless I get a call from the police, I guess. They might be following up with me on this latest case, the one I'll be doing the post on. So you can tell them that we're on top of it and will have details back to them as soon as possible but, if it seems like it's pretty urgent and they can't wait, then put it through to autopsy and I'll deal with it."

Julie nodded. "Okay, sure. No problem. Anyone else that I should put through?" She gave Kenzie a wink.

Kenzie supposed she meant Zachary, who she had dealt with on the phone before. Kenzie didn't usually want any personal calls being put through to her while she was meeting with Dr. Wiltshire or doing an autopsy, but Zachary was an exception. Only he wouldn't be calling her. He would just wait for her to visit him tonight.

"No, Zachary doesn't have his phone with him. I don't expect to hear from him."

What about her mother? Or her father?

If Walter reappeared, did she want to talk to him?

She did, but not right away. She would need to talk to him at length, getting all the details about why exactly he'd had to break contact and couldn't even let her know where he was. That was not a call she wanted to take over the speakerphone in the autopsy.

"I think anything else can probably wait," Kenzie told Julie more authoritatively, not wanting to deal with more detailed questions. Julie was perfectly capable and could take messages.

42

Kenzie entered autopsy and started washing up and preparing herself for the postmortem.

"Hello, Kenzie," Dr. Wiltshire greeted, glancing over at her.

"Hi. I'm sorry about all of this stuff…" Kenzie shook her head. "I wasn't planning to stumble across a body over my lunch. I'll tell you what happened, but…"

"Yes, we'll go over all of that."

"Did you get something to eat?" Kenzie wondered how long he had been there and if he had skipped lunch. His eyes were tired, a bit bloodshot. Like he hadn't been sleeping well.

"Oh yes, no need to worry about me," he assured her. "Tell me about your victim."

Kenzie went to the table when she finished washing and suiting up. George was still there tagging clothing, personal items, and a few trace evidence envelopes that she would have to review at some point.

"Did the victim have identification, George?"

"It's on the tag and on the screen," George pointed out what Kenzie should already have seen. "Mikhail Bronski."

Kenzie frowned and shook her head. "Are you sure? Mikhail Bronski?"

"Yes, that's what his identification said."

Kenzie closed her eyes, replaying the phone call in her head. "No… on the phone, he said his name was Alexei."

Had he been lying, just giving her a false name? Or was this not the man she had spoken to on the phone? It couldn't be a coincidence that a man meeting the description of the man who had described himself on the phone had been murdered where and when she was supposed to meet him. It had to be the same man.

"Well, he might have said that," George said with a shrug. "But his identification says Mikhail Bronski."

"Is it legitimate? Actual government ID?"

"I'm not an expert. It's not obviously forged. Looks like every other driver's license we get through here."

Kenzie nodded. "Okay. So… Mikhail Bronski." More than likely, he had given her a false name. Who would give their real name when setting up a clandestine meeting like that? Kenzie would have picked a different name too, given the opportunity. She couldn't, of course, because Mikhail had already known her name. But if he hadn't, Kenzie might easily have been a Katie. Or a Mary. Or whatever other name suited her at the moment.

Kenzie tapped the record button on the floor with her toe and started to dictate, introducing herself and identifying the victim, giving the date and his physical description. He was not as old as she had expected him to be. She had thought that he would be older, like Maksim. The other Russians she had autopsied had also been older. Mikhail was perhaps in his mid-to-late thirties. Kenzie had George bring up the driver's license on the screen and read off the statistics it gave. Thirty-six years old. The height and weight from the driver's license looked close, though Kenzie knew he would weigh in at a higher weight. He had blue eyes. And a red ring around his neck.

Kenzie stopped the recording for a moment. She looked at the cops sitting in the observation area. One of them was Sanchez, the detective she had seen at the murder site. He would have to hear the full story sooner or later anyway; it didn't matter if he overheard her discussion with Dr. Wiltshire now.

"I got a phone call this morning. A man with a Russian accent identified himself as Alexei, saying he wanted to meet me to give me some information."

"Why would you agree to meet him? That's the kind of thing you should kick upstairs. Let them handle it."

"He acted like he knew something about my father. And… I wanted to find out if the information he had was about him. Maybe nothing to do with any of the deceased Russians we've dealt with over the past few days, but to do with my father. Or somehow, with both. It's possible that he might be mixed up in the middle of all of this."

Wiltshire rested his hands and looked at Kenzie, frowning. "What would your father have to do with Russians?"

"I don't know where he is. I have been trying to reach him since Christmas Day. And as you know, when I went to see my mother, Maksim was at the house."

He considered this, brows drawn. Kenzie kept looking at the body on the table in front of her rather than the cop in the observation room. She didn't want to see his scowl as he learned the details she should have revealed earlier.

"You don't know where your father is, and Maksim, one of the Russians we autopsied, was at your mother's house," Wiltshire repeated.

"Yes. I've been trying to get ahold of my father, but he's not responding to my messages. I don't know how he is involved in any of this. It isn't like he has anything to do with the Russian mob. He's a lobbyist, not involved with organized crime. He is friends with the governor. He's not some gangster. He's never been in any legal trouble."

"Have you reached out to your mother? Any of his friends?"

"Yes. My mother doesn't know anything. She only knew Maksim slightly. He made a donation to our family foundation, and he showed up to see her on Christmas Day. But they weren't friends. They weren't close at all. She didn't even know his full name. And who knows, he might have used a fake name, like Mikhail here."

Kenzie tapped the button on the floor to record a few more observations and began to do a full body survey, looking for any other bruises, tattoos, or other markings or notable observations. She clicked off the recording again.

"This one is well-nourished, like Maksim. Not the others. He does have some inked Cyrillic letters, but nothing as extensive as the other men. And they are newer tattoos with sharply defined edges. I don't think they're prison tattoos."

Dr. Wiltshire left his table to look at the victim and to put a magnified view of the tattoo on one of the video screens where he could examine it and the cop could also see it on the observation room monitor.

"I agree. Probably done here, not in Russia and not in prison. A professional. Those look like standard commercial inks and a proper tattooist's needle. Not something that was jury-rigged in prison."

He returned to his table to continue with his autopsy, which appeared to be nearly complete. Kenzie noted these comments and turned off the recording.

"I talked to Walter's—my father's—friends too. The ones that I could remember and track down. We haven't been close the last few years and I haven't been to a lot of events that he has. I talked to the governor and he said he would look into it."

Wiltshire looked up from his table, one eyebrow raised. He looked over at the cop in the observation room.

"So someone *has* been looking into this."

"Not on an official basis, I don't think. And I haven't filed a missing person report. Governor Smith said to keep it quiet and just let him handle it. So… I was obeying him when I didn't report Walter missing and didn't report this phone call from Mikhail. I was trying to do the right thing."

"Well… that's understandable. I would expect you to do what you were told to do by the governor. Even though he doesn't have any jurisdiction over this office."

"I know." Kenzie had run into that issue once before when the governor's office was pushing for answers and a cause of death long before they were available. It was a balancing act, trying to stay on his good side while, at the same time, not letting it affect any of their work. Not allowing bias to creep into what they were doing. "It wasn't anything to do with my work here. That would be different. It was just to do with my dad. A personal thing."

Except that her missing father and the dying Russians seemed to be inextricably connected.

"So you got this call this morning," Wiltshire said, "and you decided to meet with someone you didn't know by yourself? When you know that there is likely an organized crime connection to these deaths?"

"He suggested the place and it was very public. I didn't think that would be a problem. What is he going to do in front of so many people? But I wanted to be doubly sure, so I asked George if he would come along with me. To be an extra set of eyes and let people know I wasn't alone and vulnerable. I didn't think there would be any violence, but I didn't want to look like a pushover."

"And what was Mikhail supposed to tell you when you met?"

"I don't know. Mikhail—or Alexei—was asking about where Walter was. He said that he thought we could help each other. I guess some exchange of information; only I didn't have any information to give him. Since I didn't even know where Walter is."

"What if he had asked you for information about an autopsy?"

"I... didn't think about that. I wouldn't tell him anything confidential. I wasn't planning to tell him anything... just to find out what he knew about my father or these cases."

"I'm sure he would have been delighted with that answer."

43

Kenzie shrugged and sighed. She turned the recording on again and dictated as she proceeded with the Y-incision. There was nothing remarkable in the initial examination of the organs. Nothing missing that should have been there. He seemed to be in pretty good health and functioning normally. Until he had been strangled, of course.

"Do you want me to do the same request for parasites? See if we get the same results as the others?"

"Wouldn't hurt. He's younger and looks more… Americanized. It will be interesting to see whether he has actually lived in Russia or not."

"If he is the man I talked to on the phone, he had a thick Russian accent. So he must have grown up in Russia."

"Yes, *if* this is the man you talked to on the phone."

Kenzie was hesitant about that too. There was no proof that the man she had talked to and the man that had been killed were the same person. Alexei might have described someone else. He might have added the scarf to the other man's outfit himself. It might have been a setup from start to finish.

But she felt like it had to be true. She had difficulty finding a logical scenario in which Alexei set up a meeting with her on the phone, somehow got someone else to go to the meeting dressed in a green scarf, and then had killed him. Why set up the meeting in the first place? Why not kill the man in the green scarf somewhere else, father away from crowds, without any dramatic setup? That would be safer.

Was Kenzie supposed to find the body? Was the whole thing designed to make her see she was in danger? Just like the email had told her?

It seemed like a stretch to kill a fellow Russian to warn Kenzie off instead of just killing Kenzie or one of her family members or friends. It would be harder to kill one of his own, wouldn't it? And it wouldn't mean anything to her, even if she was intended to find the body.

So that brought it back around full circle. It must have been Mikhail who had called her. He *had* intended to give her information. Data that someone did not want her to share. He had been right about being in danger if he was seen talking to her. He had been in danger just from arranging to meet with her. Maybe he had stepped over the line before and they were already watching him, already suspicious and taking note of every move he made.

Kenzie was quiet while she removed, examined, and weighed each organ, then took slides to be sent to the lab for analysis. "The heart and lungs are congested with blood."

Wiltshire nodded without looking up. "That is common in all kinds of strangulation and suffocation."

"Do you want me to dissect the neck tissues?"

"Wait until I'm done for that. I'd like to go over it with you. We need to review all of the structures and the usual presentation. Make sure you know how to find them and what to expect. What might prove or disprove strangulation in a case."

"Okay." Kenzie continued with what she was doing.

Dr. Wiltshire was finally finished with his postmortem, which must have required a lot more attention than the one that Kenzie was doing. He gave instructions to George and went to the sinks to wash and change, then returned to Kenzie's table to help her with her dissection of the neck tissues.

"Tell me what you expect to see," Wiltshire instructed before the first cut was made. Kenzie tried to dredge up everything she could remember about ligature strangulation and the signs and structures to look for. Dr. Wiltshire listened without interrupting.

"Good. Now before you cut, have you made a thorough examination of the external bruising? Photographs under room light, photographs with alternative light source, swabs for any trace or transfer, close and microscopic examination?"

Kenzie nodded. She went through the pictures she had already taken, showing them to Dr. Wiltshire so he could vet them. They both stared at the enlarged images, trying to find anything else that might give them additional leads in the case. But it all looked pretty straightforward.

An intercom beep indicated someone in the observation room wanted to talk to them. Kenzie turned the channel on, turning to look at Detective Sanchez. He was looking at the monitor, brows drawn down.

"I was expecting something with a more recognizable shape."

"It's a long, thin ligature," Kenzie said. "Not the scarf and not hands. That much is pretty clear."

"I expected to be able to see chain links or the weave of the rope. Maybe rope fibers driven into the skin."

"If this was TV, I have no doubt they'd be able to tell you exactly what was used to strangle him," Kenzie agreed. "The killer always uses something that causes a distinctive pattern, or wears a signet ring that leaves its imprint in the victim's skin, or they can match the killer's hand size to the bruising in a manual strangulation. But in real life… the bruises are much less distinct than that. We can't tell much more than the type of tool used. Some kind of strong cord in this case. But we can't tell much more than that. It was not sharp and didn't cut into the victim's skin. It didn't break. I haven't heard anything back from the techs yet. They were going to check the bins for any discarded cord, but I don't think they will find anything. I think he went after Mikhail prepared to kill him and took the cord away with him."

"You think it was professional."

Kenzie looked at Dr. Wiltshire for his opinion. "I think it's a possibility. There was no sign of a struggle. No defensive wounds. Minimal bruising anywhere else. The weapon was not left at the scene. The killer got in and got out at the busiest time of day without anyone seeing him. It must have been very quick."

Dr. Wiltshire nodded his agreement. "It could be a professional," he agreed. "Either a hired gun or part of the organization. We'll have a better idea after we get the tests back whether he was Russian or not. That will give you a better idea of how he ties into this case."

"He has a Russian tattoo, so he probably is," Kenzie reminded him.

"He may be," Wiltshire agreed. "Or he might have just picked it out of a book at a tattoo parlor because he would like people to think he is Russian mob." He smiled and raised his eyebrows.

"Well... I guess I never thought about that. Isn't it sort of dangerous to get a tattoo of a gang you don't belong to?"

"I wouldn't recommend it."

Kenzie chuckled. She nodded to the detective and turned the communication channel back off.

"I think we are ready to proceed with the dissection of the neck," Dr. Wiltshire told her.

Kenzie took a deep breath and let it out slowly. She focused the camera on the area they were working on and restarted the voice recorder.

44

They had run late on the autopsy, but Kenzie knew that Zachary wasn't waiting for her at home, so she wasn't worried about it. She was happy to have something to occupy her attention so she wasn't just banging around the house for as long.

After they finished with the postmortem and were tidying up, Dr. Wiltshire put his hand on Kenzie's arm to stop her from going back to her desk.

"Now that we're alone... I'm a little concerned about you being involved in all of this, Kenzie."

"I know... I never meant to get in the middle of it. Believe me, I don't want to be involved with Russian mobsters any more than you do."

"You really do need to take care... Those of us who work with death and murder can attract the wrong kind of attention. And we need to remain unbiased and not be influenced by those who bring pressure to bear."

Kenzie nodded. She worked her way through the samples she had taken, ensuring they were all properly labeled. She remembered once in the not-so-distant past when she'd wondered whether Dr. Wiltshire himself had buckled to outside pressure and released a body before he should have. She had never thought this would be a problem in the Medical Examiner's Office. They were sheltered there. Not part of the police force. She had never expected to encounter a dead body outside of her job. She had never expected the outside pressures she had been experiencing in this case and some of those in the past. She had pictured herself behind the scenes, coming up with the brilliant theories and evidence to help put murderers behind bars without ever having any contact with them.

"I'm not going to have anything to do with the Russians," she assured him.

"And the governor's office?"

"Well… I guess I've already disobeyed the instructions that he gave me. But… like you said, he's not law enforcement and, even if he is powerful in the state… he's not my boss. I can't keep holding back on involving the police in Walter's disappearance."

"No. I'm not sure why he would ask you to do that. I don't think it is wise to keep anything from law enforcement on this. That's how people end up in trouble. How are you going to find your father or know if he is okay if you don't report the fact that he is missing?"

"Well, Sanchez knows now, so I might as well go all the way and report him as a missing person." She shrugged, frustrated. "It isn't like keeping quiet has done me any good. The people who shouldn't know where he is seem to know more about it than I do. If the governor has found anything, he should tell it to the police."

"You don't want to get personally involved in this. It seems like people are already targeting you. Being contacted by the Russians to meet with them personally… That's very disconcerting. I don't like it. We need to keep a shield between you and the public. This office shouldn't be under pressure from third parties. Or from the governor."

Kenzie couldn't disagree with Wiltshire on any of the points he was trying to make. She did not want to be personally targeted by anyone. She wanted to remain anonymous and outside of the action.

"What has your mother had to say about this? Has she given you any explanation about what happened on Christmas Day? Why

Maksim was visiting her or what they discussed? Has she told you anything about him?"

"No." Kenzie thought back to the latest conversations she'd had with Lisa about the entries in the family foundation's database. Lisa knew something. More than she would admit. Kenzie had always admired her mother's diplomacy, her ability to deal with all kinds of people and groups without causing offense. Even making them feel good about themselves. Kenzie always found herself saying the wrong thing. She was too blunt and didn't seem to have inherited or learned her mother's talent for speaking softly. "The most revealing thing she's ever said to me was that he reminded her of Dr. Proctor, one of the doctors who treated my sister before she passed."

"Dr. Proctor." Wiltshire raised his brows. "I don't think I know him. What is his specialty?"

"He's not practicing anymore. He was in general practice, but behind the scenes, he was involved in organ transplants."

Was that what Lisa had meant when she mentioned Dr. Proctor to Kenzie? Was she giving Kenzie a heads-up that Maksim was involved in organ procurement or something equally shady? Kenzie couldn't help thinking about the Russian she had autopsied who had been missing his kidney and lung and liver tissue. Was there a connection? Had Lisa been trying to convey that to her without saying it out loud? Kenzie had talked to Lisa since then, and she hadn't given Kenzie any clues that Maksim had been involved in anything medical.

"So what do you think that was supposed to mean?" Dr. Wiltshire asked, his mind following the same lines as Kenzie's. "What do you think she was trying to tell you by saying that?"

"Well… Maksim was still there when she said it, listening in on her call. So if she wanted to tell me something without him under-standing it, then it would make sense to mention someone that we both knew, but he didn't, to communicate a message…"

"And that message was?"

Kenzie rubbed her forehead, thinking about it. "At the time, I was just thinking about how Dr. Proctor was when Amanda was alive. He was always happy to include me in discussions about medical issues.

He said that I had a quick mind for that kind of thing. He was the only one to ever recognize that I had an aptitude for medicine. Back then, he seemed like a kind old man who understood and supported me. I have quite fond memories of him. So when Lisa said that he reminded her of Dr. Proctor, that was what I thought of. That she trusted him and thought he was a kindly, interested person."

"But now you're rethinking it?"

Kenzie nodded slowly. She raised her head and met his eyes. "Yes. He turned out… to be a murderer."

45

It was already getting late and Kenzie knew that if she began the process of reporting Walter as a missing person, she would not be able to get to the hospital to see Zachary. Walter had been out of touch for so long, and one more night probably didn't make any difference. There wouldn't be a practical difference between reporting him missing Thursday night or Friday morning.

Still, she mentally apologized to him, hoping that he wasn't being held prisoner somewhere, wondering if anyone cared about the fact that he had disappeared from off the face of the earth. She cared about him, but knowing how to put that love into action with someone like him was hard.

Like him? She wasn't sure what she even meant by that. Private? Self-centered? Walter was like a master chess player who was always thinking four moves ahead of where he was, and every scenario had to be considered against what his desired outcome was. He was manipulative. He used other people as pawns in his game, smiling and telling them how helpful they were. Opening herself up to him or trusting him at his word were dangerous propositions and not something that Kenzie had let herself do for years.

So after finishing at the Medical Examiner's Office, she headed over to the hospital to see Zachary, stopping at the vending machine for a granola bar that she gulped down on the elevator ride to his floor and while checking in at the psych reception desk so that she wouldn't be starving when she arrived, but would be able to be relaxed for their visit. Only, of course, the vending machine didn't have anything that pretended to be a healthy choice, and it was a candy bar, not a granola bar, that she inhaled on the way to her visit. Zachary seemed to be doing well, with no concerning symptoms and maybe even a little less vigilance than he usually exhibited while sitting in the common room.

On Friday morning, she got up early, managed to stay awake for her shower, and had two cups of coffee before going to the police station to file a report on Walter Kirsch. She figured it should take no more than an hour to file the paperwork if she got there early, and she would be able to get downstairs to her own desk by the usual time. Maybe even early, if all went well.

But she had been mistaken. Opening a missing person file involved much more than just filling out a short form with the person's name and birth date. They wanted to interview her, to know when she had seen him last, who she had talked to, where she thought he might be, what their relationship was like, how he got along with Lisa and why she wasn't the one making the report, and everything else they could think of.

Kenzie should have been happy that they were being thorough, but she hadn't expected it to attract nearly the amount of attention that it did, and had not thought that they would do much more than read it through and enter it into the computer with a "be on the look-out" alert sent out to patrol cars.

But apparently, Walter was a much bigger deal than she had thought and there had already been rumblings as people noticed his absence. The shock waves of his disappearance had already been felt all over the state. Not just in Montpelier, where he normally resided, and in Burlington where Lisa was, but all over. The fact that she was filing the report in Roxboro didn't seem to be a problem, as she had been worried it would, since Roxboro was the last place he had been known to be. It was the natural starting place for an investigation.

The door to the chilly interview room that Kenzie had been

sitting in for hours opened, and Sergeant Campbell walked in. Kenzie sat up quickly, but she was exhausted from several hours of questioning and soon had her head on her palm, supported by her elbow on the table, as she talked with him.

"What's this I hear about your father being missing?" Campbell asked.

"Well… yeah. You heard right."

Campbell sat down in the chair across from Kenzie, where one of the detectives had been sitting—Kenzie couldn't remember all of their names—until just recently. He had promised more coffee, but Kenzie had yet to see it.

"And you knew about this when you talked to me?"

Kenzie nodded slightly, wishing that she had said something when she first talked to Campbell about the telephone threat. Then she could point to it and say that she had mentioned it. He just hadn't seemed to have been interested in pursuing an investigation in that direction. But she knew she had said nothing that could be construed as reporting that Walter was missing, because she had been trying to follow the directive she had been given.

"Yes… I'm sorry I didn't say anything about it at the time. I told you everything I could."

"Except that your father was missing."

"I was told not to tell anybody about it."

"By whom?"

"By the governor." Kenzie lifted her head to look into his eyes and see how he took this news before lowering her head again and closing her eyes, wishing that what's-his-name would return with some fresh coffee. Or even day-old coffee that tasted like it had been strained through dirty socks. She would have taken pretty much anything at that point.

46

W hat does Governor Smith have to do with it?" Campbell asked, the hint of a growl in his voice.

"I called him because he and Walter are friends. Or at least acquaintances. They run in some of the same circles. Sometimes Daddy would see him or talk to him over Christmas while the Senate was out. I thought it was worth a try to see if he had seen Walter or knew anything."

"And he told you not to tell anyone he was missing?"

"At first, he said to keep it to myself so he could look into it privately. Which I thought was okay because I didn't want any publicity. Walter wouldn't want a bunch of people to know that something had happened to him."

"So you agreed to wait for a few days. But it has been over a week, if what I'm reading is true."

"Yes. Since at least Christmas Day. I don't know about before that. I still don't know when the last person saw him. He's independent, doesn't share his calendar with other people. I don't know how to access it. So I let it go for a couple of days, but then I asked the governor what was going on and if he had found anything out. He said that I needed to keep quiet about it. That I shouldn't talk to anyone about it or go to the police. Or I could put myself or Walter or someone else in danger."

"The governor threatened you?"

"No. He didn't put it that way. Not like *he* was going to do something if I blabbed about it. But that someone else might do something."

"You're sure that's what he meant?"

Kenzie shrugged tiredly. "I wish I knew for sure what he meant, and what Lisa meant, and where Walter is, and all of those things that I am just guessing about. People seem to think that I know a lot more than I do. I don't know if I'm a lot more dense than people think and should have figured out more than I have from what other people have said, or if they are just paranoid. I don't feel like I know anything more now than I did on Christmas Day."

"So as far as you know, you are the first person to realize that he was not where he had expected to be, and you have been trying to reach him since then without any luck. And you don't know of anyone who has seen him since then or who has had legitimate information about where he might be."

"Right. Good summary."

"You've tried all of his numbers. All of his friends."

"Everyone that I know. But I haven't been close to him in years, so as far as 'all of his friends' goes, I'm really at a loss there. I've called the people I know are in contact with him regularly, but there are probably a ton more that know better than I do where he should be or who he could be in contact with. And 'all of his numbers' is just his work phone and his cell phone. And it sounds like his work phone is forwarded to his cell phone, because the voicemail greeting is identical."

"Was it always forwarded to his cell, or did he just forward it when he closed his office for Christmas?"

"I don't know. I haven't had occasion to call him."

"At all?"

Kenzie's face was warm. She was sure she was flushed. She couldn't even blame it on a hot room because of how cold it was.

"At all. Sometimes he would call me, but I rarely called him except to return his calls. I had his office number in my contacts from years back, but I don't know if he uses it at all anymore. It might be permanently pointed at his cell phone number."

Campbell sat back in his seat, rubbing his chin as he thought about the situation.

"You really should have told me about all of this. I don't know that it would have made a difference to the case, but the sooner someone is reported missing, the better our chances are of finding them. When the first forty-eight hours have already passed… The chances of our finding any evidence of what happened to him go down significantly."

"It's not my fault that he didn't have a girlfriend, secretary, or other colleagues who would call it in or know something about his movements. I'm the last person in the world who should be reporting him missing. Lisa or someone that he worked with should have called it in."

"That must be frustrating."

"You can tell?" Kenzie challenged, sarcasm finding its way into her voice.

Campbell smiled. "Yes, I can tell," he agreed. "But I'm going to continue asking you questions that you've already given the answers to, in various different ways, in the hopes of triggering one memory or association that would help us."

At least he was up front about what he was doing. Not pretending that he didn't already know everything he was asking her about.

"I really need to get downstairs. Everything is going to get backed up."

"Dr. Wiltshire is aware of the situation. If he needs other help, he can call someone else in or get a temp to watch the phones. It doesn't need to be you. If this takes all day, it takes all day."

Kenzie groaned. "Tell me it *isn't* going to take all day."

"I'll do my best. The more you can tell us, the better our chances will be."

Kenzie rubbed the bones around her eyes, trying to relax the muscles that were giving her a tension headache.

"When you got the threatening phone call, was Walter's name mentioned?"

"I don't remember. I don't think so."

"They just told you to mind your own business. Stop asking questions."

"Yes."

"And were you asking questions about your cases at the morgue or about Walter?"

"Both. And… I think they're connected. I don't know for sure, but it seems like they are."

"How?"

"One of the dead Russians, Maksim, he was at Lisa's house when I went there on Christmas Day. I expected Walter to be there. He's almost always there every Christmas. But he wasn't, and Maksim, a total stranger to me, was. And then the next day, he was dead. It seemed like… it could all be related. Then when I went to the family foundation and saw that he had been a donor—"

Campbell held up his hand to stop her. "What family foundation? Who had been a donor?"

"The Kirsch family foundation. Lisa asked me to fill out some paperwork that needed to be done. And I had been talking to a couple of charities that I might target with donations from the foundation, so I had to enter charity profiles for them into the foundation's database."

Campbell nodded for her to go on, keeping up with the scenario so far.

"That's when I discovered that Maksim's name was in the database. In association with some heritage society. Russian friendship… I don't remember what it was called."

"He received money from your foundation?"

"No, he *gave* money to it. I don't know what that has to do with anything. But when I talked to Hillary, the office administrator, she said that she thought the money was to go to one of Walter's causes, not Lisa's. She thought it was something to do with lobbying."

"And that's the first real connection between Walter and the

Russians. Other than the fact that Maksim was at your mother's house Christmas Day and Walter was not."

"Yes."

"Maksim was giving Walter money to... what, exactly?"

"I don't know. I didn't get any further than that. There has been so much going on and, after getting threats to leave everything alone... I've backed off on the inquiries. I didn't want to get anyone else killed."

Only then, Mikhail had called her to trade information about Walter and he had been killed. Kenzie just couldn't keep out of it.

"Threats?" Campbell repeated.

"Yeah. Like I told you."

At least she had stepped forward and reported that.

"You told me about one threat. Singular."

"Oh. Right. The phone call."

"What other threats have you received?"

"There was... one in email yesterday."

"Why didn't you call me about it right away?"

"I... I guess I should have. It was at a bad time."

She had just seen a man killed almost in front of her and was anticipating having to explain everything to Dr. Wiltshire and to do the autopsy. It couldn't have come at a much more inconvenient time.

But then, it wasn't like there was ever a *good* time to receive death threats. She should have called Campbell about it right away. Or forwarded it to him to have his team investigate. Instead, she had just gone on with other things and tried to forget it.

47

You need to send the email threat to me," Campbell said sternly, echoing what Kenzie had just been thinking.

"Yeah, sorry." Kenzie reached for her phone, then realized that would do her no good. He still had her smartphone and all she had was a burner that didn't have any of her information on it. "I'll have to do that when I'm at a computer."

"You know your email login?"

"Yes," Kenzie nodded. "Of course."

Campbell chuckled. "There's no 'of course' about it. You would be surprised at the number of people who have no idea of their email login credentials. They're saved on their computer or their phone; they don't have them memorized."

"Well, those I do, luckily."

Campbell delved into the messenger bag he'd brought in with him and came out with a tablet. He unlocked the screen and opened the browser before handing it across the table to Kenzie. "Log in, send me that email, and make sure there aren't any others. Check all your email addresses and don't forget the junk or spam folders. Which address did this threatening email come to?"

"My work address. I'll check my personal too."

"Is your work email address available to the public?"

Kenzie hesitated. "I think that on the website, they can only reach me through a form, not direct email. But all of the emails for state employees are constructed the same way, so if you know it is first initial, last name, at... you know, you can guess what someone's address is pretty accurately. Unless they go by something other than their first name."

"So you are kkirsch at..."

Kenzie opened her mouth to reply, then stopped and shook her head. "mkirsch."

"mkirsch?"

"For MacKenzie. My legal name. No one calls me that, though."

"So whoever sent you this email would have had to know your address already. They wouldn't be able to guess it. It's not on a public-facing website and the name you usually go by is Kenzie, not MacKenzie."

Kenzie thought about it, trying to remember everything she could about the Medical Examiner's Office website and the information available to the public there. "Yes and no... I think." She found the email she had filed into a folder to deal with later and opened it, looking at the To and From addresses. She could only process one question at a time. "Let me just send this to you. It was sent to my mkirsch address... and they address me as MacKenzie. So it must be someone who doesn't know me personally. They just know who I am. My name and where I work."

"Your legal name."

"Right. A friend or even just an acquaintance would know that I go by Kenzie. So it's more likely to be someone I *don't* know than someone I do."

"And where would they get the name MacKenzie from?"

Kenzie logged out of her email address and typed a new URL into the search bar. The Medical Examiner's Office website loaded slowly, considering how little information was on the page. She skimmed through the front page and clicked through to several secondary pages, looking for her name or address.

"This one. There is an 'Our Team' page that includes my name as 'MacKenzie.'" She turned it around for him to see. There was also a picture of her with her dark, wildly curly hair. Maybe she should ask them to take that down so that people like Mikhail would not know what she looked like.

Campbell looked it over and nodded. "So that was probably how they figured out your email address." There was a ding, and Campbell dug his own phone out of his pocket. He tapped on the screen, unlocked it, and then read through what he had received. "It came through an anonymizer service."

"Yes. I assumed that means you would not be able to trace them."

"You never know. Some of them the techs can get further information from, even though they are supposed to be anonymous. And there is always the chance that we could get a subpoena for the information from the anonymizer company. It's tricky, but sometimes you can get the necessary information."

"Well… I hope so. I don't like people out there… sending me threats."

He skimmed through the rest of the information. "This one doesn't actually make any threats."

"It says I am not safe."

"Yes. Which could be an implied threat. Or could just be a statement of fact or how they see the situation. Without knowing more about the sender and what information they have available to them, it's impossible to say."

"It makes sense if it is someone who is not a native English speaker. Other languages use other constructions. 'You are not safe' could be the English translation for something more like 'You'd better watch out' in Russian."

Campbell nodded. "Could be. I'm not saying it isn't a threat, just that it isn't an overt threat and is subject to interpretation. Which makes it harder to prosecute if you manage to catch them."

"I'm not concerned with prosecuting… just with finding Walter safe and staying far away from these guys, whoever they are."

"That's a healthy attitude."

Campbell was tapping something else into his phone. Maybe forwarding the email on to his tech guys and giving them instructions. Neither of them said anything for a little while as Campbell was obviously in the middle of something. He eventually looked back at Kenzie, lips pursed thoughtfully.

"What?" Kenzie asked.

"Well… I thought I would look at what bills have been before the Senate that might have something to do with Russia. It makes sense that if they are paying your father to lobby for them, there must be something to lobby for. Something that affects the Russian community in particular."

"Or it affects a lot of people, but that's the approach the Russian community is taking to combat it." Kenzie had been around Walter and his political agendas all her life. She knew far more about the way he approached things than Campbell did. "A lot of times, it is just one particular splinter, company, or special-interest group that hires a lobbyist to try to defeat a bill. The others who are affected by it might just be fighting it in other ways. Prayer, writing to their representatives, staging a rally… lobbying is just one of many ways to try to sway public opinion or lawmakers."

"All good points," Campbell said agreeably. "What do you know about cryptocurrency?"

Kenzie blinked at him. "Practically nothing. I mean, I've heard of it. But I don't know anyone who uses it regularly, and I don't understand exactly how it works."

"We're on the same page, then. I haven't ever followed the subject very closely either. I figure that one day it will either become a part of mainstream currency or end up as a failed social experiment that everyone rolls their eyes at a hundred years from now."

Kenzie laughed. "Yeah, pretty much. I know that people use it. But I don't really understand why. They say it is untraceable, but other people say it can be traced. But maybe that's just in thrillers and TV shows. I don't really know."

"There is a bill before the Senate right now, or when it goes back into session, about legislating changes to the way that cryptocurrency is handled under the law." Campbell's eyes dropped to the phone again. "People are using crypto for illegal operations, like the Russian mob, because it is not subject to investigation the same way that accepted currency is. With all of the money laundering and know-your-client rules, it gets harder and harder to move money around and keep it out from under the noses of the authorities. Even if all you want to do is to deposit ten thousand dollars in your bank account that you inherited from your Aunt Millie's estate, you have to prove to your banker where it came from and that it is a legitimate income source. He has to know you, who you are, what is usually in your accounts, what you do for a living, what your risk tolerance level is, and if there are any red flags on the transaction. He has to know where the money is coming from and where it is going."

"So that they know it isn't from illegal activities."

"Exactly. Like with many other laws, the non-criminals have to go through a whole lot of runaround to prove that they are following the law, and those who are criminals find ways around it. Offshore accounts, layers of corporate structures, and using cryptocurrency."

"So how does that work?"

"It is not recognized by the government as actually being currency, so it isn't regulated. When you deposit ten thousand dollars in crypto, no one asks where it came from or whether it was obtained legitimately. It falls outside the regulations."

"And that makes it good for organized crime. They can still collect money and pay people, but as far as the government is concerned, no money has changed hands."

"A lot of criminal organizations are hiding behind crypto. Groups you don't want to even investigate, they are so ugly. And apparently, crypto is being used by a lot of Russian oligarchs. Not just in Russia, but in the United States."

"And someone wants to change that. Make it so they can't transact business here with untraceable money."

"Right." Campbell's lips pressed together as he looked down at his phone. "Apparently, some of these guys aren't just millionaires; they are billionaires." He shook his head. "Can you imagine how much they can do with money like that? And how much they want to prevent a bill like this from going through?"

"Yeah." Kenzie felt a little nauseated at the thought. She thought about the dead Russians. About Walter being missing. About the check from the Russian friendship society to the Kirsch family foundation. Barely even a drop in the bucket to a billionaire. Money they wouldn't even know they were missing. What were tens of thousands of dollars to someone who had billions? "So you think... that Maksim approached Walter to get him to lobby against regulating cryptocurrency."

"It's as good a theory as any."

"Walter wouldn't do that," Kenzie said, sure of herself. "He has always seen himself as a white hat. He wouldn't align himself with a criminal organization."

"Maybe he didn't know that they were. Maybe he thought that they were just Russian immigrants who wanted to be free to earn a living using whatever means they could. Maybe he doesn't have any idea of who or what is behind the money."

48

Kenzie thought about that. she shook her head slowly. "No... I don't think he was that ignorant. He didn't just take the money. He put it into a segregated account and didn't touch it. So he must have been checking things out. Doing some kind of background on the organization, maybe, or on Maksim himself."

She thought about Zachary, eager to get out of the hospital and back to his private investigations work. If Walter ever approached Zachary to hire him for something like this... She shook her head. She would have to warn him.

"Sounds like a possibility," Campbell admitted. "If he deposited the money but didn't use it, he must have had some concerns. I'm not sure why he would take it in the first place. It's a little harder to back out of it if you've already taken the money."

"He didn't put it into his account; he put it into the foundation account. They haven't paid it out yet. And I guess if they don't like whatever they are investigating, they'll just refund it to Maksim... well, to his organization or whoever is running it, since he's dead now..."

Campbell tapped his finger on the table. "And why did Maksim get killed if he paid money to your father—or the foundation—to lobby against this bill? It sounds like he is trying to defeat the bill, which is what the oligarchs or the leaders of the Russian mafia would want. So why would anyone kill him over it?"

Kenzie opened her mouth and closed it again. "Yeah. Good question. Even if it was a rival organization, they would still want the same thing, wouldn't they? Anonymity and a way around the money laundering laws. They would want to defeat the bill too."

Campbell nodded. "Cryptocurrency." He blew out his breath. "I guess I have some research to do."

"Me too. I really don't know anything about it. You just covered what I know and more. I had no idea that it was a big thing with Russian oligarchs. I thought it was just a computer nerd thing. Gamers and anarchists who want to upset the world order. Not… dangerous people who could buy and sell small countries."

The sergeant slid his phone back into his pocket. "I don't suppose you had any information for the detectives on what your father was wearing, when or where he was last seen, what he was driving…"

"No. None of that. I can't even swear that he's missing, but after not returning my calls for this long, I have to think that he is."

"He normally returns your calls?"

"Yes, the same day, usually within a few minutes. It's never been more than a few hours."

"We're going to do what we can to find him. If he's mixed up in all of this stuff with the Russians… that is growing into a bigger and bigger investigation. It's multi-departmental now, with Major Crimes, BCI, and VIC all involved. I imagine we'll need FBI in there as well, and then when we're looking at overseas…" He trailed off, shaking his head. "Bigger than anything I want to be in charge of. But I will definitely keep my hand in and let you know if we find anything to do with your dad. He's very well-known and liked in Vermont, and people are not going to be satisfied with a 'We don't know what happened to him' answer."

Kenzie nodded. "I appreciate that." She looked at the time on her phone. "I've been here since early this morning. I'm going to head downstairs. I've given you guys everything I can. Just email me or leave me a message if you have more questions. I'm going to have to put my phone on 'do not disturb' to get caught up with my work this afternoon."

Campbell pushed out of his chair and stood up. He offered his hand, which Kenzie took and shook firmly. "Thanks for staying so long; I know this has been a big pain in the butt. We'll do our best to find Walter."

Things were not quite as bad as Kenzie worried they would be when she got down to her desk. Julie was minding the phone and public inquiries, so there was no line of disgruntled people to calm or call back. There would be a lot of emails to sort through, since she didn't let Julie process those. She couldn't be sure that everything would get into the right files, onto her task list, and printed for the paper files. If Julie did it, Kenzie would just have to double-check everything anyway and would be in danger of missing something.

"Lots of people wanting to know where you are," Julie said with a welcoming smile. "I didn't say anything, but I think when they started to hear that you were upstairs talking to the police, they were worried."

Most of the inquiries that people came down to the morgue for were from law enforcement, since no one else but next of kin or someone authorized by next of kin could get autopsy reports. There were some other general searches that Kenzie could do for members of the public or press, but no records could be released without the authorization of the next of kin. Kenzie could well imagine that news that she was there to make a missing person report would spread quickly amongst the law enforcement officers who knew her or her father. The phone threat had been a minor report made on a holiday when there was really no one around to spread the gossip. Reporting Walter Kirsch as a missing person was a much, much bigger deal.

Julie vacated Kenzie's chair. "Let me know if you need anything else. If you need someone to handle the desk while you work on a postmortem this afternoon…"

Kenzie nodded her appreciation. "Probably not today. Too much other stuff to catch up on. But if I do manage to clear the decks so that I can assist, I'll give you a call."

Julie smiled and waved. She was a floater who had contracts with several different departments and could move among the police department filing room, the Medical Examiner's Office, Vital Statistics, and a couple of other smaller departments as she was needed. That way, she got to do a variety of work and usually had enough hours to get by from one week to the next. And it was easier on departmental budgets than each department hiring part-time staff or having to call a temp agency at the last minute.

Kenzie settled in, opening up her email and starting at the top. Julie had cleared all of the voicemail messages and entered them into the computer log, so Kenzie skimmed them while her email loaded, mindful of Dr. Wiltshire's instructions always to check phone messages first. It really didn't apply so late in the day and was more to make sure that she didn't mention a message from him left overnight or in the small hours of the morning as he headed out to a call. But it was best to maintain the discipline.

Most of the calls in the log were either for Dr. Wiltshire or public inquiries that Julie had answered already. There were only three messages for Kenzie, and they were automated messages and things that could be handled later.

"Kenzie, you're back." Dr. Wiltshire was on his way to the kitchen and stopped to greet her, smiling. "How are you?"

"Exhausted. Sheesh, you think this job is tiring, you should try answering detectives' questions all day!"

He nodded. "I imagine the emotional toll is what is making you the most tired."

"Yeah. I thought it would be a relief to hand it over to someone else… that it's not my responsibility to make inquiries and track him down now, but it wasn't what I expected."

"Were they helpful? I assume there was no problem convincing them that he was missing?"

"No, they were really good about it. Everyone agreed that he'd been out of contact for way too long to think he might just be on vacation or off with a woman for a few days. I mean, the man has never taken a vacation in his life, so the chances that he went on a holiday without his phone for over a week are practically zero."

"Now I know where you get your work ethic."

Kenzie smiled. "He really loves his job. Taking time away from it just for Christmas or another holiday is practically torture. He's one of those guys who just thrives on being around other people, persuading them to follow him on something, and stirring the—stirring up drama wherever he goes. He's always at the center of things, and he loves it."

"I don't really follow politics; I have less than zero interest in most of the bills heard at the Capitol, but even I have heard about the colorful Walter Kirsch from time to time. He's an icon in this state."

Kenzie swallowed a lump, nodding. "He's a character," she agreed with a cheerful smile that she didn't feel.

Why hadn't she spent more time with him when he had sought her out? Why had she always turned down his invitations and told him she didn't have time for him? Just because she didn't agree with his ethics or politics, that didn't mean that she had to cut herself off from him. Surely they could have a personal relationship that didn't hinge on those things.

Had she left it too late and it was a regret she would carry with her for the rest of her life?

"Let me know if you need anything," Dr. Wiltshire said, as if he were her assistant instead of the opposite, "and if you need to go home early, go ahead. It's been a long day for you already, and I understand if you need to crash or have some time alone. Just give me a heads-up that you're going out. We can shut down the desk early for once."

"I don't think I'll need to, but thanks. Right now, I just want to be doing routine stuff, so I don't have to think about everything else. If I went home, I would just be sitting or lying around with my own thoughts, and that's not a place I want to be right now."

She thought about Zachary briefly, knowing how he battled his ever-busy brain. Kenzie's concern over her father's whereabouts and what was happening in the Russian community was not even close to the hyperactivity and hypervigilance that he dealt with. What was amazing was that he operated on such little sleep. With so much on her mind, she would have wanted to sleep to escape it.

Dr. Wiltshire got himself a cup of coffee from the kitchen and put one on Kenzie's desk where she wouldn't knock it over, then went back to his office. Kenzie continued to process the emails and filing, giving herself an hour to get through as much as she could. Then she would take a break to walk around and make sure that everything in the cold room had been properly checked in and cataloged. Samples should be back from the lab as well, and she would need to let Dr. Wiltshire know if there was anything significant in the results if he hadn't looked at them already.

49

Kenzie had left her phone on "do not disturb" for the afternoon, so it wasn't until the end of the day that she picked up her personal messages, including a message left by someone on staff at the High Street Hotel.

"If you would please call us back," the woman's thin voice requested, "we have items belonging to your father here and would like to arrange for you to pick them up."

Kenzie's stomach clenched and her heart raced. Items belonging to her father? What did they have? And how had they known to call Kenzie? Especially since she was still using the burner phone and waiting for the police department to return her regular phone to her. Her father would not have her number unless he had picked up the voicemail where she had left it for him. Other than that, only those she was the closest to her had that number.

She dialed the number left by the woman at the hotel. "I'm looking for Marja?" she asked when she reached someone.

"One minute, I'll see if she's still here," a brusque man's voice told her.

Kenzie waited a minute or two on musical hold before there was a click and she heard the woman's plaintive-sounding tones again. "Hello, how may I help you?"

"My name is Kenzie Kirsch. You left a message for me this afternoon."

"Yes." There was recognition in her voice. "About your father's things."

"That's what you said. But… how do you have my father's things and how did you know how to contact me?"

"They are his personal items that were still in his hotel room. The police gave us your number."

"So the police know about this already."

"Yes. They were here this afternoon to look through what he had left and to see if there was any evidence in his hotel. Evidence of what, I'm sure I don't know. It is our policy to cooperate with the police—" she started in a somewhat stern tone, as if Kenzie had protested the invasion of her father's privacy.

"That's fine. Really. I was talking to them all morning. They're helping me."

"Oh, okay." The woman let out a breath. "Sometimes people do not appreciate police involvement in their affairs."

"If they can find him, I'm all for it."

"They took his laptop with them, but that was the only thing. I got a receipt for that. You should know what they have and how to get in contact with them. That's what I figured, anyway."

"So the rest of what he left behind is there? Clothing, suitcases, that kind of thing?"

"Yes. His toiletries and things for a few days. We have carefully packed everything away. You're welcome to take a last look at his hotel room to make sure that we didn't miss anything before we rent it out again."

"That would be great. I'll head over there now. Do I just ask for you at the front desk?"

"I'm on my way home. Just tell them who you are. They'll have your father's things for you and someone can take you up to his room."

"Okay. Thanks very much."

Kenzie hung up the phone and sat there for a minute, her body shaking. Hillary had been right about Walter being in Roxboro, not

Burlington or Montpelier. Had he been there to see Kenzie or someone else? More than likely, he was there because of someone else, though he would have stopped in to see her as well, when time allowed. He'd been at her house once before. Or they could meet over a meal at a restaurant. He liked to treat her to good food. He would want a short Christmas visit, like they'd had before, though some years Kenzie denied him even that.

Was it too late now? Had her most recent visit with Walter been the last they would ever have?

———

She had collected herself once more by the time she got to the hotel's front desk. She smiled and introduced herself to the young woman who greeted her.

"I'm Kenzie Kirsch. I'm here to collect my father's things?"

"Yes, of course. Marja said that you wanted to go up to the room as well to make sure that there wasn't anything left behind? We should do that first, rather than you having to carry the luggage up and down again."

"Makes sense," Kenzie agreed. "Let's do that, then."

There was some back-and-forth with a male desk clerk to explain why the young woman was leaving and where she was going. Then the woman let herself out through a swinging door under a counter that folded up on a hinge to allow her egress, and she led Kenzie to the elevator.

"Is your father okay?" she asked. "We were concerned when we heard from the police that a missing person report had been filed."

Kenzie thought it a very stupid question to ask about a missing man. But she supposed that showing concern was just a reflex reaction.

"I don't know. He hasn't been located. This is the closest that I have gotten to him yet. When did he book the room?"

"The twenty-fourth, I believe. Christmas Eve. He put it on his credit card, and he hadn't checked out, so we just keep charging…"

And that was undoubtedly how the police had found them once

Kenzie filed her report and they pulled up the records for his credit card charges.

"When was the last time anyone saw him? Do you know?"

"We haven't kept track. It's not unusual for people to only be here to sleep and be gone the rest of the day. We don't necessarily see guests every day. They have other things to do and come and go on their own schedules."

"What about maid service? Can you find out from them whether he was here at all since he checked in?"

"The police asked that too. The custodial staff was not sure, but it doesn't look like he stayed at all. His toiletries were unpacked and the towels were on the towel bars, but it didn't look like the bed had been slept in and his clothes were in the suitcase, not hung up."

Walter would never show up at a Christmas party looking rumpled. He would have been sure to hang his clothes at least a day before he needed them, and to iron them too.

"So he's been missing since Christmas Eve."

The woman looked sympathetic. "I couldn't say for sure. But maybe?"

"Was there anything in the garbage cans? Did the maids know?"

"They couldn't remember. Sorry. They clean a dozen rooms each day, and it's been more than a week. They wouldn't remember unless it was something really unusual or disgusting. Something would have to make it stand out."

50

S he used her key card to open the door of Walter's former room for her. Kenzie stepped in and looked around slowly.

She really could have used Zachary's eye. Zachary would know what to look for, and Kenzie was at a complete loss. Had Walter just set down his luggage, brushed his teeth, and gone out somewhere? Had someone been following him? And if they had, did he know they were? Did he know who it was? Surely if Walter had thought that he was in any danger, he would have called the police. He knew people. He could call in a favor. He could have started with the governor or the police chief. Someone who he knew would listen to him and help ensure his safety.

He couldn't have known that he was going to disappear that night.

Kenzie looked at the small kitchenette. She didn't know why he'd bothered to get a room with a kitchenette. As far as she knew, Walter didn't cook. But it had been a long time since she had lived with him. Maybe he had picked it up. Maybe he'd decided he liked to cook or to have control over his own meals. Maybe it was relaxing for him. She opened the fridge but, of course it was empty other than a lone box of baking soda. Not even a drink. She opened a couple of drawers and cupboards, but knew there was no point. The hotel staff had already cleared out the room. Walter had probably never even stepped into the kitchenette. She walked through the small sitting room area, checking under the couch and under the cushions for anything that Walter might have dropped or wedged in there. She turned on the TV to see what channel it was tuned to. It was an all-news channel, currently streaming some court case. That figured.

There was an untouched pad of paper and a couple of stick pens in the drawer under the TV. No clothes. Nothing that any of the previous residents of the room had left behind. She walked through the doorway into the bedroom. The lighting was a little darker, the furniture darker and more stately. But she could see nothing of her father there. She couldn't even picture him sitting on the end of the bed chatting on the phone with one of his contacts.

She felt guilty doing so, but stripped back the blankets and top sheet on the bed, looking for any sign that Walter had been there. That he'd had a woman there with him who might know something about what had happened. That he'd eaten his favorite flavor of Doritos chips in the bed. Anything that could tie him directly to the room other than the fact that he had left his luggage there and charged it on his card.

"Did anyone see him? Do you remember checking him in?"

The woman, following her silently and staying out of her way, looked surprised by this. "I don't think I did it personally, no. I'd have to look back at the records to see who set it up. Usually, reservations are called in ahead of time, especially around Christmas. People don't want to take the chance that the hotel will be full, and sometimes it is."

"He would still have had to check in, though. To get a room key." Without the room key, he could not have left his luggage there. He had been in the room. Unless someone else had left them there. What if someone had used his credit card and left his luggage there, knowing that it would create a false trail? That it would keep the police looking in the wrong direction for a day or two longer. Long enough for them to torture him or dispose of his body. Kenzie swallowed, trying to keep the emotions and what-ifs at bay.

"Yes, of course," the woman said. "I'll look at the computer when we go back down. Look up who checked him in. I wish I could do more to help…"

"Do you have surveillance cameras? At your registration desk, elevators, hallways…?"

"Yes… but the footage is recycled every four days. If you want something, you have to get it out of the system before it is over-written with the next cycle."

In the age of digital recording, Kenzie had no idea why anyone would still be using magnetic tape or overwriting previous recordings. They could have afforded to keep much more than four days' worth.

"I need to know that it was really him. That he was really staying here," Kenzie insisted. "If anyone can remember seeing him, talking to him. Anything that happened while he was here."

"Of course. We'll do whatever we can to help. Can I ask… does he have dementia? Maybe he wandered off and forgot where he had checked in?"

"No. He was in perfectly good physical and mental health. He wouldn't have just wandered away."

Of course, she hadn't seen him lately, other than in October when he had stopped by the house and Kenzie had seen him at the Halloween Gala. He'd seemed to be perfectly in control of his facul-ties then. Hale and hearty. The same man she had known her whole life. She hadn't seen any sign that he was declining.

There was a Gideon Bible on the shelf next to the bed, along with a red LED clock showing the wrong time. Kenzie checked the closet, boosting herself up so that she could see the very back of the closet shelf to confirm to herself that he hadn't left anything behind in the closet. It was bare. She went into the bathroom. It was larger than the bathroom he would have gotten at the typical family hotel. A jetted tub that would comfortably hold two average-sized people, and a separate shower cubicle. An upgrade. A small luxury, to soak in the big tub at the end of a long day of work.

The towels and washcloths had been removed from the room and it had not yet been resupplied. Kenzie assumed that the police had probably taken the towels. Test them for DNA, see whether they could confirm that Walter had been in the room. Maybe find out if there had been someone else there with him. A woman or a guest. Hotels tried to keep people from leaving things behind by not having a lot of places to hide them. No cupboard under the vanity sink. No medicine cabinet. No storage shelves. Just the bare countertop that was barely big enough to hold a comb and a razor at the same time.

Kenzie looked around the base of the toilet anyway, eyes sharp for anything that he might have dropped. Some tiny scrap of paper that would give her some clue as to where he had gone. What he had been thinking when he had checked in. On TV, there would always be something that the maid service and police had missed.

But the place was clean. There wasn't some obscure clue for her to find. He hadn't left her a message. He probably hadn't had any idea what was going to happen to him in order to leave one.

51

I 'm sorry there wasn't anything helpful in the room," the woman said to Kenzie, giving her a shrug and another one of her sympathetic smiles. "I'm sure if there was anything to see, the police would have found it. From what I can gather, he didn't spend much time in the room."

"Didn't look like it," Kenzie agreed, trying to keep her tone as flat and unemotional as possible. She didn't want to engage at an emotional level. She just wanted to get out of there. There was nothing to find, so it was time to move on to other things.

The clerk retrieved Walter's suitcase and soft-sided carry-on bag and handed them to Kenzie, shaking her head at how sad it was or that she could do so little to help Kenzie. The desk phone rang, and the clerk answered it brightly, cutting her eyes toward Kenzie. Kenzie raised her hand in a goodbye and twitched her shoulder toward the door. The desk clerk nodded, satisfied that she had done everything she could, and focused on the new caller.

Kenzie was about to go out the front doors, the same way she had come in, when she suddenly thought about Walter's car. Where was it? No one had said anything about it. Had the police found it in the hotel parking lot and impounded it? Or was it still waiting there for him? Or had it been towed away when the hotel staff had thought that it was abandoned?

Rather than returning the way she had come, she decided to walk around the side of the hotel. She didn't want to have to deal with any more sympathy. She was quickly rediscovering that sympathy was the hardest response for her to handle without getting all tied up in her own emotions. She had learned that after Amanda's death, but had forgotten some of the lessons she had learned after Amanda's passing. She could be stoic in the face of loss, concentrate on the practical, smile through her sadness and focus on the other person's needs. But dealing with genuine sympathy was something altogether different. Anger, apathy, disdain—she could deal with those. But someone who truly felt for her and wanted to share the moment with her... a whole different story. And she didn't need it. Not yet. She didn't know what had happened to Walter and, until she did, she wasn't going to put up with any sympathetic smiles.

A brisk walk around the side of the hotel brought her into the parking lot. Not a paid lot, and there did not appear to be any assigned stalls, so Walter might have parked anywhere and it would be easy for his vehicle to stay in the same place and be overlooked for an extended length of time. She started walking up and down the aisles, trying to remember what his car had looked like when he had come to visit her.

Eventually, she found a black Lexus like the one Walter had driven to her house. Zachary would have had a better idea, but Kenzie wasn't about to call him and ask if he remembered what Walter had driven when he had come to visit Kenzie. That would lead to questions and eventually to Kenzie having to explain that Walter was missing. Zachary would probably check himself out the minute he heard it, and Kenzie needed him to stay in the hospital until he was properly stabilized and his doctor believed he was ready to reengage with his life on the outside. As well as he was doing, he wasn't there yet, and Kenzie didn't want to say or do anything that might affect his progress.

Was there any way to be sure whether the car was Walter's or just a lookalike? Kenzie walked around it, alert to any clue that would indicate that it was her father's car or that it was definitely *not* his.

There was a small sticker with a QR code on it in the corner of the windshield. The graphic in the center of the QR code looked like the capitol building. It could be some kind of parking authorization for the capitol. It would make sense for him to have something like that. She looked in through the windows of the car. But Walter had always been very neat and tidy with his personal possessions, and there was little in the car to indicate who owned it. The console tray was empty and clean. There were no special cups in the cupholders or even old coffee cups from Starbucks or another favorite coffee shop. Walter had always preferred little mom-and-pop shops to the big chains. This was funny, considering how often he worked with big chains, lobbying for or against their interests, depending on who was paying him. He wouldn't lobby for something he outright disagreed with but, if he did not already have a position or it was not solid, he could often be persuaded to take a particular stance. That was what men like him did.

Kenzie put down the suitcase, which was getting heavier the longer he stood there. She rested the carry-on on top of the suitcase, considering her options. She should probably call Campbell to check the license plate of the car and see whether it was, in fact, Walter's car. There was no point in worrying over it if it was not.

The question would be easily answered if the car had been left unlocked or if she had Walter's keys. She tried the door handle but, as she had expected, it was not unlocked. Walter didn't generally leave his car unlocked, even though many people in small-town Vermont did. Walter had always been more careful with his property than that. "If you won't take care of your property," he told a younger MacKenzie, "you don't deserve to own it."

Kenzie opened the side pocket of the carry-on bag and felt for a key. She didn't expect to find one. He would have taken it with him, on the key ring in his pocket. And he didn't believe in keeping a spare key in a magnetic box stuck inside the wheel well or anywhere else on the vehicle. Like leaving his doors unlocked, that was asking for trouble.

The side pocket was empty. But the bag had a lot of pockets. Kenzie opened each of them to search inside. Her fingers encountered something hard and thin, and Kenzie pulled back her fingers, then advanced, snagging a set of keys and pulling them out.

Walter did, apparently, keep another set of keys in case he were to lock his usual key ring in the car. It made sense to keep it in his travel bag. Otherwise, he would have to pay for a locksmith or towing service to come to him. Kenzie flicked through the various keys. One looked like a car door key, so Kenzie took a deep breath and thrust it into the lock. With her luck, it would be for a totally different car, and it would get jammed in there or would set off an alarm because the car thought someone was trying to break in. Car manufacturers used all kinds of tricks now to try to nullify threats.

But the key slid in easily and, when Kenzie gave it a twist, the door lock popped up, and there was not even an alert to indicate she had unlocked the car without first disarming the burglar alarm.

Kenzie opened the door, again prepared for the klaxon of a burglar alarm, but the car was silent, as if it had been sitting there waiting for her. She slid into the driver's seat and looked around. She had no idea what she was looking for. There was no note indicating what Walter's plans had been. No map with locations circled on it. The car was almost as clean as a fresh rental, with all traces of the previous renter removed and extra detailing done to be sure that everything was sanitized. Kenzie checked under the sun visors for any papers or directions. She opened the glove box but found nothing except the car manual and a pair of sunglasses. She opened the various hatches in the center console and found spare change and a small box of breath mints. She opened the box and smelled the mints, and visions of her father bending over her to kiss her goodnight flooded her mind. She put them back where she had found them. Nothing out of the ordinary there. Nothing at all wrong. She checked under the seats, hoping that something had fallen to the floor and been missed. She even got out of the car and ran the driver's seat as far forward and as far back as she could, but there was nothing there but another dime, wedged under the seat leg so tightly that she could not pry it out. Which was probably why it was still there. Walter hadn't been able to get it out either. There was nothing else under the seats. She forced her hand down the crack of the back seat and didn't find anything hidden there. No cell phone or secret notebook with an emergency message scribbled there for her attention.

If she had been on a TV show, there would have been *something* in the car that would have led her to what she was supposed to do next. What was wrong with the world that those important clues didn't actually pop up in real life and she was still left without a clue as to what to do next? Kenzie popped the trunk and didn't find anything but an emergency kit with a first aid pouch and road flares in it. And a spare tire under the carpet. No hidden USB drive. No blood, hairs, or shred of clothing indicated that the trunk had ever been used for anything but luggage and boxes of research files.

Kenzie locked everything back up and leaned against the car as she left a message for Campbell about its location, asking him if he wanted to send some forensic techs to examine it or if she should get it towed. Where she was going to tow it to, she wasn't sure. Her own house? She couldn't tow it all the way to Walter's. Zachary's car was normally parked in front of her house, and Kenzie's convertible was in the garage, but there was still space for one more car in front of the house without angering the neighbors by encroaching on their spaces.

She hung up again and headed back toward her car.

There were a couple of young women walking along the sidewalk in front of the hotel, and Kenzie wasn't paying any attention to them until she realized that they weren't speaking English to each other. It wasn't Spanish, either. She didn't know the language, but it certainly sounded like Russian or another Eastern European language. Kenzie stopped and looked at the women. Was there any chance they knew Maksim or one of the other men who had died? Even if they were all Russian, there was no guarantee that any one Russian in Vermont would know another.

52

W hat is it?" One of the women demanded, noticing Kenzie's stare. "What do *you* want?"

"Is that Russian?" Kenzie asked, smiling as disarmingly as she could. "It sounds so beautiful."

The woman looked at her suspiciously, but at least did not seem to be angry. Maybe the comment about the language being beautiful had helped.

"It is none of your business," the other young woman said in a harsh tone. "We are having a private conversation."

"Yes, of course. I just thought... I thought I recognized it. A friend of mine is Russian..."

"There are many Russians," the woman snapped.

"Yes, of course. It seems like there are more of you in Vermont all the time," Kenzie gushed. "I am running into you everywhere."

"We do not know you." The woman motioned to Kenzie's luggage. "Go home. Put your things away and have a nap. Maybe then you will not be so curious."

They turned away from her.

Kenzie had stopped walking, and it was curiously difficult to get going again. She looked at the two women. Another connection to the Russian community. Kenzie couldn't just let it go, even if she was wrong. She couldn't let any lead slip by her. Who knew where Walter was and what they might know about him, if she just asked?

"I'm here looking for my father," Kenzie said, swallowing hard. "He was staying here, and then he disappeared. A friend might have been staying with him. His name was Maksim."

Both girls turned to face Kenzie. "What?" the first demanded. "What are you talking about?"

"Do you know Maksim?"

She waved this question away. "There are many Maksims. Very popular name."

"In Russia, maybe. Not here in Vermont."

The second woman shook her head. "We do not know any Maksim. Do not know who it is you are looking for. You have to find him yourself."

Kenzie had classified them as young women in her mind when she first saw them walking down the street. But looking at them as they answered her questions, she grew anxious. Young women in their twenties? No. Despite their long legs and the sophisticated makeup they wore, they couldn't have been older than sixteen. They were model-thin, a look that was even more popular in Russia than in North America and Western Europe. They looked both too young and too old and jaded.

She wasn't sure what to say to them.

"Hey… are the two of you working?"

They looked at each other and didn't answer.

"I help to run a foundation, and I could help you to get off the streets if you want out. You might think that there is no way out, that you have to do this, but I could help you."

"Go away," the taller of the two told her. "We do not need any help."

"Is this what you thought was going to happen when they brought you here from Russia? I'm sure this isn't the life that they promised you. I'd like to help. I could get you into homes, back to school, job training. A lot of organizations are willing to help with situations like this."

"I said we do not need you," the girl insisted again, her voice sharp.

The younger girl looked less certain. Maybe Kenzie's words were getting through to her. She hoped she could convince the girls that she could help and that they didn't have to prostitute themselves to pay back the people who had smuggled them into the country, or that she could get them away if they were being held against their wills. But she knew how hard it was to get teens out of the life. She and Zachary had already had some experience with that. Traffickers had a lot of ways to keep girls under their thumbs even when the police or someone else offered them a way out. Loyalty to boyfriends, addiction, money and clothes, physical violence, threats to their loved ones, and, in some cases, actual shackles. Just because the girls didn't look like they were being held against their wills, that didn't mean they weren't. Or that they knew they had any other choice.

"There are ways that you could be safe," Kenzie tried once more. "I can help you. I know people who can help. I have helped get girls out of situations like this before." That was a bit of a stretch, but what were they going to do, ask for references from satisfied customers?

The taller girl called her names in Russian, short guttural sounds under her breath. Kenzie didn't need to understand Russian to know what she was saying.

They both turned their backs to Kenzie.

There wasn't anything else she could say or do. Getting those two girls—and however many more the organization was trafficking— away from the organization would take a lot more time and effort than Kenzie had. It would take many man hours on a task force somewhere to identify all of the players in the trafficking ring and to assemble enough evidence to bust them, with serious enough charges that they would not be on the street again the next day. Even if they managed to break the ring that had turned out the two girls, chances were that once they were freed, they would end up in the stable of another trafficker. It was not an easy life for them to break away from, even with all of the professional help Kenzie could connect them to.

"There are people who can help," Kenzie said to their backs, keeping her voice low in case someone was nearby watching and listening to the conversation. "If you want out, you can reach me through the Medical Examiner's Office. Or call 9-1-1 and the police will help get you away so that you can get the help you need."

One of them looked back at Kenzie over her shoulder, sneering. "The police! Police are worse than the family."

Maybe Kenzie should have remembered how corrupt the police force in Russia was rumored to be. She had always assumed that the stories were exaggerations, borrowed from TV movies about spycraft in Russia. But if the oligarchs were as powerful as Campbell suggested, then what was to stop them from buying the local police force? Police officers too needed to eat and feed their families. They were just as poor and starving as anyone else in Russia, unless they aligned themselves with the right factions.

"Not here," she assured the girls. "Maybe in Russia the police are corrupt, but they are not the same here. They will help you. They will make sure that these men can't touch you."

The taller girl shook her head adamantly. "Police here too. You think I am blind? You think I don't see anything? Don't hear anything? *You* are dangerous because you talk like this and have no idea what could happen." She looked at the younger girl beside her, scowling fiercely. "She has *no* idea what the family would do if you tried to get out. *I* know. You don't listen to her. You listen to me."

The other girl nodded, adopting a thousand-yard stare toward the traffic driving past the hotel. All of those people who just drove by as if they didn't know the girls were in trouble. With so many people ignoring the danger they were in, the terrible ordeals they had to go through while being trafficked by the Russians, how could they believe that anyone would be willing to help them? Or would be able to do anything for them if they accepted her offer of help. Kenzie wasn't even sure she believed it herself. With Zachary's experiences trying to help Madison and Luke, she knew how hard it was to keep the teens away from the men who would track them down and bring them back, even if they tried to escape.

53

Discouraged, Kenzie knew it was time to head for home. She could talk to Campbell about the girls and make sure that they were aware that the Russians were trafficking them out of the hotel. He could at least pass it on to the appropriate task force, and maybe someone else would be able to make contact with the girls or start building a case so that they would be able to get them out sometime down the line.

She walked back toward her car much more slowly than she had walked around the side of the hotel to get to the parking lot Walter's car was parked in. She'd had a purpose then, a mission, and she'd shut everything else out—tunnel vision. Walking toward the front of the hotel again, she was aware of things she hadn't been before. It had been snowing steadily from the time Kenzie had arrived at the hotel, and there was a man shoveling snow from the main walkways, his movements slow and deliberate. Kenzie watched his progress. At first glance, she had thought him an old man from the way that he moved. He had on a hat with flaps over the ears and a bulky coat so that she couldn't see much of his face or build. But he threw a couple of glances in her direction that suggested he was nervous about her being so close to him, which made her stop and take more conscious note of him. His facial features were narrow and sharp. His eye sockets were deep and there were hollows in his cheeks. The pant legs that hung below his coat were very narrow. She was reminded of the homeless man she had autopsied. Wasting away. Starving even while he performed physical labor, obvious from the muscles he had developed even with no fat visible on his body. She glanced at his face again, taking it in small bits. Hollow-cheeked because he was an old man or because he was malnourished? Were the deep eye sockets natural? Or the result of dehydration?

She walked up to him, carrying Walter's suitcases. "Excuse me, can you help me?"

His eyes turned toward her and he didn't say anything.

"I'm all turned around. Which street is this?" She pointed toward High Street.

His eyes turned toward the street, and he shook his head. "Sorry, no English."

He had that same accent. That same Russian accent she had heard from the women, from the voice on the phone, from Maksim.

"Do you work here?" Kenzie motioned to the hotel. She knew it was a ridiculous question. Why would someone who did not work for the hotel be clearing their sidewalk? But she just wanted to keep him talking. To get more information about him.

"This is High Street Hotel," he said, motioning to the hotel. "High Street."

"Is this High Street here?" Kenzie motioned to a side street.

He shook his head in confusion.

"How long have you worked here?" Kenzie asked him.

He shoveled a short pathway through the snow and tossed the shovelful of snow to the side.

"I clear," he told her. He waved his hand at her to go away. But Kenzie did not take the hint.

"I guess you must be used to snow like this in Russia."

He blinked at her, his watery blue eyes questioning, still confused. Wondering, she was sure, who this strange woman was and what she wanted.

Kenzie pulled out her picture of Walter and showed it to him.

"I'm looking for this man. Have you seen him here? He was a guest."

She motioned to the hotel.

"No English," the man repeated stubbornly, shutting down again. Kenzie held the picture there in front of him for a few seconds.

"Please. This man is my father. He is very important to me and has been missing for a week. Can you please help me to find him?"

"No English, no English!" He pushed her back with one gloved hand. Not hard. He was not in danger of pushing her over or of hurting her. But the physical contact reminded Kenzie that she could be hurt. That people she knew could be hurt. Walter himself, if he was not already dead and disposed of.

"Excuse me," a stern male voice spoke at Kenzie's elbow. She jumped and looked at him, her heart speeding even faster than it already was from her confrontation with the snow-shoveling man. "Can I help you with something?"

Kenzie turned her eyes to the man who had interrupted them. He wore a uniform, but she wasn't sure whether he was supposed to be a doorman or security. Maybe both. A bouncer to get rid of anyone they didn't want hanging around.

"I was just asking for directions," Kenzie explained, motioning to the man who had moved ahead with his shoveling, moving much faster than he had been a minute before. With so little fat on his body, he would be in danger of burning through all of his stored energy and succumbing to the cold if he were not careful to preserve what little he had.

The picture of Walter flapped in her hand. The bouncer looked down at it, eyes sharp. She said she was asking for directions, but she had been showing him a picture, not a map.

"What is that?"

"That's just a picture." Kenzie folded it quickly and tried to shove it into her pocket, keeping it from him. But he'd probably seen all that he needed to.

"Are you a guest at the hotel?"

"I was just picking up my things." Kenzie indicated the suitcase and carry-on. "I've checked out and am heading home."

"Then you do not need to be bothering the staff. Do you need help in locating your vehicle?"

He did not have a strong accent. But it was there, faint, behind his carefully articulated words. No contractions. Perfect English.

"No, I just ended up going out the wrong door, so I got turned around. I'm parked around front."

He walked beside her to the front parking lot. Kenzie pointed to her car. "I'm just over there."

He nodded and withdrew, heading back to the front doors of the hotel. "Good. Have a nice day."

The way he said it, she was pretty sure it was meant as a curse rather than a blessing. He did not like people coming to his hotel and interfering with the staff.

If the man shoveling the sidewalk could actually be referred to as staff. If he was like the men who had died, he was probably starving, suffering from exposure, and being paid nothing. He was probably barely holding body and soul together. One mistake in their care of him, and he would be dead. What they were doing couldn't even be called care. It was clearly neglect. How many other people at the hotel were part of "the family," either paid or unpaid labor? If she walked through the hotel, how many Russian voices would she hear? The girls walking the street, the man shoveling the sidewalk, the bouncer, Maksim. Walter had stayed there. Had he known what was going on? How could he have stayed there without having some idea? He hadn't deposited Maksim's money, so he must have had doubts about what was going on and how much of the Russians' business was illegal.

Had he walked right into a trap? Or was he in on it all? She didn't want to know if he had ever hired a prostitute or had an eye for the younger women. Whether he would have turned a blind eye to the use of unpaid labor—after all, they had been brought to the United States, the land of milk and honey, what more did they expect?

54

A man was standing near the entrance to the hotel, watching Kenzie. He held a hand up to his face, shielding himself from her gaze, in a gesture that made it look like he was cupping his hand around his cigarette to protect it against the wind, but she was pretty sure that he didn't want her to get a good look at his face and remember him later. She had seen him before, but it took a minute before she could remember where she had seen him. She put Walter's luggage into the trunk of her car and studied him for a moment.

He was one of the front desk clerks. Or at least, he had been at the front desk when Kenzie had arrived. He watched her now, waiting for her to leave. So he could report back to someone else? Just because he was curious about the daughter of the man that the police had been looking for? Or was he just gazing across the parking lot at nothing while he smoked his cigarette?

Or maybe the bouncer had told him to keep an eye on her and let him know if she did anything suspicious. Like going back into the hotel.

Even though she was sorely tempted to go inside and ask more questions, to demand to know what was going on and to get a feel for how much of the staff had been replaced with Russian immigrants and what they were all up to, she didn't. She forced herself to open the car door and slide into the driver's seat as if she suspected nothing and had just gotten turned around going out the wrong exit.

In her rear-view mirror, she could still see the young man smoking a cigarette was watching her as she drove away.

She tried to zone out as she drove back to the house, as Zachary would have done driving down the highway. Just to allow her mind to ignore the worries and let the thoughts float around inside her head at random, looking for connections or things that she might have missed.

But she couldn't shut off the worries about the Russians at the hotel. She knew there was bad stuff going on there. Men had died. The girls walking the street believed they were trapped and could not get out of the business, even with police help. Kenzie was afraid that they were right.

And Walter? What had happened to him? Who had taken him from his hotel room before he even had the chance to hang up his clothes? And why? What had they been so concerned about? What made him a threat to them when they had been trying so hard to get him to fight the cryptocurrency bill? Had he turned on them?

She couldn't help thinking that maybe things were even worse than she had imagined. That she hadn't even begun to dig up all the bodies yet.

Kenzie parked the car at the curb in front of her house and got out. She popped the trunk to take Walter's luggage into the house with her, already planning to search it thoroughly. Even though everything appeared to be normal and the police had not found anything of significance, she was sure that if she pulled everything apart, if she tried hard enough, she could find a clue to what had happened to Walter. So that she would at least know where to look next.

She bit her lip, thinking about the serial killer Zachary had caught, who had been burying the bodies of his kills in a cemetery and the lands around his cabin in the woods. Places they would never be discovered unless he was caught red-handed, as he had been. The Russian mafia family would have somewhere to dump bodies where they would never be found. There were surely lots of such places in the wilds of Vermont where someone like Walter, who had turned out to be an irritant could be disposed of. They had just dumped the other bodies without regard for how or when they would be found, but someone like Walter, important and well-known, would be a different story. Best if he just disappeared forever and no one ever knew where he had gone. Like Jimmy Hoffa.

There was a racing car engine and Kenzie half-turned to look at it, irritated that someone would be speeding in the quiet suburban neighborhood. There could be children around. A white van was speeding up the street. With a screech of tires and fishtailing wildly from side to side, it pulled up right beside Kenzie. She stood there frozen, her brain not computing why it was there. Did they want directions? Were they angry at her? Maybe she'd had her head in the clouds; had she accidentally cut them off in traffic?

The side doors of the van were thrown open and two large men jumped out.

Kenzie didn't believe it was really happening. She had seen such dramatic kidnap attempts on TV so many times, she didn't think it was something that could really happen. It just didn't happen in real life.

But they both grabbed her, one grasping her arm and putting his other arm around her waist, and the other gripping her other arm and tightening his elbow around her throat, cutting off her breath and forcing her to move along with him to lessen the pressure as much as possible. They both threw her into the side opening of the van, and the momentum carried Kenzie inside, tripping over the edge of the doorway to land face down in the van. Her forehead banged the uncarpeted metal floor, making her see bright flashes of light. Then they were with her, the doors of the van slammed shut, tires screeching as it peeled off down the street, leaving Zachary's car and her house behind. Kenzie tried to move, to right herself and figure out what was hurt and what wasn't and how to deal with the men who had just abducted her.

But they were on her. One of them shoved her down into the floor with a shout to shut up and stay down, even though she hadn't said anything. The other pressed a heavy, booted foot into the middle of her back, his weight on it, which prevented her from being able to get her arms under herself to lever her body up again. Her breathing was restricted and she thought about all of the stories she had read, all of the autopsies she had reviewed, where arresting officers had placed a suspect prone instead of supine or had put too much weight on the suspect for too long, causing positional asphyxiation.

She needed to breathe. She forced herself to take long breaths even though it hurt, to try to use her arms to create a little space between her body and the floor to give her lungs room to expand. They hadn't put handcuffs on her, so she still had some freedom of movement, however slight.

She didn't yell at them to let her up or demand to know what was going on. She knew what was going on, didn't she? Being confrontational and fighting them wasn't going to help anything. If she didn't fight back, maybe she would learn where they had taken Walter. Maybe Walter was still alive somewhere and they would take her to the same place to hold her.

Campbell would know that Kenzie hadn't just taken off on her own. He knew she was stable, that she wouldn't have just run off or gone away to pursue a lead without telling anyone.

Never mind that she had just gone to the hotel alone, exposing herself to the scrutiny of all kinds of baddies there. But she'd thought it was safe. The police had told her to go there to retrieve Walter's bags.

Except they hadn't, really. It had been the hotel that had called her. Was it true that the police had been there and searched everything already, or was that just a story cooked up for Kenzie? Had they all been in on it, laughing at her behind her back for being so taken in by the whole drama?

She had no idea what was true and what was not. If it hadn't been Walter's hotel, if he hadn't slept there at all, then Campbell and the rest of the police would have no idea where to go to begin looking for her.

She shifted her weight slightly, trying to turn partially onto her side.

"Don't move!" the man with his foot on her back snarled.

"You're suffocating me. I'm not getting up. I just want to breathe."

"Down!"

"Yes. I'm staying down. Just let me breathe!"

He pressed harder, putting what felt like all of his weight onto the foot holding her down. She shouldn't have asked. She shouldn't have said anything. She should have known that he would do the opposite of whatever she asked.

The other man spoke, letting out a rapid spate of foreign words. There was a bit of back and forth between them, and then the foot had been removed from her back.

Kenzie drew in several deep breaths. She felt a little nauseated and didn't know whether it was the lack of oxygen or because she had hit her head. Or if it was just her confusion at the whirlwind of events.

"You stay still and obey," the second man told her, his words barely understandable through his thick accent. "You fight, you die."

"I'm not fighting," Kenzie assured him, pressing her face into the floor, trying to hide the tears that flowed from her eyes at the throbbing pain in her head. "I don't know what's going on... but I am doing what you tell me to."

The governor had told her to stay out of it. Various anonymous threats had been made. And Kenzie had stopped. But that hadn't prevented her being pulled into the middle of whatever was going on. Would the next body on Dr. Wiltshire's autopsy table be Kenzie?

She didn't plan to be. She would do whatever she could to survive. Dr. Wiltshire was not going to do her postmortem. Her mother was not going to lose another daughter. Zachary was not going to lose another loved one.

55

Kenzie lay there, trying to be as still as possible so that her captors would not have any reason to think she was trying to escape or fight back against them. The tears continued to flow down her cheeks. She tried to think of everything she knew about how to survive a kidnapping. How to get through it alive.

There were actually training classes for those who worked for companies operating in South America or other places where Americans were sometimes kidnapped and held for ransom.

But this was not a ransom. They weren't kidnapping her because they wanted money. They were happy to pay for what they wanted. Proof of that was sitting in the Kirsch family foundation's account. What they wanted was for Kenzie to stop getting in the way.

She had been warned; she couldn't say that no one had told her. But it really wasn't her fault that she had been at the hotel. They had called her to the hotel. The police reports... she had been guilty of making those. And of using the family foundation to try to figure out what was going on in the Russian community. But she had stopped when they had said to. Sort of.

Kenzie hadn't been able to track where the van was going. It always sounded like a good idea on TV. The kidnappee would keep track of all of the turns and all of the sensory clues and would know exactly where they were so that when they managed to get a message to someone, they would know where to go. But there was no way that Kenzie could know where she was. Right from the start, when her head had hit the floor, she was far too scattered and scared to keep track of their progress. It felt like they had been traveling for hours and it only felt like a few minutes. Was she all the way in the next state or within blocks of the house, circling to give the goons time to do whatever it was they had in mind?

She was pretty sure that they hadn't left the city. So maybe she wasn't quite as useless as she thought. She hadn't felt them driving any highways. But other than that, she wasn't sure. There had been starts and stops, not just stop signs but traffic lights. No gravel roads. Not anywhere near enough clues for Kenzie to figure it out. Where were all the clues she would have had in a TV show? A clock tower, train tracks, river, mountain road, rare calling birds. She would have made a pretty lousy silver screen hero. She couldn't even figure out where she was being driven to.

The car stopped. There was chatter back and forth, several voices outside speaking with the driver, and the driver yelling information back to the men in the van with Kenzie. No English, of course. That would have foiled any TV hero too. On TV there would at least be subtitles. Kenzie tried to assign meanings to the exchanges, trying to picture the speakers, what they were angry or upset about, and what they were planning to do. Were they happy that Kenzie had been kidnapped? Was it something that had been planned out or spur of the moment when she had gotten too close to the truth?

Eventually, the van doors slid open. The man who had been stepping on Kenzie's back kept her head pressed to the floor so she couldn't move it to look around.

"Do not move!"

Kenzie stayed frozen. He released her head, talking to the men outside of the van. Then he pulled a bag or a hood over Kenzie's head.

She gasped and held her breath like she had been dunked under water. She couldn't help flailing around, trying to keep everything she could no longer see in place.

"Stay still. Do you want to be handcuffed?" the other man in the van ordered.

"No!" Air escaped Kenzie's lungs. "No, please. I'm trying. I'm just scared!"

"Stay still." He grasped her arms, forcing her to obey. Kenzie tried to school her emotions until she could hold still by herself. He let go again.

"You will come with us. You will not take the hood off. You will not fight or run. Do you understand?"

Kenzie swallowed and nodded. "Yes. Where am I? Can you tell me what's going on? I won't tell anyone. I promise I'll just go home. I'll mind my own business, and I won't do anything to get in your way."

"Shut up."

Kenzie shut up. The two men inside the van stood her up and walked her out of the van, keeping her upright even when she walked off the edge of the world to fall six inches to the ground.

It was fine. She had just stepped out of the van. She was no longer trapped inside the vehicle. That was a good thing. But the hood was disconcerting. She didn't know how big the area outside was. Was she in a forest? The inner city? Were they going to dump her in the river or put her in a dungeon? Despite the fact that she wanted to walk free, and for the men not to touch her, she felt unanchored and vulnerable without their hands directing her. They kept her from falling over the cliff every time she took a step.

She was walking on pavement. But not for long. There was the click of a door latch and squeak of hinges, and the outside noises were dulled as she stepped into a building. She was taken through the first room she entered, a right turn down a hallway, and then into another room. Smaller, by the way the sound bounced off the walls and the feel of the air around her. She was pushed down and landed on a bed. Thin mattress. Squeaky springs. A metal frame.

"Stay there."

Kenzie nodded her head, not trusting her voice to be audible. She felt very small in this new place. She had no idea who else might be there or what the room looked like. She didn't know what to expect.

She had often wondered how Zachary had felt when Archuro had taken him to the cabin in the woods. Was this what it had been like? It was terrifying. And yet, she still had hope that things would work out. She wasn't stuck in the middle of nowhere with a sadistic serial killer. There were a number of people, an organization where the men were expected to follow the rules and instructions they had been given. There was still some hope that the hood over her head meant she would be released. There was no need for them to hide their identities from her if they were going to kill her.

56

Kenzie sat as still as she could, listening to the noises of the house and the voices of the men who came and went, which meant nothing to her. She had never felt so out of place, like she was in a foreign country. Or even worse, like she was an alien on the planet. She had been to foreign countries before. She had always been able to talk to people, to find a way to communicate, to get from one place to another. There were always ways to gesture, use the few words she had learned, speak English, use her phone, get someone else to help to interpret for her. Stuck in the middle of the house with the Russian men who had kidnapped her, she had no idea what was going on.

She thought that if she listened long enough and hard enough, she might start to recognize patterns. Other languages adopted foreign words. The Russians were bound to use a few English supplement words. Or to talk about people or places she knew. Maybe some of them would speak different dialects and would rely on English to communicate with each other. Or maybe it would all just gel and she would be able to understand the Russian words.

But that wasn't going to happen in a couple of hours. Learning a new language by immersion would take months. And she wasn't going to be kept there for months.

It seemed like a long time had passed. The bedroom door opened and heavy footfalls told her that someone had entered. Kenzie had been able to smell cooking food for some time and, now that the door was open, it was much stronger. There was the clank of a dish on a table or desk nearby.

"You will wait until I go and the door is closed," the voice told her. "You will count to thirty. Then you will take off hood and eat."

She nodded obediently. Five minutes before she would have said that she could not eat, but the rich, savory smells that started to fill the room made her stomach growl. When had she last eaten?

The man said nothing else. The footsteps retreated, and then the door shut. Kenzie counted slowly. If there was a guard nearby or someone was watching her on camera, she wanted them to see that she was being obedient. That she was being very careful to do everything they said to.

Eventually, the prescribed time had passed and more. Kenzie tentatively pulled the hood off of her head. She looked around, blinking in the dim light.

It was like a monk's room. A single bed, bedside table, and bulb hanging from the ceiling. Bare floor and walls. No other comforts or signs that the house was normally occupied. She refrained from calling it a cell, even in her mind.

There was a bowl of stew on the table with a spoon in it. Kenzie picked it up, took a spoonful, and blew on it. For a few minutes she just savored the smell and was too scared to eat it. What if it was drugged? Poisoned? What if this was her last act, and she would be in excruciating pain? Or knocked out? Or dead?

What if there was Flunitrazepam or something else in the soup that would make it impossible for her to control herself, but allow the men to do what they wanted with her without any fight?

But what would they do? They already had her at their mercy.

Though Zachary had never said so straight out, Kenzie knew that he had been drugged when Archuro had captured him. That he had been conscious, but unable to defend himself. Zachary had gotten halfway to saying so more than once. Sometimes he would describe being paralyzed in a dream, and she wondered if that was what had happened in real life. But he wouldn't talk to her about that night.

She thought she had understood before. That she knew what he had gone through and what it must have been like for him.

She'd had no idea at all.

As sympathetic and empathetic as she had tried to be, she couldn't *know*.

Eventually, she broke down and put the first spoonful of soup into her mouth. It was warm, but not too hot. She'd been blowing on it for long enough. It was delicious and rich and a layer of the defensiveness and vigilance that she had felt since she'd been grabbed fell away.

Safe, and warm, and cared for. That was how she felt.

They were taking care of her. They weren't going to let her starve. They weren't poisoning her. They were nourishing her, giving her what her body needed and craved. She could rely on them.

Even as these feelings rushed to her brain, Kenzie recognized that they were not logical. Nothing had changed. She was still being held captive. She still had no idea what her captors planned to do to her. They could have terrible tortures in mind. They could traffic her. They could addict her to drugs so that she would do anything they asked her to. Or they could kill her.

But her logical brain's arguments lost to the waves of reassurance that her body sent over her. She was being taken care of. The food was good, and safe, and nourishing. She was cared for.

Eventually, the delicious chicken stew was all gone. Even though she was full, Kenzie wished she had another bowl or two to eat. She wondered whether they had put something in it to give her that overwhelming feeling of well-being. Some happy brain drug. But whether they had, or whether it was just a psychological reaction to her kidnapping, she felt better. She had hope that it would work out.

She didn't know if she should put the bowl near the door for them to pick up or back on the side table. Whether she should put the hood back over her head, or maybe lie down and close her eyes and go to sleep for a while. The man hadn't given her any other instructions, and she grasped at straws, trying to anticipate what he would want her to do. Looking at her own brain processes dispassionately, it was amazing to her how much she wanted to be a good hostage and please her captors. It had only been a few hours, but she was totally focused on them and how to make them happy. It was no wonder that people who were hostages for days or weeks became so attached to their captors.

She lay down on the bed and turned her back to the door. She would be quiet and sleep, facing away so that she would not see their faces if they came to the door and woke her up. Her brain felt wrung out, unable to evaluate the situation or try to plot an escape. The spot where she had hit her head still throbbed and when she touched it with gentle, exploratory fingers, sent lightning bolts of pain through her brain. It was best not to touch it. She didn't think she was concussed, or at least not too badly. She was tired, but she wasn't seeing double and wasn't dizzy or nauseated. When she laid her head on the thin pillow, the room didn't wobble or spin. Those were all good signs. Just a bump on the head. Once her captors released her, she would be fine.

57

hen Kenzie awoke, the room was dark, lit only dimly from outside. Maybe a security light or the full moon. Was it a full moon? She had no idea what phase it was in.

"What is it going to take?"

The voice was male. Measured, reasonable. Not one of the snapping Russian voices. Kenzie lay there listening, wondering if she was dreaming or hallucinating.

She knew that voice.

She knew that reasonable, willing-to-negotiate tone. The ultimate lobbyist, finding a way to make everyone happy, even when they had to give something up. All of the steps and swaps and machinations, as complex as a public merger or series of connected NFL deals. Every step carefully considered, the outcome of every step tabulated and then factored into the next move. The chess master, always three or four moves ahead of anyone else, with every eventuality weighed and calculated.

She couldn't hear the Russians' responses through the door. She could hear their angry tones and the flow of their words, but their words were too heavily accented for her to make out with the muffling effect of the closed door. Kenzie sat up slowly, careful to avoid a head rush. The bruise on her head felt like it was going to burst open. A throbbing, knifelike pain made her suck in air over her teeth as she tried to avoid crying out.

She wanted to call out to her father. To tell him that she was right there, and make sure that he was going to save her. She was sure that was why he was there. To negotiate for her release. Despite everything that had happened in the intervening years, he was still a hero figure in her life. The sword of truth. Banisher of monsters. Light in the darkness. When Kenzie was sick, Lisa would stroke her hair and give her ginger ale or whatever else she could think of to ease Kenzie's symptoms, but Walter would pick her up and hold her in his lap, cuddling her and holding her face against his strong chest, asking about her day and trying to entertain her with silly stories of how he had spent his day. She knew by the time she was ten that the dragons he slew were only symbolic, but it didn't matter. He was still her hero.

But she bit her lip and forced herself to stay quiet. Walter undoubtedly already knew she was there, or he would not have been negotiating for her release. If she called out, it might change the direction of the negotiations or put more pressure on Walter. Or it might anger the captors. She would not do anything to anger them.

"I'm here," Walter repeated calmly to the angry Russians. "You wanted to find me, and here I am. Let's move forward."

He had been hiding all the time? Not kidnapped as she had feared? Obviously not murdered, unless she was hallucinating. Had the whole disappearance been a ruse to prove some point or to pressure the Russians into making some concession? Had he known the whole time that Kenzie had been looking for him and had refused to answer her calls even just to let her know that he was alive?

"Daddy," Kenzie whispered soundlessly to herself. "Daddy, Daddy, Daddy."

She might have fallen back asleep during the negotiations. Only being able to hear a few muffled words from Walter every now and then, it was hard to keep herself awake and aroused, ready for him to come into the bedroom and take her home. She might have been drifting in and out of consciousness, or just seeking a safe, isolated place in her brain when everything became too overwhelming. Was that how Zachary felt when he dissociated?

Eventually, there were heavy footsteps up to Kenzie's door and the doorknob moved, just visible in the moonlight. Kenzie put her hand over her mouth, trying not to react emotionally or to blurt anything out. She didn't want them to see her distress and fear. She didn't want to cry out in anger or disappointment when it wasn't Walter.

There were a few Russian words exchanged back and forth. Then the door swung inward.

58

The moonlight was just enough for Kenzie to recognize the shape of her father. She wouldn't have thought she knew his build and stance sufficiently to identify him by those things alone, but she did. She couldn't see his face or how he was looking at her. She swallowed, waiting for him to tell her what to do or explain the situation. To tell her that she would have to stay there for longer until he could do what they wanted him to and return. That they needed something he could not give them, but he would be back, he would work it out somehow.

"MacKenzie." His voice was hardly a whisper.

"Daddy?"

"Are you okay?" He stepped toward her, crossing the small room in just a couple of steps, and he bent down to look at her, to cradle her face between his hands and turn it in the moonlight to get a better look at it.

"Yes."

"You're not hurt?" His thumb touched the sore spot on her head, making her gasp with the pain, but she gave her head a slight shake that he would feel.

"No. It's fine. It's minor."

"If they hurt you, I will have something to say to them!"

"No. No, please don't. It's okay. It was an accident. I tripped."

He pulled her to him, embracing her for a moment as he leaned over her, sitting on the edge of the bed. She could feel him take a couple of deep breaths and let them out. She could feel his heart thumping in his chest, not as slow and calm as his voice would have everyone around him believe.

"Come. Can you stand up?"

Kenzie swallowed. Was he really taking her out of there? Or to another cell? Some new prison?

"Yes." She put her feet on the floor and stood slowly, still mindful of not moving too quickly in case her head wasn't quite as steady as she believed it to be. Walter held on to one arm, steadying her, making sure she was not going to pass out and drop to the floor.

"That's a girl. Come with me. It's okay. It's all over."

She couldn't believe it. She didn't dare believe anything he told her. It would be too crushing to be told that she was getting out of there and then to find out that there were conditions attached.

When he gave them what they wanted.

After she was transferred to a more secure facility.

But he didn't add anything else. He continued to escort her gently along the hallway, through a dark and undecorated living room, and then out the front door.

She didn't see anyone else. The Russians had all decided to disappear rather than to let her see them. She was thankful there was no need for a black hood over her head this time. She didn't know if she could have handled that.

Walter took her to a car parked on the gravel pad outside. Not the Lexus that he had left in the hotel parking lot, but a white sedan, not that different from Zachary's car, unmarked and anonymous. Probably a rental.

Walter escorted Kenzie to the passenger door and opened it for her. Kenzie gratefully slid into the seat and he shut the door behind her. She heard his feet crunching on the gravel as he walked around the car and then opened his door. He climbed into his seat, then stopped to examine her again in the bright light of the cabin dome

LEDs. "You're okay? Are you sure? We should take you to a doctor to have that looked at. You might need stitches."

Kenzie moved slowly, grasping the visor flap in front of her and flipping it down to find a cosmetic mirror on the other side. She turned her head back and forth to look at her injury.

"It's just a minor scalp lac," she told him. "It's hardly even bled. I just bumped my head."

"Someone should still check you out."

"No. It's fine. I'll put a bandage on it."

"Maybe some ice," he fussed, touching the puffy skin next to the laceration very lightly. "Take down this swelling."

"Yes. And it will be fine."

"Okay." He pressed his lips together, looking at her for a minute longer, then nodded and turned to face the steering wheel squarely. He started the car and reversed, completing a three-point turn to get turned back around in the right direction, then shifted into drive and started for home.

"What happened?" Kenzie asked after they had driven a few blocks, away from the dark, lonely area the house she had been held in was situated and into a neighborhood that looked more familiar and certainly safer. "Where have you been? I've been trying to find you."

"I know. But you should have just left it alone."

"I couldn't. You were missing. No one knew where you were!" She paused, considering. "Did they?"

"No. No one knew," he agreed.

"Why? Why did you disappear like that? I was scared to death that something had happened to you. That they had killed you, like Maksim."

He shook his head a little. "I can't believe that Maksim is dead." He rubbed his forehead. "I did not anticipate that."

So even the grand master could make a mistake.

"Tell me where you were," Kenzie insisted. "And why you disappeared. You owe me that."

He glanced sideways at her. "I had to go into hiding. I had a tip-off that they were coming. That they weren't going to take 'no' for an answer this time. But what could they do if they couldn't find me?"

"A lot, apparently," Kenzie said dryly.

He raised an eyebrow. "Apparently," he agreed. He shook his head. "You were never supposed to get mixed up in this, MacKenzie. I wanted you and your mother to be safe, not the target of these men."

"Mother? Is she okay?"

"Lisa is fine. At the end of her rope with me, maybe, but she is home and safe. No one has dared to lay a hand on her."

Unlike Kenzie. They *had* dared to lay a hand on her. But maybe that was understandable. Lisa had said not to ask questions. She had warned Kenzie. Reminded her of what had happened with Dr. Proctor. But Kenzie had kept looking, kept asking, filing a police report. Told the police everything she could about where they might find Walter. Everything that she thought he might be mixed up in.

She had done it because she had wanted to help and protect him, but she had a feeling he didn't exactly appreciate it.

All along, he had been hiding from her.

"Why didn't you just tell me?" she demanded, frustrated. "Why didn't you just find a way to get a message to me and tell me you were okay? Then I wouldn't have had to keep looking."

"I did try," he said flatly.

"You *tried*? How?"

"When the governor's people started asking around, I told them to back off. They told you, didn't they?"

"Well…" Kenzie grimaced, the expression pulling at the tight skin around her scalp laceration. "Yeah, he told me just to stay back and let them take care of it. But they weren't doing anything."

"They weren't supposed to."

"You still could have told me."

"You didn't get the email?"

Kenzie's heart gave a hard throb that made her cough. "What?"

"I sent an email."

She thought about the anonymous email message. *MacKenzie, you are not safe. Stop asking questions.*

That had been *Walter?*

"You couldn't put your name on it? Something to tell me that it was from you and not one of the Russians?"

He raised his brows and glanced aside at her. "Who else calls you MacKenzie? Other than your mother and I?"

Kenzie let her breath out in a puff. "Well… anyone who knows me calls me Kenzie, other than you and Mother. But… it's my legal name and the name that's on the Medical Examiner website, so also *anyone who doesn't know me.*"

Walter opened his mouth, then closed it. "Oh."

Kenzie shook her head. "I thought it was the Russians. After getting the phone threat, I thought it was more of the same. I gave it to the police to try to trace it. I had no idea it was from you."

"Maybe we'd better establish a protocol for getting in touch with each other. When there is need for… discretion."

"This had better not happen again," Kenzie said sternly. "You don't think it will, do you? You're not going to let something like this happen again?"

The streets outside were familiar. She was getting closer and closer to home. She hadn't asked Walter to take her there, but he clearly knew that was where she would want to go. Not to the hospital or the police station. Not to the house in Burlington. Home. To her own home, where she felt safe and secure.

"I'd rather not," Walter agreed. "But having happened once, I can't promise it would never happen again. I would do anything I could to prevent it, of course, but… we can't control the future. We can't control what other people do."

"How did you get mixed up with these people? I don't understand why you had anything to do with them in the first place. How did you even meet them?"

He shrugged. "They were looking for help. That's what I do. I agree with the premise. I don't think the government should interfere with people's lives. I don't think it should be the government's business to regulate everything, especially what people and companies choose to do with their money. The government has gotten too big, too powerful, and tries to have its fingers in too many different pies.

We should not be trying to push legislation for more government oversight and regulation. We should be trying to defeat those bills."

"So they came to you to get you to help them with that. To hire you to lobby against the cryptocurrency bill."

He looked at her, sucking in his cheeks, apparently surprised that she knew about that detail. He gave a single nod.

"And you took their money. Or the foundation did. You're using the foundation to launder money now?"

"Launder it? No. Absolutely not. I needed an intermediary to hold it while I looked into it further. I wanted to know more about who Maksim was and whose money was behind him. It was obvious that it wasn't his own money. I like to know exactly who I'm working for."

"And who was it?"

Walter pulled up behind Zachary's car, parking at the curb. "Here we are. Let's get you settled."

59

Y ou don't need to come in," Kenzie told him. "I can take care of myself."

He looked at her and didn't say anything.

Sure she could look after herself. That was exactly what she had been doing when Walter had come after her, wasn't it? Kidnapped and held hostage, helpless to do anything but eat and sleep when they told her to.

Kenzie got out of the car. She was dizzy for a moment and pressed her hand to the top of the car, waiting for the sensation to pass. Then she walked up the walk to the house. Walter followed close behind her. She wanted to tell him again that she was home and could manage everything from there, thank you very much, but he had just rescued her from a dire situation. She should show him some measure of gratitude. He was her father, and he had cared more about her than about anything else that had been going on. He didn't reveal himself over Christmas when he'd missed his usual appointment with Lisa. He had kept quiet when Maksim and the others were killed. He hadn't done anything when she had talked to the governor and opened the police investigation. But when Kenzie was clearly in danger, he had revealed himself and had gotten her out of there.

Kenzie opened the door and disarmed the burglar alarm.

"What did you tell them?" she asked Walter. "How did you get me out of there? Did you promise them something?"

Walter went into the living room without an invitation, looked around, and then went into the kitchen and started opening and closing cupboards.

"You must have something to drink."

Kenzie had never been a big drinker and, with Zachary, drank even less than before. He had to be careful about mixing medications and alcohol, so he usually abstained, and Kenzie followed his lead, not liking to drink in front of him. But there were exceptions. Kenzie opened one of the cupboards Walter had missed and pulled out a bottle of wine. There was no Scotch; Walter would have to deal with it.

They were both quiet as Kenzie opened the bottle and poured a splash into each of two wine glasses.

"What did you tell them?" Kenzie repeated.

"I told them I would lobby against the bill."

Kenzie sipped her wine and closed her eyes. Because of her, Walter had given in and agreed to work with the Russians. Would he have eventually done it without her being kidnapped? If she had just stayed out of the way, under the radar, so that they didn't have her to use as a bargaining chip, would he have done it anyway? Or had he made the decision solely to free her from her captors?

"I'm sorry," she told him.

"You were doing what you thought was best. You should always do what you believe to be the right thing."

"I know. But I wasn't trying to derail your plans. I didn't know you had any plans. I thought that… something had happened to you. After nine days…" Her voice cracked despite her intention to keep it flat. "I thought you were dead."

"Oh, sweetheart." Walter hugged her around the shoulders. "I am so sorry. I didn't think… I honestly didn't think you would be concerned. You don't keep track of my movements. We have always been very independent. I would never assume something was wrong because I didn't see you at your mother's at Christmas." He shrugged. "I would just assume that you had taken a vacation."

"Yeah, except *you* don't take vacations. I wasn't worried at first. I figured you were just at some event somewhere else. We never agreed to meet anywhere; it's just that I usually do see you if I stop in at Burlington around Christmas. But when you didn't call me back, I kept leaving messages and you didn't respond. I started calling around and no one else had seen you or knew where you were. It just got to be too much."

"I never meant to concern you. I didn't think you would care where I was."

"Couldn't you tell from my messages?"

He cleared his throat. "I was... out of range of communications most of the time."

Kenzie studied him, trying to figure out what that meant. There was a lot that he was choosing not to tell her. She didn't want to pry. As he had said, they were independent and didn't check up on each other or insist that someone had to know where they were at all times.

Walter seemed paler than usual. She thought it was because it was winter and he hadn't gotten much sun. Or he had been worried about his daughter being kidnapped. But he also appeared to have lost weight.

That didn't mean anything. He could be on a diet. His doctor might have told him he needed to start eating properly and lose the paunch. It put him at a higher risk for lifestyle diseases like cardiovascular disease and type two diabetes. Or he might have a girlfriend that he was trying to impress.

But Walter's explanation that he'd been "out of range of communications" for over a week was difficult to believe when considering his pallor and weight loss. Had he intentionally disappeared to keep Maksim and the other Russians from finding him? Or had he been kidnapped, like Kenzie, and had been living in a bare, cell-like room, surviving on a bowl a day of stew for the past week? Maybe he had refused to compromise his values despite being held captive, and they had snatched Kenzie, forcing him to make the decision for his daughter's sake that he wouldn't make for his own.

"Let's sit down. I don't think I can stay on my feet any longer," Kenzie suggested, motioning to the living room. They sat down close to each other, Kenzie on a chair and Walter on the couch. She knew she should watch him carefully. He had tried planting a bug in her house before. But she was too tired to keep her eyes open and focus on him. And he had no reason to listen in on her. She wouldn't even be discussing anything with Zachary. It could be weeks before he got home and, when he did, they wouldn't be discussing anything that Walter would be interested in.

"Zachary!" Kenzie said aloud. She sat up straight and pulled her phone out to look at the time. She swore. It was, of course, way too late to make it to the hospital for a visit.

Zachary had always told her that she didn't have to visit him every day. He would understand if she needed to work late or take a break, and he was okay there on his own. On the other hand, Kenzie had always insisted that she would be there if possible. And of course, she would let him know ahead of time if she was not going to make it there.

But she had not foreseen being abducted.

Walter cocked his head at her. "Where is Zachary? Out on surveillance?"

"No." Walter should realize that. He had parked behind Zachary's car, which he would have had if he had been out on a job. "No, he's in the hospital and I missed visiting hours. He's going to be wondering where I am, what happened."

She hoped Zachary didn't have a panic attack over it or insist that he be released. He was in the psych ward voluntarily and could sign himself out if he wanted to, though he might have trouble doing it if the staff believed that he was having a meltdown and might be a danger to himself. Kenzie rubbed her forehead, trying to decide what to do. She couldn't go over there. Even being a doctor, she would not be able to get into the ward after lights-out. They had tightened up security significantly.

"What is he in the hospital for?" Walter asked.

"His depression. And a med change. I can't believe I completely forgot about him."

"You couldn't exactly have demanded that they let you go so you could go visit your boyfriend."

"No. But as soon as you got me out, I should have realized. I should have called to tell them... I don't know."

She should have at least thought of him while she'd been sitting in that bare, cell-like room. She should have thought of him being at the hospital and wondering what had happened to him. How could she not have?

"What should I do?" She was asking herself more than she was asking Walter. "Should I call them and explain? Leave a message for Zachary?"

"You don't owe the staff any explanation. Just let him know tomorrow that you were... unavoidably detained. You don't need to give him the details."

And it was probably best if he never found out about the abduction. He worried about her too much as it was. She couldn't imagine how paranoid he would be if he thought she could just be snatched off the street by Russians at any time.

Kenzie groaned and found the number for the psych unit she had entered into the burner phone. She tapped to dial through. She probably wouldn't even be able to get anyone on the unit—just an answering service.

"Psychiatric Services," a musical voice answered. "How may I help you?"

"Oh, this is Kenzie Kirsch. My boyfriend is in the unit. I was a little worried because I didn't get over there today. Would it be possible for me to talk to someone on the unit just to make sure everything is okay?"

"I'm on the unit, Miss Kirsch."

"Oh, good. Do you know how Zachary Goldman is doing tonight? I just got home, and I wasn't able to give him a heads-up that I wouldn't be visiting today. He might be upset about it."

"Everyone is down for the night."

"Can you check the records? See if he had any issues tonight? Maybe I could get a message to him so that he'll know when he gets up in the morning that everything is okay."

"I can't give you any confidential patient information." There was the clicking of keys in the background. "Has Zachary signed a form releasing us to give information to you?"

"I don't know... I've always been able to talk to the doctors and nurses without any problem. But I'm not asking for any treatment information. Just whether he was okay tonight."

There was a brief silence. Kenzie waited for the nurse to read through whatever showed up on her computer screen. "Your name is on the file... and everything looks fine. I don't see any extra meds ordered tonight, just his usual cocktail. I've been on for an hour, and no one has been up or making a fuss."

"Okay, good. Would you have someone check on him, just to make sure he's not lying awake worrying, or pacing or anything? And if he's asleep, leave a message for him in the morning?"

"I'm sure you don't have any reason to worry, Miss Kirsch," the nurse soothed. "Mr. Goldman is under medical care. If there was a problem, it would have been dealt with."

"Can you just ask that someone check on him anyway? I'll call in the morning if you don't want to take a message for him."

"I'll take a walk around the ward in a few minutes. What's your cell number? I'll text you when I've looked in on him."

Kenzie let out her breath, relieved. She knew that they would take good care of him. He'd been in the unit before and assured her they had always looked after him when he was having issues. But with some of the things that had happened before Christmas, she just had to know for sure that he was okay for the night and not panicking that something had happened to her. He was a grown man and didn't need to be babied... but that didn't mean she couldn't just double-check.

"Thank you. I'd really appreciate that." Kenzie gave the nurse her phone number and terminated the call.

"And you should get ready for bed," Walter said, draining the rest of his glass. "You've been through an ordeal. You get a good rest tonight and call in sick tomorrow. Spend some time with Zachary at the hospital. It will be good for both of you."

"Maybe." Kenzie closed her eyes briefly. She knew he was right about her getting to bed soon. She would fall asleep in her chair if she didn't get into bed. Then she'd wake up with a crick in her neck on top of everything else. "And you?" She opened her eyes and studied him again. "Will you be okay?"

"I'm perfectly fine," he said, as if it had been a normal day for him. "I'll call you tomorrow, if that's okay?"

She knew she should probably invite him to stay the night. She had a guest room, which was rarely ever used. But she didn't want anyone else in the house with her.

Not even her father.

60

Despite a strong drive to go to work each day and never call in sick, Kenzie decided to do as Walter had suggested. Even though they had postmortems left to do, they could wait until she felt more like herself. Feeling as she did, any work she did would be suspect, so it was probably best to leave it until she could put the abduction and her father's disappearance and reappearance behind her and focus on other things again.

As it was, she was still feeling confused about everything that had happened, trying to work it out and understand everything that had happened and how it all fit together.

Besides, it was a Saturday and, while she usually worked at least a few hours on a Saturday, she wasn't officially required to unless something important came up. Dr. Wiltshire brushed her apologies aside and told her to enjoy the weekend.

Kenzie also wanted to see Zachary and reassure him that she was fine and apologize for having missed the previous evening's visit without even a phone call to let him know she wouldn't be coming. In couple's therapy, they had tried to structure their relationship and communications so that they kept each other informed about their plans without having to give detailed explanations or excuses. Zachary knew that Kenzie had to work late some days, without needing to know whether she was working on administrative work or a postmortem, or details of whatever autopsies were being done. Though he generally liked to hear about any interesting cases she was working on, there were privacy issues, and she couldn't say anything that would give away any identities or information that the police were holding back from the public. Similarly, if Zachary was out on a surveillance job, he couldn't usually tell her how long it would take or anything about the target. He might tell her whether it was an adultery case or insurance fraud, or what part of the city it was in, but his client confidentiality was important, as well as avoiding any accusations of slander if his words somehow got back to a subject of surveillance.

And, of course, both of them needed their own space, time to themselves, and the ability to come and go without having to report every detail of their schedules.

But they tried to keep each other apprised with at least the general shape of their days and when they would be home or out. Kenzie felt like she had really let Zachary down by not giving him a call, even though she had been physically unable to do so. He would be worried, even if he felt like their relationship guidelines didn't allow him to inquire about where she had been or what she had been up to.

The nurse at the reception desk wasn't familiar to Kenzie, since she was probably normally on mornings and Kenzie usually visited in the evening. She paid attention to Kenzie's identification and didn't chat familiarly with her as the nurses who knew her did. She wrote everything down carefully and motioned to an orderly to escort her to the visitor room.

"I know where to go," Kenzie said, trying to wave him off.

"It's pretty quiet," the tall, dark-skinned orderly told her. "I need something to do."

So Kenzie let him escort her to the visitor room where, of course, Zachary was not waiting for her. He wouldn't sit there all day when she only came in the evenings.

"Do you mind if I go by his room? I'll suggest we come out here to visit."

"I will get him for you."

Kenzie opened her mouth to object, then let the man do his job. If it was that quiet, she might as well let him do something.

Zachary's expression was wary when the orderly returned with him. His eyes alighted on Kenzie's face, and he brightened. "Kenzie!" He stepped forward eagerly to greet her with a hug and a quick kiss; then he withdrew slightly to be able to look her in the face. "What day is it? Are you off today?"

"Well, it's Saturday, and I was up late last night, so I decided just to go ahead and take the whole day off. I thought you would be proud of me."

He chuckled. "Playing hooky from work? Of course I'm proud of you. Even though... it's not *really* playing hooky when you just decide not to work overtime."

"Don't burst my bubble."

They both laughed and sat down together. Zachary's brows drew together, and he indicated the laceration on her forehead that she hadn't been able to disguise with makeup. A couple of sterile strips held it closed, and she had managed to tone down the bruising with a little foundation around the mark, but it was still clear that she had hit her head.

"What happened there?" Zachary asked.

Kenzie rolled her eyes. "It's still icy outside. I tripped and hit my head on a van."

All of that was true, but she knew she was still constructing a lie, keeping from Zachary what had really happened. There was no way she was telling him she had been abducted. Not while he was still in psych and not fully stabilized on the new meds. Maybe down the line, when he was home and everything was back to normal, and all of the drama with Walter and the Russians was just a memory. Then she *might* tell him a little bit about it, in a casual way, as if it had just been a minor blip. She wasn't quite sure yet how she would pull that off, but she had time to think about it.

"Ouch." Zachary grimaced. "But you're okay? No concussion?"

"No. I'm perfectly fine."

She hadn't actually been checked for a concussion, but she knew the signs well enough, and she thought that the brain fog and feeling of watching herself from outside were more the results of stress and her concern over Walter than signs of a concussion.

If she did have one, it was very mild, and they would just tell her to take it easy and not do anything too strenuous. And she didn't plan to. She was taking the whole weekend off and would not be moving any bodies around.

"Good." He raised his hand and touched the other side of her face gently, letting his warm, dry palm rest on it for a second or two. "I don't like to see you hurt."

"Nothing to worry about," Kenzie assured him. "And I'm sorry about not getting here last night. Things were… kind of crazy."

She would let him think she was talking about work. All true. No lies. That was another rule they had established in couples' therapy. Never to lie to each other. They could say they didn't want to answer a question, could not force one another to reveal anything they didn't want to, but no lies.

"That's okay." He nodded to emphasize this. "I've said before, it's okay if you can't make it here every day. Sometimes other things come up. It's not exactly convenient to come here every night. If I was at home, there would still be nights that we didn't see each other that much, either because you had to work late or run errands or whatever, or because I had surveillance or something to do. If we wouldn't be home every night, why should you have to be here every night?"

"Well… because if we were at home, I would still see you in the morning before work and touch base during the day, and we would sleep together for at least a couple of hours even if you were doing night surveillance. When you're here… I don't see or hear from you the rest of the time either. *I* miss you, and you must feel isolated too. I just want to make sure… I want to support you and not let us drift apart."

"We're not going to drift apart because you missed visiting one night. It's okay."

Kenzie swallowed and nodded. He was saying and doing all the right things, but she still wondered whether he was hurt or upset that she hadn't been there the night before. He was the kind of guy who buried those feelings, hid them even from himself, and insisted that everything was fine. But he had been abandoned by his parents. Rejected by numerous foster families. By Bridget, his ex-wife. Kenzie's absence must send up red flags for him. It must have triggered some kind of anxiety that she would abandon him just like everyone else.

But she couldn't insist he feel bad about it or share those feelings. So she just smiled and acted as if she was reassured by his words. "Good. Because you're important to me. I don't want you to worry."

"It's fine, Kenzie. I just hope you didn't wear yourself out. It is still the holidays. You should be taking time to relax and recharge."

"We don't take holidays at Christmastime at the morgue. That's our busy season." She grinned and repeated one of their well-worn jokes. "People are dying to get in."

Zachary chuckled. "Still, don't let Dr. Wiltshire work you too hard. Or I'll have to have a word with him. It's not like they're going to get sicker if you don't see them right away. Your waiting room is a lot bigger than most doctors'."

"And colder."

61

Kenzie sat in the car, thinking about Zachary and analyzing whether he suspected her of keeping something from him. She didn't like keeping him in the dark about what had been happening with Walter and about the previous day's abduction. But it would have been a lot worse to tell him about it. He had seemed okay, despite her worries about how he was going to react to her missing a visit. Maybe he was secure enough in their relationship that he could accept her missing a visit here or there without getting overly anxious about it. But she knew enough about him to know that he didn't necessarily show what he was feeling.

Kenzie's phone rang. She pulled it out and looked at the number for a moment before recognizing it. Another conversation that might be rather difficult.

"Hello?"

"Sergeant Campbell, Kenzie. Good news!"

Her mouth went dry, and for a moment she was afraid that something else had happened. She didn't know why she would be anxious about new developments when Campbell said that it was good news. Maybe there had just been too many negatives lately for her to take anything at face value.

"What's that?" she asked tentatively.

"I heard from your father this morning. And he said that he had seen you last night."

Kenzie let her breath out slowly. "Yes," she agreed. "Really good news. I was beginning to think… after nine days…"

"Of course," Campbell agreed, not making her put it into words. "After so much time has passed, things didn't look good. But in the end, things worked out."

"How much did he tell you?"

"Well, I can't say that we got all of our questions answered. And of course the investigations into the deaths of the Russians and whatever criminal activities are going on in that community will continue to go forward. But as far as his missing person case goes… obviously, that can be closed."

"You don't need anything else?"

"What else would I need?" He sounded amused. Kenzie supposed it was a stupid question to ask. But she had wondered whether he would need sworn testimony or affidavits, whether she needed to go in and sign off on a report, saying that she was satisfied that the case had been resolved, or some other official action.

"Nothing, I guess. You know that he is no longer missing, so you obviously won't keep looking for him!"

"No. I think I have enough to do without looking for people who are already found. How are you doing? A little… irritated with him?"

Kenzie laughed a short, sharp bark of laughter. She hadn't really thought about how she felt about what Walter had told her the night before. She was still trying to process everything and to figure out what was true and what was not. But his question triggered a sharp jab of emotion. Irritated? She was irritated as hell. Walter claimed that he had just been in hiding. That he had voluntarily chosen to drop out of sight to avoid trouble. He had, apparently, talked to the governor, but he couldn't be bothered to talk to his own daughter. Despite her increasingly worried phone messages to him, he hadn't made a simple phone call to let her know that everything was fine and she could stop looking for him.

"I don't think irritated begins to cover it," she admitted.

"I can understand that. If I'm irritated to have him show up and say that it was all voluntary after I've deployed so many man hours trying to track him down and ensure his safety, I can only imagine how you would feel after searching for him alone for days and worrying about what might have happened to him. You have a lot more emotionally invested in it than I do."

"Yeah," Kenzie agreed. "Even though I've tried not to…"

"I can't see how you can help it when it's your own father. Even if you don't see eye to eye on everything."

It was interesting that Campbell, who she wasn't that close to, had recognized the emotional distance between Kenzie and her father. She didn't recall saying anything to him about how they didn't get along. Though maybe she had, in explaining why it had taken so long for her to file a missing person report on him.

"So if the case is being closed…" Kenzie looked at her burner phone, feeling its unfamiliar weight and shape in her hand. "Can I get my phone back from you?"

"Yes, of course. We're finished with it. I'm sure you'll want to get it back as soon as possible. And since Walter was the one to write you that email, and it was not a threat, we don't have any reason to investigate where it came from. I can tell you, though… that it was quite sophisticated. There are sites you can go to if you want to send someone an anonymous email, and you just use their web interface and everything is taken care of. This… wasn't that. On a preliminary basis, it looks like it was initially routed through Russian servers."

Kenzie's stomach tied itself into a knot. What did that mean? Had someone other than Walter sent it to her, and he had just covered for that person? Or had he been working with the Russians when he had sent it to her? Or being held by them against his will, but managed to negotiate with them to let him send her an email to try to get her out of their business?

"Oh. Well… that's interesting."

"Yes," Campbell agreed, his tone light and non-accusatory. "I thought so too."

"I'll stop by and get my phone in the next couple of hours. Your front desk is open?"

"Yes. I'll leave it in an envelope at the desk for you. Stop by at your convenience."

"Thanks. I appreciate it. And let me apologize for having started an inquiry when there was apparently no need for one. For wasting police time. I doubt if Walter apologized."

He chuckled. "No, you would be right in that assessment. Don't worry about it, Kenzie. I know it wasn't frivolous. You had good reason to be concerned."

Before Kenzie drove over to the police station, she got out of the car and checked the trunk.

It was empty.

She had been abducted just as she got out of her car to take Walter's luggage into the house. She was pretty sure that she had already popped the trunk when they had grabbed her, but the adrenaline-filled excitement and confusion around the abduction had muddied her memories. She might have popped the trunk, or she might not have.

Either way, the luggage was gone.

Did that mean that the Russians who had kidnapped her had taken it? Or had Walter taken the suitcases at some point?

She had never given Walter the keys or opened it for him. It was possible that the trunk had been unlatched when he'd brought her home after the abduction, but how would he know that? She hadn't seen him retrieve the luggage. He could have after she sent him on his way. If he'd known that the trunk was open or had jimmied it himself.

More likely, it had been the Russians. Just because she hadn't seen them take the suitcases, that didn't mean that they hadn't. They hadn't thrown them into the back of the van with her, but there might have been a follow car. Or she might simply have been unaware of it, face down in the van with her head spinning and one of them standing on her back.

Kenzie closed the trunk and made sure it latched. She slid back into the driver's seat, feeling every bruise and pulled muscle from the abduction. She should just go home and relax, like Zachary had told her to. Like Walter had suggested. Like anyone who knew what she had gone through would have recommended. But she wouldn't feel any better lying in bed at home. Then she would just be thinking with nothing to do. It was better to stay busy and not think about her aches and pains and all of the questions that had not been answered.

62

After retrieving her regular phone from the police station, Kenzie hit the road.

It was funny how much better she felt once she had the phone in her possession. She had never been one of those people who claimed that "her whole life" was on the phone. She had a life, and a phone wouldn't change that. But she had come to rely on it for her contact list, both the phone numbers and emails she didn't have memorized. And her schedule. And it came in handy when she wanted to play music in the car and didn't want to mess around looking for something good on the radio. She wasn't sure when the last time she'd actually listened to the radio was. Growing up, that had been what she'd listened to all the time. It was strange to think that the technology was becoming obsolete with the rise of cell phones and streaming music subscriptions.

And, of course, the phone gave her a way to look up her emails while on the run. And to quickly text a message to Zachary or another friend when she wanted to touch base, maybe to get an answer to a quick question when she didn't have the time for a visit.

And she sometimes wound down playing a quick game or reading a book on her reading app.

It wasn't her whole life, but it made accessing her life easier. And she felt much better having it back in her possession. It gave her a sense of security and belonging, as strange as that seemed.

She played her music with the volume turned way up, far louder than she would have if she had been driving with Zachary. No need to hold a conversation. All the reasons in the world to block out her thoughts. She was careful to stick to the speed limit, or at least within ten miles per hour of the speed limit, taking her time. Nothing was going to be gained by speeding. Getting there ten minutes ahead of schedule would make no difference.

The highways were cleared of snow, and traffic was moving at a good pace. No accidents, no slowdowns. Working in the Medical Examiner's Office, she always wondered when she saw a traffic accident whether anyone had been killed and she would see them later in autopsy. It was an eerie feeling and one she didn't share with anyone. She couldn't have shared it with very many people who would understand, other than Dr. Wiltshire himself.

Eventually, she pulled onto the familiar lane and slowed to drive the last leg to the house. When she pulled into the circular parking area, she saw a white sedan already parked there, as she had expected to. So he hadn't picked up his own car from the Front Street Hotel parking lot yet. Was he afraid to be seen back there? Maybe he had been warned off? Or had the hotel had it towed to an impound lot and he hadn't paid the fines yet?

Kenzie parked neatly beside the other car and walked up to the front door. She rang and then, after a moment's consideration, tried the handle. The door was unlocked. Kenzie let herself in. Lola barked frantically and dashed into the hall. Lisa followed at a more sedate pace.

"MacKenzie!" Lisa smiled and hurried forward to give her a brief hug and buss both cheeks. "It is so nice to see you. Come in. Your father is here."

"I saw the car," Kenzie said with a nod.

"Ah, you're very observant." Lisa held Kenzie's arm companionably as they walked back into the sitting room. Walter looked up from the newspaper that lay open on the coffee table.

"MacKenzie. Fancy meeting you here."

Kenzie imagined that the last week had never taken place. That it was Christmas Day again and she was arriving at her mother's house for the first time. That Walter was there as he usually was every Christmas, giving his ex-wife a box of chocolates or some other sentimental gift, acting as if he still lived there. Could she wipe out the rest and pretend it had never happened? That they were just a happy little family, enjoying the festive season?

"Are you okay?" Kenzie asked, unable to push her anxiety over his safety aside as she wished.

"I'm fine." Walter looked down at the paper and turned the large, folded sheet. "Did you get a good night's sleep? You're looking a bit better today."

She hoped she looked better than she had after being violently abducted and held hostage for several hours. She imagined she must have been a mess the night before. Even with Walter cleaning her cut head, she had still found dried blood in her hair, making a lumpy mess out of everything. But with a hot shower, her hair washed, and the cut tended to and brushed over with foundation, she looked presentable, at least. Zachary hadn't noticed anything other than the taped cut on her forehead.

Kenzie studied Walter for a moment, trying to evaluate everything about him, from his skin color to the way that he was sitting and holding himself. Paler and thinner than usual? In pain?

She turned her attention to Lisa. Walter had been trying to keep anything bad from happening to Kenzie and Lisa, he had said. Unlike Kenzie, Lisa had kept her questions to herself and had not been causing trouble for the Russian underground. She had known to stay out of the way and pretend that nothing had happened. That there had been nothing at all to be concerned about. Kenzie had broken through that mask of unconcern once, when she had told Lisa that Maksim was dead but, other than that, she had been able to stay cool and collected.

Kenzie thought she probably got her more headstrong demeanor from Walter. Neither one of them went on screaming rants about things, but Kenzie's nature made it difficult for her to ignore injustice and keep her questions to herself. To always keep that cool head that Lisa had and not try to take matters into her own hands.

Walter was a take-things-into-his-own-hands kind of guy. He didn't like to sit around and wait for things to happen. He was the kind of person who made things happen, and Kenzie was afraid that she was too. It wasn't a failing, exactly, but it could certainly make life interesting for them and those close to them.

"How are you, Mother?"

"Glad to know that everyone is well and safe." By saying this, Lisa acknowledged that she had been worried about Walter, which Kenzie hadn't expected her to admit.

"Yeah. Me too. So…" Kenzie sat down, choosing a seat close to both of her parents, feeling like she needed to be within reach of them, anchored by them. Lola lay down at Lisa's feet. "When Maksim was here… he didn't do anything to hurt you?"

"No." Lisa smoothed the wrinkles in her pants, not looking Kenzie in the eye. "Of course not."

"Did he threaten you? Or Dad? I want to know what happened."

"All of that is in the past, now, MacKenzie. I don't think we need to keep going over it."

"I do. I'm really confused about a lot of things and I want to know what happened. I came here, thinking that we would just have a nice, quiet Christmas Day, and then… everything just happened. I didn't know who this guy was, where Dad was, or why you weren't telling me anything." She shook her head. She felt like a little girl whose parents had avoided giving her bad news in the hopes that being ignorant of the truth would make her feel better and safer than if she actually knew the big scary thing.

They had told her about Amanda's kidney disease when Amanda had been diagnosed. They had refused to let her donate a kidney while she was underage, but she had done it as soon as she was old enough. She had hated the fact that they had tried to protect her and keep her from doing that. They had hidden the truth of their separation and divorce from her. They had hidden the truth of Amanda's second transplant from her.

It was always better when they told her the truth.

Lisa sighed, looking at Walter and then back at Kenzie. "Maksim came here looking for Walter. When I said he wasn't here… Maksim stayed. There were no threats, but… your father and I had already talked about Maksim and the people he worked for. I knew that he might be a dangerous person. That he was not someone to be trifled with. I didn't lie to him. I told him I expected Walter but didn't know when he would arrive."

"And when he didn't come?"

"Maksim tried to reach him on the phone. Had been trying to reach him before he came here. He was… sweating a lot. Nervous. Swallowing, licking his lips."

"Was he just nervous, or was he high on something?" Her description could indicate either.

"I don't know." Lisa looked at Walter again. "Was he… a user?"

"I wouldn't have thought so when I first met him. He seemed to be in control, everything straightforward and calm. But that has changed over the last few months. He became more agitated. He was making mistakes. Things that he said, sometimes erratic behavior… I knew that something was wrong."

"Was that before he gave you the money or after?" Kenzie asked. "Was he upset that you took the money and then wouldn't do what he wanted you to without checking everything out first?"

"That was definitely a turning point. I had begun to be suspicious and didn't want to jump into anything without checking it out first. When I told him he needed to wait until I'd had a chance to do my due diligence… he definitely was not happy."

Kenzie could well imagine. Not just because Walter was suspicious of him and wanted to dig more deeply into the background of the organization Maksim was working with, but because he had taken the money and then balked. Maksim must have wondered if he was going to lose everything.

"So what happened when Daddy didn't come home?" Kenzie asked Lisa. "Did he… eventually leave here?"

There was no other option. Eventually, Maksim had left. His body had not been found in Burlington.

"Yes. He asked me to let him know when I heard from Walter. Left me with numbers to reach him at."

"And then…?"

Lisa shrugged. "It was the end of the day. Walter hadn't come. You had been and gone. The house was empty once again. I went to bed."

Kenzie couldn't imagine trying to sleep after spending the day with Maksim hovering over her, waiting to hear from Walter, planning to do who-knew-what to him. It would have taken several sleeping pills, prescription strength sleeping pills, not the over-the-counter ones she normally picked up, for Kenzie to get to sleep after a day like that.

"And when did you hear from Walter?"

Lisa blinked at Kenzie. "I didn't. Not until today."

"You never heard anything from him in the last nine days."

Lisa shook her head. "No."

Kenzie frowned at Walter, trying to read the truth in his face. "You never contacted her? Not once? To let her know that you were okay and hadn't been killed by Maksim or some other Russian thug?"

"No, I didn't call." Walter hesitated, looking at Kenzie. "Why would they kill me? I couldn't very well help them if they did that."

"Because you took their money and then wouldn't do what they asked you to. Russian mafia…"

"I didn't say I wouldn't do what they wanted me to. I wanted to look into things further. To have… certain assurances. There was no need for anyone to kill me, MacKenzie. That threat was never made."

"They threatened me. Told me to back off. *Kidnapped* me."

He sighed. "I'm sorry that happened to you, MacKenzie. It was never my intention for you to get tangled up in this. They are rather paranoid about some things, and I never anticipated that you coming here on Christmas Day could set off such a series of events."

Kenzie's heart thudded heavily. She tried to unwrap what Walter had just said. "Me coming here? Why would *me coming here* cause problems?"

"Up until that point, they were holding steady. But having someone show up here who worked at the police station… Perhaps the problem was not with you. It might have just been Maksim… he had been getting increasingly unstable. He made mistakes that… some unfortunate mistakes that did not go unnoticed. When you work for someone *like that*… You must be very careful. Accidents are not tolerated. Losing control. Using the products they trafficked himself." Walter shook his head tightly. "I did not know all of this at the time. Some of it I have learned from the Russians since. But you have had several people through the morgue…"

Kenzie nodded. "A man who died of starvation. Another who was hit by a car."

"Mistakes. Accidents that could not be overlooked."

"Maksim's mistakes?"

Walter nodded.

Had he let them escape from his custody? Wherever he was supposed to be holding them? He should have been able to tell that the man who had starved was not getting enough food. He had been rail thin. Had probably fainted at some time. He was no longer able to perform the tasks he had previously. Maksim should have been able to see that. And the man who had run into traffic? Who had he been running from?

"So… someone… whoever Maksim's boss was, decided to make an example of him. To make sure that no one else made any mistakes."

"That would appear to be the case."

Kenzie sat there, thinking about it. She couldn't help feeling a little sorry for Maksim for his blunders and very painful death. And even more sorry for the others who had died and those still working for the organization, being trafficked, put into dangerous situations, and worked to death.

"How did you know… what happened to me, and how to get me out?"

"I had eyes on you whenever I could." Walter shook his head. "Going to the hotel was not smart. I would expect you to have more sense than to go to… the center of the spider's web."

Kenzie shuddered at the image. "What do you mean? They called me there. They said that they had your belongings and that the police had asked me to pick them up."

"You should not have gone there. I knew there was going to be trouble when you showed up. And you couldn't stop there." Walter shook his head. "You interfered. Asked questions. Tried to… *help* people."

And they had been watching her. Walter had been watching her. The Russians had been watching her. She remembered the bouncer who had pulled her away from talking to the man shoveling the sidewalk. He had probably not been the only one watching her. There had been others as well. The man at the check-in counter. Maybe others throughout the hotel. Who could be sure how many eyes they had?

"I'm sorry. It was just… natural."

"You are like your mother," he smiled forgivingly. "Always thinking of other people. Always trying to help."

Kenzie didn't see herself as being like Lisa at all. She always had to be talked into helping Lisa with one of her causes. Bullied and blackmailed into it. It didn't come naturally, and she was always resistant to getting involved with yet another foundation, another cause, another campaign.

"You like to help people one at a time," Lisa said, watching Kenzie's face. "Face to face. In a personal way."

"Well… yes, I guess so."

Lisa nodded. So did Walter.

"But you need to be more aware. You can't just walk into the middle of something like that and expect people to just back off and let you do what you want."

"I didn't know I was walking into the middle of anything."

Walter licked his lips. "The man who runs this organization, the one at the top. He is *there.*"

"At the hotel?"

Walter nodded.

"The top guy? The oligarch or whatever you call him? The guy in charge of this whole… family?"

"Yes."

"I thought he was in Russia. Why would he be here?"

"Conditions are much nicer here than in Russia," Walter pointed out. A simple evaluation. Kenzie had never been to Russia, but her mental picture of it was bleak. A vast gray wasteland, full of suffering, starving people. Not like Vermont, green and vibrant and alive. Of course he would prefer living in the United States to a bleak place like that. Living like a king, with all of his cryptocurrency.

63

S unday was usually Kenzie's day off. That wasn't to say she hadn't worked Sundays in the past, especially before she and Zachary had gotten close. But since they had been together and had started couple's therapy, she tried to make Sunday *their* day. The day that she could sit down and spend time with him, run a few errands together, go out to eat, or maybe drive down to Lorne Peterson's and Pat Parker's house for family dinner.

She had slept in, had a leisurely visit with Zachary in the morning, and had a cup of specialty coffee at the hospital coffee shop when her phone vibrated with an incoming call. Kenzie pulled it out and glanced at the screen. Dr. Wiltshire. It was pretty rare for him to call her on a weekend or holiday.

"Hello?"

"Kenzie. Sorry to bother you on a Sunday."

"What's up?"

"I'm in autopsy, catching up on a couple of the routine post-mortems to try to ease the overcrowding."

"Did you need me to come in and take a couple of them as well?" Kenzie knew they had a few more bodies in the cold room than Dr. Wiltshire liked, even though they weren't actually crowded for space.

"No. It's fine. I meant for you to be able to take the day today.

But a situation has developed, and I would rather not have to leave these two to take care of it..."

"Oh, right. What's going on? How can I help?"

"Got a call on a man down. Sounds like natural causes, no apparent violence. Paramedics were called, but the victim was DOA. Normally not a problem. I'd send a couple of death investigators to check it out and have the body transported here. But the police are on the scene and have flagged it as a suspicious death."

Kenzie frowned and sipped her coffee. "It looks like natural causes, but the police think there is something suspicious?"

"Yes." Wiltshire sighed. "I was called by someone on a task force. There is a multi-departmental investigation, and this guy goes down in the middle of it, so even though it looks natural, they are paranoid that it could be something relating to their investigation and want to go full-out on a detailed investigation."

Kenzie's heart sped. Roxboro was a small city in a small state, and she was not aware of a lot of task forces or multi-departmental investigations that were ongoing and would have anything to do with Roxboro.

"Where is this?"

"High Street Hotel."

Bingo.

Kenzie tried to keep her breathing calm and even so that Wiltshire would not hear any emotion or anxiety in her voice.

"Okay. I can head over there. Would you send a van and a couple of techs to meet me there, and we'll take care of it?"

"Thank you, Kenzie. Yes, I'll get things going on this end and have someone meet you. I appreciate this. You know how I hate to be interrupted when I've already got a body open."

"Of course." None of them liked anything that might compromise their work. Dr. Wiltshire was meticulous in his work, and leaving a body in the middle of a postmortem was not something he would tolerate.

It was a natural death.

Kenzie would get there and find that a businessperson had suffered a heart attack and collapsed in the lobby. Or some old guy had expired in the hotel bed overnight. People died in the most inconvenient of places, and it was their job to see that every unattended death was properly investigated, just in case it was not as natural as it looked.

When she got to the hotel, she could see that the death had not occurred in the lobby or restaurant, or in one of the hotel rooms. There were several police vehicles with their lights on lined up along the side street beside the hotel, and pylons and yellow tape had been set up to establish a perimeter and keep people away from the body.

Kenzie showed her identification when she got close enough to be stopped by one of the officers at the scene. He directed her to a place where she could park and escorted her to the perimeter, introducing her rapidly to several plainclothes detectives that stood around with coffees and red cheeks.

One of the detectives stepped forward to greet Kenzie, and they shook hands. "Agent Arnold," he told her. "With the FBI. Don't freak out; I'm sure this is nothing at all. We just have to be sure, with the investigation going on, that this is not significant and doesn't affect any of the aspects of our case."

Kenzie nodded. "Sure, no problem. That's my job."

She turned to the taped-off area and the dark form crumpled in the middle. Too bad for the hotel and the multi-disciplinary investigation that he had happened to collapse on the edge of the hotel property instead of a few feet away. Kenzie suited up and ducked under the tape. The paramedics had left him where he was and were seated nearby in the open rear of their ambulance, watching and making themselves available to answer whatever questions Kenzie had for them.

Kenzie realized as she got closer that it was the man she had seen shoveling the sidewalk just a couple of days earlier. She had talked with him, had shown him Walter's picture and asked whether he had seen him. If she found out that he had been killed because she was seen talking to him... She already had Maksim's death on her conscience. He had been judged to be a liability because he had been seen talking to her, someone who worked in the same building as the police department was housed in.

She couldn't take another death on her conscience.

She remembered the sharp angles of his face. How thin and frail he had seemed, working hard to remove the snow, trying to wave her off and not answer her questions. Kenzie felt for a pulse in his wrist, as she was sure the paramedics had already done, watching for the rise and fall of his chest. She was sure they hadn't made a mistake, but mistakes had been known to have happened in the past, and it wasn't going to happen on her watch. She gently unwound the scarf from around his neck and felt for his carotid pulse. Again, no flutter of movement through her thin gloves. Kenzie reached to check the carotid on the other side and stopped, frowning at the lump and rash on the man's neck.

She undid his coat, put on her stethoscope, and listened to his chest for any breath sounds or heartbeat, mentally reviewing textbook and website pictures and descriptions. She sat back on her heels and pulled out her phone, giving the voice command to call Dr. Wiltshire so that she didn't have to take off her gloves and unlock it.

"Kenzie. How does it look?" Dr. Wiltshire asked without preamble.

"On a very preliminary look, it does look like natural causes," Kenzie said.

"Very good. And...?" He knew that she hadn't called him just to tell him that.

"I haven't seen very many cases, just pictures in textbooks, but there are some distinctive marks on his neck. I think I am looking at scrofuloderma."

Dr. Wiltshire muttered something under his breath. Then, "Are you sure, Kenzie?"

"Can I send you a picture?"

"Please do."

Kenzie positioned her phone close to the man's neck and snapped a picture, which she then forwarded to Dr. Wiltshire by text. She could hear the ping on his end as it arrived. A louder curse this time.

"Yes, I concur," he agreed. "You're properly protected?"

"Yes. But… I saw this man a couple of days ago. I had to come by here to get my dad's suitcase. He was coughing then."

"You'll have to be tested. Keep everyone well away if they are not wearing the proper protection. Was he alive or dead when the paramedics got there?"

"I haven't talked to them yet."

"Inform everyone at the scene. I'll call the CDC. You'll need to talk to the hotel—this man is an employee?"

"He's Russian. So I don't know if he was actually employed or if they had him providing unpaid labor. If I ask questions like that… it might derail the police investigation."

"Explain the risks to them. Everybody who worked or lived closely with this guy will have to be tested. Maybe everybody who has stayed at the hotel in the last week or two, depending on what kind of contact he might have had with the guests. It will take the CDC a day or two to get their investigation going, but they'll need a way to talk to everyone involved."

"Okay. I'll do what I can on this end. We'll bring him back to the morgue."

"Talk to you when you get here."

Kenzie rose to her feet when the call terminated. She turned back toward the detectives and the FBI agent. Agent Arnold reached for the yellow tape to cross the perimeter, now that she had confirmed the man's death and seen the site. Kenzie held up her hand to stop him.

"Don't go any further," she snapped.

Arnold stopped, frozen. His brows went up, and his face turned a little more ruddy. "Why? You've had a chance to look at him. You can see that this was just natural causes. The man had a heart attack."

"No." Kenzie shook her head. "The man had tuberculosis."

64

Things got very busy very fast. Kenzie explained the risks to Agent Arnold and the fact that if this man had been housed in close quarters with other people, as she assumed the trafficking victims were, then they might all have active TB infections. While healthy subjects who were exposed to the bacteria were unlikely to get sick, the victims that she had seen recently who had been malnourished and had little or no medical care were ripe for the disease. They could have quite an outbreak.

Kenzie talked to the paramedics while she waited for the techs to arrive with the medical examiner's van. They had been gloved and masked when they had approached the fallen man, though one of them admitted to pulling his mask away from his face when it became obvious that their patient was deceased.

"But you can't get it from a dead body, right?" he asked anxiously. "You get it from someone coughing on you."

"Transmission from a corpse has been known to occur, if you've been exposed to any of the bodily fluids or moved the body in such a way as to compress the diaphragm and expel residual air from the lungs. Funeral directors and embalmers have been shown to have a higher infection rate than the general public."

He swore under his breath. "Dead bodies aren't supposed to be dangerous."

Kenzie shook her head. There were plenty of things that a person could still catch from a dead body. TB wasn't the only one, not even the most likely.

"You need to treat them as hazardous materials."

"Well, thanks. That makes me feel a lot better."

Kenzie shrugged. "Sorry. Get a TB test. It will probably be negative, but you need to make sure, especially if you're immunocompromised in any way."

After ensuring that the death investigators understood the danger of contamination, Kenzie left them to their work and went to the front doors of the hotel, where the various law enforcement officers were talking to each other and the staff, trying to get things organized and come to a landing on what was to be done. Kenzie sensed frustration from the LEOs, who didn't seem to be getting very far in convincing the hotel administration that they needed to do something to contain the infection.

"He did not live here. He only worked here, and only outside," a severe-looking woman told one of the police detectives. "He was never in the hotel; there's no reason to cause a panic."

Kenzie looked around and did not see the prostitutes that had previously been there, or any others walking the street in their place. She didn't see anyone else who appeared to be involved in any groundskeeping activities.

"What is *she* doing here?"

Kenzie turned to see who had spoken. A tall, pale man with short-cropped hair was looking in her direction, though Kenzie couldn't be sure he was looking directly at her. He wore a suit that Kenzie recognized as not just an expensive menswear label, but bespoke. Tailored just for him. That kind of thing did not come cheap, but he wore it as casually as if it were a t-shirt. She glanced surreptitiously at his shoes and saw that they too were expensive, probably handmade, and polished to a high shine.

The man he was talking to was the bouncer who had shooed Kenzie off the premises a couple of days before. He scowled, clearly not happy with the turn of events. He shook his head and said something in a voice too low for Kenzie to hear.

"I want her off the property. This disruption is unacceptable."

They were going to have a hard time forcing Kenzie to do anything when she was there in her official capacity. Or to keep the CDC from descending on the hotel like a swarm of locusts when they heard about the dead man and the possibility that he had been housed with a large number of other people in very close quarters.

The bouncer continued to talk to the rich man in low, subservient tones. But he was not giving the man the news he wanted to hear. His face grew red as he stood there, face a tight mask.

"We cannot stay," he said finally. He wrinkled his nose in disgust. "These vermin, carriers of filth and disease. I want them housed far away from my operations."

The bouncer's patience was wearing thin. "If you want them to work for you, then they can't be that far from the organization. They need to be… accessible."

"Not *far* then. But not close. Never again. I do not want to be under the same roof as these disease-laden dogs. Can't you keep them clean?"

The bouncer shook his head. "That was Maksim's job. Not mine," the man insisted.

"Well, he did a wonderful job, did he not? I wish he was not dead."

The bouncer raised his brows at this comment, and Kenzie found herself confused by it as well. He was clearly being sarcastic about the wonderful job that Maksim had done, letting prisoners escape, die, or catch a highly contagious disease. But he didn't sound sarcastic about wishing Maksim were not dead.

"You wish he was *not?*" the bouncer repeated, perhaps thinking that the Russian had mistranslated his thoughts into English.

"Yes," the tall man agreed. "Then I could kill him *myself.*"

"Excuse me." Kenzie found Ralph, one of the death investigators at her elbow. "We're ready to roll, Dr. Kirsch. Did you want to come back with us?"

"Oh." Kenzie looked at the tall, rich oligarch once more. "Yes. It's probably best if I don't hang around here any longer than I have to. I've got my own car, so I'll follow you back."

He nodded. "Sounds good. Thanks."

Ralph and his partner didn't need any help getting another body checked in and situated in the cold room, but Kenzie found herself following them in anyway. She didn't supervise their work, but went to one of the bodies awaiting cremation.

She didn't unzip the body bag, but simply stood there, picturing Maksim on the stairs at her mother's house, looking down at the two of them. He had been healthy and strong, poised, well-dressed. Not as expensively as the man at the hotel, of course, but he had seemed to fit into her mother's house perfectly. A wealthy social influencer like Kenzie's mother, secure in his belief in what he was doing. Sure, perhaps, that if he stayed there long enough, he would find Walter. Walter, who he needed to lobby against the cryptocurrency bill coming before the State Senate.

He had not expected to be killed for a series of mistakes that had culminated in being seen with a woman known to work at the Medical Examiner's Office. Someone who worked hand-in-glove with the police.

Now, they had come a full circle. Kenzie was the one looking down on Maksim, at the end of his story. Christmas forgotten. The Senate session reopening and Walter lobbying against the bill, as he had agreed to do from the start. He didn't believe in government oversight, and now he was poised again to fight them, with a large bankroll in his pocket.

And if she knew Walter, he would be successful.